Manuel Vázquez Montalbán was born in [...] the Spanish Communist party in his studen[...] three he was imprisoned for four years by a military tribunal for supporting a miners' strike. He started his career by writing satirical articles for a left-wing magazine in the last years of Francoist Spain and then went on to become a respected poet and novelist. Renowned for creating Pepe Carvalho, the fast-living, gourmet private detective, Montalbán won both the Raymond Chandler Prize and the French Grand Prix of Detective Fiction for his thrillers, which are translated into all major languages. He died in October 2003.

Also by Manuel Vázquez Montalbán and published by Serpent's Tail are *Murder in the Central Committee*, *Southern Seas*, *Off Side*, *An Olympic Death*, and *The Angst-Ridden Executive*.

Praise for *The Buenos Aires Quintet*

'A suitable requiem for a character and his writer' *Guardian*

'The most metaphysical gumshoe on the streets' *The Times*

'This is nothing less than world-class crime fiction, packed with three dimensional characters, honest appraisals of the contemporary world and vivid writing' *Big Issue in the North*

'The ambitious scope of Vásquez's subject matter is reason enough to love his work but it's the unique charm of Carvalho that seals the deal' *Leeds Guide*

Praise for the Pepe Carvalho series

'Montalbán does for Barcelona what Chandler did for Los Angeles – he exposes the criminal power relationships beneath the façade of democracy' *Guardian*

'Pepe Carvalho is a phlegmatic investigator. His greatest concern is with his stomach, but when not pursuing delicacies, he can unravel the most tangled of mysteries' *Sunday Times*

'Montalbán writes with authority and compassion – a Le Carré-like sorrow' *Publishers' Weekly*

'Montalbán is a writer who is caustic about the powerful and tender towards the oppressed' *TLS*

A complete catalogue record for this book can be obtained from
the British Library on request

The right of Manuel Vázquez Montalbán to be identified as the
author of this work has been asserted in accordance with the
Copyright, Designs and Patents Act 1988

Copyright © Manuel Vázquez Montalbán 1997
Translation copyright © Nick Caistor 2003

First published as *Quinteto de Buenos Aires* by Editorial Planeta,
S.A., 1997

First published in this English translation in 2003 by
Serpent's Tail, 3 Holford Yard, Bevin Way, London WC1X 9HD
website: www.serpentstail.com

This 5-star edition first published in 2005

Printed and bound by CPI Group (UK) Ltd, Croydon, CR0 4YY

10 9 8 7 6 5

Translation funded by the Arts Council of England

ISBN: 1-85242-783-3
ISBN-13: 978-1-85242-783-2

The Buenos Aires Quintet

Manuel Vázquez Montalbán

Translated by
Nick Caistor

For Liliana Mazure and Luis Barone

To my mind, it's just a tale that Buenos Aires began one day. I see her as eternal as water and air.

Jorge Luis Borges
The Mythical Foundation of Buenos Aires

That city offered no easy destinies. It was a city that left its mark. Its vast dryness was a warning; its climate, light and blue skies were a lie.

Eduardo Mallea
The City Beside the Unmoving River

Chapter 1

The American Uncle

A pair of eyes glances furtively at the proof on the sign: 'Behaviour Laboratory. The Spirit of New Argentina'. The man walks as though stealth has become second nature to him. Rats and chemical retorts, but on the wall the surprise of a huge poster. A cow with a beautiful young girl proudly pointing to it:

ARGENTINA WILL ONCE AGAIN BE THE WORLD'S MILCH COW: FOUNDATION FOR A NEW ARGENTINA

The eyes come to a halt on the poster. They're part of a haggard face twisted with pent-up anger. The mouth mutters through its teeth: 'A New Argentina'.

All at once the man's rage spills over. He lashes out around him. Knocks over the retorts and test tubes, flings open the rats' cages. The animals emerge into the larger prison of the room. Fascinated, he pauses to contemplate the results of his unleashed power. One rat seems to be seeking him out, and he picks it up carefully, almost affectionately: 'rat, my little sister'.

He puts it into his torn jacket pocket and slips out of the laboratory just as lights start to go on and voices can be heard shouting: 'What was that?' 'What's happening?'

The loudest voice belongs to a man who's Fat with a capital F. His face, chest and stomach are mounds of blubber and forgotten acres of flesh.

His face is theatrically old, so it seems only natural he should ask pessimistically: 'What d'you know about Buenos Aires?'

Betraying neither pessimism nor optimism, Carvalho responds: 'Tango, the disappeared, Maradona.'

This answer only increases the other man's despondency: 'Tango, the disappeared, Maradona,' he repeats.

Carvalho looks out on to a Barcelona roof terrace. The old man is sitting in an armchair; behind him the city fills the horizon as if the more he gazed at it, the more it grew. The older man seems to be having trouble finding the words he's looking for. Beyond the window blinds, two middle-aged women are whispering and glancing surreptitiously at them. Carvalho is stuck in a cane chair like something from an *Emmanuelle* film, although it looks as if it were left behind by a being from outer space rather than a Filipino.

'For the sake of your father's memory, nephew, go to Buenos Aires. Try to find my son, Raúl.'

He points to the two women spying on them from the roof terrace.

'My nieces have got me in their clutches. I don't want them to end up with what by rights belongs to my son. Who knows where he might be. I thought he'd got over the death of his wife, Berta, and his daughter's disappearance. That all happened in the years of the guerrilla. He went crazy. He was caught as well. Though I've been a Republican all my life, I wrote to the King. For my boy's sake, I asked for things I've never asked for in my life. I made deals I would never have made. And finally I got him here to Spain. Time is a great healer, they say. Time doesn't heal a thing. It just adds more weight. You're the only one who can find him. You know how to: you're a cop, aren't you?'

'A private detective.'

'Isn't it the same thing?'

'The cops guarantee order. All I do is uncover disorder.'

Carvalho gets up, walks out on to the terrace and looks down at the city. Its jumbled roofs offer him a proposed merger of the old and new Olympic Barcelonas, the last stores in Pueblo Nuevo, and Icaria, the Catalan Manchester, just waiting to be demolished, then the outskirts of the eclectic architecture of the Olympic Village, and beyond it, the sea. When his uncle's voice drifts out to him, Carvalho can't help but smile.

'Buenos Aires is a beautiful city hell-bent on self-destruction.'

Carvalho's father had always told him his American uncle had a way with words.

'I like cities that destroy themselves. Triumphant cities smell of disinfectant.'

He goes back inside to face the old man.

'So, will you do it? I don't really understand what you meant about private detectives, but will you go?'

'Welcome to Buenos Aires. We know you come here because Argentina is up for sale to foreigners. But it's not only the Japanese who are buying us: even the Spaniards are here, although Spain itself is for sale as well. It's being bought by the Japanese.'

He unstraps the watch from his wrist and starts to auction it. 'I'm not asking a million pesos for it, not even a thousand, not even a hundred, not one.'

He falls to his knees, sobbing. 'Take it from me, I beg you, just take it. We Argentines love people to take our watches, our sweethearts, our islands. So we can write tangos about it afterwards!'

The presenter rushes round the room compulsively offering his wristwatch to different members of the public, who react either with hollow laughter or dismay at this face dripping with make-up and eyeliner. The spotlight follows the presenter until it paralyses him, as if he suddenly felt there were no point trying to give away the watch any more. The presenter looks down at it as though it has become a viscous, strange object, then all at once apparently realizes he's in the middle of an audience, and nonchalantly asks them: 'By the way, what d'you know about Buenos Aires?'

Outside his window he can see the Ramblas, looking even darker than usual. The statue to Pitarra he's finally got used to. Pitarra, my old friend. His face twists in a grimace of disgust as he stubbornly asks himself who he is, where he came from, where he's going to. The Llompart file is on the desk in front of him, and in his mind's eye he can see the scene from two days earlier. He signals to the doorman, and the Moroccan understands perfectly, even though he's probably not all that intelligent and knows there· may be only five thousand pesetas in it for him. Hands over a key. The stairs and the corridor bring back the memory of every stinking rotten boarding house he's visited here in the armpit of the city. By the top step he's out of breath. He puts it down to the mixture of tension and disgust that is the only way he can keep up this crotch-sniffing role of his. But it's too late to back out now. Here's the door. The number in chipped porcelain.

'Better get it over with.'

He thrusts the key into the lock and, as if a curtain is torn in front of him, a terrified woman of an age to know better covers her flabby nakedness with the bedcover. A red light on the wall. A wardrobe door ajar. Carvalho switches on the main light. He's carrying a camera. He opens the wardrobe door. A nude, bald man. One hand covering his sex. Carvalho takes a picture.

Someone knocks at his door and the memory fades. That will be Llompart, come to sniff the crotch of his wife's lover. Carvalho sits behind the typical desk of a typical private detective; on the far side of the desk sits a man with the look of a typical deceived husband, depending of course on how deceived husbands look around the world. What could a deceived husband in New Zealand look like? Carvalho spreads the photos out in front of him. Photos taken when he burst into the room: the half-naked woman, the wardrobe, the ridiculous lover trying to hide. Señor Llompart's face crumples as though he's about to cry. But he doesn't. Instead he spits: 'Whore!'

By now his face is contorted with laughter, not tears. The more he studies the photos, the louder he laughs. 'My wife's a whore, but a stupid one. Now I've got these photos she won't get a cent out of me when we divorce.'

As if by magic he brandishes a chequebook, and a MontBlanc fountain pen probably given to him by his wife on Father's Day. 'How much do I owe you?'

'Two hundred thousand pesetas.'

He doesn't like the price. He doesn't like Carvalho. He doesn't like the photos. He frowns. He pauses in mid-flourish of his pen. He looks down at the photos, then at Carvalho, as if weighing their worth.

'Shit!'

'Regaining your honour is an expensive business.'

'What honour are you talking about? You're not giving me back my honour; on the contrary, you're showing me what an asshole I am.'

'But you're doing well out of it. You pay me two hundred thousand pesetas, but your wife'll be left without a bean when you get the divorce.'

'That's true.'

So he signs contentedly, and hands over the cheque with a smug feeling of self-satisfaction. Then he leaves, thanking Carvalho profusely for his professional expertise. Standing by the window again, Carvalho is on the point of wallowing in his nausea once more, but Biscuter interrupts him. When he pulls back the sliding curtain separating the office from the kitchen, his look of a superannuated foetus only serves to increase Carvalho's sense of melancholy. Biscuter's reedy eunuch voice grates on his ears, and he's annoyed by the way he wipes his hands on a dishcloth that's begging to be put out to pasture.

'Has he gone?'

'He thought it was expensive. He wanted to avoid paying anything to his wife, and paying me as little as possible.'

'There are a lot of cheapskates in this world, boss.'

'Cheap's the word. All he's interested in is leading the old cow off to the slaughterhouse, and he's managed to catch her out. Now he'll hitch up with a young heifer who'll bleed him dry. Nobody believes in anything in this society of ours. Everything is corrupt. When there's no morality left in society, what can we private detectives do? Take it from me, Biscuter.'

'This is dreadful, boss. We haven't got a single customer. No work at all.'

'I've got work.'

'Since when?'

'Since this morning. But not here. In Argentina. Buenos Aires.'

'So we're going to travel, boss!'

'*I'm* going to travel, Biscuter. If I take you I won't make anything on the deal.'

Carvalho looks through some papers. Finds his passport in a drawer. Biscuter can't believe his eyes. 'Just like that you tell me? Without sorting things out with Charo? Before you even try what I've cooked for you?'

'Charo. Did she phone?'

'No. But she sent you a radio as a present, d'you remember? And you didn't even respond. Maybe you should make the first move.'

'I prefer the second one.'

But his eighth sense, his guilt complex, tells him he's going too far with Biscuter. He softens his voice and his gestures, and goes over to the little foetus, stiff as a board from hurt pride. 'Let's see what you've made.'

'Aubergines with anchovies, a seafood hollandaise sauce, and to top that culinary monument a poached egg with a spoonful of caviar.'

'A real crisis menu.'

'It's lumpfish caviar.'

'Lead on, Biscuter. Argentina can wait.'

One of the advantages of living in Vallvidrera is that you can say goodbye to a whole city with a single glance, as if it were someone forced to attend a ceremony. In the days when he still did so, he had read, possibly in a book by Bowles, that the difference between a tourist and a traveller is that the one knows the limits of his journey, while the other yields to the open-ended logic of the voyage. Buenos Aires. For now, a one-way journey with the return vaguer than ever, just like in the days when travel was more important to him than life. His landscapes and his characters all destroyed. Bromide dead, Charo in voluntary exile, Biscuter left as his only connection with what had once been the fragile ecosystem of his close friendships. Above all, Barcelona after the Olympics, open to the sea, scored with expressways, the Barrio Chino being pulled down with indecent haste, the aeroplanes of political correctness circling the city, spraying it to kill off its bacteria, its historic viruses, its social struggles, its lumpen, a city without armpits, robbed of its armpits, a city turned into a theatre in which to stage the farce of modernity.

'I'll see everything more clearly from Buenos Aires.'

He pushes aside the things on the kitchen table, carefully lays down some sheets of writing paper, tries out his ballpoint. He sets himself to write, then hesitates. Time and again. Finally he screws up the courage: 'Dear Charo: I'm just about to leave for Buenos Aires on a job, but don't want to go without first trying to clear up our misunderstanding...' He lifts his head. Sniffs. Abandons the writing paper and runs towards his food, urged on by a smell of burning oxtail. He stirs his oxtail stew in a sauce. He's in the nick of time, and takes it off the stove for it to cool down a little. He separates the flesh from the bone adroitly, then puts the meat back in the sauce. He doesn't allow himself the luxury of setting the table, but settles for eating on a free corner, slightly disturbed by this total disrespect for his usual liturgy. Perhaps that's why he bolts his food, as if embarrassed at his own lack of consideration, and drinks no more than half a bottle of Mauro. Full but not satisfied. The sight of the half-finished letter keeps him from clearing up the plates or straightening out the mess on his table. He goes back to the letter, picks up his ballpoint, is about to write something more, then changes his mind. He feels like burning a book, and his hands stray towards *Buenos Aires* by Horacio Vázquez Rial, a personal guide he has almost finished. But he still feels indebted to what he's read, and it might be useful to him in the future. Instead he goes over to the bookcase. Chooses a book. One of the volumes of *Cuba* by Hugh Thomas. He starts to tear it up, and builds up the fire as it should be: first the book pages, then on top the covers. It begins to burn, then the whole hearth lights up the face of a thoughtful Carvalho, who glances over his shoulder in response to the call from the letter and the mess on the table. Finally he clears the table and the letter he's begun recovers all its presence on the polished surface. He picks it up, takes it with him to the bedroom where his suitcase is open to receive any last-minute additions. The letter falls gently on to his crumpled clothes. He reconsiders. Picks it up again. Puts it in his hand luggage. And it's from there that he recovers it a few hours later, on board an Aerolineas Argentinas jet, his nostalgia blunted by four whiskies and a bottle of Navarro Correa red wine, a Pinot Noir with a hint of burgundy. 'Things weren't the way you imagined, Charo...' He grows weary of it. Lets it drop. Picks up a paper. Glances casually at the front page of an Argentine newspaper: anodyne stuff, unimportant, second-hand, corruption Argentine-style in a world where all the hidden filth is busy exploding, Maradona playing he loves me, he loves me not with the latest football club he's chosen to complete the destruction of his legend with. The man in the seat next to him offers a cigarette, which Carvalho refuses with a friendly gesture. 'No, thanks. I only smoke cigars, and they're not permitted here.'

The man is plump, red-faced. He complains bitterly: 'Nothing's permitted these days. Everything that used to be good for you is bad now. Smoking. Eating. This your first trip to Buenos Aires?'

'Yes.'

'Business?'

'More or less; yes, business.'

'Good for you. Buenos Aires is a paradise for business. Quick and easy. What d'you know about Buenos Aires?'

'Maradona, the disappeared, tango.'

The bulging red face takes on an air of complete incredulity. 'Disappeared? Who's disappeared? Oh, you mean those subversives, the ones who died during the military government. My word, what a strange view you have of Buenos Aires. The disappeared are history, history distorted by anti-Argentine propaganda. Maradona falls, hauls himself up again, falls on his face again. The disappeared aren't going to come back, and the tango is a museum piece. But you'll see, you'll get rid of your clichés. A new Argentina has been born, a new breed of Argentines.'

He puts his hand into a black briefcase and pulls out a plastic bag, which he gives to Carvalho. 'D'you know what this is?'

Carvalho studies the contents of the bag. 'I can hardly believe it, but they look to me like lupin seeds.'

'That's right. They're *Lupinus albus*. The basis of future human nutrition.'

'We're all going to eat lupins? In Spain, we soak them and eat them with salt. They're food to nibble at, for kids or at parties or when you go to the circus.'

'No, it's the cows that'll eat the lupins, then we eat the cows. Up to now we've had all the grass we need to feed all the cows in the world, but recent scientific studies suggest that lupins are the perfect cow feed for the future. Everyone used to think that lupins, and especially the leaves, were harmful to cattle. D'you know why?'

'No idea.'

'Because bitter lupins contain a poisonous alkaloid, which is why they were used for fertilizers. But now we've produced lupins without the alkaloid. Cows eat them like cakes. Yum, yum! And Argentines are at the cutting edge of research into animal behaviour and nutrition. I'm on my way to see deputy minister Güelmes, who's one of the Argentine politicians most interested in the idea. Have you heard of him?'

'My knowledge of Argentine politics is strictly limited.'

By now, the man's bag is back in his briefcase. Carvalho pretends to doze off. The fat man goes on with what is now a monologue, driven by an irrepressible inner enthusiasm. As Carvalho is drifting into a real alcoholic sleep, his uncle's face appears and asks him: 'What d'you know about Buenos Aires?'

'Maradona, disappeared, tangos.'

'And scroungers, lots of scroungers. If a million Argentines weren't such thieves, the rest would be millionaires. And scientists, brilliant ones. It used to be one of the most educated countries in the world. My son was brilliant. Is brilliant. Things didn't go badly for me, nephew, it wasn't politics that took me there, it was hunger. Before our Civil War. I made a fortune. I made my son a scientist, a brilliant one. But my daughter-in-law got mixed up in politics. I managed to get my boy out of it, but I was too late to help her and their daughter. The earth swallowed them up. Disappeared. They say Buenos Aires is built on the disappeared. Lots of the men who worked on 9 de Julio Avenue, the widest in the world, are buried under its asphalt. A lot more disappeared when they built the metro system, the "underground" as they call it. Disappeared. It's a kind of destiny there. I managed to get your cousin Raúl out to Spain, hoping he'd forget. Then one fine day he escaped, went back. Don't worry about not knowing Buenos Aires. You'll be met at the airport by Alma, my son's sister-in-law. She's his wife's sister: she went through the whole business as well; she was married to a Catalan, or rather a

Catalan's son, a psychiatrist. A shrink who lives in Villa Freud. You'll find out what that means. She'll help you, though she doesn't much like Spaniards.'

The fat man has trouble getting his seatbelt undone, standing up and moving out into the aisle of the plane. Carvalho helps him get his hand luggage down. Several stickers on a bag proclaim 'The New Spirit of Argentina'. He wheezes off ahead of Carvalho, who loses sight of him in the process of picking up his baggage and going through immigration. He opens his passport at the back page with his photo, but the cop prefers to shut it and open it again for himself. He flicks through the pages, looks carefully at some stamps, then peers up at Carvalho. 'Pepe?'

'Yes, that's me. Do you know me?'

The cop points at the name written in the passport. 'It's the first time I've seen anyone called Pepe in a passport.'

'That's because I'm a private detective.'

The policeman says 'Ah!' as if that settled the matter, and stamps the document.

Carrying his luggage, Carvalho stares round Ezeiza airport and recalls what he knows about it. The bloody fight between people from the right and left of Perónism when Perón returned from exile. A foretaste of what López Rega and the military junta were to dish out to left-wingers a little later on. Carvalho stands with his suitcase between his legs, looking for the woman his uncle had mentioned. The fat guy passes him smiling broadly and waving a bag of lupins. Carvalho follows him with his gaze as he goes into a phone booth. The earpiece is soon covered in sweat from the abundant tufts of hair the man has round his ears, as if in compensation for his bald crown. He stares back at Carvalho while he makes a call. 'Hello, Captain? I got it out of him: he doesn't know a thing. Not a thing, although he could find out. Wait, guess who's come to meet him? The Modotti woman, Captain, the Modotti woman. The old man's made a move. I told you he would.'

A woman's voice behind his back. 'Are you the Masked Galician?'

Carvalho turns round, and what he sees interests or attracts him. A blonde woman is gazing at him. Fortyish, beautiful in a disturbing way. A wise-eyed Argentine woman with blonde hair carefully moulded in between visits to her psychologist; not that she needs to see one – she probably knows more about psychoanalysis than he does. Her age showing some attractive wrinkles and an ironic filter for everything she sees. But her smile quickly changes from ironic to open and friendly. She holds out her hand to Carvalho. 'Alma Modotti. Married name Font y Rius, but I got unmarried a long time ago. I don't like double-barrelled names.'

'Was that why you broke up?'

'We broke up because husbands with double-barrelled names are even more unbearable than those with straightforward ones.'

Carvalho would like to be able to study her at leisure, but she strides off and he can't get a good view of her face, as if she were deliberately keeping him at a distance with her smile. It's only when she's hailing a taxi that he gets a good look at her, as she turns to face him with green, ever-ironic eyes. She's about to give the taxi-driver an address, but Carvalho butts in. 'Could you do me a sentimental favour?'

'This is the capital of sentiment.'

Carvalho talks to the driver. 'Corrientes 3…4…8.'

The driver looks round with a wry smile and takes up from where Carvalho left off: *'Second floor, with a lift…!'*

Alma bursts out laughing.

'It's my favourite tango.'

'Tangos are like novels. They never tell the truth.'

'So you're a tango expert?'

'No, a literature expert. I teach at the University. How come you're such a tango fan?'

'Carlos Gardel was a myth in Barcelona. So were Irusta, Fugazot and Demare.'

'I've never even heard of them. Although I might not look it, I'm from the rock generation. Tango always seemed to me like Argentina for export. It's only recently I've got closer to it. In fact, I often go to a place called Tango Amigo, perhaps because the presenter and the singer are friends of mine. Adriana Varela. Have you heard of her in Spain?'

'I don't keep up with these things. As far as tango goes, I didn't get much beyond Gardel and Discépolo. The one who did reach Spain is Cecilia Rosetto, who's a wonderful actress. I hope to see her here.'

Carvalho has managed to produce a cigar straight from its cardboard packet inside his pocket, and Alma praises his skill.

'My fingertips can locate a Havana cigar wherever it's hiding.'

He lights it and opens the taxi window. For the first time he can get some impression of Buenos Aires, which seems too big for its own possibilities, as if it had grown too quickly or there hadn't been enough money to preserve its grandeur. 'It all looks so promising but somehow rundown.'

'Could be. Every neighbourhood is different. Borges said that when you cross Rivadavia Avenue you cross the frontier into another world. Rivadavia runs from one end of Buenos Aires to the other and splits it in two.'

The Calle Corrientes. A chaotic, old-fashioned scene, with shops and apartment buildings in clashing styles jostling each other for attention. Alma's distant voice acting as tour guide: Corrientes, home of the tango you love so much. The taxi pulls up outside Number 348. Carvalho gets out, oblivious to the withering looks the driver and Alma are giving him through the windows. Carvalho is looking for something, surprised he can't find it. Finally he spots a placard stating that this was the spot for which the world-famous tango was composed, but there's no sign of the original building now, not even a trace of the perfume of adultery. It's a parking lot. A desolate open space with battered blue gates, like a last distant memory of the love nest mentioned in the song. Carvalho turns round and accuses the two people smiling at him: 'It used to be a tango, now it's a parking lot.'

Alma says a few words to the driver: 'When our friend comes back from his tango fantasies, take us to Entre Ríos 204, would you? But first, show him the obelisk.'

The driver follows her instructions, but as compensation sings, at the top of his voice:

> Corrientes three...four...eight
> Second floor, with a lift...
> Décor courtesy of Maple's
> Piano, rug and bedside table;

A telephone that rings
A Victrola crying to the sound
Of old tangos from my youth
A cat, but in porcelain to ensure
It doesn't disturb the love-making.

Corrientes comes out into 9 de Julio Avenue, and the obelisk is there to prove the fact.

'Look, the widest avenue in the world, and the world's least significant obelisk. It's so wide – a hundred and forty metres – it's almost unreal, but I like it because of all the trees. Buenos Aires is full of trees that are just too beautiful – too much altogether – ombus, gum trees, araucarias, palos borrachos. In spite of all the traffic, 9 de Julio in November is full of blossom from the purple jacarandas, in September it's pink from the lapachos, and in February it's the turn of the white palos borrachos. The obelisk is never in bloom. It was erected in 1936 to commemorate four hundred years of the city's foundation. But the real reason was different. We had no reference point for our dreams about the city. They had to fill all this empty space somehow. Someone described it as the phallic symbol for Buenos Aires machismo. Someone else called it the city's shameless prick. Now it's the obelisk. Nothing more, nothing less. So, here's the obelisk. And here's a Spaniard.'

It could have been an apartment in the middle-class Ensanche district of Barcelona or in Madrid, without the wooden stairs the inhabitants of Madrid have, or the art nouveau design details of the Catalan capital.

'Entre Ríos, round the corner from Callao. The apartment belongs to your uncle. The centre of the world.'

Carvalho goes round opening and shutting doors, always coming back to the tiny living- and dining-room where Alma's waiting for him disdainfully. Carvalho is satisfied finally, and points to a fireplace that has a gas or electric radiator in it. 'I'd like to have a wood fire. Can I use the fireplace?'

'You could, but do you have any idea how much firewood costs? Or are you going to burn the doors?'

'What I burn is my business. Do you live here?'

'Here? No. I'm not part of the contract. Your uncle told me to do this – the flat was rented out. He asked me to show you round the city, that's all.'

Alma has big, sad, green eyes. She looks down at her bag and starts rummaging for something in it. Eventually she pulls out a photograph and a piece of paper, and hands them to Carvalho. 'Here's my address – it's not far away – and a photo of your cousin Raúl.'

It's the same photo of a family reunion that his uncle has already given him, but here in Buenos Aires it looks different. As if it were more recent. Sitting round a table loaded with plates of food, an older pair, two young couples, a little girl. Carvalho looks intently at the faces. Alma peers over his shoulder, and he can sense her female warmth, the feel of her breasts on his back, then her voice as she points out who's who. 'That's your uncle, that's Aunt Orfelia; there's me, my sister Berta, and my brother-in-law, Raúl.'

The image of Raúl stays with Carvalho. A gaunt-looking man with huge eyes and prominent cheekbones. In the photo, Raúl and Alma are sitting together. Alma's voice breaks with emotion when she says: 'That's their girl. Eva María.'

'Why on earth a double name like that?'

'You don't understand a thing, do you? Eva from Eva Perón, María because of María Estela Perón. At the time we didn't know what a traitor María Estela would be.'

Carvalho has to shut his eyes to forget the child; it's the only way he can concentrate on the others. 'You and your sister are very alike.'

'Physically, yes.'

'Otherwise, no?'

'Not spiritually: by which I mean personality, disposition, feelings, emotions, hopes and fears. Berta was intolerant and uncompromising. Alma on the other hand...me...I was always less confident, more dependent on Berta since childhood. Berta was good at making people dependent on her – me, Raúl, the rest of the group. People always praised her for her "character". She's got such a strong character! they'd always say. Even my father, who was one of those unbearable rich bullheaded patriarchs, turned into a softie with Berta.'

'Can you get anything to eat in this city?'

'You can eat to your heart's content: this is Argentina.'

'Marx said you only get to know a country when you've eaten its bread and drunk its wine.'

'Are you a Marxist?'

'In the gastronomic faction.'

Alma didn't have a car, and was against the idea of taking another taxi. She believed in public transport. Carvalho didn't. 'Some Marxist you are.'

In the end they took a taxi. On their way to the Costanera by the river, Alma got the driver to go through the Palermo neighbourhood – it doesn't really exist, she said, Borges invented it, and the park in Palermo shows how the pre-Columbian idea of the noble savage has been reincarnated here in Buenos Aires as the ignoble one. 'As soon as the sun comes up, they all strip off and head for the park to get a tan.'

It's true. On the grass, under the trees of Argentina that to Carvalho seem as unbelievably large as the rivers of America, men and women are soaking up the sun, busily pretending they're as free as birds in nature. The taxi leaves them at the Costañera, where they look for a decent 'Argentine' restaurant. Alma is no great food expert, but has a dim recollection of a restaurant that's 'not so bad' along here. But first she forces Carvalho to look at the boundless river and follow the flow of its dirty waters. 'You can't swim in it. It's so polluted it must be almost a hundred per cent chemical waste.'

'But it's beautiful. I love big rivers, perhaps because in Spain we call any little stream a river. I can spend hours watching how rivers like the Mississippi, the Nile, or the Mekong flow.'

'Have you seen all of them?'

'Yes.'

'Does the Mekong exist?'

'Of course it does.'

When the waiter arrives, Carvalho reels off a list of what he'd like to eat, despite Alma's wide-eyed surprise at his appetite.

'To start with, some meat pasties, meat roll, black pudding and sausage. After that, a big steak, rare. Oh, and lots of *chimichurri* sauce.'

The waiter has served lots of meals in this restaurant, but still he asks: 'Are you sure?'

'I'm only ever sure of myself in restaurants.'

Alma looks on passively as the table fills and empties with all that Carvalho has ordered. Gradually her astonishment turns to horror: 'Where do you put it all?'

'I've got a bottomless spirit. When my body is full, I eat with my spirit. You've hardly eaten a thing.'

'I eat to live.'

'I eat to remember and drink to forget, or perhaps it's the other way round, I've always hated poetic mottoes. This Mendoza wine is excellent: I thought only the Chileans had good wine, although apparently these days there's decent stuff even in places like New Zealand.'

'It's all part of the new international order. Are you a leftie?'

Carvalho looks down at his hands.

'I mean in politics.'

'I used to be. What about you?'

'What sort? I mean what kind of leftie.'

'Marxist-Leninist, gourmet faction. Then I joined the CIA. I killed Kennedy. I overthrew Goulart, and Allende. Then I went home and became a private detective. And you, what kind of a red were you?'

'A left-wing Perónist, I think. Does Perónism seem picturesque to you?'

'There was a long interview with him on Spanish TV just before he came back to Argentina from exile. He said he was a follower of the doctrines of Christ, Marx, José Antonio Primo de Rivera and Che Guevara. The only reason he didn't mention Mother Teresa of Calcutta was that she wasn't famous then.'

'I already told you. Some of us were Perónists in spite of Perón.'

'So what are you now?'

'A survivor and a teacher of literature earning a monthly wage that wouldn't allow me to buy many meals like this one.'

The waiter is delighted at Carvalho's appetite and the fact that he's drunk a whole bottle of Cautivo de Orfila, a sharp wine in the best sense of the word. He's even more delighted at his tip. Alma approves of neither the appetite nor the tip. 'What if after I've given a class on Steiner or *Tel Quel*, the students gave me a tip? It's a petit bourgeois invention to keep waiters as slaves. To ensure the customer is always right.'

Then they're by the river again. Carvalho is fascinated once more by the sluggish brown waters. He searches in vain for the far shore. 'Is Montevideo over there?'

'That's what they say.'

'Have you ever been there?'

'I think so.'

'You're not sure if you've ever been in Montevideo?'

'I was in a city called Montevideo once, I was in one called Buenos Aires, and I'm pretty sure I reached another one called Santiago, but…'

'But what?'

'They disappeared.'

'The cities?'

'The cities, that is the cities full of people who mattered to me. A lot of them died, and the survivors are all dead.'

'Do you divide yourselves into those who suffered and those who didn't?'

'Who do you mean?'

'The friends in your group. I suppose you did form a group.'

'Forty-six of them didn't live to tell the tale.'

'What about those who did?'

'A bit of everything. Let's just say they're a mixed bunch. We're divided into the holy innocents – literature teachers and failed artists – and those who've made it. We have friends who got married to partners from the upper classes. Even some who married sisters of people who'd once been kidnapped in the name of the revolution and historic change.'

'Who are the artists?'

'There's me, an artist with words; there's Pignatari, a superannuated rock singer, and Silverstein, who's a mixture of actor and liar.'

'And those who made it?'

'Güelmes, who's almost a minister. Does the name mean anything to you?'

'I've heard it recently, but I can't remember who said it or when.'

'It might have been your uncle. My ex-husband Font y Rius has a private clinic and is one of the leading lights in Villa Freud. Only in

Buenos Aires could you find a neighbourhood full of psychologists they call Villa Freud. When he started out, Font was all for Ronnie Laing and his anti-psychiatry. He wanted to tear down all the asylum walls. He said madness was nothing more than a metaphor. He was a psychobolshie: did that word ever reach Spain? In those days we used it for people who mixed revolutionary socialism and psychoanalysis, people who combined Wilhelm Reich and what they could take from Marxism. Now he's rich thanks to madmen: thanks to metaphors, I mean. But madness isn't a metaphor to him any more. It's a vein of gold. Raúl's partner, Roberto, has done the same. He's a weak type who's never really committed himself to anything. He continued with the same line of research as Raúl to make money, that's all. To him, it's as if nothing has happened. He's one of those scientists who reckons that science is neutral.'

'And Raúl?'

'He's a fugitive, always has been. Running from my sister, from his own scientific discoveries, from any commitment, from the military, from me.'

'From you?'

'Well, from my sister really. She was the strongest personality of us all.'

Carvalho takes the family snapshot out of his pocket. He stares at Raúl's features. Looks across at Alma. 'Where do we start?'

Alma refuses to look at the photo again. Instead she glances all around her with something like amusement. Until finally she stares down at the river in front of them. 'What about there?'

The shacks are perched above reed-covered riverbanks that stagnant waters seem to have condemned to an eternity of dismal uselessness. In one of them Raúl is lying flat on his back on a straw mattress, staring up at the ceiling. He turns to look towards the only window, through which float the sounds of nearby music. He gets up and looks out towards the rows of other shacks. A group of outcasts is trying to keep warm round a fire; on a hillock there's a wretched little bar which is where the music is coming from. Several couples in leather are dancing to rock music. Hundreds of muscular rats cover rubbish tips like a moving carpet. Then four motorcyclists appear. Their faces are invisible, but they look like medieval warriors in their helmets and chainmail. The fat man appears, looking even more monstrous in this wretched landscape and because of the silver-plated luxury of the limousine he's just got out of. He shouts to the motorcyclists: 'Make sure you find him! Don't let him get away!'

Raúl looks wrapped up in his own thoughts. He's not exactly clean, hair unkempt, several days' growth of beard. He's clasping a steaming iron pot. He turns round startled when the door to the shack opens. Looks to see who it is.

'You have to get out of here. There's some strange people outside.'

'Are you sure, Pignatari?'

The shadowy face nods. Raúl's gaze moves to the window, judging its size. All of a sudden, Raúl Tourón stands up, steadies himself in the window frame, then dives into the open air. The other man watches him fall, roll over and then run off between the maze of shacks. The motorcyclists are trying to search their way among the huts of corrugated iron and cardboard, but their wheels sink into the dank puddles. Oblivious to everything, by the bar the same couples seem to want to go on dancing to the same tune.

There are photos of Freud, Jung, Lacan and Reich on the walls. An eclectic, Carvalho decides. Font y Rius is a man of around forty, with receding hair that only serves to emphasize what half a century ago would have been called 'noble features'. He's smoking a pipe, signing papers and talks to Carvalho without pausing in his task. 'D'you know what I'm signing? Psychological reports? No. Butchers' bills. The mad have to eat too.'

'They eat meat? I thought you were supposed to give mad people fish.'

'If you take meat away from an Argentine madman, it'll only make him even madder.'

Carvalho studies the photos of the masters of psychology. 'What about your masters here? Would they agree you should call mad people mad?'

'I didn't call them mad either in the days when I believed in anti-psychiatry. By the way, it wasn't Laing who invented the phrase. It was

Cooper who started using it to describe what Laing and other experimenters like Basaglia were doing. But madness does exist. Evil exists.'

'And good?'

'No.'

'Why did your brother-in-law Raúl come back?'

Font y Ruis stops signing his bills. He seems to hesitate, looks up suspiciously. 'I don't know. He sat in that chair you're in, and stared at me. He didn't say a word. Then he left, and never came back. Typically depressive behaviour, a mixture of discharge and concealment; but not necessarily pathological.'

'You mean to say that your former brother-in-law Raúl manages to escape to Spain some years after the death of his wife and the disappearance of his daughter, and then one fine day he comes back. He pays you a visit. And according to you, you say nothing to each other. He gets up and goes, and that's that.'

'It may seem incredible, but that's how it was. We didn't talk of anything because he could hardly get a word out. All he did was shout insults and cry.'

'Who did he insult? Why did he come to see you rather than Alma? Why was he in tears?'

'He insulted the murderers of the Process.'

'What Process?'

'In Argentina we invented a euphemism for our dictatorship. The military called it the Process of National Reorganization. To some it meant the process of returning the country to normal. To others it meant the process of extermination. All dictatorships cover their image in a mask, and language is a means to help the cover-up. If you call cruelty firmness, it's no longer cruelty.'

'That's true. In Spain we had a king who right-wing historians called "The Lawmaker", and others called "The Cruel".'

'See what I mean?'

'Who else did he insult?'

'All of us. He's suspicious of those who survived. Maybe he didn't go to see Alma because she reminds him too much of Berta, or because he didn't want to insult her.'

'What or who was he crying for?'

'I think he was crying for himself. Although sometimes it seemed it was for his daughter.'

'Did he make a point of insulting you in particular? Why would that be?'

'Because I refused to disappear. All of them are the disappeared. Have you met Alma? She seems real, doesn't she? But she's not. They all disappeared more than twenty years ago. When they refused to grow up.'

'Is that why you separated from Alma?'

'The military separated us. In other words, history. Because all that's history now. History that interests fewer and fewer people. All you have to do is calculate the difference in numbers between those who disappeared and those of us who didn't. Those who refused to disappear will always win.'

'And the girl?'

'Alma searched for her desperately. She's still looking for her through the grandmothers of disappeared children.'

'The mothers of the Plaza de Mayo?'

'No, they're just symbolic folklore these days. They really are mad.'

Through the garden window they can see the more conventionally mad people walking round and round. The psychiatrist grasps the association of ideas and images that must be going through Carvalho's mind. Perhaps he's sorry for what he said. 'Those women are crazy from loneliness and impotent rage. Every time they meet up in the Plaza de Mayo it's as if they were calling up the ghosts of their children. It's a magic rite.'

This is Carvalho's baptism into the culture and love of Buenos Aires cafés. Their wonderful atmosphere is far removed from the ghastly functionality of most Spanish cafés; they're like serpents biting their tail on past time: art nouveau, art deco, modernist styles abound. And wood, wood, wood. Argentina's generous forests converted into décor to have tea or coffee in, while the conversation flows along in a musical Spanish that's full of Italian overtones. It's Carvalho's first café. It's called the Café Tortoni, and when Alma says the name, it's as if she were describing a temple. In the Avenida de Mayo. Marble, painted skylights, interior lights softened by the carved wood, prints on the walls, romantic mirrors, red leather upholstery, at the back, billiard tables and private rooms for regulars. Also on the walls, pictures of the café through history, in the very place which seems to have managed to impose its own logic on time.

It's not far from the Plaza de Mayo where the mothers plod round and round, but emotionally those protests are at the far ends of the earth from these docile-looking ladies chatting over their coffee or hot chocolate. Carvalho wonders if any sense of the demonstrations down below in front of the Casa Rosada has seeped in here. But in among the noble woods perfumed with the smells of excellent coffee, liquors, cakes and ice-creams, there's no room for History, and as ever men and women seem like nothing more than cheap traders – in their lives, in any other goods. 'A few yards from here, there are mothers protesting about their dead children, but nobody in here spares them a thought.'

'Nor out there either.'

Alma seems taken aback at Carvalho's sense of surprise. 'As individuals we tend to forget the harm we do or that's done to us. Why should it be any different for a society?'

'Sometimes I get flashes of my old naïve secondary school feelings of revolt.'

'Ah, the ethics of revolt. They'll die with my generation, and my generation is on its last legs.'

They set off down to the square. They come across a small group of women walking round and round. Some are holding placards, others wear photos of their disappeared children on their chests, like medals. Some seem as if they have a whole universe of emptiness on their shoulders. Few local people are looking on; only a few tourists who perhaps are ethical tourists, perhaps not. Feelings of emotion, curiosity and indifference in equal measure; there's even a certain annoyance in the air among the passers-by, because of the 'bad reputation' this insistence on historical memory gives the city.

'Have they explained why they go on doing this? Don't they know their children are dead?'

A flash of anger appears in Alma's eyes. 'If they accept their deaths, they can't accuse the system any more. If they accept money in reparation, it would be exonerating the system. How many accomplices did the military have to help them do what they did? But you're right, the mothers have almost become just another tourist attraction. I work with the grandmothers. They're searching methodically for all the children adopted – that is, kidnapped – by the military. Like Eva María. Those children exist. They're not spirits. My niece, for example. She must be twenty years old now. How could anyone recognize her?'

The demonstration is almost over. Hébé Bonafini, the leader of the Mothers, grabs a megaphone and delivers the political message for today: we will come back again and again so that our children are not wiped from the memory of infamy. They were taken from us alive. They must be returned alive. In other countries of the world, mothers are looking for their children. The system and its barbarity goes on and on. Carvalho and Alma cross the street separating the square from the entrance to the Casa Rosada. Carvalho searches in his memory for everything stored there about one of the most famous presidential palaces in the world.

'Do you want to go in? Or would you rather walk up to the Congress building? The old-age pensioners demonstrate outside it once a week. It's like a complete collection of fantastic old people. Or would you like to see inside here?'

'Is it that easy to get in?'

'It's full of former friends of mine. Some of them ex-revolutionaries. Menem wanted to undermine the left by incorporating them into the system, like the PRI did in Mexico. All I have to do is give my name in reception and all the doors will be opened, even at the highest levels.'

'I don't have the time to see any politicians.'

'Well, when you need me just whistle, and I'll come running.'

True to her word, Alma turns on her heel and leaves him standing there. She's strangely annoyed with Carvalho or with herself or with the backdrop of the Casa Rosada and the Mothers. Carvalho catches her up.

'I want to see Raúl and Berta's place. Will you come with me?'

'Who do you think I am? I've had more than enough tragedy for one day. No, thanks. Do you think I've nothing better to do than follow you around?'

'What did I do wrong?'

But by now Alma is far away, running to catch a bus, and it would be too violent to try to catch up with her. A taxi appears from Puerto Madero, and Carvalho tells him to go to La Recoleta. He tries to remember what he's learnt about it in the book on Buenos Aires he read by Vázquez Rial before leaving Barcelona, with all the mixed feelings he gets when he reads these days. The well-off area of north Buenos Aires comprises more than one neighbourhood, the author says, and several have a very definite character of their own. This is the case of La Recoleta, which is bordered on one side by a cemetery celebrated in a poem by the young Borges. The rich people of Buenos Aires arrived here in the mid-nineteenth century, fleeing the plagues of the port area; later they continued their exodus towards even more select neighbourhoods, as has happened in every city in the world that can lay claim to be something more than a mere city. Carvalho finds himself in front of the huge gum trees mentioned in the book, with their enormous cement crutches holding up the centuries-old branches. And beyond them is the Recoleta cemetery Borges wrote about – Borges here as everywhere else in the imagined world of Buenos Aires. Carvalho goes in, looking for the family pantheon of Eva Duarte de Perón, which contains all that's left of a body that was embalmed, tortured, broken, even raped by a crazy necrophiliac military officer who hated Perón but fell in love with the icy soul of his dead enemy. The severity of the marble is softened by bouquets of flowers, and two women are talking to Evita as if she could hear them in the depths where she's been buried to avoid any further desecration. 'Oh, poor Evita! So far from Chacarita, where Perón's buried!'

The sober pantheon obviously belongs to a rich family that fits in well among these long, broad avenues of a cemetery that itself is a reflection of the rich, well-appointed houses of the neighbourhood outside, where houses with gardens boast bronze doorknockers on doorways made of the finest woods – the external signs of having arrived for people who live protected by porters, like the one on duty in the apartment building where Berta and Raúl lived until the night they were raided. In his smart uniform, the porter is busy polishing the brasswork on the stairs and makes it clear he doesn't have time to waste talking to someone so obviously Spanish. While Carvalho is waiting for some kind of response, an old woman tries to use the lift.

'It's out of order.'

Resignedly, the old woman starts to climb the noble marble staircase. For some reason, this loosens the porter's tongue. 'The only thing that works around here are us porters.'

'Did Señor Raúl ask for his key by any chance?'

'Which Raúl would that be?'

'As I tried to tell you, I'm the cousin of someone who used to live here, Raúl Tourón. I'd like to see him, and I thought he might have called in here.'

'Ah, you mean Professor Tourón? He lived here a long time ago. But not for long.'

'Has he been back recently?'

'Yes, but I didn't give him the key. He didn't ask for it. If he had, I wouldn't have been able to anyway. After the night of the raid, the apartment was sealed off. Later it was handed back to its owners – Doctor Tourón was only renting it. The owners are selling loads of apartments in the neighbourhood, especially to Europeans and North Americans. Lots of Spaniards bought bargains. Argentina was for sale, although now the prices have gone up again, and it's become very expensive for foreigners.'

'What did Señor Tourón do exactly when he came back?'

'At first he stood there for a while on the pavement opposite, as if he was scared to come any closer. A good while. Then he crossed the street and opened the door. I went up to him to see what was going on, because although I sort of recognized his face, he'd changed a lot. He replied with my name: "Mattías." I asked him: "You're Doctor Tourón, aren't you?" He nodded. Then he asked me: "What about the girl?" "I don't know, doctor, I never knew anything about her." So then he left the same way he had come.'

'Is it true you never knew anything?'

'A porter knows everything and nothing. I see people come and go. I nearly always know who they are, and when I don't, I ask. For many years now. I polish the metal and dust the carpets. If you were to go up to one of those luxurious apartments today, they probably couldn't even offer you a coffee, because their coffee-makers are electric, and there's no electricity. Am I making myself clear?'

'Yes, you are. Not that I understand a word of it.'

'That's what I wanted, to be clear and yet leave you guessing.'

'Fine. So after years in exile, Doctor Tourón comes back, turns up here, asks you obvious questions, then disappears again. And in all this time has his sister-in-law Alma never been here?'

The porter doesn't seem to want to continue the conversation. His eyes have turned cold, and he is clinging on to his shammy leather cloth as if his life depended on it.

'I can't tell you any more, because I don't know any more; and anyway, I've already said too much. Ninety per cent of Argentines wouldn't have answered your questions at all. What went on in the Process had nothing to do with us porters. All we ever did was see who came and went.'

It's a slogan which is also the name of a company: 'New Argentina'. Carvalho suddenly remembers the conversation he had with the fat man on the plane. Small world. The food and animal behaviour institute his cousin had worked in before the dictatorship is now called New Argentina. But even though that's its name, it is housed in a neoclassical 1940s building with more than a whiff of Mussolini, and nationalist pride is evident on all sides. Production statistics, pride in Argentina's cows, its horses, even its human beings. Carvalho is led down scrupulously scrubbed corridors by a girl dressed in a white coat that cannot hide her splendid ass or legs, and Carvalho gives in to her obvious charms.

The laboratory door opens and one of the fattest men in the world appears. It takes Carvalho a few seconds to identify him with the photo file his brain sends him in a flash: of course, the passenger next to him on the plane. The man pretends not to have seen Carvalho, who also busies himself looking around what appears to be a typical laboratory, with its rats' cages and scientific equipment that's always seemed to him should be used for alchemy. Eventually Roberto Améndola comes up. He's big in every way: physically, cynically, playfully. In his hands and mouth everything seems small. He looks at Carvalho as if he were a tiny mouse. 'Raúl and I studied biology together. We got our professional qualifications together. We ran this laboratory together. Fortunately, I didn't get married; unfortunately, he did. His wife Berta was like a cross between Marta Harnecker and Evita Perón. Do you know what females I'm referring to?'

'As far as females go, I'm a real encyclopedia.'

'He let Berta do whatever she wanted, he just accepted it. He was brilliant. I was stubborn. That wasn't right. Why not? Because he was the son of recent immigrants, so he should have been the stubborn one. I'm from a family which has been here since the time of Rosas in the nineteenth century. That's a long time for Argentina. So I should have been the brilliant one.'

'He got into a political mess; you didn't.'

'That was where his being an immigrant betrayed him. He was a rebel, but a rebel who wore silk Italian ties, had an apartment in La Recoleta and an imported European car. The ones who got him mixed up in politics were his wife and his sister-in-law. Those two had a very masculine view of history.'

'And you have a feminine one?'

'Let's just say I take the conventional female position. I'm passive with regards history. I'm more interested in the biological memory of animals than in the historical one of men. What use is historical memory to us today?'

'Did he come and see you when he returned to Argentina?'

'Yes.'

'What did he want?'

'I don't know. To tell you the truth, I've no idea. He talked of his work, and how far he had got with it. We've come a long way since then, but I offered to help him get his job back here. We don't make as much as before, because we can't get any contracts with private firms, and the state pays badly. He was very angry we call this New Argentina. He said it sounded Fascist. But I needed new partners, and they as well as all other Argentines need to believe in Argentina after all the crap we threw at each other or had thrown at us. It was easier before. Can you guess how we managed to live well, very well, and still do? We apply some of what we've discovered to making rat poisons.'

With his interior gaze, Carvalho tries to stand back from himself alongside the biologist, to take in the whole of this laboratory built as a prison for rats perhaps out of fear that otherwise they might imprison men. The animals scamper around looking for a way to escape, or perhaps they're simply imagining it. He hears Améndola trying to tell him something.

'These rats' behaviour teaches us not only what we have to do to get rid of other rats, but also what's needed to save mankind. What we have to do to save the only animal that doesn't deserve to live. For example, by improving his diet. What do you know about lupins?'

'That's strange. It's the second time I've been asked that. Next to nothing. Should we be eating them?'

'No, the cows will eat lupins, then we'll eat the cows.'

'That seems like an idea that's been tried often before in history.'

Roberto has fallen silent, and Carvalho respects his withdrawal for a few seconds. 'Raúl. Did he say anything about what his plans were?'

'What he said was quite a jumble, but he was calm. He talked about rats. He said that when he was a rat he'd been kept in an underground dungeon with a small grating in the roof for air. Sometimes he'd look up and imagine he could see the two of us examining him. You and me, he said, we were there above the grating, looking down at me the rat – and I wanted to behave properly, like a well-behaved rat, even though I might get impatient sometimes, like a rat who looks at his watch, but...'

'But what?'

'But he didn't have a watch. Apparently they wouldn't let them have watches.'

Améndola seems to be enjoying the thought of the imaginary scene. The well-endowed young woman, possibly an assistant, passes by. Carvalho can't help admiring her ass and legs again. Roberto notices his interest. 'That comes from a lot of meat protein. Lots of steaks. Our asses are full of the best of Argentina. Do you want to see the real Argentina?'

Roberto's eyes go to the poster showing the contented cow. Carvalho follows his gaze. New Argentina it says on the door. Outside the window, motorcyclists dressed as if they intend to terrify circle round. Roberto leads the way and shows Carvalho to cowsheds that look like something out of a Hollywood film, with all the latest equipment. Unbelievable cows. Superbly looked after. 'First the lupins, remember...then the cows, then mankind – riches, plenty. We have a future again.'

He goes into the pastures, strokes the cows, kisses them. Carvalho doesn't know whether to laugh or be concerned. He looks round to see if anyone is watching, but doesn't see how behind a Venetian blind a gaunt-faced man with pale grey ice for eyes is staring at them. Next to him is the fat man from the plane, who's clenching his teeth so hard he almost seems to have a jawbone beneath the rolls of fat. The gaunt, athletic-looking man of around fifty stares out of the window and says: 'He's a fool. Why did he let the Spaniard in here?'

'I told you Captain, he's unreliable. He's going to cause us trouble. The mess that crazy guy Raúl caused here the other night has knocked him off balance.'

'I should have finished them all off twenty years ago. That son of a bitch isn't going to cause me any trouble. I wish I'd never even thought of doing a deal with them.'

Out in the field, Roberto is still spouting his theories about cows and the future. All of a sudden he falls silent. He's spotted Raúl a bit further on, peering at them from a ditch. Roberto tries to say something but fails, as if Raúl's hidden gaze had paralysed his body and his voice. Then he snaps out of it, mutters an excuse to Carvalho, turns on his heel and runs into the Foundation. He bursts into the room where the fat man and the Captain were observing them. They stare angrily at him. 'He's here! I've just seen him!'

The fat man rushes up to him and asks: 'Who?'

'Raúl!'

The Captain turns to the window. All he can see is Carvalho philosophizing with the cows. The fat man hurries out of another door and runs waving his arms towards the motorcyclists. The bikes roar off round the building, and zoom towards Carvalho, who is taken by surprise at their determination to catch him. He doesn't have time to ask them why. Two black leather angels throw themselves on him and knock him down. They start punching, and as he is trying to avoid the third one landing on top of him as well, beyond their masked faces he thinks he sees the fat man from the plane come panting up, shouting at the top of his voice: 'Not him, you assholes!'

Carvalho loses consciousness.

Raúl runs along the ditch and falls panting by an irrigation channel. He raises himself on his elbows, and can't see any immediate danger. Kneels down again to cup some water from the channel, and is brought up short by the image of himself reflected in the water. The wild, staring eyes of a man: Raúl. Himself. In a bad way. Several days' growth of beard, as if he were still down in that cement hole with a narrow grating on its roof. He remembers how when his mind wandered in those days, he would sometimes see himself on top of the grating with Roberto, commenting on the behaviour of his other, imprisoned self, the laboratory rat. The two of them would stand there, in their white coats, staring down at the tortured Raúl with the same indifference as they would study a rat. Perhaps it was because he was able to stand outside himself and see that Raúl, that rat in a torture laboratory, that he managed to grasp the situation more objectively, that he managed to survive. But what was Roberto doing there, always alongside his other scientific self, the rat torturer? Passing neutral comments on the rat's squeaks of fear. Raúl, beside himself, about to succumb mentally from the pain and fear. Then all at once the Captain appeared alongside them, with his refined, subtle cruelty.

'Would you like to go out into the street, Doctor Tourón?'

Or: 'Who would you kill, son of a bitch, to be allowed outside?'

The same Captain. The one who once took him out for a ride in his own car. That was no guarantee you would survive. It just happened that sometimes the torturers took you out of the cave where all you saw were shadows of reality, and allowed you a glimpse for an hour or two of the life you had left on hold. They took you to the cinema. Or showed you the bills for flowers they had sent in your name to their wives, or to your mother. The Captain took him to see *Being There* with Peter Sellers, and within a few minutes both he and his torturer were laughing, taking time out from their real roles. But then back in the underground cell, there was no guarantee that the good mood would continue, that a beating or a torture session with the cattle prod would not immerse you once again in the only possible reality. And you couldn't take advantage of being outside to escape, because your family was facing all kinds of threats, as were you, and then beneath or beyond those threats was the syndrome of the grateful hostage.

'That's an excellent idea, Señor Tourón,' the Captain said to him on one of these outings. 'And it was you who first thought of it. The grateful hostage! I remember that in your research into animal behaviour you wrote brilliantly about awarding a prize arbitrarily and very rarely, as a powerful exception to the rule of constant and equally arbitrary punishment.'

Then one day they let him see his father. That was a sign they were not going to kill him, that he wasn't going to disappear – or if he was, his father would disappear too. But he seemed in control. He was very sure of himself, and the Captain seemed to respect him. Raúl was allowed to speak alone with him, but they didn't manage to say anything to each other. They never managed to say anything ever again. Not when a few days later the two of them returned to Spain. Not for almost twenty years in Spain. Only when Raúl, his mind made up, told him he was leaving the next day for Buenos Aires. And then all the old man had said was: 'What will be, will be. And all I've done is useless.'

The students listened to her perhaps because she had the look of a mature Madonna, with scars on her face that looked gentle or traced with her permission. The lecture room of a university fallen on hard times, in keeping with a pauper culture. Alma is sitting behind a table up on the platform. Carvalho has slipped in through the half-open door, behind the backs of the carefully scruffy students sitting in this carelessly scruffy room, a rundown, cheap and mercenary scene that is completely at odds with the words coming from Alma's pale, sensual lips.

'The criticism that the language of marginalized people is a non-language merely disguises the fact that all language has now become non-language. Look at all the usual messages we get from politics or advertising. They are not trying to convey knowledge, truth, or a sense of mystery. All they want to do is convince us. And we all pretend we have been convinced, because we doubt whether there is any point in doubting, suspecting, or still less, denying. Steiner asks himself the Romantic question of whether it is still possible that words can reacquire the mystery they had at the dawn of tragic poetry.'

The lecturer is as beautiful as she is sure of herself, and sceptical.

'But why does Steiner ask himself that question? Isn't he doing it from a position where his own language has become false? Isn't he laying claim to an impossible nostalgia?'

Silence.

'Thank you for your attention. Tomorrow we'll look at the topic from the point of view of Roland Barthes' *Mythologies*.'

Carvalho pushes his way forward through the scrum of young bodies. He observes how Alma rhythmically collects up her books, straightens her cardigan, stands up and accommodates her dainty muscles to her remarkable forty-year-old frame. She smiles briefly to dismiss everyone, and when she raises her head to decide which corridor she should make her escape down, she sees Carvalho standing by the platform.

'The masked Galician. Are you interested in Steiner or Barthes?'

'Are they a tango duo? Or do they play on the left wing for Boca Juniors?'

'Don't make me talk any more. I'm thirsty. Thirsty for water.'

'The thirst for water is a primitive one. Thirst for wine means culture, and thirst for a cocktail is its highest expression.'

Only now does Alma notice the bruises on Carvalho's face, and a transparent bit of plaster on the corner of his mouth.

'What happened?'

'I got beaten up by mistake. They thought I was Raúl.'

Alma's ironic mask slips. She looks around as though Raúl's name could only bring alarm and disaster. Carvalho leads her out and she allows herself to be taken along without realizing exactly where they are going, until she finds herself in a club inevitably lined with precious woods, and with a cocktail list in her hands. She doesn't even glance at it, still horrified by Carvalho's face.

'Are you going to explain or not?'

But the presence of a waiter hovering over them cuts short their conversation. Carvalho surveys the list of cocktails, shuts it with a sigh, and hands it back.

'Surprise me.'

'Would you like to try a Maradona?'

'What's in it?'

'Bourbon, peach, lemon and orange juices, with a sprig of fresh mint and some strawberries.'

'What's that got to do with Maradona?'

'Nothing, probably. But if you are Spanish...'

'How can you tell?'

'You Spaniards are almost as unmistakable as we Argentines are.'

'Oh, you don't say. Go on. If I were Spanish, what would you offer me?'

'A "fifth centenary", perhaps.'

'Tell me about it.'

'Pisco, white wine, and a few drops of sweet sherry.'

'Help!'

Alma laughs despite herself, but when the waiter moves off, her eyes are again full of concern and enquiry.

'I went to see Raúl's former associate, Roberto. My cousin had been there, and paid him another visit. Their experiments are part of a foundation which calls itself The Spirit of New Argentina. I've been hearing about it since I started my trip here. The man in the seat next to me on the plane is one of their promoters, he told me about the foundation and about Güelmes.'

'Güelmes?'

'Yes, your almost minister Güelmes. While Roberto was showing me the pride of Argentina's cows, he thought he saw Raúl and ran off. All of a sudden, two motorcyclists leapt on me and started to beat me to a pulp. Before I lost consciousness I saw my flight companion, a fat guy out of a B-movie. He was giving the orders.'

'What did Roberto say?'

'He patched me up. He said he was sorry, and explained how obsessed Raúl seemed to be with returning there. First he paid them a call, then one night he got into the laboratory and trashed it, and now he's been back a third time. The strange thing is that when I mentioned the fat man, the man I'd met on the plane and who was in charge of the motorcyclists, he looked at me like a scientist faced with some far-fetched theory, and told me the only fat things around were the New Argentina cows. I reckon the meeting in the plane was a set-up. They knew I was coming from Spain. They must have been monitoring your letters or your phone calls to my uncle. How else would they know?'

Although she's on the verge of it, Alma has no time to be scared stiff. Two 'fifth centenaries' fall from the skies and put a stop to

Carvalho's confessions. She waits until he's tried the cocktail, winked at the waiter and given his verdict.

'Very refreshing.'

The waiter glides off, pride assuaged.

'Ghastly, isn't it?'

'I've drunk worse. What d'you make of my adventure?'

'Why did they beat you up? I mean, why did Roberto let them beat up the person they thought was Raúl?'

'He said Raúl's night-time shenanigans had annoyed them.'

'And you believed him?'

'No; but I've no better idea. By the way, I won't be attending your classes any more.'

'Why? Are they that bad?'

'You're pessimistic about language, but you earn your living discussing and analysing other people's language. Don't you believe in what you're doing?'

'I use words to earn my living, and say what people expect to hear. Aren't you a pessimist?'

'I'm supposed to find a cousin I don't know in a city I don't know either. Those of you who were closest to him could help me. Are you sure you haven't seen him?'

Alma sustains his gaze.

'No.'

'Why not? I don't understand.'

'He didn't want to see me. Perhaps I remind him too much of my sister. We're very alike.'

'Perhaps.'

Alma changes the subject. Sips at her drink.

'I've tasted worse too.'

'What did you make of your brother-in-law?'

'An industrialist who used science. All he wanted to do was make money from his discoveries. He was a behaviourist who taught how to treat people like rats.'

'Did Berta agree with him?'

'No. At some point she thought perhaps the discoveries could serve the cause, but she often expressed her doubts to me. Like all of those who come from the working classes, Raúl had a twin brother inside him who wanted to be rich, even though his father was already rich enough. But that's enough about Raúl.'

'What happened to you?'

'You mean, in general?'

'No. I mean the night you were arrested. How did you survive? What exactly happened to the little girl?'

Alma shakes her head, but eventually thinks about it and starts to speak as if she has no need for an audience. As she tells the story, she takes on the role of the different people involved that night.

'They forced their way in, shouting, insulting us, guns in hand. We were in Raúl and Berta's apartment. There were more people there, who didn't survive. Font y Rius, my husband, was there. Pignatari had written a piece of music dedicated to Eva María, and I'd had it recorded in a music box. Have you ever heard a rock song in a music box? Then they burst in. It was like a full-scale battle. Berta grabbed a pistol and faced up to them. They hit the walls of the entrance hall and crawled their way towards us. Raúl shouted at Berta not to resist. "Don't be stupid! They'll kill us all, the child too! Don't be so stupid! We surrender! Just spare the girl's life! The little girl!" I remembered Eva María in her cot, so I dropped my gun and ran in there. She was only a year old. I picked her up. My mind was a blank – perhaps that's how I managed to get out, by being completely blank. I got out with my Eva María – it was as if the bullets stopped to let us through.'

Slowly Alma comes back to reality. She's cradling her arms as though the baby were still in them. Carvalho gently stops her movements, but encourages her to go on with the story.

'Some days later I read in the papers that Berta had been killed in the shoot-out. I thought it was the right moment to go home or at least to my parents' place to hand over Eva María. Until then I'd been in hiding, like an insect, not knowing who to turn to. So I went to my parents' apartment. The goons were there. I didn't even get to see my parents. I was arrested. They took the baby away.'

She's about to break down. Carvalho comforts her.

'It's all right. That's enough for today.'

'You're right. You made me talk about something I never wanted to mention again.'

Now it's not an emotional Alma opposite him, but a woman furious with herself and with him. She's had enough of confessions and of being there. She stands up abruptly, and leaves Carvalho open-mouthed when he realizes she's stood him up yet again.

All human rights offices look the same, especially if organized by a group of victims of crimes against humanity. They are down-at-heel apartments full of second-hand furniture and posters proclaiming hope beneath garish neon lights. The people there act as if they were in a convent, fired by the secret joy of those who have succeeded in freeing themselves from at least a tiny part of their innate selfishness. In other words, people who feel solidarity: in this case, almost all of them women, somewhere between old and very old, well-dressed middle-class ladies who discovered in their own families during the Process how cruel history can be. Anyone who goes into the office hands over and receives an invisible ethical credit card, a solidarity Mastercard. Carvalho can feel its presence in his jacket pocket just above his heart as he explains why he has come to an impossibly short-sighted old woman, behind whose pebble glasses he can see at least five pairs of eyes superimposed on each other, and with a tiny mouth painted a gentle pink to chime in with her oh! so nice way of talking. She turns away from him and makes off down a corridor to the room where the grandmothers keep all the painful memories of the grandchildren they hope to find alive, even though they are just as disappeared as the parents who were snatched by the armed forces during the years of the military junta. Carvalho is moved by everything he sees around him, even the routine inertia of what has become an office, the veneer of habit laid over the most sensitive skin, the rawest of wounds. Then the old lady comes back with a big white folder. She sniffs it before opening it. 'I told them to put in those little white balls for damp.'

Then she plunges her inadequate, ocean-deep eyes into the pages of the file, until... 'Ah, yes...I remember...I remember...'

She remembers and looks up at Carvalho.

'Eva María Tourón Modotti. No trace of her from the moment she was taken from her aunt, Alma. A disappeared baby, disappeared without trace. The raid was led by a Captain Ranger, although his prisoners knew him as Gorostizaga. No one is sure of his real name. Do you want to see him?'

She hands him a press cutting. Someone is giving Captain Ranger a medal. All muscle and fibre, eyes that command obedience, a disdainful smile on his lips, triangles where his hair is receding. 'A hero of the Falklands War.'

'Has anyone talked to him about the raid?'

'Nothing was ever officially proven about his taking part in it or the kidnapping. There's nothing in the archives. We know that from information given us by the girl's aunt, Alma Modotti, and from other survivors. But it wasn't always the officers in charge who were responsible for this trafficking of babies. Sometimes it was their subordinates. Ranger is a pseudonym he was given because he was always boasting about how he was trained in the US Marine school in Panama – the place where the Yankees trained all the Latin American butchers.'

'Are there no leads?'

'Nothing. It's one of those obscure, baffling cases which if and when they are eventually solved, prove to have been right in front of our eyes the whole time. Sometimes we can't see for looking.'

Even though she's so short-sighted, she is aware of Carvalho's ironic smile at this.

'I'm not talking about myself. I know I've got the worst eyes in the world – every time I got pregnant, my eyes weakened by three dioptres. And I had four pregnancies.'

That's when Carvalho notices she has three photos pinned to her dress. The woman would be entitled to cry, but her voice is firm as she comes to the end of her train of thought.

'Only one of the four is still alive. A girl, who lives in Sweden. She reckons she'll never come back to Argentina even if President Menem sends his Ferrari to fetch her.'

'D'you have any grandchildren in your files?'

'A boy we found, and a girl we're still looking for.'

Carvalho wishes her luck with a vague gesture. Then gives her his card. 'If you ever hear anything about the Tourón Modotti baby.'

'Baby? By now she'll be almost twenty years old.'

It's no easy task to open a door with a bag in each hand and with your mind set on the idea of saving time by not putting the bags on the floor, opening the door, and then picking them up again, and going in. Carvalho prefers to do it all at once, wondering how he could manage things better, but when he succeeds in depositing his bags safe and sound on the table he is delighted that he has not only overcome his own sense of how things should be done, but has achieved the feat without even putting the light on. He goes over to the window, opens the shutters and smiles at being free from the weight of the bags and at the light streaming in from outside. But there's something unexpected filling the space behind him, so he turns round. An angular, strongly built man is calmly going through the bags Carvalho dumped on the table. Another man is standing there, hands in pockets, staring at him menacingly. The first one tips up a bag, and books pour out. Then the other, which is full of food. A tin rolls across the floor towards Carvalho, who stoops to pick it up. A foot appears, and kicks the tin out of his reach. Carvalho looks up at these threatening figures, and slowly straightens. A police badge is thrust into his face, and when he peers beyond it he can see that this Argentine cop is just like any other cop in the world. A cop isn't a face. It's a state of mind.

'Inspector Oscar Pascuali.'

Carvalho stares at him suspiciously. Gives him his best hard-boiled private detective look – sometimes it's best to start where you mean to leave off. But this Argentine cop is one of the sarcastic ones. 'Been shopping, have we?'

The second man is still watching carefully. Carvalho moves away from Pascuali, picks up the tin, and puts it on the table. Pascuali goes over, and starts to examine some of the things from the bags. 'Salted cod, tomato sauce, peppers, rice, a guide to Buenos Aires, olive oil, cloves of garlic; *Who Killed Rosendo? The Open Veins of Latin America, The Cafés of Buenos Aires, The Complete Works of Jorge Luis Borges, Adam Buenosayres, A Funny, Dirty Little War,* two bottles of Chilean wine – ah! just as well, *three* bottles of Argentine wine: Navarro Correa, Velmont; *The Tragic Decade, Flowers Stolen from Quilmes Gardens, Perón's Boys,* a large portion of offal, black pudding. Have you got someone to cook all this for you?'

'I'm quite a good cook.'

'And a good reader.'

'I hardly look at the books. Reading them would be too much like hard work. I like to buy them, and then burn them.'

'To burn them? Did you hear what he said, Vladimiro? Señor Pepe Carvalho here burns books. That's a job for us police to do, isn't it? Because we are Fascists, aren't we? Isn't it true we're Fascists? And book-burning is for Fascists, isn't it? Are you a Fascist too?'

'A bit, like everyone is, like you are.'

'No, I'm only a cop. But I respect books. Even ones like these, which I would probably never read. Do you know why I respect books?'

Carvalho gives a shrug.

'Because as a child I only ever had one.'

'*Trueheart*, by Edmondo de Amicis?'

'How did you know that?'

'It was the only book working-class kids ever had, and you look as if that's where you came from.'

Pascuali thrusts his face right up against Carvalho's, then spits at him: 'When you come into this country, you leave your balls at Customs. Pick 'em up when you leave.'

He steps back to survey the effect these words have had on Carvalho, but sees only a face trying its best not to betray any emotion. Pascuali signals to his assistant to follow him, and they head for the door. He turns round in the doorway.

'The best thing you can do for Raúl Tourón is to stop looking for him. If his family wants to find him, tell them to go to the police.'

'Where's that? I'm a foreigner here. Where can I find the police? Wouldn't you like to leave me your card?'

Vladimiro is about to launch himself at Carvalho, but Pascuali stops him.

'Let him be. Assholes like him bring it on themselves.'

While he is busy fussing over a steaming pot, Carvalho can't get this phrase out of his mind. 'Am I really one of those assholes who brings it on themselves?'

He adjusts the seasoning. Snatches a handful of the steam rising from the pot, and sniffs at it.

'Appearances are deceptive. I've always had a good instinct for self-preservation.'

He glances occasionally at a book open on the stove. *The Open Veins of Latin America.*

'But what exactly am I trying to preserve? What have I got that's worth preserving? Myself?'

The table is set in the dining-room. A single plate, one set of cutlery, one cod stew, an open bottle of wine, one glass.

'An instinct to preserve this?'

Carvalho goes over to the fireplace. Puts on some logs. Picks up the book he was reading. His hands tear it to pieces, and toss it on to the wood. As he lights the fire, the flames light up his face. He can see it as if it were someone else bending over in his place. He looks across at the table, where he dimly senses the smell of the stew calling him, but all he feels is nostalgia as he gets a sudden mental picture of his grandmother, her face enveloped in steam, carrying a pot of this same stew. Then when he sinks his fork into the rice it tastes of exile, as if there is some special ingredient missing to make it like the dish he remembers. To cut short any more self-pity, Carvalho's fork hastily scoops up the last of the food, then his hand reaches out for the half-filled glass of wine and raises it quickly to his mouth. A satisfied sigh in honour of the other Carvalho who's accompanied him throughout this solitary meal. He gets up. The fire is still blazing in the grate. Carvalho sinks into an armchair. Then he changes his mind, struggles up, and goes over to the writing desk to find the letter to Charo he has so often begun and abandoned. 'Perhaps we ought to admit we're not kids any more and that what's at stake is choosing whether or not we're going to enjoy the years left to us.' He reads it through. Gives up yet again. Then decides to pick up the phone and dial a lengthy number.

'Biscuter? It's Carvalho, in Buenos Aires. It might seem I'm close by, but I'm not. Ten at night. Oh, I'm sorry, I didn't think of the time difference. Cod stew. No, no. Pure nostalgia. What's the weather like in Barcelona? Any news of Charo? Good. This city's still full of forlorn Argentines. Listen, is it true you sometimes put sausage in the base for cod stew with rice? Be careful with our funds.'

Alma is waiting in the bus queue. From a nearby taxi, Carvalho

watches her get on. He leans forward and tells the driver to follow her:
he's not surprised at the request, but his eyes light up with excitement
and he obeys the instructions as if this were the most normal thing in
the world in Buenos Aires. He tails the bus with professional skill,
only cursing out loud when another driver pulls in front of him. 'See
that? Good job I'm the calm type, otherwise I'd give that guy a good
crack across the head. Is your friend going to the Caminito? Is this a
tourist contest?'

The bus heads for the Boca. On their left, the modern ruins of
the Puerto Viejo. Yard after yard of empty dock warehouses, falling
into ruin, poetically obsolete and useless, although perhaps at night
they're put to some use, when all cats and tramps are a dark shade of
grey. Alma gets off her bus. Carvalho pays his driver.

'You should pay for this kind of joyride in dollars,' he comments,
screeching off.

But Carvalho has already set off in pursuit of Alma, who's
running along a street with brightly painted walls and full of
pavement artists. When she reaches a part lined with a mixture of
tourist and cheaper restaurants, she seems to have doubts. She looks
all around, as if unsure whether to go on, or whether she's being
followed. Eventually she disappears inside the corrugated iron door
of a rusty store. Inside it's as if, as the tango says, twenty years are
nothing: it's full of antiquated implements and useless gadgets, all of
them abandoned to the dust, dirt and rats. Alma climbs an iron spiral
staircase. Waiting for her on the floor above is a wretched room and a
white-haired man who looks older than his years. His nervous
twitches abate when he sees her. They gaze at each other. Smile. He
flings himself on her. Alma's face is perfectly calm, she even smiles a
little while the man is stripping her roughly to the waist, working
himself up into a frenzy.

'You can't live without my prick, can you? Can't live without little
orphan Norman? There's nothing like Norman's little prick, is there?
Circumcised like a baby's dummy, or a big red strawberry. Is there?'

Alma lets him push her over to the camp bed, stretches out on it
and opens her legs when Norman frantically leaps on top of her,
unzips his trousers and starts thrusting at her. Despite this sexual
assault, Alma's face loses none of its calm self-control, as if she were

doing him a favour. Five thrusts, five groans, and it's over. Alma seems to be counting silently. After the fifth groan, the man's body collapses on top of hers. Alma strokes his head and tries to look him in the eyes.

'You were much better today, Norman.'

Norman sits up on the side of the bed. He smiles, pleased with himself. Alma, like a charcoal sketch, encourages him.

'How many times did I manage?'

'Five.'

'I'm getting better. The last time it was three. D'you remember the good old days? No, you weren't my partner then, but d'you remember what they used to call me?'

'The insatiable ferret.'

'I'll be one again some day.'

Alma strokes his hair again.

'You're good because you don't put me off. But if a woman starts shouting before I can get it up – "Give it to me, do it" – and to shake about like a foodmixer, I can't do it, Alma. I used to fuck anyone. Half an hour at least. Half an hour without stopping.'

'What about Raúl?'

Norman shrinks from her, as if the question has brought him up short.

'I don't know.'

Alma is no longer calm – she's furious and indignant.

'What d'you mean, you don't know?'

Norman points to a cage where a laboratory rat is moving nervously about.

'That's all that's left of him.'

'What are you talking about, you idiot?'

'He brought the rat with him when he came, and when he disappeared again yesterday, he left it. I brought it here from the theatre.'

Alma pushes Norman away and stands up. She grabs a blanket to cover her body. Her stockings are down round her ankles like a pair of socks, and her bra is round her midriff. She swaps the blanket for a sheet.

'You're an asshole, a bastard, an irresponsible lout!'

'That's the way I am. There's nothing I can do about it.'

'How long ago did he leave?'

'I don't know. I couldn't watch over him all day long. I couldn't stand any more monologues about rats, about Berta, or Eva María. He's a grown man. A free man.'

'You're meant to be grown-up too. And we're all meant to be free. Didn't you stop to ask yourself where he got that rat? Can't you guess? Can't you see he's in danger? When did he leave? Where did he go?'

'About four days ago.'

'Four days! Why didn't you tell me?'

'Who do you think you are? Still the one giving orders?'

The man bursts into tears.

'I don't know. I was sick of him, of myself, of all of us. He said some very strange things. That he'd been back to his laboratory, that some men on motorcycles were following him, that they'd tried to run him over or push him into the river. That he was really close to finding out where Eva María is. I thought he was raving. I had to go out to audition an actor. I couldn't miss it, it was the first dress rehearsal. I told him to go and see Pignatari. What are you doing?'

Alma is throwing on her clothes. Suddenly a look of alarm appears on Norman's face, and he gets up from the bed.

'Who's that?'

Alma looks in the direction Norman is pointing. Carvalho appears from the shadows of the staircase.

'Carvalho, the Masked Galician.'

Norman is about to throw himself on the intruder, but comes to an embarrassed halt when he realizes he's naked. Carvalho says scornfully: 'Mind you don't damage the insatiable ferret.'

'Calm down, Norman. He's just a voyeur.'

'A disgusting voyeur!'

'No, a very respectful one who's only come on to the scene once the young lady had finished and was almost dressed again.'

Alma's face reflects her efforts to control her indignation, but she is still only half-dressed, so Carvalho takes charge of the situation.

'Now let's talk quietly and calmly about Raúl, and I hope this time you don't lie to me. Why did you tell me you hadn't seen Raúl when you knew where he was hiding?'

'I didn't lie to you. Raúl didn't want to see me. You didn't ask whether I was helping him or not.'

'Why didn't he want to see you?'

'That's what I'd like to know. I thought Norman here was looking after him, but he's gone.'

'From here?'

'No. Norman kept him more or less in hiding in a theatre he runs. He was pretending he'd hired him to do the cleaning.'

'And who are these mysterious motorcyclists who are out to get him, and beat me up by mistake?'

Alma shrugs. Norman is dressed by now, and when he speaks, his voice is self-assured: 'Now it's my turn to ask a question: who is this Spanish bullshitter who's messed everything up for us?'

But like an English gentleman from a Noël Coward comedy, he immediately adds:

'Anyway, you two must have lots to talk about together. A gentleman is someone who instinctively realizes when he's not wanted. Good-day to you, madam.'

At which he kisses Alma's hand, and turns to bow his head slightly to Carvalho. He makes to walk past him, but as he does so, he swiftly punches him in the genitals and then runs out laughing. Carvalho is bent double as the other man clatters down the staircase, shouting: 'Next time go watch your mother fucking, you queer!'

Carvalho is trying to get his breath back, seated on the bed. Alma looks at him quizzically, uncertain what to say.

'Did you see anything?'

'Everything and nothing. Don't worry. By the time we're forty, everyone has the face and the arse they deserve.'

Carvalho stares at the rat in its cage.

'Raúl's partner didn't tell me the whole truth. Or perhaps he didn't tell me any of it. Raúl was definitely there, but I wonder what really happened?'

'Roberto is a piece of shit, always was and always will be. Deep down he's jealous because Raúl and Berta were brilliant.'

Alma goes over to the bed and sits next to Carvalho. She puts her hand in his jacket pocket and takes out his packet of cigars. Pulls out a cigar, lights it for him, puffs on it, then gives it him. The detective draws deeply on the cigar with obvious pleasure.

'Friends?'

Alma hesitates at the proposal, but then offers him a hand and a smile.

'Friends.'

'Are we going to help each other?'

Alma agrees, more tender now.

'We artists are going to help each other. Norman's not such a bad guy. In spite of the low blow, he's an artist too. He's an actor, always playing some role or other. So we artists are going to help each other. Me, Norman, Pignatari.'

'Who's Pignatari?'

'Perhaps it's time for you to meet him. But you should also go and see Güelmes, because he has power. He's almost a minister. He will be one some day.'

A thin, statuesque actor, his face painted white and with slicked-back hair, is cutting off a finger on the stage of a tiny theatre which has never seen better days, is somewhere never chosen for the first night of any play.

'I'm getting rid of you. A quick mutilation. Because you pointed out impossible people, things and desires.'

He redoubles his efforts to cut off his finger. A booming voice is heard offstage.

'Son of a bitch!'

The actor shakes his head furiously, throws the knife to the floor, tears off the rubber finger and makes to leave.

'No, no, you're not getting out of it that easily!'

Norman leaps on stage and throws himself at the actor. He pulls him to the floor, kicks him, puts a foot on his neck.

'Go on, say it: I'm a son of a bitch!'

'I'm a son of a bitch.'

'Louder!'

'I'm a son of a bitch!'

'That's better. Now get up, and pick the knife up again.'

By now he's got the actor by the hair, and thrusts his face at him.

'You're going to cut off your finger properly! Because you're a son of a bitch! Tell me again what you are?'

'I'm a son of a great bitch.'

'No need to boast about your mother. It's enough you admit what you are.'

Norman leaves the stage. The actor spits after him and shouts: 'I hate you, Norman!'

Norman's voice sounds strangely calm as it floats up from the stalls.

'That's more like it!'

The actor can barely hide his hatred for Norman, but he puts the rubber finger back on again, picks up the knife, and shouts with all his might: 'I'm getting rid of you. A quick mutilation. Because you pointed out impossible people, things, desires.'

Applause from the stalls. Norman's voice again.

'That's great, son of a bitch, fantastic!'

Norman is sitting, elbows on the back of the seat in front, cupping his head in his hands, muttering the lines to himself as the actor speaks them on stage.

'Obscene reality! If I don't point you out, do you exist?'

Norman seems a bit happier, until he hears Carvalho's voice next to him.

'Is that the Stanislavksi method?'

Carvalho and Alma sit down on either side of him. Alma places her hand on his arm to try to keep him calm. Carvalho is finishing his cigar.

'It's my method.'

Alma puts her arm round Norman's shoulders, as if she is both protecting him and presenting him to Carvalho.

'Norman is an impostor. He's an architect, not an actor. When he was in exile in Barcelona he pretended he was a psychotherapist because there were lots of architects but not many therapists.'

'You can only know about your own nation's madnesses. Freud could only cure Austrians, because he himself was a crazy Austrian struggling to come to terms with the crisis in the Austro-Hungarian empire and in the bourgeois ego. So how could I hope to cure any Catalans? The only patients I had any success with in Barcelona were two Siamese cats. They had suicidal tendencies because I was sleeping with their owner – and she was a psychobolshie.'

Alma tries to put in a good word for Carvalho.

'We have to help our friend here.'

'If you start helping private detectives, you end up collaborating with the police. Private detectives are simply the embodiment of nostalgia for a supposed golden age, an ancient civilization organized around a collective myth and ideology, a way of life governed by unshakeable authorities – the laws of the aristocracy and the Church, or the dogma of a political leader heading a single-party state. There's no real difference between one of Chesterton's detectives and a Marxist one. Both of them are reactionaries, nostalgic for a lost order.'

Norman is very pleased with his little speech.

'I must write that down. It's fantastic. Remind me, will you? But now I expect you want to see the scene of the catastrophe. Follow me!'

They follow him to the tiny staircase leading to the basement dressing-rooms.

'Just imagine you're living a mixture of *Le Dernier Métro* by Truffaut and *Phantom of the Opera.*'

Norman leads the way, with Carvalho and Alma following. They descend a spiral metal staircase that looks as if no human foot has touched it in centuries. They come to a halt in front of a metal door. Norman lights a match, opens the door, and they find themselves in a tiny space that only has room for a camp bed, a wash-basin, a tiny wardrobe, a few books.

'Raúl spent almost a month in here.'

Carvalho tries to pick up some trace of the fugitive, some message left imprinted on the objects in the room. But he doesn't feel the slightest vibration.

'Did he tell you what he wanted to do, or why he had come back?'

'He said it was on impulse. Partly it was because he was horrified that the military leaders had been pardoned, but I don't know if that was the real reason. He talked about getting his daughter back, but I think it was he himself he wanted to rediscover, to find his role in the film of events again. He also talked about his father. The old man surprised me, he said. He didn't realize that everything came to an end that night. In that freeze frame.'

When Alma speaks, it's with a bitter voice.

'Write that down too, it's brilliant.'

She is caressing some of the books on the table. Picks up *A Universal History of Infamy* by Jorge Luis Borges. Then suddenly puts it down and turns to face the two men.

'We have to start at the beginning. Some day he's bound to come back and visit you, Norman, or the other two.'

'Why not you?'

Alma cannot look Carvalho in the face. Instead, she glances towards Norman, as if they're sharing a secret. Norman replies for her: 'It wouldn't be good for him to see Alma. She looks too much like Berta.'

But Carvalho cannot help staring at Alma's tortured face, or listening for the words she finds it impossible to say.

The dim lights of the Boca seem to have been reluctantly lit. They illuminate restaurant fronts that would be garish were it not for the eternal damp of the river. Away from the lights, the rest of the neighbourhood is mostly corrugated iron, with rusty patches that speak of having to survive without any sense of greatness apart from the soccer victories of Boca Juniors in a stadium that's seen better days, and stands in the midst of a desolate hotchpotch of wasteland. The restaurant doors cast oblongs of yellow light on the pavements where Alma and Carvalho are walking. From inside they hear snatches of secret bandoneon music, smell the charcoal embers and the crucified carcasses of roasting lambs.

'Remember Pignatari's address, but don't keep my piece of paper.'

'We're in a democracy now.'

'A controlled one. People are frightened of having any memory. Raúl's return has stirred too many memories. Don't think it's a political problem: it's a fear of remembering.'

'The victors appropriate the memory of the defeated, and when they finally do get it back, it's changed beyond all recognition. Do you think someone is really out to get him?'

'It's possible. Those rats, the ones he spent so long studying. He wrote a treatise on animal behaviour in completely alien situations. Theoretically, he was the best prepared of all of us to face what happened, but he broke down.'

'What about Norman?'

'He broke down too, but we all knew he would; Berta had already foreseen it. She thought she knew as much about militant behaviour as her husband did about rats. Norman was never a threat, and the military understood that. Now he's abandoned architecture for the theatre. As a student, he wanted to build the utopia Le Corbusier had imagined for Buenos Aires. He wanted to create the *Ville Verte* here where the soil is so rich and the trees are larger than life. Now he puts on plays in our Off Off theatres, plays that will probably never get a proper audience, and earns his living as a showman, presenting the acts in a tango cabaret in San Telmo: Tango Amigo, it's called.'

'There you go with the tango again. You refuse to accept it, you want to get away from it, and yet you always come back to it.'

'The whole country's a tango. The city's a tango. I remember a phrase of Malraux's, which sounds like the words of a famous tango: "Buenos Aires is the capital of an empire that never existed." I used to hate the tango. I'm from the rock generation – people who followed the Rolling Stones, people like Pignatari, who had the balls actually to become a rocker. We thought we'd be young for ever, but now I'm forty I find myself blushing to admit I like rock music. It's as if I liked polkas or something. But what comes after rock 'n' roll, eh? What d'you like?'

'Boleros most of the time, Mexican corridos, tangos sometimes.'

'That's because you prefer words to bodies. Rock is music for the body, the sorts you like all have words you have to listen to.'

Carvalho stares her up and down. Alma smiles and shakes her head.

'No chance. Pignatari – grey ponytail and all – is still singing rock music, in some of the poorest neighbourhoods down by the river here. In Barracas or La Boca, but not the Boca for tourists we're in now, all the painted housefronts of Caminito. Perhaps Raúl's gone to ask him for help. Another loser. Norman. Pignatari.'

'Are you a loser too?'

'He doesn't want to see me, and I don't want to see him.'

'Will you take me to the tango place where Norman performs?'

'I'll take you when you're ready.'

'Ready for what?'

'Just ready, that's all, my little Masked Galician.'

Walking aimlessly has its limits and its cost. Carvalho is suddenly surrounded by a mass of bodies, and in all the confusion thinks he spots a police badge. A voice confirms this, shouting: 'Police!' Then things get even more confused because he's being shoved around, then pushed up against a wall and forced to spread his arms and legs. He's searched by knowing hands he only notices when they feel his balls. Then they go through his pockets. A long switch blade and a plastic bag full of a white powder fall to the ground. Cocaine, Carvalho says to himself with a grimace. Rough hands turn him around. Carvalho finds himself faced by Oscar Pascuali and two plainclothes policemen, one of them the excitable Vladimiro. Pascuali stares down at the ground, where the knife and the plastic bag look as if they're drawing attention to themselves. Pascuali's voice is cold; his breath is warm.

'Weapons and drugs.'

'How d'you know they're drugs? It could be detergent. I live alone, I have to do my own washing. I use Surf.'

Pascuali's hand grabs the bag, opens it. He pokes a finger inside, sniffs it, thrusts it under Carvalho's nose.

'Surf? Omo?'

'I don't know the names of brands in Argentina.'

'Detergents are the same the world over.'

Carvalho feels it's time to show his impatience. 'You've been reading too many cheap thrillers. Any doctor, even a police one, could tell you I haven't sniffed a thing since my first communion. The knife is mine, the drugs are yours.'

Pascuali hands him back the blade, and puts the plastic bag in his own jacket pocket. 'We'll leave it there for now. But it would be easy enough for you to turn up one day with your nose full of cocaine and snot, and your apartment stuffed with bags like this. Did you tell your friend I'd paid you a visit?'

'No.'

'Why not?'

'It was men's business. The less we tell women about our affairs, the better.'

'Ask her about me.'

'Are you a dirty war veteran?'

'Yes, from a really dirty war: the Malvinas War.'

'So we're all losers. When I was a boy, I lost the Spanish Civil War. Alma lost the dirty war, and you lost in the Falklands. Why don't we get together and form a veterans' association?'

Someone behind Pascuali spits an insult at Carvalho. But it's not Vladimiro, who is staring at the detective with something like respect. It's the other cop, an inexperienced-looking youth. Pascuali shakes his head disapprovingly.

'Don't let him get to you. He's a wise-guy. Look at Vladimiro. He knows how to take people like him.'

'A cop called Vladimiro! Was your old man a follower of Lenin?'

Pascuali is not interested in idle chat.

'I'll be clear and concise. The sooner we find your cousin, the better for him, for us, and for you. We're not the only ones looking for him. Your cousin saw too much, and escaped by the back door. Fifty years will have to go by before all those involved in that nightmare have vanished. Someone wants him, and if they get him, he's a dead man. And you're too old to be playing Philip Marlowe.'

'You're right, I used to imitate Marlowe. Now I'm too old. My model is Maigret – he's timeless.'

'What were you after in the Grandmothers' Association?'

'A little girl.'

'And in The Spirit of New Argentina?'

'Information about cows.'

'And what were you talking about with that Jewish clown?'

'About theatre and suicidal Siamese cats.'

'If you feel someone breathing down your neck, don't worry, it'll be me. But if you get a bullet in the back of your head, it won't be me, and you'll be the only one to blame.'

The three men turn into dark shadows beyond the glare of their headlights.

Not since killing Kennedy has Carvalho been so close to power. He has never set foot inside a ministry: the nearest he's got is a security headquarters, when he was investigating the murder of the general secretary of the Spanish Communist Party. But perhaps in some other life he had even been in power himself, because there's something very familiar about all the comings and goings of officials, clients, victims and pests in a building that would look obsolete if it were empty, and full, seems somehow unbelievable. Simply mentioning Güelmes' name has opened all the doors for him, until he reaches his waiting-room, where the secretary tells him she's Spanish as well.

'But from Galicia, not Catalonia. Here all Spaniards are Galicians, even those from Andalusia. My parents came after the Civil War.'

'Were they Republicans?'

'No, just dirt poor.'

Güelmes tells him to come in. Carvalho is confronted by a still young, aristocratic-looking man, who almost dances round his desk as if reluctant to sit down again. As the secretary opened the door for him, Carvalho had time to see the deputy minister snorting a line of coke and then wipe up the remains and rub them quickly on his gums. No sooner has Carvalho entered the room than he's on his feet, shaking his hand, asking after Alma and Norman. Carvalho can't take his eyes off a framed poster on the wall: The Spirit of New Argentina, with the inevitable cow.

'Everybody here wants to get out to Spain, and yet you Spaniards seem to keep on coming to Buenos Aires.'

'It's cheaper that way.'

'Not any more. Thanks to Menem and his policies, Argentina isn't bankrupt now. Every day I see a hundred projects from people wanting to invest in Argentina. People feel confident about our future. Alma called, and her wish is my command, but I don't know much more about it. What is it you want?'

'Were you one of the guerrillas?'

'Thanks to Menem, those who were and those who weren't are all Perónists again now. Anyone who wasn't a revolutionary at twenty had no heart, but anyone who still thinks he is at forty, hasn't got a brain.'

'Power.'

Güelmes immediately understands that Carvalho's brief remark is the result of taking in this magnificent office compared to the rest of the shabby building.

'Someone has to wield it, and it's much better that it's someone who answers Alma's calls.'

'Has Raúl Tourón been here?'

'No. Is he in Argentina? I thought he was in Spain. I spent some time in exile in Spain, then in Germany, the United States – it was a long journey out and back. A lot of us Argentines, Chileans, and Uruguayans went to Spain hoping we'd get a warm welcome in the motherland. But you Spaniards find it easier to go into exile yourselves than to receive others.'

'It's an old historical tendency.'

'Raúl was a different case. He never lost his Spanish nationality. Now there's a crazy Spanish judge who wants to put all our military officers on trial for the people who disappeared. Raúl, who's just as crazy, managed to escape, but now he's back and out to get himself hanged, apparently.'

'Apparently, the whole world is after him: me, because his father sent me, then there's the police, and some strange people who won't come out of the shadows, but who aren't exactly well-wishers.'

'Why did Tourón come back?'

'Some say to get revenge; others say not even he knows why he's here.'

Güelmes laughs politely, and Carvalho concludes this is the way deputy ministers usually laugh.

'To get revenge? In alphabetical order?'

'Perhaps he's looking for his daughter.'

Güelmes doesn't seem convinced.

'What would you like me to do?'

'You could ask the police to help me.'

'I have influence in social and economic spheres. I can't get involved in police or military matters. They have a memory too.'

'Perhaps you could find out who's out to get him. They're something to do with that poster, it seems.'

Güelmes turns to look at it.

'The Spirit of New Argentina? We've high hopes in that project, there's talk of Japanese investment right away. Raúl's colleague Roberto is in charge of it.'

'But there are people involved who don't like Raúl.'

'Did they tell you that?'

'It was the impression I got. Could you find out why?'

'That would be difficult, but not impossible.'

'And if he shows up here, perhaps you could tell us.'

'Tell who exactly?'

'Alma, or me, or Norman Silverstein, or...'

'Silverstein! D'you know what his *nom de guerre* was? Camilo Cienfuegos. What a great actor! Some nights I go to Tango Amigo to relax, it's a wonderful place, the penultimate bastion of tango. No, that's not true. You're a tourist. You can go to the Viejo Almacén or the Café Homero in the Calle Cabrera.'

'I don't want to be just a tourist. I'd like to be a traveller. Even though I don't have enough time to fully get to grips with this city.'

'Ah, if you're a traveller rather than a tourist, then you must go to Tango Amigo. Silverstein introduces the show. Sometimes it's fantastic. The more hysterical it gets, the better it is. Haven't you been there yet?'

'No, Alma says I'm not grown-up enough yet to see the show. Were you a rock 'n' roll fan too?'

'Anyone who wasn't a rock 'n' roll fan at twenty had no heart; anyone who still is one at forty has no brain. There was a famous rock'n'roller in our group: Pignatari. Have you met him? We were more like brothers than comrades. We loved each other. Pignatari adapted one of his songs for a music box he gave to Eva María, Berta and Raúl's daughter.'

He falls silent. Stares at Carvalho openly. Eventually, after the detective has written down the name Pignatari in his notebook, he asks him: 'But tell me, if it isn't asking too much...why are you so keen on finding Raúl?'

'His father hired me for the job. My uncle, that is. My American uncle.'

'Want to know something? Anyone who twenty years ago didn't have an American uncle was someone with no past. But anyone who still has one has no future. Now it's much better to have a European uncle.'

He guffaws with laughter, but Carvalho can only raise a faint smile. The detective gets up. As he turns away from Güelmes, the politician's laughter quickly subsides. Carvalho hears his voice behind him.

'D'you know the only thing that compensates me for this damned power game?'

Carvalho shrugs. Güelmes invites him out on to the balcony. He points down at a couple making love on the grass.

'To be able to look at life from the perspective of history. At sex from a position of power. I remember that one of our slogans was "to change history in the way Marx and Eva wanted, and to change life like Rimbaud wanted".'

The couple are writhing around passionately.

'Look how beautiful it is!'

Güelmes shows him to the door, but doesn't have time to open it. The bulk of the man Carvalho met on the plane fills the doorway. The fat man's face shows consternation; Güelmes' is a picture of controlled indignation.

'I'm sorry, nobody told me...'

Carvalho holds out his hand to the newcomer.

'How are the lupins doing?'

The other man feigns surprise.

'Are you talking to me?'

'The lupins. On the plane, remember?'

The fat man continues to plead ignorance, increasingly irritated: 'What lupins are you talking about?'

A long but fleshy face, its length accentuated by a heavily receding hairline, and a grey rug of hair that ends in a greasy-looking ponytail. Deep creases round the eyes. One ear-ring. The grease on the tuft of hair over his ear seems to have spread to the telephone. 'Yes, this is Pignatari.'

He listens, then covers the mobile phone with one hand and turns to his right. Raúl Tourón is playing solitaire at a metal table, inside a shack. Beyond the window, reedbeds and swarms of mosquitoes on a riverbank. Pignatari tells him in a loud whisper: 'It's the Spaniard! Your cousin!'

Raúl dismisses his cousin with an airy wave of the hand. He goes on with his game, but with the eye on the same side as Pignatari's ear pressed to the phone, seems to be following his half of the conversation.

'I might be able to help you. I'm playing tonight in Barracas. Pignatari Rock. I'll see you after the show.'

After he finishes on the phone, Pignatari considers what he's heard and what he should say. 'You ought to talk to him.'

'I don't trust him.'

'You don't really think your father would send him as bait for you to swallow, do you?'

'How do I know it was my father who sent him? Anyway, even if it was, that's no guarantee.'

'Alma got in touch with your old man. Don't you trust her either?'

Raúl pauses in his game to decide whether or not he does trust Alma and his father. But can't decide. Pignatari has filled a bowl with water from a barrel; he takes off his shirt, soaps his hands, face, his armpits, then rinses himself with water from the bowl and dries himself on a dirty towel after lifting it to his nose and resisting the impulse to throw it away. Raúl has been watching all this, and their eyes meet.

'Are you surprised at all this poverty?'

'My ability to be surprised is not what it was.'

'Rock 'n' roll means something to me, and protest rock means you live among people who protest.'

Raúl looks all around the shack, and what can be sensed outside.

'So who's protesting around here?'

'Nobody. But they should be. You know as well as I do that an external awareness is needed to make the popular classes conscious of the way they're being exploited.'

'Rock music is for dancing. Not even Mexican corridos helped create a revolution.'

'I could live like a comfortable bourgeois; but then what songs would I be entitled to compose?'

'But the lumpen don't ask their idols to live in poverty. They prefer to see them arriving at concerts or football matches in their Mercedes. Take Maradona for example.'

'I'm not interested in those lumpen.'

Pignatari carefully puts on a red silk shirt with black polka dots, a studded leather jacket and a pair of tight leather trousers, then a pair of grey cowboy boots with silver decorations and spurs. He takes a hairpiece out of a cardboard box and fits it in place on his head to cover his bald patch. He checks it in a mirror, and when he turns round thinks he sees a sad glint in Raúl's eyes. Pignatari says not a word. Picks up his electric guitar from an ancient, broken chair.

'The best thing would be to come with us in the van. You could pretend to be one of the crew. Those motorcyclists might come back.'

Raúl obeys in silence. A silence that lasts the whole trip to the abandoned chicken farm in Barracas where Pignatari is giving his concert. The rest of the band is waiting for them: they're a bit younger than Pignatari, but none of them is under forty. Their gestures show a tired professionalism, until they pick up their instruments and start warming up. On stage they peer out at the half-full arena, where the audience participates with a mixture of mockery and enthusiasm. At the end of the set, they shout for more. They want one song in particular. The singer is exhausted, but agrees. The band starts up. It's a song dedicated to a young girl: Eva María. It's a song of victory, written just before the deluge. Raúl, who's going round the audience with beers in a wire basket, feels tears come to his eyes.

> Eva for Eva,
> The bright star María
> The little girl shines
> Eva María.
> Eva María
> Will finish off the CIA
> The guns of justice
> Will have their day.

Pignatari is sweating. There's not enough applause for another encore, so he jumps down from the stage into the audience with a leap that leaves him cursing silently and his knees creaking. A notebook and a pen. He signs an autograph. He winks at the beer seller, Raúl, who comes over to him.

'Have you decided then? Are you going to meet your cousin?'

'I'll see.'

A girl steps in front of them. Shyly, she pushes a piece of paper and a pen into his hands.

'It's for my mother.'

Pignatari smiles ruefully. He leaves the concert hall. In the bare wasteland outside, the tiny hut where his CDs and cassettes are on sale seems even smaller and more desolate. A slovenly-looking youngster is doing the selling, not exactly convinced he is a salesman.

'How did it go today?'

'As usual.'

'Badly, in other words.'

Pignatari looks at his brightly coloured watch. There's still time, but his body is crying out for a rest after all the tension on stage, and the caravan is there waiting for him as if it were one huge bedroom, a welcoming country. Pignatari climbs in, tired but relaxed. Two fat men-insects or insect-men are waiting for him. Two motorcyclists. One of them grabs him by the studded leather jacket. The other punches him with a fist full of knuckledusters. Pignatari has no time to protect himself, and all the objects in the caravan start to fly through the air or crumple into trash, with in the foreground the swollen, bleeding, slashed face of the rock singer. Either he hasn't shouted for help or his shouts can't be heard because someone has turned up the volume on the loudspeaker to full blast:

Eva for Eva,
The bright star María
The little girl shines
Eva María.

These are the last words Pignatari hears as he succumbs to terror and horror. The motorcyclists show no emotion. They're breathing hard, hitting him with deadly precision. One of them pummels him without asking any-thing at all. The other is also punching away, but he's more than a cut-out figure and still betrays a certain curiosity.

'Where is Raúl Tourón?'

Pignatari tries to say something, but is too far gone. His head lolls on his chest. The two motorcyclists call a halt. One of them places the back of a hand full of brass rings against the singer's neck.

'We've gone too far.'

'We've got our hands full of shit all for nothing.'

He gives Pignatari's body a soft, scornful kick. It topples to the floor.

Two police cars with their flashing lights whirling. Onlookers pushing to get to the front of the crush around the caravan. Pascuali is framed in the doorway. His face is an expression of disgust. Vladimiro asks: 'Now what do we do?'

'Hold a vigil for him, Vladimiro, what else?'

At the back of the watching crowd, Raúl is both fascinated and terrified. His fear increases still further when he hears Carvalho's voice beside him, speaking out of the corner of his mouth without looking at him.

'Raúl. Don't be alarmed. Your father sent me. Alma. Norman. Pignatari told us to come here. I'm your cousin Pepe.'

Raúl's face has completely altered. He looks calm and collected, in control of the situation. 'My dear Alan Parker, I only hope we can meet one day in happier circumstances. You'll be hearing from me. And say hello to Zully Moreno from me.'

Carvalho nods. 'I will. But I think he retired from the film world years ago.'

He decides to risk looking at his cousin. But by the time he does so, Raúl has vanished, and suddenly Pascuali pushes in front of him, preventing Carvalho from going anywhere.

'A coincidence?'

'I had an appointment with Pignatari.'

'When did you get here?'

'About the same time as the police.'

'Can you prove it?'

'It's not a theorem.'

Pascuali shouts for Vladimiro.

'Take this clown's statement.'

Just trying to annoy me, Carvalho thinks, as he peers for his cousin in among the crowd being dispersed by the police. Vladimiro pushes him into one of the squad cars, and when they're both inside, he turns to the detective.

'How come you got yourself mixed up in this mess?'

'It's my job.'

'My father's from Spain too. He came after that war of yours; now he refuses to leave his house. He's scared they'll come back: Franco, Perón, Videla. Who knows? Politics ruins everything.'

'So that's why you're called Vladimiro; your father was a Leninist when you were baptised.'

'I haven't been baptised.'

'Are there many unbaptised cops?'

'More than there are unbaptised priests.'

So Vladimiro has a sense of humour. But it vanishes when he takes his notebook from his pocket. He can't find a pen. Carvalho lends him his.

'Come on, make up some nonsense so we can get this over with.'

So Vladimiro is human as well. Carvalho simply tells him he had arranged to meet Pignatari, that he arrived on time, but everything was already in turmoil.

'The meeting was to solicit information as to the whereabouts of a cousin of Don José Carvalho, Don Raúl Tourón, who is apparently somewhere in Buenos Aires.'

The formalities over, Carvalho makes to leave the car. As he is getting out, the young policeman gives him a piece of advice.

'Don't go looking for trouble, my friend.'

It seems he wants to say something more, but doesn't dare.

'Is that all?'

Vladimiro looks all around him, and when he realizes no one can hear, adds in a low whisper: 'My father's a distant cousin of yours. Carvalho is my third or fourth family name.'

He winks at the detective and that's that.

Twenty-four hours later, when Carvalho sees him trailing along behind Pascuali at Pignatari's wake, Vladimiro has again become the tough, scornful cop who eyes him suspiciously. But things are different now, because the corpse is laid out in its coffin in a back room, while in the parlour two conventional-looking widows and three equally conventional-looking adolescents are busy exchanging the conventional condolences. The only person who looks really affected is Alma, slumped on a sofa. Norman is trying to console her, console himself, or say something, but it's too much for him. Alma finds the words.

'D'you remember? D'you remember the music box he made for Eva María with the song he wrote for her on it?'

Carvalho comes in. He looks from Alma and Norman to Font y Rius, who is with Roberto. They appear to be arguing. Font y Rius is saying something through gritted teeth, and Carvalho thinks he can make out: 'So it's the hunting season again, is it?'

Then he hears quite clearly what Roberto replies: 'I told you it would all get complicated if Raúl came back.'

And he hears what Roberto adds, staring straight at him. 'That detective was all we needed.'

'Why can't he just take Raúl back to Spain?'

Forty-year-old rock 'n' rollers crowd round the parlour door. They want to see the body, sign a petition on behalf of the body, applaud the body. A radio reporter is talking into her recorder as if it were an essential part of her anatomy.

'So great is the consternation caused by the brutal assault and murder of the man who was the leading figure in Buenos Aires protest rock that the deputy minister for development, Doctor Güelmes, is here in person to say farewell to someone who was both a friend and an outstanding artist.'

Güelmes shows he knows how to control the situation. He strides through the photographers' flashes, goes straight up to the elder of the two widows, gives her an emotional hug, dries a furtive tear, then turns back to the reporters for his interview.

'I trust you understand my feelings of grief and will respect them. Pignatari and I, together with other friends of ours, lived through hard years of struggle that also promised hope. We wrote the words, he sang the songs of freedom. I've lost a friend, but all of us have lost a great musician. Thank you very much.'

He makes as if to leave, but with one ear still alert for any questions. There's a hubbub of confused suggestions, then one voice imposes itself on all the others.

'Was his death a settling of accounts from the time of the Process?'

'What accounts are you talking about? Thanks to Menem, all our accounts have been settled.'

A sudden silence, followed by Güelmes' exit. As he passes by, he glares at Carvalho. The detective notes the tension and scorn in his face.

'A Señor Tourón would like to speak to you. Shall I put him through?'

Font y Rius is taken by surprise by his own intercom. It takes him a second to recover and react.

'Who did you say? Who's calling me?'

The voice on the intercom repeats the same name with the same intonation.

'I said a Señor Tourón would like to speak to you. Shall I put him through?'

Font y Rius thinks over his reply, staring at the four walls of his office as if they might supply him with inspiration from someone less dumbstruck than himself.

'Keep him on the phone, make up whatever excuse you can think of so he doesn't hang up.'

He frantically dials a number, as frantically as only a psychiatrist overwhelmed by his own psychosis can do. Before he speaks, he takes a deep breath, like a basketball player before shooting a free throw.

'The biologist is trying to contact me. I'll keep him on the line as long as I can. Trace his call.'

He hangs up the phone and flicks the intercom.

'Put him through.'

All of a sudden Font y Rius' face is wreathed in smiles.

'Hello? Hello? Is that you, Raúl? Where have you got to? Hello, Raúl, Raúl Tourón?'

The silence at the other end of the line disconcerts him. Then all of a sudden a noise comes through the receiver. Someone is whistling the same song for Eva María that Pignatari sang at his concert.

'What's that? Raúl? Are you crazy? Who do you think you are? Raúl! If you're a man, come and see me. Where are you calling from?'

His face flushed, Font y Rius jerks his head away from the receiver. When he listens again some moments later, the whistling is still going on. He stands up angrily, the music filling his brain, as though it were not just a distant whistle, but the overpowering sound of a rock group inside his head. Then there's silence.

'Raúl? Are you still there? I'm sorry for shouting at you, but I don't like it when you play at being mysterious. Raúl? Raúl?'

The psychiatrist stares at the telephone in his hand as if it had turned into something useless yet dangerous. He hangs up, then takes an address book out of the top pocket of his white coat, and firmly dials another number.

'Captain? The net's closing in. We're being surrounded by one man. Raúl's out to get us. We have to do something. But nothing violent, as we agreed, not your usual methods.'

All intercoms are pretty much the same. So are the voices they transmit, and sometimes even the messages they relay.

'A Señor Raúl Tourón would like to speak to you.'

Güelmes thinks this over.

'Is he here?'

'No, sir. He's on the telephone.'

'Put him through.'

He adopts a gentle smile so that his words will be gentle too.

'Raúl? Raulito?'

All this forced tenderness does not seem to evince a reply.

'Raulito? It's me. That shit Güelmes, as you used to call me.'

From the telephone, Pignatari's song gushes like a wave of nostalgia, whistled with feeling.

'Raúl. Stay right where you are. Raulito. For old times' sake, trust me.'

The only reply he gets is the whistled tune.

'Trust me, and don't move, will you, Raúl?'

By now all he can hear over the phone is the crackle of a dead line. Güelmes slowly replaces the receiver. A worried look steals over his face as he takes a phone number out of his desk drawer, dials for an outside line, and then the number.

'Doctor Font y Rius, please. He's not there? D'you know where he's gone?'

The voice does know, and Güelmes hurriedly gets rid of it so he can make another call, one he needs to make as desperately as a fire needs water.

'Captain. Things are getting complicated. Font y Rius is nervous :
he's gone to New Argentina to talk to Roberto. The son of a bitch.
Both of them are sons of bitches. We don't want to bring attention to
ourselves.'

But the Captain has already hung up.

Roberto casts an expert glance over his animals. He calls out to several
couples by name. 'Hermann and Dorotea, you're noisy this morning.
Yeltsin and Gorby, I hope that's the last time you'll fight. Galtieri,
Galtieri... you drunk again? Raúl, Raúl, where do you think you're
going?'

He tries to prod the rat out of its hiding place with a glass rod. A
shadow appears over his shoulder. He turns round.

'You?'

He doesn't get to say any more because an iron bar crashes against
his skull, splitting it and the room into two hemispheres. His head is
chopped open like a ripe fruit, and the scientist's body topples over,
though his hand inside the glass tank full of rats prevents him from
falling to the floor. The rats scurry about, terrified, and then start to
climb up the arm, searching for a way out. Someone opens the
laboratory door and calls out: 'Roberto? Roberto?'

Font y Rius looks in, trying to make out the scientist.

'Roberto? Roberto?'

Font y Rius enters the laboratory cautiously, as if afraid he will
break some of the fragile glass apparatus, or as if trying to calm down
the rats' compulsive movements.

'What's the matter with you, damned rats?'

In the darkness he notices Roberto's body slumped across the
bench.

'I think Raúl knows about the report. Roberto?'

Roberto's body does not move. As Font y Rius takes a step back
in alarm, a motorcyclist fills the scene and punches him hard in the
face. Font y Rius gasps with pain and tries to protect himself. The
motorcyclist stands over him menacingly. Takes off his helmet and
goggles. It's the Captain.

'You haven't seen a thing.'

Alma has her glasses on. She's sitting at her desk, gathering up scattered notes and books, then adjusting a small computer until it's exactly right for her. She sighs briefly, satisfied that everything is in order before she begins work, but just then she is interrupted by the doorbell, and goes to open it. She is about to say something, but a towel thrust over her face and suddenly anxious eyes makes it impossible. When she comes to, she finds she is sitting naked, tied to a chair, with a motorcyclist standing each side of her. In front of her there is a sheet with a light shining on it. Behind the sheet there's a shadow figure of someone sitting comfortably, so comfortably this in itself is a threat. Alma's eyes try to compensate for being unable to move her body, and rove desperately around the room. She cannot make anything out. The gloved hand of one of the motorcyclists is pressing a screwdriver to her throat. Then she hears a voice from the far side of the sheet.

'Alma? Do you remember my voice? It's me, the Captain, Alma! We meet again. The world turns and turns, and here we are again. We've arranged everything so that you can forget what's happening. And we've stripped you naked so you'll remember what happened in the past. You were lucky. Your sister died. Poor Berta: she was so sure she could change history and all she did was lose her life! But you spent a few months in prison and then years of golden exile.'

'My baby!'

'Your baby?'

'My niece.'

'She's disappeared, unfortunately, but I'm sure she's in better hands than yours or her mother's.'

Alma tries to look down at her body, seeking out the feeling of freezing cold that has invaded her, but the screwdriver point jabs into her neck, and the impotent fury in her eyes gets her nowhere.

'Where is Raúl Tourón?'

Alma wants to say something, and swallows, finding it hard to get the words out. Finally she says in a broken voice:

'I don't know.'

'I believe you, Alma. Do you remember how we became friends? How often my voice consoled you in those difficult times? I believe you, Alma. Perhaps you know what Tourón is looking for? Who is he looking for? His daughter? Me? Who am I?'

'I don't know. I don't know!'

Alma has raised her voice, and suddenly the screwdriver breaks her skin and a drop of blood appears. Alma bites her lip, and expresses all her despair through her eyes.

'I believe you, Alma. I believe you. I've always believed you. But listen carefully to what I'm going to say to you. If Raúl Tourón does get in contact with you, hang the blouse we've taken off you in the window – just the blouse. What colour is it, Alma?'

Alma tries to remember. The hand of one of the motorists thrusts it in front of her eyes.

'It's blue. Light blue. Sky blue on a fine summer day. Sky blue, the same blue as you're going to see in a few seconds. Remember, put the blouse in the window. That's all, Alma. Goodbye. See you soon.'

The shadow figure disappears, and Alma waits for the sheet and all it stands for to fall to the floor. Then a towel covers her face, stealing reality from her instead.

Pascuali stares lengthily at Font y Rius' horrified face. The psychiatrist appears to have suffered a momentary paralysis which prevents him moving backwards or forwards, from thinking or talking.

'You stated you came here looking for a report. What report is that?'

Slowly, Font y Rius lifts his eyes to Pascuali, who is standing next to the legs of the dead man, which are dangling from the laboratory bench as if counterbalancing his head and arm, still plunged inside the tank full of rats.

'It's an old story.'

Pascuali is on the point of saying something but hesitates, waiting for Font y Rius to emerge from the depression that hangs heavily in the air of the room.

'We're the only ones here. You can talk.'

Font y Rius starts to speak, at first overcome with emotion, but gradually recovering his calm.

'It all happened twenty years ago. We were already one year into the military government and what had at first seemed like just another routine coup had clearly turned into a "dirty war". We heard news of all the atrocities being committed. Torture. Disappearances. I wasn't really involved, but my wife, my sister-in-law, Raúl and Roberto decided to draw up a detailed report on mental and physical resistance to pain and brutality. They had been working on it for years. They knew everything about pain in rats so they drew up a comprehensive list of situations. They looked at every possible variable that could help resist interrogation. The report was meant to be kept a complete secret. After they read and memorized it, people were supposed to destroy it. Nearly all the group were captured. I was there the night they raided Raúl and Berta's apartment in La Recoleta. But Roberto and I were only there by chance.'

'And the report?'

'Someone handed it over to the military.'

'Roberto?'

'I'm not sure. Nobody knew what was going on. I could swear it wasn't me, but it could have been any one of us, trying to buy our freedom. The fact is that all of us who were in the Berta Modotti group saved our skins, apart from her. She was killed in the shoot-out. And there's something else.'

Pascuali doesn't ask him to go on, but he does anyway.

'I helped the goons interpret the report.'

'And the others didn't?'

'I couldn't say. We've never talked about our experiences in the Navy Mechanics School, which is where we all ended up.'

'Nobody's perfect. Everyone has something to hide.'

'Some more than others. I suddenly thought maybe Raúl believed it was Roberto who gave the military the report. I wanted to talk it over with him.'

'You haven't had time for that since 1977?'

The forensic scientist comes in, and Pascuali signals to Font y Rius to follow him. They walk down a corridor full of curious onlookers; both Font y Rius and Pascuali note with surprise that the director of The Spirit of New Argentina is among them. But whereas Font y Rius tries to avoid contact, Pascuali stares at him, racking his brain to try to recall where he's seen that angular face and its disdainful look before. The two of them reach the police car. Pascuali uses the car phone.

'Headquarters? I want you to put out a call for the arrest of Raúl Tourón as the prime suspect in the murder of Doctor Roberto Améndola Labriola. Dig out the most recent mugshots from the files.'

'D'you think Raúl did it?'

Pascuali turns towards Font y Rius and growls: 'If you're sure you didn't see the murderer, then yes, I do. For the moment, he did it. Strange, I thought I recognized the New Argentina director. He said his name was Dónate.'

Font y Rius doesn't seem interested.

The blinding light hurts Alma's eyes. She thinks she can see a dirty blue sky: a sky that's immensely dirty, intensely blue. She hugs her body as if she were naked. But her clothes have been thrown on. Her blouse is unbuttoned, she has no stockings, her skirt is undone. She can feel the indents of the ropes she was tied up with on her arms. She gets up from the sofa, turns her head, can smell or taste chloroform. The chair she was tied to stands there alone. Everything else is where it should be: her books, her notes. She cries with a mixture of panic and joy. The door bell rings. She bites her fist to avoid shouting out. Then hears Carvalho's voice.

'Alma? It's me. The Masked Galician.'

She laughs tearfully and runs to open. Carvalho has to hold her tight until she can recover the thread of what she wants to tell him: the words, her breathing all come out in a rush, her eyes are still rolling with fear. He sits next to her on the couch and hugs her again. He conveys sympathy, she her need for protection.

'Are you going to tell me the truth once and for all?'

'I don't know what the truth is. There are so many different versions. I'll tell you my own. I told you what happened the night of the raid. But it didn't really happen exactly like that. When they burst in we were having dinner and doing political work. But most of all, I'm not Alma. I'm Berta.'

Carvalho cannot and will not hide his stupefaction.

'Let me speak. I was Berta. Now I don't want to be her any more. That night, I tried to fight back against the people raiding us.'

Deep down inside her, the film of those events reels out as she describes what happened. Her voice changes with each character:

'Raúl shouted at me from the other room – "don't be such a fool! They'll kill us all! The baby!" Alma stood up to grab hold of her, and was cut down by a machine-gun burst. I couldn't believe my eyes. Alma's body, her husband Font y Rius and I were all lying on the floor in one room. My brother-in-law shouted, "Get the baby and escape through the bathroom". I turned Alma's body over. Her face was destroyed by the bullets. My brother-in-law was insisting: "Get out with the baby! I'll tell them it was you they killed. Save the baby! Do it for her! I'm surrendering! Don't shoot!" I crawled to the bedroom where my baby was. I picked her up: she was such a delicate thing, and smelled so sweet, but she was such a weight. I climbed out of the window and down a folding fire escape we'd put up for an emergency like this. I carried the baby down. She was so heavy! She weighed so much I was scared I'd drop her! The street was blocked off by more soldiers. There was a light on in the porter's apartment. I went in there. He confronted me. He stared at me, then at the baby: at first he was angry, then sympathetic. He pushed me inside a big wardrobe, but not before he told me, "I haven't seen a thing. If they find you, I haven't seen a thing." The rest is pretty much as I told you. Now I'm Alma, and glad to be her. It's the only way I can fight off my sense of guilt. My baby Eva María is the only one who really disappeared. I hate Berta. I hate myself. I know I shouldn't, but I do hate myself when I remember what I was like then.'

'Memory sometimes doesn't deserve us, sometimes we don't deserve it.'

Alma throws herself into the haven of Carvalho's arms and chest. But her relief is short-lived. The door bell rings again. This time it's Carvalho who goes to open it. He finds himself faced by a sarcastic Pascuali and a worried but scowling Vladimiro.

On the way to the police station, it's Vladimiro who gives the orders. Pascuali doesn't deign to speak, even when they reach his lair: he walks up and down in front of Carvalho, Alma and Font y Rius, who are sitting on benches opposite each other. Alma and Font y Rius try to communicate silently with their eyes. Pascuali signals for the three of them to follow him. His office smells of metal furniture and ketchup. Pascuali stares each of them up and down slowly: three complete idiots, his look says. He frowns at the other cops to leave the room. When he's on his own, he remains silent for a few moments, then growls: 'A murder. A raid on an apartment, with the owner kidnapped in her own home! It's like something from a sado-porno film. What are you hiding from me? What's this all about?' Pascuali bangs his fist on the desk. 'I've had it up to here with your stories! First we've got a madman who's trying to recover his past, his own discoveries. And he arrives at the worst moment, just when none of you needs him.'

He stands up, beside himself. Goes over to Carvalho.

'And you, you snooping asshole, why don't you get out of here, get back to Europe and stop making things even more difficult for us!'

Then it's Alma's turn.

'And why don't you go for a trip down to the Plaza de Mayo, like a nice little old widow, a history widow! Just don't give me any more headaches! And when your brother-in-law does show up, make sure you hand him over to me, for his own sake, for all our sakes! Or do you want the hunting season to start again?'

For a few minutes, Pascuali says nothing more. Finally he shouts: 'Get out of here!' As Font y Rius passes by him, he hisses: 'Psychiatrists!'

'What's the weather like in Barcelona, Biscuter? Are the Olympic Games over yet? Five years ago? I've lost all track of time. Has Charo phoned? No. I'm cooking. Well, it's an Argentine dish that nobody in Buenos Aires makes any more. Its called *carbonada argentina*. It's like a beef stew with maize, sweet potatoes, pumpkin and peaches. The city here? It's fine. Still full of depressed Argies.'

He hangs up. Wearily picks up the letter he can never finish. 'Charo. What would a normal solution be for me and you? Are there any normal solutions after fifty, or is there only the fear of growing old alone and losing one's dignity?'

He makes as if to tear the letter up. Changes his mind and drops it again. Goes back to the kitchen. It takes him a while to realize that Alma is standing by the stove, carefully supervising the cooking.

'Is everything all right?'

'D'you call this cooking?'

'What else would you call it?'

'It's cooking itself.'

Carvalho uncorks a bottle of wine.

'Are you opening it already?'

'It's a fine Cabernet Sauvignon from Mendoza. Four years old. You have to let it breathe. But you're from a good family, you ought to know that.'

Later, with the remains of their meal still on the plates, Alma holds the wine glass up to the light.

'I've learnt something tonight. That you have to look at wine, to sniff it, taste it. My parents were rich, but they never taught me things like that. They probably didn't know. There are rich people who don't know how to enjoy it. My parents didn't. They didn't know how to be the parents of two revolutionary daughters either. But what are we doing, talking about wines? What can have happened to Eva María? Or to Raúl?'

'If I'm not thrown out of the country, I'll find him. Do you think he killed Roberto?'

Alma dismisses the possibility with a wave of her hand.

'That's impossible. Raúl was born to be killed, not to kill.'

Carvalho is looking at her with surprising tenderness.

'What are you staring at?'

Carvalho doesn't answer. Alma looks across at the bedroom next door. When she speaks it's calmly and gently.

'Are you used to women thanking you for dinner by going to bed with you?'

Carvalho takes another sip of wine and answers unconcernedly: 'If you suggest it, I won't say no. But if I'd known you wanted to go to bed with me, I'd have chosen a different menu. You don't go with *carbonada argentina*.'

'So what do I go with?'

'Stuffed veal à la Wanda, perhaps.'

'And is that edible?'

'Very.'

'What about Charo? Is Charo edible?'

'What do you know about Charo?'

Alma gestures in the opposite direction to the bedroom, towards Carvalho's unfinished letter.

'I couldn't resist the temptation. I read it. I adore letters. I love epistolary literature.'

'Let's just say she was my sentimental companion.'

'Is she a private detective too?'

'No; she's a whore.'

Alma stares at him, not knowing whether to be shocked or angry. She's surprised at her own reaction, and offended on Charo's behalf.

'It's nothing but the truth. I've got a wayward soul. My girl-friend is a call girl. My technical assistant, waiter, cook and secretary is a car thief called Biscuter. My spiritual and gastronomic adviser is a neighbour called Fuster. He's also my manager. He manages what little I have to manage. I adore impossible families. I detest possible ones.'

'So did you detest your father and mother?'

'I detest possible families who are alive. I love dead ones.'

Alma drinks thoughtfully. Carvalho picks up the letter and crumples it. He hesitates over what to do with it. Eventually he goes over to the hearth, but quickly stuffs the letter in his pocket. Then he sets about lighting the fire. Alma watches him in a detached way until she sees him pick up a book and begin to tear it up.

'But...what? Are you off your head?'

She struggles to try to stop him, but it's too late. The book has already caught fire, and the flames spread to the rest of the kindling and logs.

'Are you crazy? Or just a Fascist? They're the only ones who burn books.'

Carvalho sinks into the sofa and lights a cigar.

'It's an old habit of mine. For forty years I read book after book, now I burn them because they taught me nothing about how to live.'

'Now you sound like Julio Iglesias.'

She contemplates Carvalho and the fire, still upset.

'I hope it wasn't an important book, anyway.'

'I think it was by Ernesto Sóbato. I've no idea what it was about. I think it was called something like: *Tango, the Song of Buenos Aires.*'

Alma reacts violently: 'But that's a wonderful book!'

'Too bad. The other day I burned *Adán Buenosayres.*'

'You're telling me you had the nerve to burn Marechal's novel?'

'I don't care who it was by.'

'But that book's our *Ulysses*!'

Alma is seriously indignant.

'You're a Fascist queer. A cook!'

'Culture doesn't teach you how to live. It's nothing more than a mask for fear and ignorance. For death. Take a cow on the pampas…'

'Does it have to be from the pampas?'

'From wherever you like. Say you kill it, and eat it raw. Everyone would point at you: look at that barbarian, that savage. If on the other hand you catch the cow, kill it, slice it up skilfully, roast it, and then put sauce on it: that's culture. A disguise for cannibalism. Cannibalism's subterfuges.'

'You mean if we ate each other raw we would be being sincere?'

'No. We have to delude ourselves. But the fact is, yes, we do eat each other raw. So from time to time I burn a book, even one I like.' He recites: 'Which of us does not fear losing what he does not love?'

'Quevedo?'

'Quevedo modified by me.'

He holds a piece of paper out to Alma.

'A message from Raúl. I found it under the door.'

Alma snatches the paper from him, and reads what it says out loud: 'Cousin, I've turned to Güelmes. I'm tired of running, and I've almost reached Eva María, just like Peter Pan reached the stars.'

She comes to a halt, and looks up at Carvalho with fear in her eyes. Carvalho puts a hand behind her head and turns her face towards him. Their lips draw close, but at that very moment Pascuali and four cops start battering on the door, and the two of them draw apart again.

'Pascuali, who else?'

Three of the men throw themselves on Carvalho and pin him down. Pascuali stands over Alma.

'The game's up. I don't want any more corpses. I have to find your brother-in-law before I don't know who; but I do know that if I don't get to him first, he's not going to like it. I recognized the chairman of The Spirit of New Argentina, and I don't like playing games with ghosts.'

Carvalho has managed to struggle free from the other men: he elbows one in the liver, and aims a kick at another one which misses by a mile. Pascuali points his revolver at him, but calms his men down with a gesture.

'That's enough. You've shown off for the lady, so now be quiet, because you haven't the first idea what's going on.'

'I know how to find Raúl.'

Alma and Pascuali stare at him incredulously.

'He's being hidden either by Güelmes or by Font y Rius. A ministry, a psychiatric clinic – they're both safe hiding places.'

Pascuali has his doubts, but not about Carvalho: 'In Argentina, ministries aren't safe.'

Carvalho adds: 'Nor are ministers.'

He hands Pascuali the piece of paper with Raúl's message.

The two men are strolling along by the river. The moon paints Raúl's face like a clown as he looks up at the night sky and recites:

> *To have looked up*
> *at the ancient stars*
> *from this bank of shadows*
> *to have looked up*
> *at those scattered lights*
> *my ignorance never learnt to name*
> *nor to arrange in constellations...*

He turns to his companion. Güelmes speaks in a slow voice, as if he was conjuring up a dream, and the dream was providing him with words.

'The ancient stars. You used to be a star, Raúl, remember how brilliant you were, how we all admired you. I was an economics student in those days, more of a militant than a student in fact; it was only afterwards during my exile in the United States I made my name as an economist. A pragmatist. Do you remember the analyses I did following Mandel or Gunder Frank, about the inevitability of the fall of capitalism? I'm sure it will fall one day, but neither you nor I are going to live to see it. So now I'm a pragmatic economist. A social liberal. Social on Monday, Wednesday and Friday, liberal on Tuesday, Thursday and Saturday. On Sundays, I have a day off. I've grown up:

you never did. What are you looking for? The memory of a feeling? Or are you after your share of the profits from your animal feed discoveries? Roberto and I agreed we'd market them when I returned from exile and found a good position, and you had disappeared. Roberto claimed the scientific rights to the formula; I was the partner who had the capital and state backing.'

He comes to a halt. Raúl doesn't seem to have understood a thing.

'Roberto is dead. He got too nervous when you came back, he wanted to explain everything. Your brother-in-law Font y Rius is mixed up in it as well.'

'What about Alma?'

Güelmes smiles and mutters: 'Alma!' as if it were the strangest of names. He pulls out a pistol, and points it at Raúl, whose surprise quickly gives way to laughter. Then he starts to squeal like a rat – even his features take on the aspect of a threatened rat, a rat twitching its long, white-haired nose. Güelmes thinks he has turned into a gigantic rat.

'Are you crazy?'

He aims at Raúl. But his eyes reveal the solution he has found. 'You really are crazy. And do you know where we put crazy people?'

Raúl tries to grunt like a less desperate rat, and carries on mimicking as he climbs into the car Güelmes has waved him towards with the gun. Once he's inside the car and has accepted the new situation, the sounds suddenly cease, as if they had a life of their own. Güelmes is on his right; on his left, there's a man he doesn't know, and another sitting beside the driver. The car pulls up outside Font y Rius' clinic. The psychiatrist is waiting for them behind the barred windows, momentarily blinded by the car's headlights. He throws down the cigarette in his hand and comes out to meet them. Headed by Güelmes, the new arrivals push past him into the clinic, and he has to turn and follow their unresponsive backs. Güelmes is frogmarching Raúl along. Font y Rius wants them to put his chaotic thoughts in order.

'D'you think this is a good idea?'

Güelmes does not even bother to turn round.

'Good ideas are always provisional.'

Several of the newcomers post themselves in the psychiatrist's office. Font y Rius rushes after Güelmes and Raúl, who is now guarded by two nurses. They stride down the clinic's most secret passages. One of the nurses flings open a metal door; the banging echoes all along the corridors. Raúl is thrown into a bare, brightly lit room. The nurses pull off his clothes while Güelmes looks on impassively, and Font y Rius winces. They put Raúl in a straitjacket. He starts to squeal like a rat again. Güelmes strides in front of Font y Rius back to the office. His wipes his sweating palms with a handkerchief. But when they reach the clinic office they find their space has been taken over. Two motorcyclists are standing guard on either side of the table. In front of them is the fat man, while behind in the shadows sits the chairman of The Spirit of New Argentina. His face is hidden, but when they hear his voice, Font y Rius' eyes narrow, and Güelmes swallows nervously.

'Do you think this was a good idea?'

Güelmes tries to sound natural.

'We couldn't kill him, could we? Too many people are looking for him.'

The voice from the shadows is unconvinced. It seems to be speaking for itself, or the fat man and the motorcyclists, rather than for Güelmes or Font y Rius.

'They couldn't kill him.'

He drives his fist into the open palm of his other hand. Güelmes and Font y Rius start with fright. The fat man laughs.

'Is that why you brought me here? To tell me you couldn't kill him?'

Font y Rius plucks up his courage:

'Captain. Too many people have already died.'

The fat man turns to the figure in the shadows and receives a whispered message only he hears. He gets up, and the two motorcyclists follow him out of the room. When they have gone, the Captain swivels his chair round and faces Güelmes and Font y Rius.

'My dear partners. We haven't had a company meeting in some time. You're still playing with death. You're still amateurs. In war, pity does more harm than good. Pity is dangerous. At stake in all this are your lives and my money – or rather, the money of our wealthy backers. New Argentina could be my chance of a lifetime, of your lifetimes; or it could all be wrecked thanks to a crazy guy who has no past and no future.'

It gradually dawns on Font y Rius and Güelmes what is going to happen.

'Where did the fat man and those two thugs go? What are they going to do to Raúl?'

The Captain doesn't even take the trouble to reply. He goes on: 'Who wrote that little novel *Beware of Pity*?'

Font y Rius makes a desperate lunge for the alarm bell. It goes off so loudly that it stops the fat man and the motorcyclists in their tracks in the underground passageways. The shrill alarm sound fills every corner. The fat man draws his gun. The two motorcyclists feel for the daggers hidden in sheaths on their legs. They search around, trying to discover where the noise is coming from. They are frightened, nervous, and their fear only increases when they hear the sound of a shot ring out from the clinic office. They run back there, and find Font y Rius still clinging on to the alarm bell with one hand, while with the other he tries to stanch the flow of blood from a wound to his hip. Güelmes is cowering on the floor, rolled up, protecting himself with his arms. The Captain steps towards him. Güelmes covers his head with his hands. The other man goes over to the window. The garden is swarming with policemen, led by Pascuali. By now the alarm has fallen silent, but there is even louder shouting. Every patient has become an alarm, screaming out their certainties, their scorn, their fears. Raúl is still in one corner of his cell, prevented by the straitjacket from shielding his ears from the uproar. The door bursts open. It's Pascuali, gun in hand. Carvalho is right behind him. The corridor is full of policemen. Carvalho leaps on Raúl to make sure he is unharmed, helped or hindered by two nurses. The Captain's voice rings out behind them.

'Good work, Pascuali.'

Pascuali turns round and salutes him, taken aback but showing respect. He sees a thin man of around fifty, with a gaunt face and a cold, self-satisfied smile.

'At your command, Captain.'

'I didn't want to miss this brilliant operation. And I'd like to question your prisoner personally.'

Carvalho examines first the fat man and then the Captain.

'I've seen your face in a photograph.'

'The Captain...' Pascuali tries to explain, but Carvalho doesn't need any introduction.

'Captain Ranger, war hero: of the Falklands War, that is.'

Carvalho steps between Raúl and the Captain.

'I've just phoned the Spanish embassy. They're sending an official to see if he can be of any assistance to you, and to my cousin, of course.'

The Captain isn't convinced.

'You've just told them? How did you know that "thing" was your cousin?'

'What's the difference between just having told them and being just about to?'

The Captain relaxes, smiles, then turns on his heel and pushes his way through the policemen. As he passes Alma, he nods his head slightly, and says in a voice so low only she can hear him: 'Now you won't need to hang out your blue blouse, Alma.'

Alma watches fearfully as the Captain leaves the clinic, followed by the two motorcyclists and the fat man. Two ambulancemen carry Font y Rius away on a stretcher, supervised by Güelmes, who all of a sudden has regained all his authority and political dignity. Pascuali is very nervous; Alma is distraught. Carvalho speaks on the telephone. Freed from his straitjacket, Raúl stares at everyone; his face shows conflicting emotions until he sees Alma, when he looks dumbstruck. Alma turns away from him. Carvalho gently puts the phone down. Pascuali is taken aback at Raúl's reaction.

'What's the matter with him?'

Güelmes responds quickly.

'It's the emotion. It's the first time he's seen his sister-in-law. And she looks so like his wife.'

Carvalho takes the initiative. He takes Alma by her arm and forces her to look at Raúl.

'Alma, look, this is Raúl. Raúl, this is Alma.'

Raúl peers at Güelmes, at Alma, at Pascuali and finally at Carvalho. Eventually he smiles and with great difficulty asks: 'How are things, Alma?'

He goes up to her, and their two faces tilt to exchange a kiss on the cheek. But as Raúl touches her, it's as if a whole hidden past seeps from their skin. Their eyes fill with pain as they hug each other tightly, so tightly their bodies seem to fuse into one, moulding flesh and bones together as if never to part. They moan: 'Eva María, Eva María.'

Pascuali does not want to be moved by the scene.

'Nobody leaves here until I've heard what I want to know.'

Güelmes seems to be on top form.

'Just ask, and we'll tell you.'

'Who shot Font y Rius?'

'It was an accident. Everyone was nervous because the alarm went off.'

Pascuali is not satisfied.

'Why did the alarm go off? And what has the Captain got to do with you all?'

Güelmes is talking a blue streak.

'We appointed him chairman of The Spirit of New Argentina. We need to strengthen links between the political, civilian and military sectors of our society if we are to avoid any more tragic misunderstandings. We need heroes to back our successful businesses. It's very simple really. Don't look for complications in your life, Pascuali, or in your service record. The New Argentina is based on discoveries that our friend Tourón here made, together with Roberto – may he rest in peace. I'm sure Raúl will want to join our wonderful team and benefit from the fruits of his labour.'

At that, Güelmes turns and addresses Raúl: 'Welcome on board, Raúl. The Captain's in charge once more. It's time for national and personal reconciliation. Your brother-in-law, me, you, all of us partners. One big happy family.'

Raúl looks as if he's smiling, but as he goes up to Güelmes a blob of spittle flies through the air almost in slow motion and lands on the deputy minister's shirt front. Vladimiro and another policeman take Raúl out and put him in the police van. Carvalho and Pascuali walk out level with each other. Carvalho is tired; Pascuali is still stunned. They have to walk past the Captain, the fat man, the motorcyclists. Carvalho questions Pascuali: 'Who is the Captain?'

'A big shot.'

'In what? Since when?'

Pascuali shrugs. 'In what, I've no idea. But he's always been in charge. Always will be. Apparently all the secret shit of power never disappears.'

'Be careful, Pascuali. That sounds almost like anarchy.'

By now they've reached the fat man who steps forward to protect the Captain. Carvalho puts a hand out to stroke his belly: 'You ought to ease up on the lupins.'

The Captain calms his companion's anger with an icy stare.

Font y Rius is taken away in an ambulance. Alma and Carvalho join Raúl in the police van. Güelmes is driven off in an official car. Pascuali watches while two policemen join the others in the back of the van, shuts the door from outside, then sits up with the driver. He gives the order to set off. In the back, Raúl and Alma are lost in thought, but with their hands entwined. Carvalho surveys them. The two policemen have their machine-guns on their laps. Raúl looks up, and gazes tenderly at Alma: 'What about the baby?'

'I did all I could, but there are no traces. The person who kept her must be a very powerful son of a bitch.'

'She must be almost twenty by now.'

'She's nineteen years, six months, and four days old...'

Alma starts to sob quietly, and then all of a sudden bursts out: 'Why...why?'

Raúl caresses her as much as his handcuffs will allow. Carvalho is still staring at them, poker-faced. Raúl murmurs to Alma: 'Thank you.'

'What for?'

'Thank you for living.'

Suddenly, Raúl starts to squeal like a rat and to shake all over. Everyone but Carvalho is dumbfounded. The policemen don't know what to do; just in case, they raise their machine-guns. Alma thrusts herself between the guns and Raúl.

'Why don't you stick your pricks back in your trousers, where they belong, you halfwits? Can't you see he's ill?'

One of the policemen decides to consult Pascuali. They knock on the window, and the inspector's face appears behind the grille.

'What's going on?'

'The crazy guy's having some sort of attack.'

'Oh, shit!'

The van brakes. Carvalho and Raúl glance at each other. Raúl's look is far more coherent than his squealing. The van comes to a halt, the door is opened and Pascuali leans in. He shouts angrily: 'What's going on in here?'

Raúl takes a sudden leap out of the van. He lands on top of Pascuali, who is pinioned beneath him. As he struggles to his feet and draws his gun from its holster, Raúl flings himself into the undergrowth separating the road from a line of trees as black as night. The two policemen raise their machine-guns. Carvalho pretends to lose his balance, falls on them, and for his pains receives a blow from the butt of a gun that knocks him half-conscious to the floor of the van. He opens his eyes when he realizes Alma is leaning over him. Carvalho sees her tearful face next to his, asking him something. He has no time to reply before he blacks out completely.

A policeman lets Carvalho out of the police station with an irritated, perfunctory gesture. The detective walks slowly down the front steps. As he takes a deep breath of the night air, he touches the bandage on his side covering the wound. He starts walking. A car draws level with him. Carvalho is suspicious, but it's Güelmes, who leans out of the car window and offers him a ride. Inside the car, Carvalho flops back alongside the honourable deputy minister of development.

'I had a hard time getting you out of there. It took all my influence and my common sense. After all, what did you do? You prevented our police getting into a real mess. Gunning down a foreign subject! And a Spaniard at that! The ambassador would have blown his top! Called in the United Nations! Amnesty International! Mother Teresa of Calcutta! Judge Garzón! Isn't that the name of the Spanish judge who's trying to lock up all our military junta? Whatever happened to our sovereignty? We're the masters of our torturers, and we've decided to pardon them. What else is national sovereignty for, in these times of economic and political globalization?'

'States are only the masters of their state torturers and murderers.'

'You have to leave us something. Pascuali is a good officer, but he takes his professionalism too far. Argentina has to regain its democratic image. Any questions?'

Carvalho shrugs. 'Do you have any answers?'

'Inside here, yes. It's your word against mine. This is the last explanation you'll get from me. We kept the switch between Berta and Alma a secret. At first only Font y Rius knew about it. Then Pignatari and Norman. We couldn't tell Raúl while he was being held, and afterwards Alma – that is, Berta – told us it would be better for him to get out and start a new life in Spain. Berta – that is, Alma – felt guilty about having dragged us into politics: she was our idol, our heroine, our pirate captain. Ah, the myths of youth! Anyone who isn't an idealist at twenty... !'

'I know that refrain. What about betrayal? What about your deals with the Captain?'

'You're confusing betrayal with pragmatism. It was the Captain's idea. While we were being interrogated, he realized he could do business with us. He was a dirty hero; now he wants to be a clean rich man. So he's the much respected chairman of a foundation: The Spirit of New Argentina. Rats, cows, men and women. It's a new humanism. Fattening mankind. The only possible kind of humanism. Besides, it wasn't a crime to put Raúl's discoveries to good use. Times have changed.'

Güelmes smiles and takes hold of Carvalho's arm.

'Let me tell you once more, and make sure you get the message. Anyone who doesn't want to change the world at twenty is a son of a bitch, but anyone who at forty still wants to change it is a fool...'

Güelmes' car deposits Carvalho on the outskirts of San Telmo, and the detective finds his way to the Plaza Dorrego and the tango bar Alma has said she'll meet him in. Inside, it's as though Gardel was just about to embark on his death flight, but Alma only lets him savour the images of bygone sentimentality for a few moments, before she leads him out along streets full of antique shops.

'They're all that's left from the shipwreck of the richest bourgeoisie in Latin America. They began to sell everything off when Perónism started to bring the workers into the political picture, and finished the sale when the armed forces let loose inflation and hunger.'

Alma and Carvalho keep their distance as they walk along. Alma is playing at stepping up and down from the edge of the pavement whenever parked cars allow her to. Carvalho gazes up at the stars above San Telmo.

'Back at home in Vallvidrera I sometimes amuse myself looking up at the constellations. If I can make them out that means I'm in a good mood, if I can't see them, it means I'm drunk.'

'What about the air pollution?'

'There isn't any in Vallvidrera.'

Alma's game up and down the pavement saves her from having to speak seriously, but eventually she makes up her mind: 'I owe you an explanation.'

'You've paid all your debts, you've buried all your dead.'

'You're a real poet.'

'There are worse.'

Alma takes him by the arm and points out the sign over a brightly-lit bar: Tango Amigo.

'Norman's tiny enchanted kingdom: Norman Silverstein. You've grown up enough. Time for you to enter.'

He's hit by a clash of lights and smoke, a distant mass of bodies lining a bar or picked out against a low stage on which a spotlight draws a circle where the magic is soon to begin. Carvalho and Alma push their way through the audience. A waiter shows them to a pair of reserved seats close to the stage. Carvalho whispers in Alma's ear: 'What's an old rocker like you doing in a place like this?'

Alma laughs out loud. Then the room goes completely dark. Calls for silence. The spotlight draws a sun on the stage, in the middle of it is the grotesquely made-up Norman Silverstein, with a grotesque smile on his face, a leering grimace. His voice is a grimace too, as he launches into a speech he cannot control.

'Welcome to Buenos Aires! We know you're here because for foreigners this is a cheap city, and Argentina is up for sale!'

He points to his audience.

'You! And you!'

His pointing finger halts at Carvalho, and the spotlight follows him.

'If anything isn't for sale, that means it's worthless!'

He unstraps the watch from his wrist.

'My old grandfather sold this to me. He was a military man, and it always showed him the time for coups d'état, firing squads, for balls for tennis or for the electric prod. I'm not asking a hundred pesos for it, not a million, not even one.'

He falls to his knees, sobbing.

'I'm just begging you to take it from me. We Argentines love people to take our watches, our sweethearts, our islands.'

Abruptly, his tone changes.

'By the way, what'd you know about Buenos Aires?'

Norman has recovered all his sang-froid, and now questions his audience like a schoolmaster.

'Come on. Show me what you know. What do you know about Buenos Aires? Shout "Yes!!!" if you know what I'm talking about.'

A drum roll.

'Tango?'

The audience agrees reluctantly. 'Yes!'

'Maradona?'

'Yes!!!!'

'The disappeared?'

Some of the audience reply 'Yes!' as if this were another routine question; others realize just what they are being asked, and stay silent. Gradually a soft drum roll is heard again. It's so gentle it almost seems as if the drums are trembling.

'Unfortunately, honoured and respectable public, Maradona has got problems because he stuck his nose in where he shouldn't have, Maradona now only believes in his family and Fidel Castro. He doesn't even believe in Menem! He's just like Zulema, Menem's ex-wife!'

Loud laughter.

'The disappeared. Have any of you ever seen a disappeared person? If you haven't, how can anyone ever say there were disappeared people?'

The audience falls silent, shifting uncomfortably. Some heads wag their disapproval.

'But we still have the tango! Our tango! We are tango! And tango is a woman: tonight, tango is a woman who no less a person than the

Polack, the great, the inimitable Goyeneche, said was the only woman who could sing tangos. Here is tango!'

He raises an arm to introduce the singer. 'Adriana Varela!'

A woman with a plunging neckline, a dramatic white face. A woman full of mystery, in full possession of her seven doors and six senses in the silvery light. The bandoneon leads off the orchestra, and as Norman withdraws, the singer fills the whole stage.

> *Searching*
> *among the shadows of a memory*
> *for footprints in the blood*
> *as ancient as the sun.*
>
> *Searching*
> *like a wounded animal*
> *hunted by a destiny*
> *that refuses to admit all pain.*
>
> *Come on in, stranger*
> *there's no pity here*
> *for anyone who missed*
> *the express train of time.*
>
> *Traces*
> *in the wounded city*
> *a landscape between two wars*
> *between being and non-being.*
>
> *Traces*
> *of a wounded animal*
> *the animal of all of us*
> *so blind, so obstinate.*
>
> *Come on in, stranger*
> *there's no pity here*
> *for anyone who missed*
> *the express train of time.*

All you'll find
Is a weary city
with its mirrors smashed
and pretending not to care.

Searching
to see if among the ruins
your face might be the face
of a time that's dead and gone.

The singer acknowledges the audience's applause with an automatic, ritual wave. Carvalho stares at her, moved and astonished. Pascuali has been watching from the back row. He sees her salute her public, turns on his heel and goes out into the street. He takes a deep breath and looks up at the constellations of stars – the same stars that Raúl is enjoying, head thrown back as he runs beside the river, loping along in a way that for him has now taken over from walking. When will he be able to return to walking normally, like everyone else? And the Captain glances up at the same stars through the window of his armour-plated limousine, ignoring the presence and continual chatter of his driver. It's the fat man who is at the wheel, attentively following the path the headlights pick out along the highway, but also acutely aware of the Captain's unshakeable presence in the back seat. The Captain looks up at the stars, then stares at the landscape outside to calculate how much further they have to go. The car pulls up on the gravel path in front of a mansion standing on its own in a clearing of a eucalyptus wood. The Captain gets out – the fat man has opened the door for him, and is standing to attention.

'What next, Captain?'

The Captain simply dismisses him with an airy wave, telling him to be on his way.

'My respects to Doña María Asunción and your daughter.'

But the Captain has already bounded off and reaches the front door of his house, which he opens without needing a key, and almost without breaking stride enters a reception room. He sniffs at the air. His gaze lights upon an almost empty whisky bottle, and through it the distorted face of a woman struggling between falling asleep, collapsing into a drunken stupor, or trying to work out who has come in. Hunting trophies. Even the few books carefully adorning the bookshelves look like hunting trophies. So does an Argentine flag, on which is placed a blown-up photograph of a group of smiling soldiers, with behind them the sea, the Falklands sea. The Captain strides over to the drunken woman in her rocking chair and almost spits at her: 'Where's the girl?'

The woman nods vaguely upwards. The Captain bounds up the stairs two at a time. He comes to a halt in front of a bedroom door. Opens it. Inside, a young woman sleeps the untroubled sleep of a twenty-year-old. The Captain tucks her in. His cruel, impassively cold features have softened into plasticine tenderness. The girl stirs.

'Nothing and nobody will ever separate us.'

The Captain lifts the lid of a music box. It's Eva María's box, the one Alma remembers so well, with the tune Pignatari sang. The Captain makes as if to caress the sleeping girl, thinks better of it, and goes over to the window to look up at the stars again. The same stars Carvalho can see from his apartment. Logs are burning in the hearth on the ashes of *Buenos Aires: un museo al aire libre* by León Tenenbaum. Carvalho, staring out of the window because he can't get to sleep. He goes back to the table, picks up a piece of paper, and reads out loud:

> *Dear Charo, As I was leaving for Buenos Aires to do some work, I started this letter to try to clear up a misunderstanding. Things weren't how you imagined them to be, Charo. Perhaps it's time for us to wake up to the fact that we're not kids anymore, and that what's at stake is trying to enjoy the years left to us, before old age sets in. Charo, what might be a normal situation for you and me? Are there any normal situations after we've reached fifty, or is all that's left the fear of disintegrating, of growing old without dignity, and all alone? Everything here has finished, but could start up again at any moment. Every end is its own beginning, here just like anywhere else in the world, but I've never been to a place I haven't wanted to leave, and I'm scared of the*

fact that you need me almost as much as I am that I need you. Perhaps I'll look for an excuse to stay here a bit longer. A professional excuse. Finding my cousin, for example. Getting paid for it. Settling my debts. Finally burying the dead...

Chapter 2

The Hidden Man

Because it's an old, old woman struggling with the tray, a dinner trembles on the brink, especially a plate of soup, like a sea with no shore. The old woman insists stubbornly, even though she finds it hard to walk and her Parkinson's threatens at any moment to spill all the liquid to the floor. She struggles to a corner of the kitchen, manages to deposit the tray on a shelf while she gropes for a bell on the wall. In fact it's a spring, and the wooden-panelled bottom half of the wall opens before her. A black hole to the unknown. After a moment, a man approximately as old as she is appears. He's wearing a dressing gown, half-moon glasses. He leans out of the hole and stares round suspiciously.

'All quiet?'

'Yes, all quiet.'

'Is the guy with the sideburns still in power?'

'Yes he is, Favila, just like he was yesterday and the day before yesterday.'

'Perón didn't come back?'

'Forget Perón, he's dead.'

'I can't believe it.'

'Come on, eat your dinner before it gets cold.'

The man picks up the tray with difficulty. His hands shake as much as hers. But he also succeeds in not spilling a drop of the soup.

He grasps the tray firmly and heads back into the darkness. Just before she closes the door on him, he reminds her sternly: 'If the Argie military, the Francoists, or any other armed bastards show up, you know what to tell them.'

She ignores him. She presses the switch again with something approaching vindictiveness, and the man disappears in his hole before he can add something more. The old woman stands rooted to the spot for a moment: 'I've completely forgotten what I'm supposed to say. I'll tell them the first bloody thing that occurs to me.'

Norman Silverstein's narrow face is sweating in the spotlight beneath the clown make-up.

'Until a few years ago you'd get some Japanese or other appearing in the jungle of a Pacific island convinced the Second World War was still going on. I reckon it was always the same one, on the same island. They'd slip him a few coins, a canteen full of *sake*, and he'd start his little number. All the tourists would say: "Ah! Here comes that stupid Japanese soldier who's still fighting for his emperor!" And he would strike his best threatening imperial warrior pose, with one of those huge swords all the best samurai have. "Ahso! Hatamitaka! Fujimori! Tanaka! Come off it, Takiri! Stop playing the fool! Commit hara-kiri and get it over with!" There's obviously no point in any Japanese hiding out nowadays. But have you any idea how many moles, how many hidden people there are in the world today? All those who can't settle their debts, all those who can't pay the alimony to the women they've divorced, all those afraid they'll be recognized as ex-torturers, all those afraid they'll be tortured again, a million Tutsis hidden from the Hutus, a million Hutus hidden from the Tutsis. All of them, all of us, are like those inscrutable Japanese soldiers – who in this day and age asks anyone to explain themselves? We accept everything. God is dead. Marx is dead. Mankind is dead. Marlene Dietrich is dead. And I'm not feeling too well myself. Anything goes! Not even nation states have sovereignty any more. We're ruled by multinationals, by monetary funds, by fixed prices, by Yankee Doodle soldiers. The only sovereignty we have left is over our torturers. When a foreign judge wants to try our torturers: it's an attack on our national sovereignty! The sovereignty of repression! It's all we have left. So are you surprised if everything gets mixed up? Guerrilleros marry upper-class girls, left-wing mayors rip off everything they can lay their hands on in Buenos Aires: trees, pavements, whole blocks of streets, building plots, lamp-posts, lamp-post lights, the shadows of dogs pissing against the lamp-posts. All they leave us are the Mothers of the Plaza de Mayo and their demonstrations, and the old-age pensioners demonstrating outside Congress. Anything goes! So what's the point in hiding? There's only one. I respect those who are hiding because they've forgotten where Buenos Aires, America, the world, are – all they can remember is the tiny corner where they were, are, and will be, scared out of their wits.'

The faces of the audience live up to the simple sociological calculation Carvalho has made about the effects of Norman's sarcasm: a few smiles, embarrassment, perplexity, annoyance. Carvalho asks for the bill and pays. He looks at his wallet and the money inside. Not much left. He stares doubtfully at his credit cards. Turns his head when he hears Alma's voice: 'Are you running out of dough?'

'Yes, I'm running out of dough, and I can't ask my uncle for any more in advance until I find his son.'

'You'll have to get a job. What can you do?'

'Look round me.'

Silverstein has finished his monologue and announces: 'We all know that as far as modern tango goes, there's a before and after, and that the watershed between the two was a piece composed by the late lamented Astor Piazzola: "Ballad for a Crazy Guy". Ladies and gentlemen, tonight we are privileged to have among us the author and singer of the words to that unforgettable song, a man who is the living memory of tango and our Buenos Aires slang: Horacio Ferrer!'

As the applause rings out, a bohemian-looking figure with eyes as streaked as his moustache stands up to acknowledge it.

'And now, a tango worthy of our illustrious guest: "Hidden Man!"'

The music starts up, but Carvalho turns away from the stage just as Adriana Varela makes her entrance.

'Are you leaving already? Aren't you in love with Adriana any more? Didn't you say she's the best tango singer you've ever heard, and the one with the most exciting neckline in Buenos Aires?'

'I've got a business meeting.'

Outside, the night is tinged with green, or silver if he looks at the moon. All the housefronts and the shadows seem bathed in a green light, as does the taxi he hails and the taxi-driver he tells: 'to La Recoleta'.

He has to blink and screw up his eyes several times until the real pale shades of the night appear before him. The green that filled his vision was the green of the metal doors and railings of the Modelo prison in Madrid, where he spent time in his youth. The colour and smell of prison repeat on him like heartburn whenever anyone mentions fugitives. But now he can clearly see the colour of the whisky in his glass, and he pours part of it into his coffee and whispers to himself the word *carajillo*, staring down at the mixture in his cup as if it could take him home. He looks up, gazes at the other people in the bar, and then turns his attention to the man addressing him. He is around sixty, with hair turned silver by the neon lighting and smoothed back with cheap brilliantine. He is dressed far too smartly, although it's plain his suit is not new, and that his shirt has been washed and rewashed many times. But his cufflinks gleam, and so do his tiepin, his shoes and one gold tooth.

'Vito Altofini's the name, Altofini Cangas; my father was from Lombardy, my mother from Asturias.'

'Don Vito, I need an Argentine partner. As a foreigner, I have no right to work here.'

'You've come to the right man.'

Don Vito spreads out press cuttings yellow with age that detail his career in crime: 'Vito Altofini succeeds where police fail. A trail to follow in the case of the kidnapped Bayer family.' Carvalho picks the cutting up. In it, a considerably younger Vito is pointing to a piece of clothing. The photo caption reads: 'The kidnappers came from Uruguay. No political motive involved.'

'How did the case end?' Carvalho wants to know.

'Unfortunately, the Bayer family was never heard of again, but no one could ever prove the kidnappers didn't come from Uruguay. The piece of cloth I'm holding up was part of a woollen waistcoat woven in the Uruguayan style, in the days when people still wove by hand. Where is your office?'

'I'll put one in my apartment.'

'What sort?'

'What d'you mean?'

'I mean: private dick from the United States in the 1940s, or chintzy furniture *à la* Hercule Poirot, or neon lighting and computers like something from a Hollywood B-movie in the 1980s?'

'Are you a film critic then? Or an interior designer?'

But Don Vito is reliving his past.

'In the good old days I had my office done out exactly like Dick Powell's in the Dashiell Hammett films – they were the best ever made, black and white they were.'

Then he considers Carvalho, his attitude to his drink and to life in general. 'Are you hoping to get rich as a private detective here in Buenos Aires?'

'I have to make money to buy time. I came to find a disappeared cousin, and my savings are running low.'

'A disappeared person? For political reasons? At this stage in the game? All that's dead and gone, my friend.'

'Perhaps he's not one of the disappeared. I wouldn't know what to call him.' Carvalho thinks before he elaborates: 'Perhaps he's just a hidden man.'

The removal people carry out the dining-room table and then as if by magic reappear almost instantaneously with a desk to replace it, plus some old filing cabinets from a 1940s office with vague traces of art deco. Alma helps Carvalho put away what had been on the table, and to place the armchairs for any hypothetical clients.

'Where will you eat?'

'In the kitchen.'

Alma consults her watch and cries out: 'Oh, I'll be late for my class!'

As she dashes out she bumps into Don Vito. Carvalho can barely recognize him in a broad-brimmed trilby tilted rakishly to one side, but then he spots his gold tooth gleaming as he rewards the young lady with a flashing smile, doffing his hat as he steps to one side to allow her past. In his other hand he is carrying a zip-up briefcase like a 1950s insurance salesman. He takes a good look at Carvalho's office installations, and comes towards him, openly disappointed.

'So you went for the down-at-heel Humphrey Bogart style in the end, did you?'

'Down-at-heel Carvalho style more like.'

'What did you do to make that interesting woman run out of here in such a hurry?'

'She's almost a cousin.'

'Fantastic. I always kept twenty or thirty cousins on the go. By now, they're all nieces.'

'It's not what it seems. She *was* in a hurry. She's a professor of literature, and she has a class to give.'

Carvalho looks down at his watch. All of a sudden he's had enough of giving explanations, so instead he almost barks at Don Vito: 'Take a seat.'

Carvalho takes a bottle of 15-year-old J&B out of a desk drawer. 'It's the best I could find round here.'

But Vito Altofini refuses the offer politely, and instead takes all the bits and pieces he needs to make a drink of *mate* tea from his briefcase.

'If you'll let me use your kitchen, I prefer to make myself a *mate*. It's what I like, and I thought to myself... 'That Spaniard won't have the first idea what a *mate* is.'

Carvalho waves him towards the kitchen, and a short while later he and Don Vito are savouring their drinks in time to each other. Carvalho appreciates the gourd with silver decorations that Don Vito is drinking his *mate* from; by the way he is cradling it and drinking from it with such reverence, it must be a very precious object. Carvalho feels slightly tipsy. His tongue is loose, but he's not drunk.

'At the moment we haven't got any clients, Don Vito. Here in Argentina you suffer from the same problem of moral relativity as we do in Spain, in the West, in the whole of the fertile North. Adultery, theft, even murder aren't taboos any more, because everyone is a potential adulterer, thief or murderer. Then again, although our public police forces are experiencing a crisis of numbers and standards which has given rise to a huge increase in private security people, most of them work for big firms, even multinationals. That's why classic private detectives like us struggle to survive.'

'Public police forces are unfair competition. I'd privatize all policing. The whole lot.'

'So you see it as a labour market problem?'

'Elementary, my dear Carvalho. At times of crisis like this, even accountants are up against it. I've got a relative who's an accountant – he's had to take on extra work. He does the books for two or three firms now. It's not only the working class that's fallen on hard times, you know. The bourgeoisie ain't what it used to be either.'

Then he begins to mutter:

> The middle class is on its uppers
> Mireya has gone, Margot is dead
> And all their lordships' suppers
> Are no more than crusts of bread.
> Tears at their farewell are falling
> Tears that times are now so hard
> The lovely Barra Florida's closing
> Nostalgia is our business card.

Don Vito does not notice Carvalho's mild amazement at this outburst, and goes on: 'If you like, we can look for your cousin in the meantime.'

'I wouldn't know where to start. A few weeks after I got here, I almost had him. My cousin left Argentina during the military dictatorship. He thought his wife was dead, and that his daughter had disappeared. The years went by, and suddenly he gets a bee in his bonnet to come back. But he chose the wrong moment. Twenty years had gone by. His wife's alive, but...sorry, I mean his sister-in-law is alive. She's the one you saw running out.'

'So she really is a cousin. Carvalho, you're a man of principle.'

'Some of my cousin's former guerrilla friends are still loyal, but others have taken over his scientific discoveries. They've had them patented thanks to a Captain, the same man who captured and tortured them twenty years ago, and who now is using more terror and money to control them. And his daughter still hasn't been found.'

'It sounds like an Argentine soap opera written by a Venezuelan scriptwriter,' Don Vito mutters to himself, suddenly serious: 'but I'm sure it's true. As true as you or me here. Is anyone else after your cousin?'

'The police. Or rather, a policeman called Pascuali. He's a professional: in other words, he wants law and order to be upheld.'

Don Vito almost chokes on his *mate*. He's saved by a knock at the door and the sudden appearance of a thin, hollow-eyed young man with a pallid face. He wastes no time in presenting himself: 'I'm Javier Lizondo. If you are the detectives whose name is on the door, I need you. Someone's killed my girlfriend.'

Vito and Carvalho exchange smiles of secret delight, but manage to keep a straight face for their first client.

'You've come to the right place.'

The youngster is plainly nervous, and swallows hard. Don Vito encourages him to go on with a tilt of his chin. Carvalho is busy surveying him. Don Vito's face reflects all the intricacies of the boy's story.

'My name is Javier Lizondo. Someone's killed my girlfriend. Well...I've already told you all that. My girlfriend...my girlfriend...'

'Your girlfriend?' Don Vito encourages him.

'Are you implying she wasn't my girlfriend?'

'Please. I was simply inviting you to go on, we're both concerned and anxious to know more.'

'My girlfriend worked in a topless bar. You know, one of those places where they dance...'

Don Vito gesticulates as if his own breasts were bobbing up and down, but never once allows his look of concern to slip.

'She only did it to make ends meet. She was a nice girl. Well-educated. Yes, well-educated, that's the thing. She was called Carmen, Carmen Lavalle.'

He shows them the photo of a pretty young girl smiling with the confidence of someone who knows they are going to live for ever.

'You don't have one of her topless, do you?' Don Vito asks. 'Strictly for identity purposes, of course.'

Carvalho steps in.

'All we really need to know is where she worked, and why you don't want to go to the police about her.'

Javier does not know what to say. He breaks down in tears. Don

Vito seems ready to sob along with him.

'I'm a fugitive. On the run. There's an arrest warrant out for me, but I didn't do it.'

'Another hidden man,' Carvalho says, to someone who isn't in the room.

Sometimes we do things, or think about them, with someone in mind who doesn't see us do them or think them at all. In Buenos Aires, Carvalho thinks and does things with Alma in mind. She or her shadowy outline in his mind is the one he directs his monologues at, is an invisible presence everywhere he goes, helps justify everything he does. But now here she is, the real live Alma, watching Carvalho perform his culinary arts with scarcely contained admiration.

'Did you always cook in Spain?'

'No. At the office it was Biscuter, my assistant, who did the cooking. He looks like a foetus – a cross between a Spielberg special effect, Doctor Watson and a cordon bleu chef.'

'Why do you call him a foetus?'

'He looks just like one. Like one of those babies who had a difficult birth and was torn out of their mother's womb with a pair of forceps.'

'You call him all the time. Do you like him a lot?'

'I feel sorry for him.'

'What about your lost girlfriend? Do you like her a lot?'

'I feel sorry for her.'

'Aren't you capable of affection? Do you only feel sorry for people? What about those poor creatures you fried and cooked in the saucepan, do you feel sorry for them?'

'No, I love them. That's why I eat them.'

They sit at the table, and Alma pushes around the pasta of the *fideua* with her fork.

'They look like worms but they taste delicious.'

'Just a simple pasta dish,' Carvalho says with a sigh.

'You cook and you eat, but you're depressed.'

'I cook and I eat *because* I'm depressed.'

'About Raúl?'

'It's more complicated than that. It reminds me of a poem I read once, in the days when I used to read poems. A driver has a flat tyre and thinks to himself: I don't like where I came from, and I don't like where I'm going to. So why am I in such a hurry to get the tyre changed?'

'That's by Brecht, Bertolt Brecht.'

'I knew it was by him. Once upon a time, I knew who Brecht was.'

'You still do.'

'No, not any more.'

'You have to unravel the metaphor. What or who is that tyre?'

'Raúl maybe. I don't know where to start. Has he been in touch with you?'

'Don't you think I would have told you?'

Carvalho pushes away the plate and stands up, in a fury.

'How should I know? I haven't the faintest idea what you think of me. Aren't I an intruder? Isn't Raúl one as well? How do I know what your intentions – you and your comrades – are towards Raúl? Do you want me to find him, or not?'

Alma also stands up, furious.

'He was my husband! He is the father of a daughter who was taken away by someone we still haven't found! He's running away from himself more than from any real danger.'

'Aren't the police a real danger? And what about that Captain and Raúl's partners who stole his patent – aren't they a danger to him?'

Alma slumps into a chair, sobbing gently. From behind the rainbow of tears in her green eyes, she blurts out: 'I don't know what's a real danger from one that isn't any more. Or real anxiety from the imaginary kind.'

By now Carvalho has calmed down, and would like to reach out and comfort her, but thinks better of it.

'I want to find my child, but so many years have gone by I wouldn't even know her. Do I really want to find her, or simply get my revenge on the bastard who stole her from me? As far as Raúl is concerned, I want you to find him and take him with you back to Spain. For good. He's not part of my life anymore. He's only part of my most terrible memories.'

'Where do I start?'

Alma smiles, as if she suddenly has the perfect answer.

'With a barbecue. In Argentina, everything starts and finishes with a barbecue. We're having one for ex-guerrillas. Raúl must be close by – it's the only place he can get any protection. Do you like *asado*?'

The fat man is driving. In the back seat are the Captain and his daughter, who is busy going over some notes, her lap full of books. The Captain looks down at her at first affectionately, then with a look of concern. The car pulls up outside the university. The girl gives her father a quick kiss. Gathers up her books, and gives the fat man a pinch on the back of his neck.

'Ciao, uncle Cesco.'

The fat man smiles with satisfaction.

'Why are you in such a hurry, Muriel? What have you got on today?' the Captain wants to know, poking his head out of the car window.

'My first class is with a pain of a teacher, a literature prof.'

'What's her name?' the Captain asks.

'Alma. Alma something-or-other,' Muriel replies, turning back as she runs into the building.

The Captain tries to smile, but cannot hide his dismay. The fat man makes as if to get out of the car, but the Captain stops him. As they drive away from the faculty building, the Captain struggles to regain his composure. The fat man is indignant.

'Did you hear that? It had to be her, didn't it...? We should have got rid of them all, Captain. Have you any idea what might happen when Muriel gets to know that woman?'

'Nothing,' the Captain says curtly.

'Nothing? What about the call of the blood?'

'Blood is silent. You if anyone should know that – you've seen more than enough of it. At any rate it's the father, Raúl, who's the main problem. He still wants to ask questions, investigate. Berta or Alma, whichever it is, is one of the disappeared. Nobody knows it, but she is.'

'I wouldn't underestimate her.'

The Captain's car pulls up outside the Ministry of Development. The Captain, still muscular and athletic despite his fifty years, gets out and runs easily up the stairs. His jawline is still firm, and he has thin, firm lips. He shows the guard an identity card and pushes past him without waiting for permission. The secretary shows no surprise at seeing him there, and makes no effort to stop him going straight into the minister's office.

'Is he alone?' the Captain asks.

'He will be.'

The Captain decides to wait. The secretary makes a call on the intercom. The minister's door opens abruptly, and a hurriedly despatched and somewhat surprised visitor appears.

'So you think it's all perfectly clear?'

The minister's voice can be heard from inside the office.

'Perfectly.'

'Thank you so much, sir,' the visitor replies, pleased with himself. 'That took much less time than I imagined.'

Still rather bewildered, he steps out of the room and the Captain darts in through the door. He stands arms akimbo in front of the minister, waiting for him to say something. Güelmes looks him up and down before commenting:

'I don't think it's a good idea for you to come here.'

'Every door in Argentina is open to me.'

'This isn't the Argentina of 1977, or 1981, or 1985.'

'No, as far as dates go, you're right. But as far as the country goes, I'm not so sure. Dates come and go, but countries remain. What did you want to talk to me about? But first of all, let me congratulate you on your promotion to minister.'

Güelmes tries to recover his ministerial authority. He sits back in his powerful ministerial armchair, and invites the Captain to sit as well. The spring-heeled man is having none of it.

'I'm still interested in a deal,' Güelmes says. 'As well as continuing with our business and making sure Font y Rius forgets everything that's happened.'

'What kind of deal?' the Captain growls.

'My deal is that I'll help you find Raúl, but you are not to kill him. We have to get him out of Argentina alive.'

'Do you know where he is?'

'No. But Alma's arranged a strange reunion. It's a barbecue at the Baroja place – you know, the intellectuals behind left-wing Perónism.

An *asado* for ex-guerrillas. Old friends. She was kind enough to invite me. I think she's getting us all together so we can help find Raúl.'

'I suppose the Spaniard's going too.'

'Of course. Remember he's the one officially looking for Raúl: him and inspector Pascuali.'

'That Pascuali needs to learn a thing or two. I can't understand why he's such a stickler for formal democracy. I get on better with terrorists. Well, you go and get what you can out of the barbecue. Keep a good lookout, and if you hear anything that could lead us to Raúl, tell me first because of all the unfinished business I have with him, and then if you must, go and see Pascuali. I want a report on all that's said at the barbecue and everyone who's mentioned.'

'Do you want to know what we all eat as well?'

'The menu's always the same at barbecues. They're better or worse cooked, that's all.'

Then as he's going out the door, without turning round, the Captain asks: 'Do you know if Alma is still determined to find her daughter?'

'She hasn't mentioned it for years,' Güelmes replies, in such a casual way it's obvious he's trying to convince the Captain it is true.

The students gradually quieten down. Alma puts her glasses on, glances down at her notes, then raises her head. The room is completely silent.

'Although the main theme of these lectures is how language is applied to literature, today I'd like to talk to you about the way in which other languages can be codified and decodified. For example, the language of architecture, the architecture of a real city – this city of Buenos Aires, for example.'

She is interrupted by the classroom door opening. Muriel comes rushing in, red in the face from having to run. Clutching her books to her chest, she mutters an excuse, and searches for a seat near the door where she can hide. There isn't one. Alma pauses in her lecture, and all eyes turn towards the latecomer.

'There's a good seat here in the front row. The last shall be first.'

Nearly everyone laughs as Muriel makes her way embarrassed to the front of the class. She sits down and looks at Alma uncomfortably.

'I don't insist students come to my classes. What I do ask is that they get here before me. If you're not interested in my course...'

Suddenly Muriel blurts out, almost in tears: 'But it's my favourite!'

All the others laugh. Alma herself smiles, and then goes on: 'That wasn't rehearsed, I swear. But let's get back to Buenos Aires. I've already told you how André Malraux called it the capital of an empire that had never existed, and that Le Corbusier wanted to make it the "Ville Verte" of his dreams. A friend of mine who was an architect – or rather, a friend who planned to be an architect, but never made it, always says Le Corbusier is much more important for all that he planned than for what he actually built. He planned a truly revolutionary Moscow, but the Soviet bureaucracy frustrated his ideas. He planned a green Buenos Aires, but in the end all we let him build was a tiny house for Victoria Ocampo. He was about to change Barcelona when the Civil War broke out. I'd like you to think about all that and to write what you feel about this apparent paradox. You can compare Buenos Aires as the capital of an empire that never existed with Vienna, which not only is, but appears to be, the capital of an empire that no longer exists. How can we compare the concept of the ruin of an imagined world, like Buenos Aires, with the ruin of a real world, like Vienna for example? Then again, imperial Vienna gave birth to the most important cultural output of the twentieth century, together with the fabulous first decade of the Soviet revolution. Is there anything similar in this Buenos Aires of ours, with its hopeless dreams of grandeur? Our best writers apparently never seem to want or dare to step outside their strictly literary knowledge; they are outsiders. Borges is the supreme example of that. The Vienna of Freud or Klimt offered the world the anguish of the crisis of the bourgeois ego; after the Revolution, Moscow offered the redeeming hope that this crisis could be overcome. What has Buenos Aires offered the world? Borges? The literary representation of a lack of identity as shown in the works of Borges, Bioy Casares, Mallea, Sábato, Macedonio Fernández? I don't want you to answer these questions directly. I want you to metabolize them, to make them your own. You could even write a tango about it if you like. Even though it's hard for me to admit it, tango still is one way of describing reality.'

One of the students shakes his head with disapproval, and his blond ponytail swings from side to side.

'Don't you agree, Alberto?'

'Football is all we've given to the world.'

Alma throws her files and books on to the sofa. She takes off her shoes and starts massaging her feet as if they were aching.

'You're crazy. You've got a headache and here you are, rubbing your feet.'

She gets up and changes into more comfortable clothes: a pair of baggy trousers, a blouse, slippers. She opens her fridge, and sees defeat staring her in the face. She gives up, and goes to find a can in the pantry. The door bell interrupts her, and she goes over to it without opening it. She peers out through the spyhole, and sees a man dressed in an overall. She can't see his face properly.

'Who's there?'

'Terminator.'

'I'm not in the mood for jokes.'

'I'm the rat man, señora. Didn't you have a problem with rats?'

She looks through the spyhole again. Sees Raúl's face, distant and distorted by the lens. Alma throws back locks and bolts, and when the door is wide open, Raúl stands there waiting until she drags him inside, slams the door, and enfolds him in a possessive embrace. There are shreds of words, greedy hands trying to recover so much time lost, both of them rushing to get out of their clothes in search of nakedness, of human contact, of shapes and volumes they knew so well twenty years earlier, panting and groaning as if from a recorder, the recorder of memory. Later, bothered by her own nakedness, Alma puts on a pair of pyjamas, and sits on the bed, her head resting on the board. Raúl is curled at her feet, and she reaches out to take his hands.

'Twenty years later, and we're starting again...'

'I never expected this. For many years, I thought you were dead. I don't understand why nobody told me the truth, not even you. I can understand you impersonated your sister to fool the military, but why me, Berta? Why me?'

'My name is Alma. I'll never be Berta again.'

'What about the baby?'

'I looked everywhere for her. You can't imagine how I looked. I joined the grandmothers' group, disguised as my daughter's aunt. It was no use. If she's still alive, she must be in the hands of someone powerful enough to destroy all the traces leading to him. Every so often I see a girl in the street, and something inside me says: that could be your daughter. I cry inside, I can't help it. Then as soon as I get back here, I cry for real. I'm tired, so tired psychologically of needing her. Sometimes I think: you don't really want to find her, what you want is vengeance on the person who took her.'

Raúl agrees.

'I'm going through something similar. Am I hiding because people are after me, or simply because I can only live hidden? From whom? From what?'

'But people are after you, Raúl, and don't forget it. The Captain, his associates who betrayed you and are selling your discoveries, even though they still care for you – Güelmes, Font y Rius. The best thing would be for your cousin to get you out of here. Argentina doesn't exist. The Argentina you and I knew, the one that gave us our identity, doesn't exist any more. Those of us who survived and go on believing in the same ideals are even more disappeared than those who did disappear.'

'You want me to go, don't you?'

'I don't know,' Alma replies, but in the end she throws herself on him again, and kisses him hungrily: 'but stay for tonight at least.'

Day breaks to find them under the sheets, with the ceiling their only horizon. Alma is about to say something, but Raúl hushes her with a finger on her lips.

'No, don't say a word. I know what happened last night, and will always happen between us. In our memory we're still the young lovers who wanted to change life, like Rimbaud, and to change history, like that odd couple Marx and Evita.'

'Don't forget Trotsky.'

'Marx, Evita and Trotsky. I was a secret Trotsky supporter. You were a Perónist nationalist. Now you're a woman in the prime of her life, with not even the name I remember, who has just slept with a depressive with no desire. One of the first signs of depression is you can't get it up, you know.'

'Sex isn't everything.'

'No, that's not true. I'm going. Perhaps one day we'll be able to meet freely, to talk and rediscover what we have in common; then perhaps it'll happen. Now all I ask is permission to see and talk to you. Like the Scarlet Pimpernel. I'm a hidden man. I'm not even going to tell you where I hide or who is hiding me. But I'm not charging ahead blindly, even though that's how it looks. I know Eva María is alive, and in the past few months I've learnt I might be able to find her. Don't ask me how: I couldn't tell you anything definite.'

They kiss again. Raúl has slipped out from under the bedclothes, and looks down contemptuously at his own nakedness.

'Are you going to come to the barbecue at Baroja's place?'

'It's too risky.'

'You're right. I organized it to talk about you, and find out what was going on, not to have you there.'

Raúl leaves the building dressed in the overalls of a pest-control company. He's carrying a box with some official-looking initials on it.

Vladimiro speaks into his walkie-talkie.

'There's a guy coming out. He looks like someone from a pest-control place.'

'What kind of pest?' Pascuali wants to know on the other end.

'Rats. It says something about rat poisoning.'

'Follow him!' Pascuali orders. 'Have you still not got it, bird brain?'

'Still not got what... ?'

Vladimiro starts up his car, and puts the siren on.

'Is that your siren I can hear?'

'Yes.'

'Stick it up your ass then! I bet the guy's vanished, hasn't he? Have you got the balls to deny it?'

Vladimiro tries in vain to find the pest-control man among the crowd of passers-by thronging the street, but the relaxed expression on his face contrasts sharply with his nervous manoeuvring of the car.

'Would you like me to try on foot, Inspector Pascuali?'

'I'd like you to drop dead. And don't worry. The most beautiful wreath at your funeral will be from me.'

A lamb split lengthwise and crucified on a stake. Placed too far from the embers of the fire for Carvalho's liking, as if the flames were playing at roasting the meat. The barbecue includes beef as well as lamb, and a terrifying list of internal organs that Carvalho picks up from his neighbours' comments: spare ribs, sirloin, intestines, sweetbreads. A group of about twenty people are either appreciating the dexterity of the men doing the barbecue, or are walking around the garden of a country house in one of the thousands of suburbs of Buenos Aires. The garden has a slightly abandoned air, and without knowing why, it reminds Carvalho more of a dacha like those he encountered in the 1960s outside Moscow than any elaborate weekend cottage in Spain. Most of the guests are relaxed professionals living a weekend in the open air. They have stopped off to pick up their children at the children store and are now trying hard to reinvent the idea of the noble savage with them. The conversations between adults are more strained when they touch on political and cultural topics, except when one of them breaks off to show the children his skills with a soccer ball.

'Closer to forty than thirty. Some, like Girmenich over there, almost fifty. The generation that started the armed struggle by kidnapping General Aramburu. The one that were still adolescents playing at revolution when they felt the full force of the 1976 coup and the military dictatorship. The whole of Argentina in arms greets you, Carvalho my friend.'

Silverstein has got into the habit of muttering in his ear as if it were a stage whisper, or simply the way that all villains behave in Shakespeare plays. Font y Rius is another guest; but all those present are eclipsed when an official car and its escort comes sweeping in and Güelmes steps out. A blond, blue-eyed man comments sarcastically: 'Well, if it isn't our old friend Güelmes.'

Again Carvalho hears Silverstein's whispered commentary, sees the scene through his darting eyes. 'That was Luis Barone, Luigi to his revolutionary comrades. And over there, look, the one with the heavy jowls and the annoyed look in his eyes, that's Girmenich. We still can't make our minds up about him after all these years. Some worship him, others wish he were dead. He's still a Catholic. They say he believes in the Virgin Mary.'

'Güelmes looks as if he owns that official car,' comments a woman with finely sculpted eyes, and a sensitive, sharp nose whom he has been introduced to as Liliana Mazure.

'Long may he reign, I say. At least he shares things out with his old friends.'

'He was the king of plastic explosives,' Barone explains to Carvalho. 'It was no good giving him a machine-gun, because he couldn't hit a barn door, but with explosives he was a real magician.'

'D'you remember when we blew up that police station?' adds a paunchy man with tired, drooping eyes.

Carvalho avoids being presented to Güelmes by walking off with Silverstein, who provides him with a rapid summary of the occasion.

'Just look how all of us turned up when Alma called, drawn by the smell of a good barbecue. The house is owned by someone who has an incredible library and I think is a descendant of the Spanish writer Baroja. They've been a mainstay of the Argentine left for several generations. Baroja! Why don't you show our Spanish friend here your library?'

Güelmes is busy greeting people, shaking hands: he is one of them, but also knows very well he is a statesman. Some of the guests bend and ironically kiss his hand, muttering with false reverence: your honour. Silverstein ostentatiously ignores him, still shouting at one of the men cooking the meat: 'Baroja, why don't you show the masked Spaniard here your library? He loves burning books, so perhaps he can help you sort out your problem of not knowing where to put them all.'

Baroja looks younger than most of the others, but he is playing his part in this nostalgic event, and he wipes his hands on his apron, then leads Carvalho off towards the house. When they enter, they are immediately overwhelmed by the presence of books. It's a mausoleum of twentieth-century left-wing literature. Carvalho pulls out volumes by Gramsci, Howard Fast, Wright Mills, Habermas and Adorno as carefully as if they were protected species, then carefully returns them to their original place.

'It's like a left-wing paradise for readers between forty and seventy,' he says. 'Everyone from Lukacs to Marta Harnecker.'

'My father was a Red before me. He still is in fact, he's always been a left-wing Perónist. He was friends with Rodolfo Walsh,

Gelman, Paco Urondo. I was still a kid in 1976, but all those people out in the garden were like my elder brothers and sisters. They were my heroes.'

'What about now?' Carvalho asks.

Silverstein is the one who answers: 'He loves us like you do all your childhood memories, from your toys to sugar lumps, don't you, Baroja?'

'Will Raúl show up, do you think?' Carvalho interjects.

'Raúl's moment will come. Alma explained why she invited everyone here.'

The three of them stare out of the window at the guests in the garden. They can see several people pointing at their watches. They seem to be in a hurry.

'The barbecue is taking its time, and some of them want to get back to Buenos Aires. Boca is playing Independiente. All I have are books – I haven't even got a TV to offer them. Is this your first Argentine barbecue? It's more than a meal, it's a sophisticated rite which started with the determination of our pioneers the gauchos to survive by eating every scrap of meat they could lay their hands on. Are you familiar with all the cuts of meat here?'

'To some extent. There used to be a fairly decent Argentine restaurant in Barcelona: La Estancia Vieja, run by two people called Cané and Marcelo Aparicio. But I don't remember all the cuts, just *bife de chorizo* and *asado de tira*.'

'There's more to it than that. The *bife de chorizo* is a sirloin, from close to the rump, but your rump steak is *bife de lomo*, and *bife de costilla* is what you call chuck steak. Then there's *vacío*, which is very tasty and is like your brisket. Then we also have the *entra ña* or offal, but we also cook the intestines, the *chinchulines*. Ah, and you mustn't forget the *morcilla* or black pudding sausages we make from the blood. Here, take this copy of the *Manual del asador argentino* by Raúl Murad.'

'Don't give it him – he'll only burn it!'

'I don't burn useful books.'

In the garden, the barbecue is ready. Carvalho has more than enough time to observe how all the guests overdose on protein: the adults eat as voraciously as the children, and even the women do not disguise their appetite for dead animals as they might in Europe.

The banquet reminds Carvalho of the great popular feasts in Spain, where the sacred alibi for eating so much was always the memory of times of scarcity. After a while, the table is littered with the remains of meat, *empanadas* and salads, and half-empty bottles of wine.

'In Argentina, a barbecue is judged not so much by what's eaten as by how much is left over.'

Alma's words reach Carvalho over another conversation he has been half-listening to: 'Tell me Font, how are the lunatics getting on in your asylum based on the principles of anti-psychiatry?' a man with moustaches is asking. 'I've been told that nowadays you even take in the rich wives of poor husbands who want them locked up so they can get their hands on their fortunes.'

'Most of them just want to get rid of their wives,' Font y Rius replies calmly, then adds: 'Or you could see it as my contribution to the revolution. I take money from rich women to give to poor men, or vice versa. Didn't you do the same in exile when you used to counterfeit Visa Gold cards?'

Barone tells Carvalho the man in question had supplied half the Argentine exiles in Europe with domestic appliances by making fake credit cards. It's the men rather than the women who laugh at this joke, and one woman comments sarcastically: 'So you're such a macho man you won't accept rich men in your clinic?'

'I must admit that statistically speaking they're a small minority.'

'I only ask because I wouldn't mind sending my husband there.'

Alma clinks her coffee spoon against the side of a cup.

'It's been wonderful to see you all again. But what we're really here for is to try to find Raúl Tourón before others do. Some of you already know he came back to Buenos Aires. We have to get together to protect him.'

Font y Rius still has his head lowered; Güelmes looks interested but remote; Silverstein is busy observing all the others' reactions. Some remain poker-faced; others are clearly moved by Alma's voice.

'You all know Raúl managed to escape from the hell here. And now years later, he's back from Spain. Nobody knows what he's looking for, perhaps his disappeared daughter, perhaps he's trying to build a new life, like the rest of us. For the moment though, he's in hiding. He's running from himself, but also from people from the

THE BUENOS AIRES QUINTET

intelligence services who've stolen one of his discoveries and don't want him around to reclaim it. It's too complicated to explain now, but if any of you know anything at all...we have to find him before the Captain and his men do.'

Some of the faces around the table look alarmed. Güelmes and Font y Rius look concerned. Several voices call out: 'is that murderer still in action, the son of a bitch?'

'Yes, he's still in action,' Alma goes on. 'There's someone else pursuing Raúl. He's what you might call a professional policeman, someone who believes in the law and in democratic rule, in the separation of powers.'

'God is dead, Marx is dead, Montesquieu is dead, but there are still some idiots who refuse to lie down and die!' Silverstein shouts scornfully.

'The ideal would be for his cousin, this Spaniard here...' Alma points to Carvalho.

'The masked Spaniard! The hidden Spaniard! The one and only Spaniard!' Silverstein shouts gleefully.

'You can trust him,' Alma insists. 'At least the people I trust can. Please, if Raúl has been in touch with any of you, remember the ideal solution would be for him to go back to Spain with his cousin here.'

Silverstein clambers up on the table, treading on various scraps of *asado*. 'A hidden man could be anywhere. But let's not think of those of us who came, but of those ex-combatants of the glorious, unfinished Perónist revolution who didn't show up here today. Let's remember them!'

Silverstein stoops to pick up a piece of meat from the table near his feet. Carvalho drinks as if all of a sudden he's extremely thirsty.

'Did any of you realize Honrubia isn't here?' Barone asks.

Some people whistle, others laugh.

'He's on his honeymoon, busy robbing the Brucker family blind, except that this time he doesn't have a machine-gun. You used to know him well, didn't you, Girmenich?'

Girmenich has said very little all afternoon, but around him there has been an ebb and flow of people, as though each of the guests had his or her own personal agenda with the best-known revolutionary.

'Knowing people in those days didn't mean you knew them well.'

'Are you still a Catholic, Girmenich?'

'Yes, I am.'

'And you believe in the Virgin Mary?'

'Yes.'

'And in the armed struggle?'

Barone is the one asking the questions, perhaps trying to provoke a dialectical argument. Girmenich doesn't answer, but a pale-faced woman with skin so transparent her veins show through steps in.

'If we win, yes, I believe in the armed struggle. But if we lose… they won the struggle…and look at the way they did it.'

'What about reconciliation, Celia? Would you kill them if you had the chance?' Barone asks.

'With these hands.'

By now, night is coming into its own. Barone is driving. Sitting beside him, Carvalho is somewhere between drunken slumber and trying to keep one ear on what the driver is talking about. But he has succeeded in asking to be dropped off at a night-club called El Salto.

'That's a strip joint.'

Barone looks round to check whether Alma heard him, but she's dozed off, as has Silverstein. Barone is still obsessed with Honrubia.

'I mentioned him on purpose. He was one of the leading revolutionaries. He had a price on his head because among other feats, he'd kidnapped the Brucker brothers, heirs to the most important family in our oligarchy. Then he went into exile, and travelled all over the world, still preaching revolution, gun in hand, ready to fight anywhere for the cause.' Barone laughs out loud. 'He was a great guy! Then he returned to Argentina, and they put him in prison for a while to balance out the joke trials against Videla and the others. He gets out, Menem gives him an important position, he's thrown out of that because he fills his pockets a bit too quickly. All of a sudden, he announces he's going to marry a Brucker, the sister of the brothers he had kidnapped, who is twenty years younger than him. And not only does he go ahead and marry her, but since then he's managed to sideline her brothers from the family business, and now he's almost in sole charge.'

Alma has woken up. She leans forward over the two men. 'Drive slowly, Luis. Remember Argentina's got the worst accident rate in Latin America.'

'We've got other records too. The highest rates for suicide, divorce, for drinking the most soft drinks and using the most deodorants. It's not that we like to smell good, we don't like to smell at all. I was just telling your friend here that Honrubia has done well for himself. He's shown he's an excellent negotiator.'

'Our political militancy made us efficient, hard-working and cynical. Our defeat made us pragmatic. That's why we were so successful in business afterwards. Well, those who went into business were.'

Barone shakes his head. 'I still get the feeling that all this is provisional, as if we were in a truce between defeat and victory.'

'Between two defeats, more like.'

'You're too pessimistic, Alma. One day it'll be cherry blossom time again, like the song by Yves Montand. Nothing can be done these days in one country, simply by wishing things to happen. Some day there'll have to be another Revolutionary International.'

Carvalho nods at this, and Barone thinks he's agreeing with him.

'So you think so too?'

'I'm worried about a few details.'

'Such as?'

'Well, nowadays it's impossible to start an international movement without a fax machine.'

'Yeah, I get you so far.'

'So, where do we put the fax machine? It can't be in Moscow any more, or in Havana, and putting it in Tripoli or Teheran would be suicide. So, where do we put the fax machine?'

The car pulls up outside the El Salto Club. The green and red neon sign is exactly the same as all the signs for strip clubs all over the galaxy.

'So all the meat you ate woke your sexual appetite, did it?' Alma asks.

'We private detectives have strange beef and bedfellows.'

Carvalho says his goodbyes. As he gets out of the car, he slams the door and wakes up Silverstein. He walks towards the club, his legs heavy from so much alcohol and protein. As he is going in, he hears

Silverstein's sarcastic commentary from the car: 'Who would have thought it? The masked Spaniard's got a prick.'

El Salto is a strip joint like a million others, with anonymous girls, dim lighting, loud music and the inevitable Brazilian transvestite who's the most beautiful woman in the place.

'But I shave three times a day,' the Brazilian pouts at Don Vito when he refuses to be picked up.

Don Vito looks as if he's tied to the bar, overwhelmed by the music and the strobe lighting, but he does not miss a chance to wink at every girl who passes by. When Carvalho touches him on the shoulder, he turns round with evident relief.

'Thank God you're here. About time. I've had a bellyful of this ghastly music. I'm going home to put on Libertad Lamarque singing some decent tangos. Something to soothe me. Then I'll watch the Boca–Independiente game.'

Carvalho watches Don Vito leering at the passing trade, trying to work out his tastes. 'You don't seem to be having such a bad time.'

'Music as loud as this leaves you sterile. Take a good look at that giant outside the bathrooms. He's called Pretty Boy, and he's the one who decides what goes on and what doesn't in here. I'm not old enough to do business with him.'

Don Vito puts on his hat, touches the brim to say farewell to Carvalho, and heads for the exit. On the way, he leans over the topless cigarette girl and tells her: 'If you give me your knickers, I'll buy half a dozen packs.'

He doesn't give her time to react, and disappears out of the door. Carvalho orders a whisky on the rocks, and sees Pretty Boy go over to talk to the cashier.

'What do you want to do? Follow him in there to see if he's shooting up? Just cool it,' the cashier advises him.

Pretty Boy grumbles. He looks the spitting image of Gabriela Sabatini. Carvalho goes up to him. 'Too many drugs?'

Pretty Boy is about to tell him to get lost when he sees the fifty-dollar bill Carvalho has pressed into his hand. 'Private dick? You're not a cop, they never pay.'

'I'm a sociologist,' Carvalho explains.

Pretty Boy looks confused, and Carvalho takes advantage of his confusion. 'What do you know about the murdered topless girl?'

'I've already told the police what they wanted to hear. The girl had a name. She was called Carmen Lavalle.'

'Is Pascuali the guy investigating the murder?'

'Do you know him, then?'

'Inspector Pascuali and I are like brothers. I already know for example you told him you were fucking her.'

'I've had every girl here,' Pretty Boy tells him proudly. 'But I'm no vulture. I have my morals. And even though we did it occasionally, I could tell she was different. She didn't enjoy it. She only did it because she had to.'

Carvalho studies the pimp, trying to bring him back on track, but the other man beats him to it.

'She studied Latin.'

'Latin?'

'Latin.'

Carvalho presses another fifty-dollar bill in his hand.

'And I'm sure you know the address of her Latin teacher, don't you? Oh, and by the way, you aren't Gabriela Sabatini's brother, are you? You look just like her.'

Pretty Boy writes it down on a paper napkin, and Carvalho demonstrates that movement is displacement from a fixed point by leaving the clip joint.

The address is in a down-at-heel neighbourhood. The building has no porter or entryphone, so Carvalho is forced to look for the name on the letterboxes. He cannot find it. There are three apartments that have no name on their box. Carvalho gazes up the staircase. A woman is struggling down as if her feet are aching a lot. She's carrying an old-fashioned radio set in a basket.

'Can I help you? Is something the matter?'

'Too much body for too little foot, that's all.'

'Small feet are the sign of a delicate soul.'

All of a sudden the woman is inordinately pleased with her feet. She stares down at them affectionately.

'Perhaps you can tell me which floor the Latin teacher lives on?'

The woman wrinkles her nose. She is still smiling at Carvalho, but there's a look of disgust in her eyes.

'We call him "the plague". Him and soap don't get on, and as if that weren't bad enough, he's surrounded by cats. There's always a foul smell from his apartment.'

'My God! How can that be? A wise man like him. A Latinist.'

'A latty what?'

'A Latinist. An expert in the language of the ancient Romans.'

'I hope they talked better than today's Romans do. My husband is the son of a family from Rome, and he's as foul-mouthed as a footballer. The teacher lives on the third floor at the back. And be careful if you take the lift, there's a hole in the middle big enough to fall through.'

At this the woman turns her back on him and stumbles off. Carvalho walks carefully up the stairs, which are lit by nothing more than the grimy panes of glass giving on to the interior stairwell. He reaches the third floor and rings the door bell. He wrinkles his nose just like the woman did. The stench from inside is overpowering, and he can hear desperate miaowing. Nobody comes to the door. He tries forcing the lock with his credit card, but it's too old and he has to try various picks before the door does not so much open as come unstuck. There's a short hallway, full of anxious cats coming towards him. Some of them rush out on to the landing; others brush against his trousers. The rooms leading off the hallway are filthy and untidy. At the far end is a kitchen cum dining-room. The sink is full of crockery with scraps of unidentifiable food on it. All the plates are third-hand or on a third life. Chipped and not exactly clean. A dining-table covered in an oilcloth. Bookshelves everywhere, full of antique-looking books. Even the kitchen is lined with books, smeared with smoke and grease. Carvalho forces the window open and takes a deep breath. One smell in particular forces him to turn back into the room. He walks over to a half-open door. Inside he sees the Latin teacher's body spreadeagled on a bed, his arms and legs out in a cross. All his blood appears to have drained into a coagulated pool on the bedcover and floor. One cat sits next to the body, licking at the dried blood. Yellow in life, and an even more livid shade of yellow in death, the face has begun to bloat. Carvalho turns away from his inspection of the body and searches in the desk drawers instead. They are full of a heap of papers and objects, including half a mouldy sandwich. There's a school notebook on which a trembling hand has written: Latin students. Carvalho slips the notebook under his shirt and goes on with his search. More books, old photos of people who are probably already dead or close to it by now: then Carvalho hears a voice behind him, and turns his head to see.

'Always looking for the same things as me.'

The voice is Pascuali's. Carvalho turns to face him, superficially calm.

'This time I've been so nice I've even opened the door for you.'

An hour later, and the apartment has become a meeting place for half the police in Buenos Aires. Carvalho wrinkles his nose again, and speaks directly to Pascuali and his other half, Vladimiro.

'I'd prefer to talk outside, if you don't mind. This stink will stick to us for weeks.'

Pascuali's face is also wrinkled up with disgust, so the two of them cross the road to a bar that has some character to it – billiard players in the back, the inevitable wood panelling, and male customers who look as if they are from sometime between the wars: shiny heads, well-dressed and talking business or seeming to do so. Pascuali orders a milk shake, Carvalho a glass of port.

'Are you allowed to drink milk shakes on duty then?'

'Don't try to get smart with me. Don't push your luck. I said I wanted you out of Buenos Aires, and here you are with a detective agency.'

'All I do is assist my boss, Vito Altofini.'

'Another bigmouth. A smartass who is as much of a private detective as I am a classical ballet dancer. Have you given up looking for your cousin?'

'He seems to be well-hidden. D'you know if the Captain is still looking for him?'

Pascuali leans over Carvalho in a menacing fashion. 'I am a public servant. I don't believe in private detectives like you. Nor in parallel networks like the Captain's.'

'Then you've picked the wrong world in this century. In the future, all the police will be privatized, and every state will be a mafia, full of parallel networks, plumbers digging in the shit, specializing in sewers.'

'Who got you on to the case of the topless girl and her Latin teacher? Her boyfriend? That other fugitive? A kid from a good family who's probably hiding under the skirts of some maiden aunt of his mother's.'

'Why would a topless girl study Latin?'

'Perhaps she wanted to become a nun.'

'That's a reply not worthy of you, Inspector.'

Pascuali looks as if he's about to launch himself at Carvalho, but he quickly calms down.

'Let's get back to the other hidden man, your cousin. Or not so hidden. Are you interested in Alma?'

'In what way?'

'A man and a woman.'

'I've got a steady girlfriend back in Spain.'

'Is she a private detective too?'

'No. She used to be a whore, one of those call girls. But she got depressed, because AIDS took all her clients. Her stable lovers were growing old, and I was too. So she left. I'm looking for her as well. That's my reason for living: to look for people.'

'I'm not the least bit surprised your girlfriend is a whore. But Alma isn't driven snow either. She pays you regular visits, has dinner with you, you go to listen to tangos and Silverstein, and then she gets a visit from her brother-in-law, Raúl Tourón, who spends the night with her.'

'Were you the third one in the triangle?'

'I heard it from a reliable source.'

'How come you let him escape then? No one's more vulnerable than a naked man in bed.'

This time, Pascuali can't control himself, and he flings a punch across the table which lands squarely on Carvalho's nose. Then he looks all round to see if anyone has seen him do it.

'That punch came from the man, not the policeman.'

Carvalho punches him back, smack on the nose. Pascuali puts his hand up to it, as blood starts to pour. Both of them sit with bloody noses.

'D'you know I could put you away for ten years for that?'

'I was returning the man's punch, not the policeman's.'

But Pascuali's blow had been the solider of the two, and so, pride assuaged, the policeman allows the detective to leave.

Carvalho's nose and his soul ache, thanks to the secret passages that link the two. Back in his apartment, his fingers stray towards the phone, and dial his office number in Barcelona. 'Biscuter? Yes, it's me. Is everything all right? Did my uncle give you the money? Tell him everything is going well, that I've almost laid my hands on my cousin, but there are a few technical hitches to sort out. Tell him Raúl is fine. Yes, I've had dinner...squid in their sauce. Yes, in Buenos Aires. Yes, they do have squid here; squid and depressed Argies. Yes, the city's still full of depressed Argies and paranoid cops. And psychiatrists. Not all of them left for Barcelona. Has Charo phoned? Did she say she loved me madly? What did you make for dinner? A tortilla with *fredolics*! So Charo didn't phone? How's Barcelona? And the Ramblas?'

Feeling sorry for himself, Carvalho clings to the phone as if suddenly everything around him has grown bigger. He is left with an imprecise feeling of loneliness, and a very precise sensation that Pascuali has broken his nose.

The mock English-style house rises from lawns straight out of an Eden catalogue, with a barbecue range worthy of Norman Foster, guests dressed as though they are Giorgio Armani gauchos posing for a photoshoot of an *asado* in the open air, the smell of roasting meat engaged in a subtle contest with the women's Cartier 'Must' and the men's 'Opium'. Carvalho descends the grassy bank and walks over to people sipping at cocktails and picking at canapés served by waiters dressed up as rich gaucho waiters, until the barbecue is ready.

'If they find us or our children with a hundred grammes of cocaine, we're paraded on television like criminals. But they discover Diego out of his head on the stuff and he becomes a national martyr. That's Perónist demagoguery for you. Don't you agree?' Carvalho hears these words from a well-preserved blonde, busy haranguing two distinguished-looking gentlemen. One of them is the Captain, who's also dressed up for a luxury barbecue.

He replies smoothly: 'Politics is always demagoguery.'

'And you were always a man of action and one of the most intelligent defenders of the state.' This time the speaker is a senator who looks as though he were born to the role.

'He was? Who's to say he isn't still? Once a warrior, always a warrior,' the lady says.

'You're too kind.'

'Well, you, as a man of action who's also had a lot to do with our intelligence services, you know better than anyone what politics is about. Can it ever be anything but demagoguery?'

'If I say no, I'll be arrested.'

They all laugh. The Captain excuses himself, and comes towards Carvalho, who turns his back on him and heads off in the opposite direction, as if he wanted to catch up with another rich-looking man dressed up as a field-marshal from Rosas' nineteenth-century army, who is spouting forth to another varied group of canapé browsers.

'The Radicals have always robbed with their left hand, but the Perónists with all four hands at once.'

'Four hands, Brucker?' asks one of the guests.

'Ha, don't you know they're all apes? Only just down from the trees?'

'Have you said as much to your son-in-law, who was more Perónist than Perón?'

'But he went to the best schools, and he's from an excellent family,' Brucker replies.

'Are you looking for someone?' a waiter asks Carvalho, blowing his cover as an invisible onlooker.

This threatening personage, backed up by two other equally inhospitable figures, blocks Carvalho's path. Two or three other groups of guests raise their heads to see if something interesting is going to happen.

'We don't want any journalists or people who haven't been invited.'

'But I told you, it was Señor Honrubia who invited me.'

'I've got someone called...' the waiter is now speaking into his walkie-talkie.

Carvalho hands him his business card. It reads 'Altofini and Carvalho. Partners in Crime.'

'...someone called Altofini-Carvalho.'

He is given the all clear, so he quickly frisks Carvalho, then says:

'Follow that path down to the lake, and Señor Honrubia will be waiting for you at the landing stage.'

The Captain is observing all that has gone on from a distance. He sees Carvalho go down the path to the artificial lake and the small pier. A bulky man is sitting there, staring down at the waters as if they were gently calling him to a gentle suicide, or were concealing a drowned man that only he can see. As Carvalho draws closer, the sheer bulk of the man and his sad bloodhound look impress themselves on him.

'Señor Honrubia?'

Honrubia looks him up and down. His melancholy turns into suspicion.

'Don't you like *asados*? Why are you all on your own down here? Are you from *Gourmet* magazine?'

Carvalho hands him his card.

'Yes, Alma already told me about you. How is she?'

'The other day we went to our own *asado* – Girmenich, Silverstein, Güelmes, at the Baroja place.'

'What a collection of dinosaurs! Do you know why the dinosaur became extinct? It's a joke. A Russian joke. You don't? The dinosaur became extinct because it was a dinosaur.'

'Well, these dinosaurs were remembering the days when they used guns and plastic explosives. They talked a lot about you.'

'All of it bad, I'm sure. I'm the traitor who married a young señorita from the oligarchy we were fighting against.'

'It seemed more as if they were very jealous of you. You married the sister of someone you kidnapped when you were a revolutionary, and you're about to be made general manager of your father-in-law's businesses.'

Honrubia gets up. His arm moves out towards Carvalho in what at first might be a threatening gesture, but finally settles on his shoulder and steers him back towards the other guests.

'I've been a guerrillero, an exile, a beggar in exile, a thief, a corrupt top official, unemployed, and now I'm an oligarch. But I'm still faithful to those lines by Pavese: "A man who has been in prison goes back there every time he takes a bite of bread".'

He's moved by his own eloquence, and raises a hand to his eyes.

Then he points to the people waiting for their *asado*. 'Look, they're all posing for *Caras*, our big fashion magazine. If that didn't exist, neither would they. From here they look like monkeys, and when they talk it's like chattering monkeys. But deep down inside, a revolutionary will always be a revolutionary. Anyone who fought on the side of history will never lose that identity.'

'Güelmes says the opposite.'

'He was never a revolutionary. He was always a shit.'

A young and studiously attractive woman comes loping down to them.

'Before my wife gets here, what is it you want from me?'

'I'm looking for Raúl, Raúl Tourón.'

Mistrust quickly replaces all trace of melancholy in Honrubia's eyes. The young woman drapes herself affectionately on his arm, and the three of them walk up to the barbecue. They arrive just as Brucker is holding forth on the science of a good *asado*. 'Roasting meat is for waiters. It's one thing to plan it, quite another to do the cooking.'

'But I just love putting on my asbestos gloves and doing the roasting.'

Señor Brucker shouts out: 'The lambs are mine! Nobody knows how to give them the final touch like me!'

Several of the guests murmur their agreement.

'Nobody can roast lambs like papa!' Honrubia's wife exclaims, and her husband nods, back with his bloodhound look. Carvalho, Honrubia and his wife follow the other guests to the spot where the lambs have been cooked. Five crucified Christs facing the glowing embers.

'*Agnus Dei tolis pecata mundi!*' Honrubia entones.

'You even know Latin!' his wife enthuses. 'What did you say?'

'Lamb of God who wipes clean the sins of this world,' Honrubia translates, with his Old Testament prophet's head.

'*Ora pro nobis,*' Carvalho completes the response.

The sunset seems put on especially for Honrubia and Carvalho as they sit in the library on sumptuously rich armchairs made from the best leather of the best Argentine cattle. In the hearth the best logs from the best forests of Misiones or Bariloche are burning. But Honrubia is drinking from a full glass of second-rate whisky. Carvalho the same.

'What makes you think I might have hidden Raúl?'

'You own half of Argentina.'

'In fact, only zero point zero nine per cent of it.'

'That's still not bad, considering how little the rest of the Argentines have.'

'Some day this house and all the others like it will burn. The revolution is bound to happen. The world can't go on being divided between a tiny majority of people like us and millions of others dying of hunger.'

'In the meantime…'

'In the meantime,' Honrubia butts in, 'I thought this was an excellent whisky until you told me otherwise. You're one of the few people who really appreciate a good malt, and this isn't one.'

'It's not even a malt.'

'Are you a revolutionary?'

'I used to be. Now I simply drink and smoke as much as I can, and from time to time burn books.'

Honrubia points to the bookshelves with a sweeping gesture.

'Burn away! They belong to my father-in-law, to his father or his grandfather. Who cares? They never read any of them.'

'Do you mean it?'

Honrubia shows him he does by getting up, taking out an obviously very expensive book, and throwing it onto the fire. Carvalho does the same, then Honrubia again, and Carvalho a second time. Before long, the smoke from this incineration of a good part of Western culture billows from the fireplace. Some servants shepherded in by Señor Brucker and followed by a few remaining guests burst into the room. They find it empty, but for a pile of books still smouldering in the hearth.

'Thank heavens. It's only books,' Brucker says.

The first to smile at this is the Captain.

Carvalho, meanwhile, is following Honrubia down stairs that lead to the wine cellar. When they get there, he's astonished and moved at the spectacular collection of bottles.

'We have some Bordeaux 1899. To look at, not to try.'

Honrubia leads the way through a small door out into the garden.

At the far end of a track stands an elegant summerhouse.

'My study. A sacred place.'

They go in, and as soon as he crosses the threshold, Carvalho feels he's entered another world. The walls are covered with posters of Evita, Che, Castro; there are revolutionary books and pamphlets everywhere, and a showcase full of weapons. Honrubia tells Carvalho to sit down, and disappears through an inner door. Carvalho casts a sceptical glance over the iconography. Then he spots a telescope pointing up at the stars through a glass canopy, which opens in the roof as he approaches. The starry night sky extends above him. He hears a noise at his back. When he turns round, Honrubia and Raúl are staring at him.

'Ten minutes,' Honrubia warns him, before leaving the room again.

Raúl remains standing, Carvalho stays in his chair. For a few seconds, neither of them speaks.

'How is my father?'

'He goes on living because he wants to see you.'

'It's all about his inheritance. He's scared my aunt and cousins will suck his lifeblood from him. That's what I've been doing all my life. I managed to become what I was thanks to him, and then lost it all no thanks to him. It's too late now.'

'Everything would be so much easier if you returned to Spain with me.'

'Everything is hard. I've discovered I'm Argentine. In Spain I felt like a dirty South American – that's what they call us, isn't it? Here, somewhere or other, is my daughter. I know there's no chance now with Alma. But my past is here, my nostalgia for the past. In Spain I had no future, and I had lost my past.'

'I'm not the only one looking for you. There's the Captain. There's Pascuali. I could do a deal with Pascuali for you to leave the country.'

'I'd be happy with just one thing: to be allowed to live here, not to leave again. And you're the one who worries me the most. You're a rescuer. You want to rescue me from myself.'

'I'm a professional. If I return you to Spain, I get paid.'

'And I'm looking for my daughter. I'm on the right track.' Raúl studies Carvalho, and eventually adds: 'In a fortnight there's going to be a big family *asado*.'

'Another one?'

'All *asados* are the same but different. This is at the house of a distant uncle of mine, in Villa Flores. He's a cousin of my father's. I won't be there. But I will give you my final answer. And by the way, I won't be here either – I can't stay here any longer, so don't even think of coming back.' He hands Carvalho a scrap of paper. 'This is where you'll know for sure whether I'm going or staying.'

Carvalho leaves the Brucker mansion in the most luxurious Mercedes imaginable. The uniformed chauffeur presses a remote control, and the imposing wrought-iron gates glide open, revealing open country beyond. As they leave this garden of Eden, the chauffeur asks: 'Did you like the *asado*, sir?'

'It was excellent.'

'Every *asado* is different. I make mine in the patio I share with neighbours in the old tenement buildings where I live – every free Sunday I have. It's really soothing, and calms me down: you get back to the really important things in life – killing and eating.'

Carvalho studies the back of his neck with great interest. 'Were you a guerrilla too?'

'I was one of the foot soldiers, you might say. I studied in a shit-awful school in Barracas, and that's where Señor Honrubia recruited me. He's brought a lot of the old comrades to work for him here.'

'Plotting the unfinished revolution,' Carvalho mutters to himself. 'The Bruckers have no idea what's in store for them.'

Several motorbikes come zooming along the outside wall of the residence. They all gather outside one of the entrances. Their riders dismount without taking off their helmets or their masks. The two guards on the door do nothing to get rid of them. Instead, one of them opens it, after he's pressed an alarm bell.

'It's disconnected in the sector around Señor Honrubia's study.'

The motorcyclists nod. They make for the lighted windows of Honrubia's summerhouse. One of them looks inside. Honrubia appears to be reading in front of the wood fire. He's also singing. The motorcyclists surround the building. One kicks in the door, another dives through the window. In less than a second, the six of them have their guns trained on Honrubia. He still has his bloodhound look, although there's a glimmer of anxiety in his eyes. Two of the intruders barge their way into the other room, and give a thumbs-up sign. A third man follows them. They seem reluctant to go into the bathroom, but their attitude changes abruptly when they see the bidet has been turned to one side, showing a dark hideaway underneath. They turn it round completely, revealing a gaping hole. A powerful torch shows just how big it is. When they are all back in the study, a neutral voice orders Honrubia: 'Stay where you are for fifteen minutes. Don't move; don't even go to the window.'

The group withdraws to the gate they entered through, where the guards who had helped them are waiting. Two of the motorcyclists pull out bottles and handkerchiefs from the depths of their leather jackets; the guards lean forward meekly to receive their dose of chloroform. As they lie unconscious on the ground, the attackers beat them with their gun butts. Then they get back on their bikes and head off towards a car hidden in the woods. The fat man is at the wheel. One of the motorcyclists takes off his helmet and the goggles covering his face. It's the Captain.

'That bastard oligarchic guerrillero got rid of his little friend.'

'Shall I put the screws on him?' fat man suggests.

'How stupid can you get?' the Captain says, collapsing on to the back seat. 'He may not be a real Brucker, but he's a Brucker all the same.'

Carvalho has the notebook he took from the Latin teacher's apartment open on the desk in front of him. The neat handwriting on the cover continues inside, where it establishes a Manichean list: the students who pay, and those who don't. Carvalho sorts out the group: Juan Miñana, post office employee; Mudarra Aoíz, student retaking his exams; Carmen Lavalle, dancer and classical philology student; Enzo Pasticchio, teacher.

'From what they paid, if he hadn't been killed, he'd have died of hunger.'

'These old-age pensioners have got amazing resistance,' comments Don Vito, seated opposite Carvalho. 'You only have to see them demonstrating outside Congress. Some of them look like skeletons because all they eat are bones. Others look tanned and fit from all the marches they've been on. Some of them are stripped to the waist, showing off muscles that the dignity of work has given them. But most of them are just surviving. Now my fifth wife's left me, I have to buy meat sometimes in the local butcher's, and I often see the old guys: "Can I have half a pound of scrag end please, it's for the dog." Get it, Don Pepe?'

'Let's split the list between us. Carmen Lavalle is dead. That leaves Mudarra Aoíz and Enzo Pasticchio for you, and Juan Miñana for me.'

'That's two to one.'

'I've still got my cousin. Or perhaps he's got me. Sometimes I think he's the one watching me.'

At that moment, Alma comes into the office, so Don Vito quickly adds her to the list.

'And you've got your other cousin here.'

Carvalho looks at Alma so scornfully she is taken aback, before she returns his stare defiantly. Don Vito notices the duel between them.

'Well then, I'll be off. We're up to here with work.'

After excusing himself in this way, he nods to Alma, and she responds. Carvalho speaks to her sharply, and points to the visitors' chair.

'Take a seat, please.'

'Are we going to play the game of detective and client?'

'That's right.'

Alma sits down and crosses her legs, staring at Carvalho as though she was hanging on his every word.

'Have you come to employ me to find your husband – sorry, I mean your brother-in-law?'

'That's your problem.'

'Perhaps it's yours as well, after the fantastic night you spent making love in your apartment a few nights ago. The whole night.'

Alma gets up indignantly.

'Were you spying on me?'

'Not me. Pascuali was though, and Raúl only escaped by the skin of his teeth.'

'What of it if Raúl was with me? Why should I tell you?'

'He was in your apartment the night before that balls-breaking *asado* with your ex-revolutionary comrades, when you cynically asked them all to help find him: "We have to get to him before the Captain does."'

'Don't try to imitate my voice. I don't talk like a queer.'

'You even managed to convince me when you said: "The best thing would be for his cousin to take him back to Spain."'

'Why is that so ridiculous? The best thing would be for him to go to Spain, and for you to go with him. The sooner the better.'

She picks up the nearest thing to hand – a file on the desk – and flings it at Carvalho. She storms out of the office, but when he runs after her and catches her on the stairs, she doesn't try to escape.

'It was all so sad. It was like the end of something that had lasted twenty years, but had never really existed. I told him the best for everyone would be that he went with you.'

'So you're trying to get rid of me as well.'

Alma smiles a little forlornly.

'I'm not sure whether Raúl will go or not, but you, Don Pepe, are bound to leave some day or other, and get back to your Biscuter, your Charo, your Ramblas. You've got the face of a man frightened he'll never find his way home.'

This hits the mark.

'I've never found my way home. And the worst of it is, I can't remember when I left, or what home I left when I did.'

Alma gives him a hug to make up for his loss.

'Since when? Since you were a little boy? This high?' She measures a few feet from the floor with her hand.

'Why don't we have something to eat in a badly lit bar I know near here?' Carvalho says, recovering his composure.

'Why not? I'm ravenous.'

Carvalho pushes his way through sacks, trolleys, postmen and foremen until he reaches the personnel manager's office.

'Juan Miñana? He doesn't work here any more. He was a novelist in his spare time. He won an important literary prize and left for Europe. He had an uncle there. Before, Argentina was full of Europeans, and now everyone wants to escape to Europe.'

'Did you know him well?'

'He was like a son to me. I encouraged him to go on writing and studying. What's better: to be a postman or a writer?'

'Being a postman is more secure; and anyway, where would writers be without postmen?'

Carvalho does not give him time to be amazed. 'Do you know he studied Latin? Doesn't that seem odd to you?'

'I can see you're not a writer,' the personnel manager says, doubly amazed now. 'What else would he study? Quechua? The only word we get from Quechua is *chinchulines*. Why study Latin? Do you think you can write good Spanish without knowing Latin?'

'Do you know Latin?'

'If I did, do you think I'd be here?'

Carvalho cannot be bothered to consider the possible destinies of Miñana's bad-tempered intellectual mentor, so he leaves to meet up with Don Vito in the place where they first met.

'It's safer to speak here than at home. I think it's full of microphones,' says Carvalho.

'They plant them just for the hell of it. Just to show they can break the rules. Whether they need the bugs or not.'

'Where have we got to?'

'Hang on a minute, why are you in such a hurry? Sometimes I think you're more German than Spanish. You have to give these things time, my friend,' Don Vito says, dancing a foxtrot with himself.

'What do we know?'

Don Vito gives in. 'The topless girl is dead. The novelist postman is in Europe. Enzo Pasticchio is a secondary school teacher trying to win a competition to get a university post. And the kid Mudarra is just that: a kid, a strange kid, the son of an invalid mother, who takes his dog for a walk every night: his dog's called "Canelo". The kid is a strange mixture of nobility and sordidness. He's fair-haired, and moves around elegantly, but he picks his nose even when people he doesn't know are around.'

He stops when he sees how disgusted Carvalho looks. 'I can't bear people who pick their noses in public.'

'The secondary school teacher gets all over the place. He teaches at school, in a couple of hundred academies, and is obsessed with winning a university post. He's gone bald from so much scratching his head over getting nowhere. Nothing remarkable there, except...'

'Except?'

'Except that Mudarra told me why he quit the Latin classes a few weeks ago. Carmen Lavalle and the professor were alone in his study. The professor leaning over the girl, hands on her shoulders as she concentrated on reading the book in front of her. I suspect that while the prof was giving her advice, he was staring as hard as he could down her neckline in search of the hidden valleys of her breasts. She reads more slowly, warming to Catullus' emotions: *bebamus mea Lesbia atque amemus...*'

'Where on earth did you learn that?'

But Don Vito won't be interrupted. He goes on with his monologue: 'As Carmen reads Catullus' love poem, the professor's hands start to caress her. She pauses, turns her head and glances at the professor with an amused look on her face. "What's got into you, professor?" "We old men have feelings too!" he says with a sorrowful face. "You mean you have sexual feelings?"'

'Don Vito, are you making this up?'

'I'm offering you a scene in three dimensions and two voices. The old professor responds: "Why not? We have sexual needs too. They're not often satisfied, but we do have them." Carmen closes the book, stands up and puts her hands on the shoulders of the professor, who is looking away in embarrassment. Carmen lifts his skull-like face towards her. Kisses him on the forehead. Then gives him another passionate kiss full on the mouth. As they draw apart, the professor looks confused, almost stunned. Carmen is smiling, enjoying herself. All of a sudden, Pasticchio and Mudarra appear in the doorway. They're astonished at what they have seen. Don't know whether to be horrified or moved. You get the picture?' Don Vito asks, but does not wait for a reply: 'Pasticchio is a man of principle. He was in a seminary, he's got six kids, he's against the use of condoms. And it goes without saying that all the children are from the same mother.'

'What about Mudarra?'

'He's got no balls. He's a kid with no balls,' Don Vito says dismissively, clutching at his own flies.

It has been years since anyone has trimmed the grass borders, cut back the trees, or interfered in the struggle between rats and feral cats, but the skyline of the house – more French than English in style – is still imposing, even though the way of life it once saw has long since gone. Marble stairs lead up to a heavy panelled front door with an unpolished bronze knocker, but Raúl has no need to use it because the door yields to his touch, revealing inside a large hall lined with doors and a pink marble staircase fronted by the statue of a welcoming angel. Hearing the sound of music from behind one of the doors, Raúl walks over and opens it: a llama comes rushing out, closely followed by the cries of a parrot hopping up and down on a perch.

'I love gays! I love gays! I love gays!' the parrot screeches as it flies round the room whose floor is dotted with brightly coloured cushions. Eventually it lands on the shoulder of a black man.

Beside him is sprawled another man, this one dressed up as an explorer from what must be the end of the seventeenth century, although Raúl has no way of being certain. The black man is also dressed like a caricature from a Romantic print. He strokes the white man's greying, lank hair affectionately.

'What scared you – the llama or the parrot?'

'Señor Honrubia said I should come.'

The explorer laughs and comments to his companion: 'If Honrubia sent him, you'd better search him for weapons.'

Raúl spreads his legs, lifts his hands in the air, and wearily drops his head to his chest.

'Don't bother, Friday. This man's been searched too often in his life. Can't you tell?'

The black man had not moved anyway, and now he's observing the newcomer with a wry smile on his face, while the explorer continues to think aloud.

'If you're a friend of Honrubia's who doesn't need to be searched, that means you're one of the losers of the dirty war. Only the losers of that war don't need to be searched – isn't that right, Friday?'

'Yes, Mister Crusoe.'

So they're playing at being Robinson Crusoe and his faithful servant Friday on a desert island. Guessing they are playing a game to see how he reacts, Raúl overcomes a desire to leave immediately the way he came. Instead he asks permission to sit•on one of the cushions, and the gesture inviting him to do so seems to include the whole room.

'The idea of private property does not exist in this house. Would you like a glass of llama's milk? Of cold water? A spliff? You won't find any Coca Cola or Seven Up here. We only have healthy, anti-imperialist drinks.'

Raúl says he hardly drinks healthy anti-imperialist drinks either, but is curious to know what llama's milk might taste like.

'I knew you were going to ask the impossible. Our llama's just got out, and there's no way of catching her until feed time. Well, you have our permission to explain why you're here.'

Raúl quickly sketches in the story of his life and the events around it. He explains the 1977 raid, the disappearance of his daughter, his desperate and useless return to Spain thanks to an over-protective father, the identity crisis he's been going through over the past few months, his need to find his daughter, and Honrubia's advice – you should go and see a friend of mine at this address, I can't tell you his name, but however odd he may seem, he might be able to help you. The explorer has been closely observing all the signals Raúl has been communicating – his gestures, his words, the different tones of voice he has adopted while telling his story. He occasionally looks over to his companion, passing silent messages only they understand, and when Raúl's speech has finished, Robinson and Friday continue their silent dialogue. It's broken by the parrot: 'I love gays! I love gays! I love gays!'

This interruption seems to have broken the spell, because Robinson raises his tall, handsome frame and says to Raúl: 'There was a time when I was powerful and like all powerful men I surrounded myself with information and files for my own protection. I have kept some of them, although I rarely need them in my new life, which is devoted to finding volunteers to set up a phalanstery on the Malvinas islands. I have to decide whether you are worthy of our help, and not just because you are a troubled man or a distraught father. If you knew me, you'd be aware I'm not a man who feels much sympathy for others. Nor am I ruled by vague emotions such as optimism or pessimism. I am a slave to lucidity. And if my lucidity tells me – help this man, then help him I will. What do you think, Friday?'

'There's too much sentiment in his story.'

'It's true, that's the weakness, but who is it aimed at? That's the interesting part.'

Friday appears to have understood, with great admiration, his master's immense talent for spotting where these things necessarily lead. He agrees wholeheartedly. Robinson exclaims: 'I'm going to help you, because you and I are both fighting the oligarchy!'

A down-at-heel bar, on Tacuari almost level with Avenida San Juan, the outskirts of central Buenos Aires. Four or five chairs, a few locals, almost no one at the bar, and behind it a tired waiter whose obvious lack of interest is what makes the café so gloomy and disturbs Carvalho, who has an Argentine grappa in front of him but is more interested in a doorway on the far side of the street. He looks at his watch. Twelve midnight. The doorway opens and an indistinct young man steps out, pulling a dog along. Neither of them seem too keen on going out. The young man has fair hair; his looks suggest TB or a prince with genetic defects. He's young, but everything he wears looks old and sad, especially his shoes. Their age betrays not someone scraping by, but real poverty disguised by too frequent washing. Carvalho wraps some croquettes in tinfoil, pays and leaves the bar. He walks along his own side of the road, at some distance from Mudarra and his dog. The youngster yanks the dog's lead from time to time, making it dig its heels in even more. Then Canelo pees. And shits. Carvalho crosses the street and pretends to bump into them by chance. Mudarra looks at him with an expressionless face.

'I could set my watch by you two. Whenever I come out from my meal, you and Canelo appear. He's called Canelo, isn't he? Canelo!' The dog seems very pleased to see Carvalho. 'There's a good boy.'

He takes the package with the croquettes out of his pocket, and tips them on to the pavement. Canelo pounces on them.

'He's already eaten,' the youngster says hesitantly.

'Animals eat whatever they're given.'

Canelo makes short work of the croquettes. Mudarra shows more interest in Carvalho.

'Where do you know us from?'

'From seeing you come out every night. Shortly after twelve, always. I'm a regular at the bar over there.'

'And how do you know my dog's called Canelo?'

'Because I've heard you call him more than fifty times. But I don't know your name. The dog never seems to call you.'

'Mudarra. My name's Mudarra.'

'That's a strange name. Sounds like something out of a medieval epic poem.'

'Out of what?'

'One of those medieval Spanish epics.'

'My father was Spanish. From Navarre, I think.'

Mudarra pulls at Canelo's lead to continue their walk. Carvalho falls in beside them as if he were headed in the same direction.

'I love animals. Years ago I had an Alsatian puppy, but it was killed; Bleda was her name. I swore I'd never have another one. It was like betraying her. How's your mother by the way, has she recovered?'

Mudarra smiles as if he's trying to conceal the reason for it.

'So you know about my mother too?'

'Waiters in bars know everything.'

'I've never been in a bar.'

'Are you sure?'

'I don't like them.'

Mudarra hesitates, then returns from his little mental trip.

'Would you like to meet her? She loves having visitors.'

'At this time of night?'

'My mother never sleeps. Nor do I. The only one who sleeps in our house is Canelo here.'

He pulls again at the lead.

'It's very late. But some other day I'll come up. Your mother's an invalid, like mine was.'

'Worse, far worse. My mother has always been much more of an invalid than anyone else.'

He tugs again on Canelo's lead.

'Listen to me carefully,' Pascuali says, and his four colleagues do so, especially Vladimiro.

Pascuali reads them the report he's holding: 'Confidential. Raid on the Brucker residence. Under cover of night. A group of non-identified individuals dressed as motorcyclists, with their faces practically covered. – Does the motorcyclists bit ring any bells? – Said

individuals beat and chloroform the guards at one of the rear gates to
the property, and broke into a summerhouse which Señor Honrubia
uses to rest and meditate in. Fortunately they did not harm anyone in
the summerhouse: that is, they did not harm Señor Honrubia, and so
there was only material damage and the assault on the guards.
Confidential! Con-fi-den-tial! Not a word to the press. Not a word
beyond this department. Confidential!'

Just touching the document appears to excite Pascuali. He takes
it and rushes through all the department doors out into a corridor of
the National Security Headquarters. He carries on past the
astonished gazes of several secretaries until he comes to an obviously
important door. He pushes it open, goes in and shuts it behind him.
A man who's too young to believe he can be the head of anything at
all is watching a video of the Boca–Independiente match.

'Hello there, Pascuali. Sorry, but I couldn't get to the match, or
see it on TV. See how they stroke the ball around? There's a lot of
stroking going on, but nobody gives it the final touch. It's as if
Bilardo's forgotten you need balls to play football. That creep
Menotti's been getting at him. Football as art! Did you read that
interview with Valdano the other day? Left-wing football! Passing the
ball all round the field, just like your lefties! It's the right-wing that
puts the balls into it! If you ask me, Bilardo's had a lobotomy.
Menotti's left him brain-dead.'

Suddenly he notices Pascuali is not joining in, and the file in his
hand suggests to the head of the service that perhaps he should switch
off the video and turn his swivel chair to properly face his subordinate.

'Thank you, sir, for this confidential information, but it seems to
me that this is a clear case of unwarranted interference in an official
police investigation being led by this ministry, by your service and by
my department.'

The service head lets him talk.

'If you authorize it, I'll teach the Captain and his motorcyclists
where they belong.'

The service head studies Pascuali, and eventually deigns to speak.

'You're not going to teach a thing to the Captain, Pascuali. The
Captain was defending the state long before you, and if he got his
hands dirty, he wasn't the only one. Every state needs its sewers and

sewer experts, especially a democratic state. What the public side doesn't want to know is handed to the hidden side. Don't be so naïve.'

'But if we keep this kind of parallel police we'll end up in the same kind of shit as before.'

'Don't exaggerate. A democratic state is never completely drowned in shit, but it does exist. Every four or six years it renews its leaders at the polls. What are the ballots? Toilet paper? Well yes, they are that too. Ballot papers can also be used to wipe away shit. You just get on with your own work – you do it very well. Let the Captain and his lads know you're on to them. But nothing more. They can be a bit – how shall I put it? A bit theatrical. You've got nothing theatrical about you, have you? You're too straight for that.'

At that, he swivels his chair back and switches the video on again. Pascuali mouths increasingly crude but silent curses. His face is a picture of contained indignation, which spills over when he is back in his own office and seated once more in his chair, faced by his four expectant colleagues. He shouts at them to leave, but keeps Vladimiro with him.

'Stay here, Vladimiro, would you?'

Vladimiro sits in silence, closely observing the emotions struggling to burst out of Pascuali's lips, cheeks and eyes.

'Tell me, Vladimiro, the day you became a policeman, did they tell you to leave your balls on the door handle?'

'Not that I remember.'

'I thought this was a profession where you had to have balls, but I was wrong. Even I have to make sure I leave my balls on the door handle before I go into a room. So that whenever any asshole politician gives me a kick in the balls for what he calls reasons of state, like Morales our beloved head of service, that idiot covered in masters' degrees, he will be surprised to find there's nothing there. D'you understand what I'm saying, Vladimiro?'

'More or less.'

Vladimiro glances down at his watch, and Pascuali notices.

'Are you in a hurry?'

'Yes, to tell you the truth, I am.'

'A piece of skirt?'

'Almost. A family *asado*.'

'Ah! *Asados* are sacred. Be off with you, Vladimiro, and forget what I said.'

'So what do I do with the balls?'

'What balls?'

'Mine. Do I leave them hanging on the door handle? Or keep them with me?'

Pascuali explodes, and looms over Vladimiro, who backs towards the door.

'The only one who needs balls around here is me!'

The open back yard of a neighbourhood villa, a villa twelve metres wide and with a hundred years of neglect showing in its iron window grilles and a tiny balcony like something out of the Marx Brothers' *Night at the Opera*. A constantly growing crowd of people, mostly married couples between thirty and fifty years old, with a varied assortment of children, adolescents and relatives; the men looking lost without their ties, the women lost in their necklaces. Some of them are busy around a modest barbecue that has already produced one lot of meat and is now being made ready to grill twice as much again. Sparkling cider is the drink of the day. Others are drinking flat Asturian cider from a barrel. While they wait for the *asado*, everyone is trying the *empanadas* or slices of spicy Spanish sausage prepared by the local Italian butcher. Favila's ancient wife is trying to make herself useful, struggling against her Parkinson's and her nieces, grandchildren and children, all of whom want to make her sit down. But she will have none of it, and lurches dangerously around with trays of meat and bottles, although she never drops a thing – no one can remember her ever having dropped anything at all. Her eldest son puts an arm round her shoulders.

'Mama, why don't you go and fetch the old man? Tell him we're all here...even the cop.'

He points to someone – Vladimiro – and everyone laughs.

'Don't let anyone ever get the idea of telling Favila Vladimiro is a cop. He thinks he's a lawyer. Well, he thinks what he wants to think,' the old woman says.

The woman who is obviously Vladimiro's companion seems rather upset at this.

'Well I don't see what's so wrong with being a cop.'

Nobody pays her much attention, not even Vladimiro, who's giving the *asado* the look-over with an expert eye. The old woman disappears into her kitchen. She struggles over to the button on the wall, presses it, and the concealed door swings open. She shouts into the hole: 'Favila! Everyone's here! It's your birthday. Favila! Come on out, will you, you old goat?'

Favila's pale, wrinkled face appears in the light. He's dressed in his Sunday best.

'Anyone can tell you're Spanish by the amount you curse.'

'I talk as I see fit.'

'Are you sure the coast is clear?' Favila asks, pausing but not completely halting in his progress out into the yard.

'In Argentina it is. It always has been.'

'Did you remember the cider?'

'Why didn't you see to it instead of playing at hide-and-seek?'

The old woman stamps off, sustained by her accumulated sense of grievance. Before stepping out into the yard, Don Favila gives his painful black shoes a final polish with a tea-towel. When he appears, he's immediately surrounded by his relatives and their guests. They applaud him, kiss and hug him, give him presents.

'Has Vladimiro come?' Favila wants to know.

Vladimiro comes up to his father, who embraces him with special affection.

'My youngest, born in hard times during the dictatorship of that assassin's apprentice, Onga...'

He's so passionate about what he's saying he can't get the words out. One of his daughters interrupts him.

'Papa. No politics. Today is your day, a year on our planet.'

'I called him Vladimiro in homage to Lenin, I called you Rosa after Rosa Luxemburg, and you Dolores were named after Dolores Ibárruri, *la Pasionaria*,' Favila insists, pointing to each of his offspring in turn.

'So why am I called Fulgencio, Papa?' another son calls out. 'In homage to Fulgencio Batista?'

'Don't try to annoy me. You're called Fulgencio because that was the name of my father, your grandfather. Revolution doesn't mean throwing away traditions. Let's see: I want to pour the cider, because you lot are a bunch of ninnies who were brought up on Coca Cola and Seven Up.'

He's handed a jug of flat cider.

'We bought it in that shop in Calle Corrientes – you know, the one that sells Spanish goods.'

Don Favila's eyes express their satisfaction. He picks up a traditional wide-rimmed glass. With one hand, he lifts the cider jar behind his head; in the other he holds the glass in front of him. With expert judgement he pours a stream of cider into the foaming glass. Everyone cheers and applauds him. He courteously offers the glass to his wife. She takes it with a trembling hand, and starts to cry softly. She takes a sip, but still manages to comment: 'I never liked cider, it tastes like piss.'

All the guests sit round the table, wherever they can find a place. The table is already overflowing with meat, salads, *empanadas*, Italian pasta dishes and a bowl full of tinned Spanish beans. Suddenly, the street door bell rings. The old woman gets up to go and answer it, but one of her daughters-in-law restrains her.

'By the time you get there, they'll have given up and gone.'

'Bitch...I hope your cunt freezes over,' the old woman mutters to herself.

A short while later, the daughter-in-law reappears, accompanied by Carvalho. Both of them seem rather embarrassed: she doesn't know how to explain what's obviously a long story, and he is taken aback at seeing so many people. He's even more disturbed when he notices Vladimiro is one of the guests.

'This is José Carvalho Tourón, a nephew of your cousin, Evaristo Tourón,' the daughter-in-law says, pointing at Favila, 'and the son of Evaristo Carvalho, brother of...'

Favila stands up with a cry of emotion.

'Nephew!'

He gives Carvalho a warm hug, and the reminiscences start to pour out.

'I didn't recognize you at first, but you're the spitting image of your uncle and your father.' He turns to the others. 'This man's father was a hero who fought Franco and paid for it with forty years in jail.'

'It was only five,' Carvalho corrects him.

'In those days, five years was like forty.'

Carvalho sees Vladimiro shoot him a silent look that pleads: keep quiet. Favila is busy presenting each of his children. Fulgencio after his grandfather. Rosa for Rosa Luxemburg. Dolores in honour of Dolores Ibárruri. Vladimiro for Lenin.

'Congratulations. You must be the last Leninist,' Carvalho comments, before he's steered to a place at the table to join the feast.

He sits down and starts to eat, more hungrily with each mouthful. As if the flavours help him find his way home, he feels more at ease and begins to enjoy himself. After a while, a scene rises from the depths of his memory – a wedding banquet in Barcelona, a cousin getting married to a girl in service. Both are from Galicia, they've been engaged for years, saving up for the wedding, and it's a real Galician feast, meat with tuna, cockle *empanadas*. This banquet fills his childhood memory – it's the happiness of abundance, of a strange moment when life or even history somehow relaxed. History had marked his childhood, lived out among hidden men and women, and now Carvalho rediscovers a similar happiness as he eats and drinks free of fear, talking and answering questions, especially from Don Favila.

'I'm still in hiding, just in case. One day there'll be another coup, or perhaps the revolution will really come, and we shouldn't be caught out. We always have been and always will be the vanguard. Revolutions fail when the vanguard disappears or goes soft, like it did in the USSR. The vanguard are people like your father and me.'

Rosa Luxemburg lifts a finger to her temple to warn Carvalho Don Favila is not quite right in the head. The feast fills the guests' stomachs and hearts, and finally makes its way up to their brains, telling them they've had enough. Slices of cake are handed round, after Don Favila has done his best to spread bits all over the table during his ten attempts to blow out the eighty-four candles on it. Carvalho looks on with his usual stony poker face, but there's a glint of emotion in his eyes. Vladimiro comes over.

'You're one of life's great surprises.'

'My father doesn't know I'm a policeman.'

'My father died without knowing I wasn't a Communist any more, and that I'd become a private detective.'

Vladimiro hesitates, but finally decides to speak.

'I knew you were going to be here, but not for the meal. Raúl told me to tell you he hasn't got a definite answer for you yet. He's gone into hiding again. The Captain raided the Brucker place.'

'So you're Raúl's contact?'

'He's my cousin. Only a second cousin, but still a cousin. Do you think I could ever look my father in the face if it was me who caught him?'

'What about Pascuali?'

'He's a cop with a good pair of balls.'

'Are there any cops who don't have them? The problem is where they put them. If they use them instead of brains, we're all done for.'

Vladimiro sits down again next to his girlfriend. She looks like a girlfriend and not a wife, Carvalho thinks. Then he is distracted by the sight of the old woman carrying out a secret inventory of real or imaginary objects in the kitchen. It's as if she's praying. She smiles at him through the window, and beckons him inside with a crooked finger. Carvalho joins her in the kitchen, and sees that Don Favila is waiting for him half-hidden in a corner of the room, out of sight of the yard.

'I have to go back into hiding. I've taken too much of a risk already. It's all right once in a while, but I mustn't push my luck. But I brought you in here because on behalf of your heroic father you deserve to know my secret. I live hidden, and only come out once a year for my birthday.'

'And whenever Boca's playing on TV,' his wife quickly adds.

'Everyone has their weak spot. Didn't Lenin like to howl like a wolf in the moonlight?'

Don Favila presses the button and his hide-out door opens. He steps inside, and invites Carvalho to follow. Carvalho stands aside to let the old woman go ahead of him.

'Me in there? Over my dead body. When this old fool comes back to bed and does his duty like a proper husband, then I'll set foot in there. It must be like the gates of hell.'

Carvalho follows the old man. Don Favila scuttles down four steps and switches on a light. They are in a fairly large basement, but Carvalho stops in his tracks, overwhelmed by all the messages bombarding him from the walls. It's like a Red cultural museum from the beginning of the twentieth century to the 1970s, plus a few examples of bang up-to-date post-Marxist protest. Some 'liberation theology' posters hang next to pacifist ones from the First World War. Others from Spanish deserters in the North African war. The Spanish Civil War. Che. Castro. The October revolution. Photos of all the icons of world revolution. Books selected for a Red shipwreck survivor on a 1930s desert island. A model of one of Lenin's giant statues. Another for the Third International by Tatlin. A photo of subcomandante Marcos in his mask. Rigoberta Menchú. The old man observes the effect all this iconography is having on Carvalho.

'The world is full of hidden people. This city too. There's always been a reason to hide. Buenos Aires is full of secret tunnels; I know of a complete network of catacombs in Calle Peru, for example. Why should I venture out? In here I know where I am. Outside, it's capitalism which dictates how everything should be. For the moment it has won, but one day a new generation will discover the old and the new disorder, and then all the hopes you see here will regain their meaning. Don't you agree?'

Carvalho agrees. He allows the old man to sit him down, and then put a bakelite seventy-eight record on a wind-up gramophone. A whirring sound, then the anthem of Thaelmann's men from the International Brigades during the Spanish Civil War rings out. The old man sings along in an imaginary German. Carvalho eventually pretends to sing along too, waving his arms about in the air.

'Those Germans have always had a genius for symphonies!'

Carvalho nods his head.

Carvalho and Alma push their way through to find two seats near the platform in Tango Amigo. Norman is just drawing his monthly monologue on hidden men to its close.

'I respect all those who are hiding because they've forgotten where Buenos Aires, Argentina, America, and the whole world are, those who only recognize the corner where they were, are and always will be frightened.' He drops his bombastic tone. 'And now at last the hidden Adriana Varela is going to sing for you "Hidden Man"!'

Adriana Varela comes on. This is tango from a woman's heart, sung as if the words of the story had been written just for her:

What's your game? Man without a shadow
What's your game? Lurking in the darkness
Your only light an age-old fear
That shelters you and numbs you.

What's your game? Owner without a dog
What's your game? Master of nothing,
You who have killed your gaze
So you cannot see, so you cannot kill.

Some fear the executioners
Some fear just being afraid
Some fear being an executioner
Some simply want to go on being blind.

Some are running from their mother-in-law
Some are running from a memory
Some are running from their dreams
In order simply to stay sane.

What's your game? Man without a shadow
What's your game? Lurking in darkness
Your only light an age-old fear
That shelters you and numbs you.

What's your game? Owner with no dog
What's your game? Master of nothing
You who have killed your gaze
So you cannot see, so you cannot kill.
But see you will in the shadows
See without fail in the darkness
The most precious of your memories
Which shelters you and numbs you.

If white was black already
When everything was so white

Why leave the hole you're in?
Why go back to the fight?

You've already killed your gaze
So you cannot see, so you cannot kill.

The tango ends, with Adriana exultant and Carvalho stupefied –
the word Alma uses to describe his fascination for the singer. Her
fingers are there to snap him out of his obsession as Adriana leaves the
stage.

'D'you know why you like Adriana so much? Because she sings
tangos, and to you she represents the typical Argentine woman, that
is, a mixture of guilt, sex and melancholy.'

'Guilt, sex and melancholy. That's not bad. I remember a one-
woman show with Cecilia Rosetto I saw in Spain. The monologue of
a poor hysterical woman. Oh, and I still haven't seen Rosetto here.'

Suddenly he gets to his feet.

'Are you leaving already? Trying to find Cecilia Rosetto? Why
don't you just look on the billboard outside?'

'I'm a private detective. We're always looking for a hidden man or
woman. But tonight it's not Raúl or Cecilia I'm after.'

'Have you got a whole collection of them then?'

'It's a never-ending collection.'

Carvalho leaves the club, followed by Alma's gaze. He has to walk
quickly to make up time and reach the outer edges of San Telmo and
enter the strange world of young Mudarra and Canelo, the dog who
loves to eat croquettes. He enters the bar. The waiter looks more
world-weary than ever, and even manages to doze off from time to
time. Mudarra has not appeared, and it's already past midnight.
Carvalho posts himself outside the house, waiting for the doorway to
open as it has done in the past. Half-past twelve. He goes back to the
bar and questions the barman, who's busy stacking chairs.

'What about the boy with the dog? Hasn't he been out tonight?'

'I've no idea. He's not a customer of ours. In fact, I don't reckon
he's a customer anywhere, they're dirt poor. The only cash going into
that place is from his mother's pension. You can imagine what they eat
– less than a cannibal in a fishtank. And that boy's always had

problems with his nerves.'

Carvalho crosses the street to Mudarra's block, and uses his bunch of keys to open the street door. He gropes his way up a staircase dimly lit from the streetlamps. He reaches the apartment. He fondles his keys, doubting, but finally puts them away and rings the bell. After a good while, the door finally opens. Mudarra stares at him, expressionless.

'I came to say hello to your mother. You told me she liked visitors.'

Mudarra steps back to allow Carvalho in. It's a flat as poor as the Latin teacher's, but this one is scrupulously clean. In what functions as a dining-room, living-room and kitchen there is a black and white television that is showing a zigzag of lines, but no programme. Opposite it sits an apparently invalid woman in a wheelchair, rug drawn over her knees. But Carvalho can see blood on her face, and her eyes stare blankly. He pretends not to have noticed.

'So she's asleep. I'm sorry…'

'Yes, asleep at last.'

'What about Canelo?'

Mudarra jerks his head vaguely into the distance.

'He's asleep too.'

Carvalho moves across the room, followed by the young man, who has a slight smile on his face but says nothing more. They go into the bathroom. A bath that in its day must have looked regal, but now stands there like an abandoned elephant that has only three legs instead of four. Inside the bath, water and blood and Canelo's dead body. His head lolls over the side, eyes clouded over and teeth bared as if he were snarling uselessly at death or were waiting for another portion of Carvalho's croquettes.

'He made too much noise. The neighbours were complaining. My mother never did a thing. The whole world is false. Take my mother. She loved me because she needed me, but if she hadn't, she would have confessed she hated me.'

'And the Latin teacher?'

Mudarra doesn't seem in the least surprised by the question.

'He was another clown. A dirty old man, who always left his flies half open. He stank of piss. I can't bear a smell like that.'

'What about Carmen Lavalle?'

'A whore. She went around boasting about how she paid for her studies by dancing, but she would let anyone slobber over her, even that disgusting old man.'

'But not you?'

Mudarra nervously rubs at his lips, as if trying to wipe them clean. Carvalho gives a last look at all the horror in this one small apartment. He lingers on his way out as he passes by the old lady.

'Goodnight, Señora.'

Mudarra follows him and opens the door. Out on the landing, Carvalho turns back to question this tubercular, emotionless prince's face.

'What will you do now?'

'I'll never go out again.'

He shuts the door slowly and carefully. Carvalho hears him shutting the bolts. He starts down the stairs.

Chapter 3

The Malvinas War

They have never seen anything like it in the Calle Florida, and how can it be that something has never been seen in the Calle Florida? A man dressed up as an explorer or a castaway, wearing clothes straight out of a nineteenth-century illustration of *Robinson Crusoe*. Behind him a black man got up in equally outlandish fashion, a Man Friday of childhood memories. The black man even has a parrot on his shoulder, and Robinson is leading a pet llama. Robinson and Friday in all their splendour, with flowing locks down to their shoulders. The white man has a well-established beard, and strides along arrogantly; Friday is the noble savage wary of the big city and its overdressed inhabitants. The passers-by cannot make up their mind whether this is a piece of street theatre, some candid camera television programme, or perhaps a prize competition. As if he were a street singer or one of the people who sold songbooks in villages before the Korean War, Robinson is speaking into a rudimentary loudhailer, little more than a funnel. Friday underscores the message with rhythmical beats on his drum.

'Citizens of the Argentine Republic! In these times of corruption and the collapse of patriotic, social and ethical values, times when man is a wolf to man, and women are the worst she-wolves to other women, it's essential to regenerate mankind and our nation, using Robinson Crusoe and his values as our starting point. We have to become islanders again. We have to rediscover pure solitude, Robinson's lonely grandeur on his island, if we are to reconquer a continent, a world. Which islands? Do we have to imagine them like Daniel Defoe did? No. We have our own islands, the Malvinas. We have to reconquer the Malvinas to save our nation.'

A mixture of applause, whistles, a braying sound here and there, the sarcastic comment of a one-armed man: 'I have to get to the Malvinas again because I left an arm there. I wonder if the Gurkhas kept it for me, if they ate it or stuck it up their arses.'

The sadness of a prematurely old mother: 'I left a son there. I wonder if they kept him for me.'

But Robinson's speech is over, and he heads off for the Harrods stores with Friday, the llama and the parrot in tow. The procession continues until they reach the barber shop, where several clients are roused from their centuries-old slumber to discover this weird apparition. Robinson in a barber's chair. The llama. Friday and his parrot. The barbers stand there, razors in mid-air. The security guards do not know whether to intervene or not. Robinson starts to speak, and the clients listen, their faces half-shaven or their hair half-cut or washed. The manicurists' hands hang in the air above their customers' fingers. Robinson announces: 'When I say the Malvinas, I'm talking about both real and symbolic islands. We have to retake our islands, but we should not think they are only ours. They are a step on the road to universal reason, to the establishment of true ethical values: fraternity, equality and liberty.'

This same quartet: master, slave, llama and parrot, walks up and down outside the Faculty of Letters until it has gathered a group around it. Robinson is making the same speech, as if oblivious to who might be listening: 'We have to conquer the Malvinas in order to reconquer ourselves, to rediscover the innocence that the torturers and their accomplices stole from us. But how can we do that?'

It's Alma who speaks up from an audience which apparently cannot decide whether to be scornful or interested.

'First of all, we have to get there. Swimming. Just like the last time, when those military bastards sent our youngsters swimming to the islands.'

As well as laughter, there's a positive suggestion from one student: 'We could make rafts.'

Robinson folds his arms and looks at them as if he pities the shallowness of their comments. 'Why not swimming? Why not on rafts? My plan is to save the world's ecosystem, so why not bring together the new ecowarriors, ecologists and "liberation theologists" so we can bring about a peaceful, universal invasion of the Malvinas. What would the British do if thousands, millions of pacifists went and took over the Malvinas?'

Again, it's Alma's voice which tries to put history back in its proper place. 'They'd machine-gun them.'

Laughter and more whistling. Alma continues indignantly: 'Where does this prophet think he's from? Are you crazy or just irresponsible? Do you think you can still stir the masses up as if this was an Argentina–Chile football match?'

'Woman, who robbed you of your faith?'

'And you – where were you when Videla and Co. stole it from me?'

Now the applause and whistles tell Alma she should get away, show her disapproval at having been drawn into the trap. She is still angry when she enters the lecture-room, and leaves her books and papers on her desk. She sits and tries to calm down. She looks up. Some students are filing in. One of them is Muriel, who comes to the front and sits in a seat that Alma is glad, was hoping, she would take, because she likes having the girl's bright face close to her. The rest of the class drifts in. They are arguing about what Robinson said. All of a sudden two of them start a fight. Alma shouts: 'That's enough! What's going on?'

But the direct intervention of other students is more effective than the lecturer's voice. One of them tries to explain: 'This one says he'd give his life for the Malvinas, and this other one says the Malvinas aren't even worth...'

'Aren't even worth what?'

'Not even...'

The student starts to blush, but the person who originally used the phrase comes to his rescue: 'It was me. I said the Malvinas aren't even worth the toilet paper I use to wipe my arse with.'

This time the whistling is louder than the applause, and by now Alma has recovered her place, her voice, the reason why she is standing out in front of this classful of students.

'There's still a difference between fantastic literature and eschatology. The Malvinas exist. They are a national reference point – for many, a nationalist one. Anti-imperialist, possibly. I'm not sure if that's a good or a bad thing anymore. But they're there. That clown outside was talking symbolically, and irresponsibly. And romantic adventures cost lives.'

Now it's Muriel who speaks up.

'Excuse me, miss, but why do you call him a clown?'

'How do you see him?'

Muriel swallows hard, but launches herself anyway.

'As a poet. And anyway, I like clowns.'

Alma looks down at Muriel with interest. She restrains herself, and does not pronounce the brilliant repartee that could crush her. Instead, she softens her tone: 'There are dangerous poems, just as there is dangerous music. Clowns may be innocent, but clowns' tricks can be criminal, like the stunt General Galtieri pulled when he started the Falklands War.'

Alma repeats the same phrase to herself: there are dangerous poems, just as there is dangerous music and criminal clowns' tricks, as she is travelling home on the bus, as she walks from the bus stop to her apartment, as she halts in amazement at the spectacle greeting her there: Robinson, Friday, the llama, the parrot. She walks past them, letting drop a commentary in the guise of a question: 'Is it carnival time then?'

Robinson leans towards her with a courteous gesture: 'We wanted to talk to you.'

Alma surveys the four of them.

'You four must be the most picturesque quartet Buenos Aires has ever seen. So now you want me to join in and make a quintet, do you?'

'We simply wanted to talk to you.'

'Well if that's what you want, it has to be all of you, including the llama.'

The quintet piles into the lift, causing stupefaction on the faces of the people waiting on each floor, who stare in disbelief at the ascension of Alma, Robinson, Friday, the llama and the parrot. Once they're all safely installed in her apartment, Alma leaves her books and notes on a table, and invites them to make themselves at home.

'Just like your own cabin. I'm sorry there's no stockade to make you feel more secure.'

Robinson sits on the couch, with Friday next to him. The parrot settles on Friday's shoulder, and the llama starts sniffing at Alma's pot plants. Alma acts the perfect hostess: 'Did you miss this kind of comfort? Would you like something: hard tack, meat jerky? What about you, Mister Robinson? Have you always been Robinson Crusoe?'

'I used to have a different name, but I chose to be Robinson. You used to have a different name, and chose to be called Alma.'

Alma becomes alert. This Robinson is very different from the crazy clown out in the street. He goes on talking calmly: 'I'm a petroleum engineer. That's my trade, and I've worked in the Middle East and in Argentina. Afterwards I trafficked arms, favours, currencies. I laundered money for some of the planet's worst assassins. My driver and favourite butler here can tell you it's all true.'

He points to Friday. Alma looks at him, back at his master, and finally settles on the slave.

'Do you talk like a grateful slave then?'

Friday responds in an effeminate twitter: 'I like crazy women like you, because next to them I seem normal.'

Robinson is very pleased at Friday's retort. So is the parrot, which starts to screech: 'I love gays, I love gays, I love gays.'

The llama is sniffing at Alma's favourite fig plant. She is worried he will eat it, but Robinson focuses her attention back on him: 'Appearances can be deceptive, but they're all we have. I could dress myself up as any kind of guru, so why not Robinson? I took part in the Falklands War, in many other wars, because I sold arms and charged my commission. And my youngest son was killed in the Malvinas. He was an idealist who believed in Videla, in Galtieri, in his father – above all, in his father. He believed in me.'

Friday leans over and kisses him on his cheek, then throws an arm round his shoulder, as if trying to protect him from his own nightmares. Alma tries to be as icy as possible: 'What has all this got to do with me?'

Robinson says, quietly and apparently guilelessly: 'I've heard a lot about you.'

'Who from?'

'Raúl. Raúl Tourón.'

A disciplined darkness in the room. A big television screen is showing a video set in motion by a pair of plump hands full of rings. In the darkness, the Captain's rapacious profile staring at the images, the fat man pausing them, a group of other men looking intently on. The fat man is stopping and starting the video like an image-hunter. The video shows Robinson and Friday in the streets of Buenos Aires. The Captain's voice rings like a stone.

'Is his identity confirmed?'

The fat man replies.

'Confirmed. Joaquín Gálvez, one of the vice-presidents of the bosses' association not so long ago: the Brucker, Ostiz clan and so on. I think he was there until early on in Galtieri's time. In those days, the black man was his driver: it was always a white Rolls-Royce. His youngest boy was killed in the Malvinas.'

The Captain spits: 'I knew him. A buffoon.'

The fat man knows the file by heart.

'Trafficking of arms, of currency, on good terms with the Yankees: he was said to be a close friend of President Reagan before he was president.'

'So now where has he built his Robinson Crusoe cabin?'

'He's kept an old mansion by the river. On the outskirts of the Tigre delta.'

'Is it a ruin?'

'I don't know. Lots of his business affairs are going well. His son Richard Gálvez takes care of them.'

'Why Richard?'

'A homage to ex-president Nixon. Homage from the days when he hadn't yet been president or ex-president, but was Eisenhower's vice-president. That was when Gálvez was linked to a lobby group in California, which backed the young Nixon too.'

The video has come to the point where Robinson is haranguing the university students. The Captain orders the fat man to be quiet and to increase the volume so that he can hear Robinson's voice: 'My plan is to save the world's ecosystem, so why not bring together the new ecowarriors...'

'What an asshole, what an irresponsible clown.'

But suddenly the Captain pauses in his litany of insults, because he spots Muriel in the front row of students.

'It's my daughter! Turn the volume down and pause the image! It's Muriel! That son of a bitch is poisoning her for me. Can you blow up the image? Have you seen who I've seen?'

'Yes, it's Muriel.'

'Blow up the photo of my daughter.'

The girl seems fascinated by what Robinson is saying. The Captain rubs his eyes as if he cannot believe what he is seeing.

'What a mess! What are you doing getting mixed up in this farce? Carry on, carry on.'

Robinson's voice starts up again: 'What would the British do if thousands, millions of pacifists went and took over the Malvinas?'

First they hear the voice: 'They'd machine-gun them.'

Then they see the face: Alma. The Captain leaps out of his seat. 'It had to be, didn't it? It had to be her.'

Alma's angry voice goes on: 'Where does this prophet think he's from? Are you crazy or just irresponsible? Do you think you can still stir the masses up as if this was an Argentina–Chile football match?'

Robinson replies: 'Woman, who robbed you of your faith?'

Alma: 'Where were you when Videla and Co. stole it from me?'

Rivulets of sweat as narrow as his features run down the Captain's cheeks. He barks an order: 'Switch it off!'

The lights are flicked on, and there is silence. The Captain is sitting head in hands; the fat man looks undecided; the rest are paralysed. The Captain suddenly realizes everyone is looking at him.

'Who told you to switch the lights on? All I said was for you to stop the video!'

He's beside himself, so all the others decide it's safer to keep quiet and simply to follow on behind him when he leaves the viewing room and goes down to the car park. The Captain flings himself into his seat at the back, and the fat man slides in the front. He gradually takes control of the situation, and voices his concern out loud to the Captain:

'I told you it was dangerous to send her to university. It's a breeding ground for subversives. Thirty thousand disappear, and another thirty thousand spring up to take their place. Those leftists grow like weeds, and the girl's in the midst of them.'

'I couldn't stop her studying, though; otherwise she'd have ended up a drunken vegetable like my wife.'

'Now we won't even be able to take her there or bring her home, in case we meet that subversive.'

Images from the video are flashing through the Captain's mind. Alma shouting at Robinson: 'Where does this prophet think he's from? Are you crazy or just irresponsible?' He also sees Muriel, staring fascinated at Robinson. Alma and Muriel's faces blend into one. The Captain closes his eyes. The fat man is following the changes in his expression in the rearview mirror.

'I could get rid of her, boss.'

'I could do that myself, but as things stand, we can't touch them. And anyway, the situation is interesting: a mother giving literature classes to a girl who is her daughter, but she doesn't know it. Though Muriel is my daughter really, because I took her away from her mother to save her from a dynasty of subversives. It's a wager. A game.'

'But you can't play Russian roulette with emotions. Let me finish her off, boss. Some day the girl might...'

'For now, keep Robinson and the lecturer in your sights. We still have to find Raúl Tourón. And be very careful, because there could be a very, very unfortunate development. Any meeting between Gálvez, Robinson and Tourón could be very dangerous indeed. I'll worry about my daughter.'

At the far end of the room, Norman is compèring his show: laughter and his voice reach Alma and Pepe, but they cannot work out what he is saying. Perhaps that is because their own conversation is a heated one, so much so that Alma gets up in mid-sentence and walks off to the side to listen to Norman instead.

'Before, if your wife went off with someone else while you were in jail or away at the wars, in the Malvinas for example, it was looked on very, very badly. The more patriotic the war, the worse it made adultery seem. Nowadays, what's badly looked on is if, when you come out of jail or return from the wars, there she is, there the silly cow is waiting for you because no one else wants her. Nowadays they're there waiting because they can't find a lover to rescue them from being a housewife. It's a crisis, an ethical crisis, the corruption of our habits. Are there no good women? Were there ever any good women? Are there any now? Listen to this tango by Adriana Varela, the woman whose voice is more than a voice, it's a whole orchestra. Goyeneche the Polack once said: "I can't stand women who sing tango, the only one who can do it is Adriana Varela."'

The spotlight picks out Adriana and plucks her like a mythic silhouette from the darkness. When the silence, darkness and her mythic silhouette coalesce, the bandoneon thumps out the start of the first verse:

> *A no-good woman has cost you your life*
> *Said your momma, that saint in disguise*
> *A no-good woman has cost you your fortune*
> *Said your poppa, that great teller of lies.*

Silverstein moves away from Adriana's singing to join Pepe and Alma. The pair of them are indignant and silent, and Alma's cheeks are still glowing red with annoyance. Pepe's anger is busily being dissolved in a large glass of whisky.

'What are you talking about?'

Faced by their stubborn silence: 'What were you talking about?'

Carvalho shrugs an expressive shoulder in Alma's direction: 'Alma's made friends with Robinson Crusoe and Man Friday.'

Before Alma can manage to coordinate her indignation into words, Silverstein kneels in front of her, takes one of her hands, and intones: 'All shipwrecked sailors are bound to meet some day.'

Now it's Carvalho's turn to cast a sarcastic eye in Alma's direction: 'She even knows where their island is.'

It's more nose-to-nose than head-to-head as Alma thrusts herself at Carvalho.

'Listen here, you fat Spaniard. Either you shut up or I'm off. It's far more simple than he makes out, Norman. Have you seen that pair who walk along Calle Florida dressed as Robinson Crusoe and Man Friday?'

'I haven't actually seen Buenos Aires for ages. I sleep every morning; in the afternoon I rehearse plays that are very rarely staged even though there must be eighty or ninety "alternative" theatres in Buenos Aires, and then at night I'm working.'

'They're either two mystics or two jokers. It doesn't matter which. They preach a new world order.'

'Just like Carlos Menem.'

'They dress up as Robinson Crusoe and Man Friday. They preach a new world order based on equality. Not that I give a damn about that. They live in an old mansion near the Tigre delta – halfway between San Isidro and Tigre. They give refuge to beggars and the homeless. And Raúl goes there sometimes. Robinson told me he's helping Raúl. Do you think it's so stupid to want to follow that lead? Can't you convince this mule of a shitty Spaniard here that I'm not a lying cretin?'

Carvalho insists, grimly: 'It's a trap.'

'Who'd lay a trap like that? Inspector Pascuali, who's got less imagination than a worker bee? The Captain? Can you see his men dressed up as Robinson Crusoe? The fact is, I've arranged to go to the house, and I'll go with or without you two.'

Silverstein has calmed Carvalho down by putting his arm round his shoulders.

'Of course we'll come with you.'

Carvalho spread his hands in a gesture of helplessness, and smiles as Norman tries to console him. 'No-good women always get what they want from us.'

Which just happens to be what Adriana Varela is singing about at that very moment:

> *A no-good woman has cost you your life*
> *Said your momma, that saint in disguise*
> *A no-good woman has cost you your fortune*
> *Said your poppa, that great teller of lies.*
>
> *Before it was droopy blondes with a scowl*
> *Now, they're skinny redheads in a thousand wigs;*
> *Before they were stuck-up tubs of lard*

Now they're skeletons on the prowl
But be they fat, thin or on the jive
They'll spit in your soup as soon as they arrive.

The Marguerite Gautiers of a thousand poems
Ended their days as tragic consumptives
Or ripped off some poor louse
Who loved them as they slit his throat
Stuck like a prick in a whorehouse.

Now they're Misses from another planet
From Cosmos, from Belgrano or from Misiones
Top models strutting their naked stuff
Designed by some pretentious creep
Who's buying and selling Buenos Aires cheap.

A no-good woman has cost you your life
Said your momma, that saint in disguise
A no-good woman has cost you your fortune
Said your poppa, that great teller of lies.

And me, the no-good woman of this shack
Can tell you I've had it up to here
With all the creeps who ask me to hurt them
To get dear wifey off their back.

Before it was droopy blondes with a scowl
Now they're skinny redheads in a thousand wigs
Before they were stuck-up tubs of lard
Now they're skeletons on the prowl
But be they fat, thin or on the floor
They'll spit in your soup as they go out the door.

As if bowing to the inevitable, the key finds its way into the lock despite the Captain's unusual hesitation. It's only on the third attempt that the door opens, and he is faced with the evidence of his wife, sitting staring at the buzzing television screen, lost in herself, drunk, her eyes desperately wide open in an effort to show that the empty bottle on the table is nothing to do with her, that she hasn't the faintest idea why her husband is saying to her: 'Sometimes I think you don't even get up to have a pee. Is my daughter back?'

Still trying to stand on her imagined dignity and clear-headedness, his wife gestures up the stairs, but when the Captain starts to climb them, she starts to mutter, gradually more and more loudly: 'You son of a bitch! Son of a bitch! Son of a bitch!'

Muriel hears him tapping at her bedroom door and quickly hides what she was writing under a pile of books. Then she says: 'Come in!'

She smiles back at the Captain's affectionate gaze. Gets up and goes over and hugs and kisses him.

'My little grizzly bear...'

'Muriel, Muriel, do you think it's right to call your father a grizzly bear?'

'Well, if he is one, and he's such a nice little one, then yes, it's OK...'

Apparently satisfied with this explanation, the Captain runs his eye over the books filling the bedroom.

'Books, books. Real life is outside books, you know.'

'But it always ends up in books. Everything that's done – good or bad – finds its way into books in the end.'

The Captain sits down. Now it is the posters on the walls that worry him. They are of rock stars like Kurt Cobain who mean nothing to him, Nelson Mandela, travel posters, especially to South Sea islands. He inspects them one by one.

'Travel, yes, that's a good idea. I have to talk to you, Muriel.'

'About Mummy?'

This briefly throws the Captain, but it is Muriel herself who sets him straight.

'I know you don't like talking about her, but she needs help. She's drinking more and more. She's completely cut off. She needs a doctor or a psychiatrist. She says some very odd things.'

'What kind of odd things?'

'She keeps insisting that one day she's going to tell me something that'll completely change our lives.'

The Captain scarcely blinks.

'She's delirious. She either doesn't know or doesn't want to know how to get help, that's all. But anyway, it wasn't your mother I wanted to talk to you about. Listen, Muriel, I heard that today a prophet, a joker, went to your faculty, preaching revolution.'

'Peaceful revolution.'

'There's no such thing. I know you're a healthy girl, with clear ideas, but you seem to be far too much into this abstract world of books: it's useless faced with reality, it's a world of myths and lies. How long is it since you've been to the club, to play tennis or swim? Sport clears away the cobwebs of the mind. I knew a lot of healthy kids from good families whose ideas got corrupted, and they ended up badly, fighting against the society that had created them.'

'The subversives?'

'Most of them weren't bad kids, until they started reading the wrong books, got into bad company, swallowed communist propaganda. The time came when we had to defend ourselves against them, because they wanted to turn Argentina into a Marxist concentration camp.'

'But they disappeared, didn't they? So in the end they built their own concentration camp.'

'They wanted to change our lives for no better reason than a few cents' worth of ideology. But they didn't all disappear. They're still active – hidden, but still at work. Nowadays they wear an ecological flower, or follow liberation theology, or belong to an NGO. And the worst are university professors. A lot of them are ex-guerrilleros who kill now with their words. What are your lecturers like?'

'Some are good, some are bad. But there's one really excellent one, Alma Modotti. I really like her, though I don't think she likes me.'

'How do you know?'

'Vibrations I get. I don't know. Sometimes I think the complete opposite, that she looks at me in a very special way. She demands more of me than of anyone else. But that's good, isn't it? Ever since I was a child, you've told me that teachers and parents should be very demanding, haven't you, my little grizzly bear?'

'Altofini & Carvalho. Partners in Crime.' So they exist, or at least that's what the stencilled words on the frosted glass of the office door say, and when it is opened, there's the back of the head of someone telling his story. He is a man of around fifty, well dressed despite the anxious look on his face, with carefully dyed hair that makes the white of his sideburns stand out all the more.

'So in short, the trouble was a no-good woman.'

Carvalho tries to sum up without too much of a smile, helped by distance and by the desk Alma has bought in a junk rather than antique shop in one of the meaner streets on the fringes of San Telmo.

'Yes, a no-good woman. And I'd like you, or you and your partner, to find her. My son was the least decisive person in the world, easily swayed, too kind-hearted for his own good. I'm sorry I couldn't be with him more. I'm a widower. I work long hours in my undergarment business. The boy grew up on his own, and he didn't always have the most suitable friends. My poor Octavio is a good person, but he's changed since he met that slut. He's become argumentative, aggressive, he always answers me back – although that's a bit difficult, as we hardly ever speak. He tries to avoid me.'

Carvalho sniffs, he can smell roses, and realizes where it is coming from when Don Vito comes in. He's perfumed like a bunch of roses. He's also got a white handkerchief in his top pocket, his cufflinks and his tiepin are gleaming, and so are his gold tooth and his broad smile.

'My associate and the owner of the firm: Don Vito Altofini, with a degree in criminology from the University of Buenos Aires.'

At first Don Vito is a little surprised at his newly acquired academic title, but he quickly accepts it and goes one better.

'A degree? How typically Spanish of you to underplay it. A doctorate, dear boy, a doctorate. And then there's the Master in Criminology and a few other baubles from the MIT.'

'So sorry, Don Vito, a doctorate in criminology, of course. We have before us a heartbreaking case. Because of a no-good woman, this gentleman's son has disappeared.'

Don Vito takes this in solemnly, but can't help murmuring: '"A no-good woman cost him his life…" Everything that's said in tangos is true! Carry on, dear sir, carry on. Only a father whose hair is turning white and who doesn't know where his own children might be can understand what you are going through.'

This speech visibly affects their client. He finds it hard to pick up the thread of his tale.

'Thanks to that no-good woman, my son has become an enemy to me. And one day – I can see it as if it were happening right now – I arrived at my office and found all my closest associates with faces grim as death.'

Carvalho explains to Don Vito.

'Don Leonardo here is a leading manufacturer of fine ladies' lingerie.'

Don Vito puts on a thoughtful, knowledgeable look.

'Ah, a woman's true skin! An important writer once said: a man's most profound attribute is his skin. And I would add: a woman's most profound attribute is her underwear.'

Carvalho invites Don Leonardo to continue.

'Well, it was embezzlement. While I was away, my son used the powers I gave him in such cases to steal a million pesos from our accounts.'

'A million before or after the 1984 devaluation?'

Don Leonardo looks offended by Altofini's estimation of him.

'Would you be worried by the theft of a million 1984 pesos? Good God, that was worth nothing – it was a single note.'

Don Leonardo ignores Don Vito's appreciative whistle, and goes on with his story.

'Now I think – what are a million pesos compared to my son's life? I didn't go to the police, but I asked the Davidson detective agency to find him.'

Altofini lifts a hand to his forehead, then tries to cover his mouth with it, but the words come out regardless: 'A big mistake, if you don't mind me saying so! The Davidsons are incompetent. Whenever they come to a dead end, they always ring me for advice.'

'I only wanted them to find my son before the police, and they did. He was in the Bahamas with that slut, that bloodsucker. I didn't want the money back, I only wanted my son. I swear to you. May I be struck down on the spot if I'm not telling the truth. I told the detectives to let them know they were being watched. That's the worst thing I could have done. She got scared and left him. He felt abandoned, and perhaps thought I despised him. He fled. Nobody knows where he's gone. I'm afraid I'll never see him again.'

At that, he bursts into tears. Don Vito sheds a few tears of his own, and puts his hand on their client's shoulder to comfort him. The distraught father soon recovers his composure.

'Find the woman for me.'

Carvalho rummages among his thoughts and asks what seems most urgent to him: 'What for?'

'I want you to introduce me to her – under a false name, of course. I want to uncover her vicious soul and do her as much harm as possible.'

He is already well out of the office by the time Don Vito asks if it is ethical to find someone just so that a client can kill them.

'That's what he wants, isn't it?'

Carvalho shows him the advance Don Leonardo has given them. Don Vito still looks doubtful, but picks the cheque up and looks at the amount.

'And this is just the advance? Well then, let's look at the case from a professional point of view.'

'My point of view is very direct and simple. We do our duty by finding the woman, and introducing her one way or another to our client. What he does then is his business.'

Don Vito is amazed.

'Why, you took the words right out of my mouth.'

'Besides, I know who the woman is.'

'Already?'

'No, I knew her from before. I had a similar case in Barcelona. Exactly the same, in fact. A father trying to find the no-good woman who had led his son astray. The only difference was that the boy had killed himself. In that case, the woman was called Beatriz, Beatriz Maluendas. But I bet you it's the same one.'

Alma, Carvalho and Silverstein are standing in silence, as if hypnotized by the waters of the river. Silverstein is skimming stones across it, like a child fascinated by the relation between depth and distance. Carvalho turns and surveys the mansion behind a wall smothered in ivy, honeysuckle and wistaria. It's a French-style house that has kept some of its former splendour, and stands out prominently among the other houses of San Isidro, near the Yacht Club. There is a wrought-iron gate topped with Cesar Borgia's slogan: 'Either Caesar or Nothing'. They go over to the gate. Alma rings a bell, but there is no sound. Carvalho pushes the gate open and they step into a garden that had once been carefully tended and still boasts statues, footpaths and hedges that no one has taken the trouble to repair or cut back. But they are not unwelcome intruders – Friday is waiting for them at the front door.

'We blacks open the door better than anyone else.'

'You're very pale for a black man.'

The other man does not respond to Carvalho's sarcasm, but leads them in with mincing, effeminate steps. They follow his swaying backside through the neglected house, empty of furniture, and with marks on the walls where paintings have been saved from the general shipwreck. Other alabaster statues have not been so fortunate. They emerge into a large living-room that looks like a cushion warehouse. Dozens are heaped together so that Robinson can play his flute sitting on top of them, and the rest are scattered about and occupied by the full range of social outcasts: adolescents with AIDS, battered old women with drink-crazed eyes, 'flycatching' madmen. In what was once an elegant fireplace, something is cooking in a large copper pot. Every so often one or other of the beggars goes over and fills his or her bowl. Robinson pauses in his recital: 'Friday, fetch them large, clean cushions will you?'

Friday throws three cushions in front of the new arrivals. Alma and Norman settle on them, but Carvalho remains standing.

'Don't you have a chair?'

'The last one we had is being burnt in the fireplace. We ought to prune the trees in the garden, but who could do that?'

'I don't like sitting on cushions. I prefer to stand up.'

'If you do that, you'll block the flow of your spirit.'

'Standing or seated, my spirit's been blocked since I was born.'

Robinson stares at him, but also notices that Alma is studying the catalogue of human misery in the room and seems disappointed.

'I was hoping – we were hoping – to find Raúl.'

'Raúl knows you're here. He'll come if he wants to. I can give you his message anyway. It's easy enough. He still doesn't know what he wants to do, but he thinks I can help him find out. If I decide to help him find his soul, then he'll find his soul. If I decide to help him find his daughter, then he'll find his daughter. It's all the same to him.'

Robinson gestures to them to follow him. He leads the way up a noble pink marble staircase, followed by Friday, then Alma, Silverstein and Carvalho in the rear. There are hardly any doors left on the first floor.

'We've burnt all the doors. Doors shouldn't exist – they're a bourgeois invention. There were no doors in noble savages' houses.'

A room used as a library. Alma is impressed by the number and quality of books lining the walls. Her words of praise amuse Robinson.

'I bought them by the yard many years ago. It's only now I'm reading them, bit by bit. This is Raúl's favourite spot. Are you comfortable? You'll see that although from the outside the house looks French, inside it's pure English. I'm one of those anglophile Argentines for whom the Malvinas war came as such a wrench. I used to play cricket at the Hurlingham, with tea, toast and jam at five o'clock. The bars I frequented were the Dickens Pub, the John Bull, the Fox Hunt café; I was a subscriber to the *Buenos Aires Herald*. Well there you are, now I've told you my secret, and I've shown you my den, Robinson's cabin. Perhaps it'll help you understand my parable about the Malvinas. Parable or metaphor. Raúl says that really I'm a utopian socialist, and that if I got the chance I'd fill the world with phalansteries.'

'Aren't you scared of being raided?'

Robinson bursts out laughing.

'Alma, my past is my protection. I was so rich that the doors of this church inspire respect in every kind of police. The police respect wealth. I can help Raúl. I think we have common enemies. But what can I do for the three of you?'

Silverstein doesn't wait for the other two.

'Have you ever thought of investing in the theatre?'

'No, it had never occurred to me.'

'Well think about it while you're helping us save Raúl. It's an old story. Half of yesterday's Argentina is after him, and half of today's Argentina has joined in.'

'What do you mean by save?'

Now it's Carvalho's turn to intervene.

'Don't go all metaphysical on us, friend. Saving means you don't get killed before it's your turn to die.'

'Leonardo. Fine lingerie'. If Carvalho ran an underwear business, what would he call it? 'Carvalho. Fine lingerie'. No: 'fine lingerie' was definitely out. He'd probably put an image, something that conjured up the female skin, his fascination with women's petticoats, slips they were called in his childhood, by the women who came to his mother's for fittings and whom he caught furtive glimpses of through a crack in the door of her tiny workshop.

Night falling in a nondescript street lined with stores and small industrial units, with the roar of traffic from the Panamerican highway nearby. Carvalho is waiting for the staff to leave, he glances at several and dismisses them, then concentrates on one slender woman about thirty years old; her legs are even more slender as they run comically after a bus that doesn't want to wait. Carvalho makes sure she misses it.

'Doña Esperanza Goñi?'

The woman takes a step back before eventually admitting that is her name, at the same time realizing she is not going to catch the bus. Carvalho flashes her a badge that seems to impress her.

'Detective Carvalho. Don't be frightened. I'm investigating the disappearance of Don Octavio. It's quite routine, for the insurance companies – but I don't need tell you, do I, you are such an efficient secretary.'

Esperanza walks on sadly, allowing Carvalho to fall in beside her.

'I used to be a secretary. But not any more. I used to work for Don Octavio, but now his father's put me in the filing division. He's downgraded me, because he thinks I knew about his son's double life, and didn't warn him.'

'A boss is always a boss. But I'm sure you were just being loyal to your own boss, Don Octavio; that was your duty, after all.'

'More than my duty, it's what I believe in.'

'As you should. You must know who your boss's companion was. You'll understand my situation too. My company is on the verge of bankruptcy, and there's no filing division to send me to. Either I solve this case or...'

Carvalho makes a slicing gesture across his throat, and stares penetratingly at Esperanza, who is suddenly on his side.

'Help me. I have to find that no-good woman.'

'A no-good woman? But she was charming!'

'Better still. But I have to talk to her. Perhaps you know how I can find her.'

The secret is too much for Esperanza to keep, and Carvalho is sure she'll let it slip before they reach the stop to wait for the next bus.

'We used to speak on the phone. Marta and I. Your no-good woman is called Marta, and has a married woman's surname.'

'Is she married then?'

'She was. To an Aerolineas Argentinas pilot. I'm sorry, I must catch this bus.'

Esperanza's thin legs scuttle off, while Carvalho recalls that Beatriz Maluendas was also married to an Aerolineas Argentinas pilot, and that it is either the same woman or the statistics very much favour Aerolineas Argentinas pilots.

'Don Vito, get over to Ezeiza as quick as you can, and ask for a pilot by the name of Fanchelli. He's our no-good woman's husband.'

The least agile or most exhibitionist passengers have clambered wearily from the plane, wanting to be the last off so that the ones who preceded them will have to wait in the airport bus; the pilots and air hostesses make for the van reserved for the crew. As they get out in front of the main terminal building at Ezeiza, an employee whispers something into the ear of the pilot leading the way. He nods. He is a heavily built, athletic-looking man. He bounds along, bag in hand, to a small office where Don Vito is smiling broadly to welcome him. Taking the initiative, Don Vito grasps his hand and presents him with his card, while explaining out loud: 'Altofini & Carvalho. Partners in Crime.'

The pilot drops his bag on the floor. He holds the card in his right hand, waiting for Don Vito to add something more.

'Señor Fanchelli, it's vitally important for us to find Señora Fanchelli as soon as possible.'

'Who did you say?'

'Your wife, Señora... '

He does not have time to finish the name. The pilot lands him a left hook to the jaw that knocks Don Vito to the ground. Then he drops the business card on top of his prone body. Picks up his bag and leaves the office calmly, even smugly.

Back in the office of Altofini & Carvalho, Partners in Crime, Carvalho and Alma try to restore Don Vito's aching chin.

'He was left-handed.'

'How do you know?'

'Because he hit me with a left without letting go of the card in his right hand. What are you laughing at, Alma? I don't understand why women always think it's funny when a man is humiliated. Careful! Aagh, don't grab it like that Carvalho, remember who it belongs to. I'll look after it – it's part of me, after all. But when you touch it, Alma, it does help.'

Carvalho gives up his attempts at being a medicine man, and apologizes for not having warned Don Vito that Marta, the no-good woman, sometimes calls herself Fanchelli, but has not been married to the pilot for several years now.

'She is from Spain, but began her career in Argentina with Fanchelli and got married to him here. After Fanchelli, she married an importer of luxury shoes. She nibbled at a few other fortunes. Went back to Spain. She tried to make it in the film world, in Spain and Argentina.'

'Did she succeed?'

'No, only a few ermine capes, the odd mink stole, never a whole outfit.'

'It must be her destiny. A no-good woman with an ermine coat. Life is tango. If you knew all that, why didn't you tell me? Where can we find her?'

'In the Bahamas, Santo Domingo, Miami, Las Vegas, New Orleans, always in the best hotels – in the Fontainebleau in Miami, for example. Her latest beau is Pacho Escámez. She's in Buenos Aires, and this evening they're having dinner at Chez Patron.'

'Pacho Escámez? The one on the television?'

'The very same.'

'It's unbelievable. In Spain she hooked a TV producer, now here she's going out with a presenter. She's incredible. She even repeats the same deal and the same situation.'

Carvalho picks up the phone and dials.

'Don Leonardo? We ought to dine together tonight in Puerto Madero. What about Chez Patron? No, it's not simply a whim. It's highly likely you'll see Señora Fanchelli there in person. We can get together a convincing table. You supply the credit card, and I'll do the rest.'

Alma wants to know: 'What's a convincing table?'

'You, Don Vito, me and Don Leonardo.'

Alma sweeps out of the office without so much as a backward glance, and shouts over her shoulder: 'Count me out. I've got my own ideas about what convincing means.'

'But it's Chez Patron. Are you going to miss it? A table without a woman isn't convincing. What if I brought a cousin along?'

Out in the front doorway, Alma looks at her watch. She looks impatiently for a taxi. One appears suspiciously quickly.

'To the university, as fast as you can. I'll be late.'

Alma stares out of the window at flashes of cars and people as they speed by. The taxi sets off towards the university campus, but all of a sudden Alma realizes they are taking a very long route, then she sees they are going down a road she does not recognize. Alma taps on the glass separating her and the driver.

'Are you sure this is the way? I told you, I'm late.'

The driver does not even bother to turn round. Alma decides not to worry, but cannot help it. Then she discovers that the doors are locked and she cannot open them. By now she is not only worried, she is frightened. She starts beating at the car windows, trying to attract the attention of the rare passers-by in this out of the way spot. The taxi speeds on down streets she has never seen before, but which she imagines must be in the Quilmes neighbourhood. It seems an eternity until the car has left the city behind, and is travelling through scrubby woodland. It turns down a track into the leafy darkness. Alma's terror does not prevent her from seeing the driver click a button to release the doors. She pushes open the right-hand side one, and leaps out – only to find herself confronted by two motorcyclists, who seize her by the arms, and stun her with a punch to the jaw.

When she comes to, she can see the tops of the trees and the cloudy sky, but also four motorcyclists and the fat man staring down at her. She has been tied to the ground, legs and arms apart, with four stakes. The fat man starts giving her gentle kicks in her sex with the tip of his shoe. Alma screams with fear or pain. The fat man leans over her. His face looms close to hers.

'Do you know what this is?'

He shows her a cut-throat razor.

'What would you like me to cut off first? Your nipples? Your clitoris? Or perhaps you prefer this.'

A gloved hand thrusts a slimy bundle at her.

'Here, eat this shit. It's cleaner than the shit that comes out of your mouth. It's my shit. Fresh this morning.'

Alma shakes her head desperately and clenches her teeth, but cannot prevent the slimy stuff dropping on to her mouth, her nostrils.

'This is your last warning. Be careful what you say to your students. Be careful with your brainwashing.'

The fat man vanishes. Once again, the tops of the trees. The sky. Alma's tears rolling down her bespattered face, Alma retching, as tears and her stomach refuse to let her vomit.

Pascuali's eyes will not let him believe what they see on the ground. Behind him, Vladimiro is trying not to throw up, and another two policemen await their orders, paralysed by compassion and shame. Alma opens her eyes to let the terror out. Pascuali overcomes his paralysis and kneels down to pull out the stakes and release the woman. His colleagues rush to help him. One of them brings a water can from their car, and Pascuali wets his handkerchief to clean off Alma's face, but there is not enough water or cloth for the job, until Alma herself snatches the can and pours it over her face and head. She is standing sobbing under the streams of water, and instinctively seeks comfort in Pascuali's arms. He does not refuse, and his Adam's apple bobs up and down in silent dismay as she sobs disconsolately against his chest. All at once Alma realizes where she is and pulls brusquely away, as though she were clinging on to something repellent. Her face and Pascuali's confront each other, suspicious and distant once more.

'Who was it?'

'You mean you don't know? Ah, of course...you were just out for a stroll in the woods and found me by pure chance. Is this your favourite wood?'

'We got a phone call. Did you recognize anyone?'

'Use your imagination. Do I really have to tell you who would have the nerve to do something like this? Who still enjoys complete impunity?'

'In today's Argentina, nobody.'

Alma screams hysterically: 'Nobody? You're telling me nobody enjoys impunity? Well I'm telling you I saw that fat man, that bastard who is the Captain's sidekick. And those others who are always on motorbikes. Are you going to arrest him? Shall I come with you?'

Pascuali persuades her to get into the patrol car. Sits with her in the back. Vladimiro is driving, and looks in the rear-view mirror at Alma refusing to say another word and Pascuali equally silent, until Alma suddenly says: 'Drop me off at home, would you?'

'I'm sorry, but I can't take you straight home.'

'I'm in no mood to make a statement.'

'You'll have to make one at some point. But there's something else too.'

Alma has to endure another lengthy trip across Buenos Aires, which finally takes shape when she recognizes the surroundings near Robinson's mansion. Pascuali's car passes through the open garden gate, and pulls up alongside other police cars and an ambulance. Alma's defiled, weary, astonished face peers out of the car window. She is told to get out and follow Pascuali. He walks quickly, far too quickly for her exhausted body, up the pink marble staircase to the first floor, along a corridor to a spacious bedroom, in it a huge double bed, and on the bloody sheets the half-naked body of Robinson. His throat has been slit from ear to ear. The llama is grazing in a far corner. The parrot on its perch calls out now and again: 'I love gays. I love gays.' Alma turns away from the bloody mess, struggling to prevent herself laughing at the parrot's stupid refrain.

'Was it really necessary to bring me here, in the state I'm in?'

'You knew each other. You were here a few days ago – you, your Spaniard and that Jewish clown.'

'What do you so dislike about Norman: the fact that he's a clown, or a Jew?'

Pascuali does not respond, and Alma starts to pace up and down the room.

'Is he the only victim?'

'How many do you want?'

'What about Friday?'

'Friday? Ah yes, Robinson and Man Friday. No, he's not here. D'you think it could be a crime of passion? A black homosexual servant slits the throat of his white homosexual master, who just happens to be Robinson Crusoe.'

The parrot appears to favour Pascuali's theory.

'I love gays. I love gays.'

'Was Raúl here when you came?'

'No. I swear he wasn't. But Robinson, or whatever his name was...'

'His name was Joaquín Gálvez Rocco, and I'm sure that means something to you. He was a member of the oligarchy that you and your friends blackmailed, reviled and sometimes kidnapped, ambushed and murdered, executed or submitted to revolutionary justice – what was the phrase you used?'

Alma stares down at the body as if recognizing it for the first time.

'Gálvez Rocco.'

'Who would benefit from his death?' Pascuali wants to know.

'Mankind as a whole. Gálvez Rocco was one of the oligarchy who supported the military junta, like Ostiz or Pandurgo or Mastrinardi. So don't waste too much time on him. What about me though? Are you going to pick up the fat man?'

'We won't be able to find him. He won't be so foolish as to wait at home for us to come calling. And anyway, we don't know where he lives.'

'What about raiding the Captain's place?'

Pascuali hesitates.

'You don't know where he lives either?'

'That's confidential information, at least as far as I'm concerned. Nobody knows where the Captain lives, no one is sure what his real name is, and that makes it all the more difficult to find the fat man.'

The brass knuckles beating the fat man's face to a pulp seem to be enjoying the cracks, tears, bumps and bruises they have been creating.

His mouth is bleeding; he lifts a hand to it and pulls out a smashed tooth. Like a whipped dog, he looks up in fear and apprehension at his assailant, but is rewarded only with two more blows, one to the spleen, the other to the pit of his stomach. He groans and collapses. Crumpled on the floor, his eyes beg for mercy. It's the Captain who is standing over him. Ice-cool. He kicks at the fallen man, then lifts him by his lapels and in spite of his enormous bulk, pushes him up against a wall, and knees him in the groin.

'Boss, please… !'

'Who asked you to get mixed up in this? Who asked you to kidnap the professor? Who asked you to kill that joker?'

'I didn't kill anyone, I swear to you, boss.'

He's a bloody mess slumped against the wall. He even looks thinner. He takes advantage of the pause in the beating.

'I admit I went too far with the woman, because I was worried about the harm she could do the kid. But I didn't kill anyone, ask them over there.'

The group of motorcyclists stand silently in the dark.

'Who has been killed, boss?'

The Captain starts the video. The screen shows Robinson's body with his throat cut, on the bed.

'It took an expert to do that.'

'But it wasn't me, boss, I swear. I know who it could be. It's well done. But it's not my handiwork. I just wanted to protect the girl.'

'Perhaps this murder will protect me more than her. But then again, if I'm protected, so is she.'

Carvalho restrains the impulse to grab Pascuali by the lapels. Pascuali had been expecting it anyway, and one of his fists has tightened to white knuckles.

'You're the perfect cop, aren't you? This woman has been kidnapped and beaten up, and you keep her here for hours without any reason.'

'She's been looked at. Our medical team has examined her. They've also given her some tablets, and if she's still here, it's for the same reason that you are. You were the last identifiable people to see Robinson and Friday alive.'

'What are we waiting for? Or do you just like keeping us in your police station?'

'We're waiting for Robinson's son. He specifically asked to see you.'

'He wants to see us?'

Pascuali does not deign to answer. He turns his back, condemning them to a further wait that Silverstein fills by stroking Alma's violated face, and Carvalho by cursing the day he came to Buenos Aires and the fact that he feels close to these human and historical wrecks. He stares at the *pietà* Norman and Alma are forming, and repeats his complaints out loud, with a mixture of rancour and compassion.

'You love yourselves too much. You feel too sorry for yourselves.'

'What's the masked Spaniard saying?'

The masked Spaniard does not have the chance to reply. It is obvious someone important has come in. A man of around forty, sportily dressed – sports fashion at its most elegant – passes by, followed by two men who could not be anything else but lawyers. He walks with the assurance of someone who has ten gold credit cards in his pocket, and speaks to the guard on the door as if he were a porter.

'Inspector Pascuali is expecting me. I am Gálvez Aristarain. Tell him I'm here.'

The guard-cum-porter shows him the way to Pascuali's office. The newcomer walks past Carvalho's bedraggled troops, lost in introspection and too weary to react. The office door opens to reveal a frowning Pascuali who listens to the announcement by the guard-butler as he reads the business card he has just been handed.

'Señor Gálvez Aristarain.'

Gálvez Jr. dispenses with the man's services and holds his hand out to the inspector.

'Señor Pascuali?'

Pascuali is drawn to his hand as if by a magnet.

'I'm sorry to be so late, but my plane was not built to cope with real storms. It's a miracle we got here at all. I went to the morgue. And yes, it is my father. Until a couple of years ago, we only communicated through our lawyers, and since he became Robinson Crusoe, we spoke occasionally on the phone.'

Pascuali invites him into the office, but pauses to point out the three people sitting outside.

'Take a look at this bunch: a university professor, a Spanish private detective and a comedian. No, I'm not off my head. These are the three people we know who last saw your father alive. The beggars who lived with him have all vanished. Friday, his butler...'

'Liberto. My father got him to call himself Liberto when he took him on. I can't remember his real name.'

'OK, well, Liberto has disappeared too, and I have to ask you a question that will go no further than just the two of us: did your father and Liberto have relations – I mean...'

'When my father handed over the running of nearly all our businesses to me, he also revealed some family secrets. You don't need to know most of them, but yes, my father told me he had always been bisexual and that from about fifty-five or fifty-six onwards, he had become openly homosexual.'

'We know that Friday – I mean Liberto – is in the final stages of AIDS. We have seen his medical records, and he has only a few months to live. And our three friends out there are people your father met for reasons which I suppose...'

'What reasons?'

'In recent months, the old mansion in San Isidro became a kind of hospice for all the dregs of society. One of them was a "disappeared" person, a crazy guy who is related to or friendly with those three, and I wouldn't be surprised if your father was the link between them. I kept them here to talk to you, to see if it throws up any clues.'

Gálvez Jr. studies the trio, then shakes his head.

'I'm not interested.'

'But you told me...'

'I know what I told you, but now I'm telling you I'm not interested in talking to them.'

Pascuali shrugs his shoulders, and is still shrugging when he releases Carvalho, Alma and Silverstein.

'You can go, but make sure you're available.'

'For you, anytime.'

'Don't rile me, Carvalho. I just might decide to shadow you everywhere, and make your job impossible.'

'After nine-thirty you'll find us in Chez Patron. *Cuisine d'auteur*.'

Pascuali cannot be bothered to get angry. Carvalho smiles smugly, but as soon as the three of them are in the street, Alma explodes with rage.

'So my masked Spaniard is off to have dinner, you are off to your tangos, and after the day I've been through, what do I do? Go home? Wait for them to come and get me again? Wait for them to come and take me off and smear shit all over my face again?'

'It's a professional dinner. You were invited, and declined the offer. D'you want me to leave it to Don Vito and the dragon of a cousin or niece he's bound to bring along?'

'Do you really think I'm in the mood to go out for dinner?'

Silverstein puts a protective arm around her shoulders.

'Come with me. You can lie down for a while in my dressing-room.'

'Then I'll come and fetch you. You can sleep at my place tonight.'

Alma allows the two men to do as they see fit with her life. As they are about to go their separate ways, one of Gálvez's lawyers comes up and hands Carvalho a business card.

'Señor Gálvez Aristarain would be delighted to talk to you about a professional matter.'

Gálvez Aristarain passes by. Carvalho goes up to him.

'Is this your card?'

'Yes.'

'Can't you hand them out yourself? Do you need a lawyer to do it for you?'

The gaggle of lawyers look uneasy, and one of them is on the point of coming over to confront Carvalho. Gálvez Jr. stops him. He takes the card from Carvalho's hand, tears it up, takes another one from his wallet and offers it to the detective.

'Is that better?'

'You are a very polite young man.'

Alma is very proud of Carvalho.

Fiftyish and in full technicolor, Don Vito presents her as his favourite cousin, a well-spoken, even cultured lady, full of class and refinement. Carvalho is on his own, and struggling like a cornered animal with her jollity and Don Vito's courteous blather, when he spots Don Leonardo entering the restaurant. Carvalho introduces everyone.

'Madame Lissieux, ballet teacher and niece of my associate, whom you already know.'

'She's my cousin, not my niece; and she dances modern dance. Just for the record.'

Don Leonardo kisses her hand.

'With someone as charming as yourself, it couldn't be any other kind of dance.'

They all sit down. Don Leonardo is expecting an explanation. Carvalho tips his chin towards an empty table and tells him: 'If my feminine intuition hasn't deserted me, at that table you'll soon see your no-good woman and her current lover, a television presenter who no longer presents very much at all, though she doesn't know that.'

'But I'm not ready for this. I don't know if I'll react properly.'

'Control yourself, and remember what Confucius said: "wait in the doorway of your house for your enemy's body to go by".'

Madame Lissieux corrects Carvalho in a low whisper.

'But that's an Arab proverb.'

'I know, but it impresses clients more if I say it's a proverb by Confucius. I attribute almost everything to him. Even the thoughts of Chairman Menem.'

They get through several courses of their dinner. The table Carvalho pointed out remains empty, and Don Leonardo turns philosophical.

'Is this what they call nouvelle cuisine? It's not my favourite food, though I can afford it. I like Italian canteens, or La Cabaña, or somewhere out on the Costanera. And if you want to eat well while you're doing business, there's nowhere like the Camara de Sociedades Anónimas restaurant on Florida, behind the Cabildo. Where's the woman got to?'

'It's the kind of food you might call *cuisine d'auteur*.'

Madame Lissieux backs him up: 'Yes, like the food Gato Dumas used to cook. I think Robuchon and Girardet have retired. *Cuisine d'auteur*. Like Bergman's cinema.'

Don Vito is proud of his companion's intellectual level.

'Claire, you're indispensable at this kind of interesting meal with interesting people.'

Don Vito and Claire link hands, and Carvalho's eyes go from her well-manicured nails to the restaurant door. In it stands the no-good woman with the presenter Pacho Escámez. She is quite tall, curvaceous, and with a skin so white it looks as though it could have been bathed in the milk that might gush from the abundant fountain her breasts offer beneath a revealing neckline. It is Beatriz, Beatriz Maluendas, but she passes by Carvalho without recognizing him. Beside her, Escámez is done up as a postmodern television hero, and looks so decrepit that Don Vito is tempted into a scatological comment: 'How ancient poor Pacho is. He looks like a mummy from La Recoleta cemetery. But on the screen he still looks good.'

Everything about Escámez speaks of a smooth televisual seducer; everything about the woman suggests someone enjoying life, from the way she walks to their table, the expectancy with which she picks up the menu, and the way she strokes the old man's veined, liver-spotted hand. Don Leonardo's inquisitive eyes follow her every move. Carvalho studies him, and suggests: 'Don't overdo it. They'll see you looking at them.'

'And to think that bitch...'

Don Leonardo takes a deep breath to contain his emotions. Containment and emotions that are far too obvious, thinks Carvalho. For her part, the no-good woman puffs cigarette smoke into Escámez's face. He tries half-heartedly to scold her. Don Leonardo congratulates everyone at his table.

'Thank you for being so efficient. So there she is. The woman who caused my son's downfall.'

Carvalho sighs and confronts Don Leonardo.

'That's nothing more than a metaphor, of course.'

'Why?'

'If I'm not mistaken, your son is thirty, and the lady in question, whose married name in Marta Fanchelli, or Beatriz Maluendas to be more exact, can't be much more than thirty-five. So it's hardly corruption of minors.'

Leonardo gives a sad smile.

'My son may be brilliant in many respects, but when it comes to women he's still wet behind the ears. We're from another generation. We had less protection. I started out selling women's underwear door

to door on credit, and ended up sleeping with half of my clients –
pardon my French, Madame Lissieux. Do you know where my son
has ended up? They tell me he's joined one of those North American
sects that operate in Central America. It was on the cards. What can I
do about it?'

Don Leonardo has been staring so hard at Marta Fanchelli that
she realizes, and rewards him with a smile.

'Did you see how she looked at me?'

Madame Lissieux has the perfect answer.

'That's because you're so good-looking.'

Don Vito squeezes his cousin's arm in a prearranged signal. She
gets up and goes over to the other table. Don Leonardo looks at
Carvalho in alarm, but without saying anything follows the
movements of the modern dancer as she skirts round tables, waiters,
and flambée trays with some style.

'She dances like Burrito Ortega!' Don Vito sighs in awe.

Claire is carrying a small notebook and a tiny gold pen. She
overcomes Pacho's reticence at her sudden approach.

'Excuse me, but I recognized you as soon as you came in. You
have always been and always will be my favourite TV presenter. And
how well I remember the days when you were the male lead in all our
films! Nobody has ever made anything more sublime than *Nostlagia
de organdí* or *La guita ensangrentada* together with Mirta Legrand. Or
was it with the Laplace woman?'

Escámez's purple lips open in a broad smile. He happily picks up
the pen and writes a lengthy dedication. Madame Lissieux turns to
Marta.

'We were saying at my table that you must be the TV channel's
next star. Channel 8, isn't it? Is this your latest discovery, Don Pacho?'

'It could be.'

The old rake kisses Madame Lissieux's hand as she leaves their
table. Meanwhile, Carvalho has leaned towards Don Leonardo, and
the instructions he whispers seem to brook no argument.

'Your name is Alvaro de Retana, you make antique reproductions
and you have several leather goods shops in the best part of town –
the Calles Santa Fe, Paraguay and so on. Take these – they're your
business cards.'

Dumbfounded, Don Leonardo stares down at the cards Carvalho has given him. He reads: 'Alvaro de Retana. Los Macabeos Leather.' An address that means nothing to him.

'I took the liberty of renting a luxury apartment in your name next to the Alvear Palace. Now we'll put you in contact with the no-good lady, and that will be the end of our part of the bargain. Go over to their table with Madame Lissieux – she'll keep Escámez busy, and you take advantage to slip one of your cards to the lady. Anything that happens after that is your entire responsibility. Including payment of our fees.'

Leonardo is unsure of whether to protest or to do as he is told. Madame Lissieux does not give him the chance to make up his mind. She gets up and marches off, with Don Leonardo in her wake. Carvalho and Don Vito watch to see if things turn out as planned. Madame Lissieux and Don Leonardo greet the couple. Pacho listens intently to Madame Lissieux, and Don Leonardo strikes up a conversation with the woman. Something passes from his hand to hers.

Covering his lips with his hand, Don Vito whispers to Carvalho: 'We could be the accomplices in a crime.'

'Or of the start of a great friendship.'

'With the woman who cost his son his life?'

'Isn't there a Greek tragedy with a plot like that?'

Don Vito cannot get over Madame Lissieux's expertise.

'How well Claire does it! I thought I might get her a present. When we get paid, that is. Not to bribe her, of course. Just as a thank you. Something nice.'

Carvalho is looking expectantly at the light aeroplanes being made ready for flight, as if he would love to go up in one. He turns when he realizes someone is standing behind him. It is Gálvez Jr. and his lawyers. They shake hands politely and the financier takes him to one side.

'I'm sorry this is so rushed, but at the moment I'm so busy, I'm like a piece of paper being blown in the wind. I want you to carry out a parallel investigation to the police's, and to keep me informed of what they have found out. I didn't like the sound of that AIDS business at all. If Friday has got AIDS, it could infect us all, starting with my father's reputation. Business nowadays depends on appearance, on having a good image. If you pour petrol on something, it becomes a huge blaze. As soon as the petrol is finished, the blaze dies down.'

'I'm afraid I'm not very good with metaphors. I don't understand.'

'Whether or not you understand my metaphors, you have understood that I am employing you, haven't you? I'll leave one of my lawyers with you to sort out the details. Money is no problem.'

He walks towards a beautiful private jet, accompanied by two of his entourage; the remaining lawyer stays at Carvalho's side.

'Don't you get to go up for a trip in the biplane?'

'It's not a biplane, and anyway, you and I have to talk money.'

'And I have to warn you that I want to loop the loop.'

The man stares at him uncomprehendingly.

'Neither of us is very good at metaphors, are we? I want loads of money, dough, bread, bakshish!'

Carvalho holds out the cheque for Don Vito to inspect, seated in what is normally Carvalho's chair.

'Loads of money! But lots of work too. First the case of the no-good woman. Now Robinson Crusoe.'

'We'll need an assistant.'

'That would make us a multinational or a lawyers' or architects' practice. I don't like multinationals.'

'Well then, let's distribute the tasks. We need to get organized.'

'You're a specialist in no-good women. I'll start the search for Man Friday.'

'And for your cousin. Don't forget your cousin.'

Annoyed that his suggestion was rejected out of hand, Don Vito makes the sign of the cuckold behind Carvalho's retreating back. Carvalho chooses not to notice, but he cannot choose to ignore the sudden appearance of Pascuali, who looms up as soon as he hits the street. Carvalho decides to walk on and leave the next move to the inspector. Pascuali falls in alongside him, with his favourite team a couple of yards behind.

'There's no denying you're a hard worker.'

'And you seem like a cop who's paid by results. You're a fine example of public sector productivity. Has Menem given you your worker's medal yet? Are you paid commission for each arrest?'

'Are you learning to fly? You were seen at the airport yesterday with Richard Gálvez. Don't get in my way again, will you?'

'It's a logical progression. The Robinson case leads on to Raúl. As soon as I can find Raúl and convince him to come back to Spain with me, it's goodnight Buenos Aires. You'll be free of me. What I don't understand is why it's me who gets up your nose so much, and not the Captain. He's the one who is really getting in your way. Who's in charge among you lot? You when you're in front of the TV cameras, or him from the sewers?'

'Don't you start with ethical considerations at this stage of the proceedings. I'm here to offer you a deal that's always been possible: Friday for Raúl. If you find Raúl, I'll open the door wide for you to take him wherever on earth you choose, the further the better; but as far as the Gálvez–Robinson case goes, I want you to tell me immediately if you find anything out.'

'Why all this interest in a Robinson Crusoe? It could have been a simple case of arteriosclerosis. Or it could have been Friday or a beggar who slit his throat...'

'To show you my good will in this, I'll tell you something you probably don't know. Robinson was a blackmailer.'

This does not stop Carvalho in his tracks, but Pascuali notes with satisfaction that it does slow him down.

'A blackmailer out of his love for humanity, of course. He was threatening the big names in finance, industry and business. He wanted to impose a revolutionary tax to win back the Malvinas, to set up his phalansteries, to redeem humanity. He knew all the slimeballs this country's oligarchy has produced in the last thirty years. Now do you understand why he got his throat slit?'

'Oligarchy. My, my, Pascuali. You sound like a policeman who believes in the existence of the class war.'

'I'm not in favour of AIDS, but AIDS exists whether I like it or not.'

The detective speeds up again, to see if Pascuali will follow him, but the inspector drops back, and signals to a nearby car to follow Carvalho.

This must be the ward for the sickest of the sick, so Carvalho finds himself tiptoeing as if to avoid having to feel too much pity. The doctor he is following appears to be sleepwalking, but his sleepiness is rapidly transformed into nervous energy once he is on his own with Carvalho in the hospital office.

'I must warn you that my friendship with Raúl Tourón and his wife Berta, may she rest in peace, was never political. And I have no intention of giving away any professional secrets by talking to you.'

'This is a case of life and death. Friday – or rather, Liberto, who used to be the Gálvez family butler – is in the terminal phase of AIDS, isn't he?'

'Yes, and as far as his medical condition goes, I won't tell you anything more.'

'He needs a treatment, a treatment you used to give him, and which he hasn't been to see you for in several days now.'

'Correct, and I'm surprised, although I do read the newspapers and watch TV from time to time. I thought it must have something to do with the murder of Señor Gálvez – of Robinson.'

'I admire your powers of deduction.'

'Science uses both deduction and induction.'

'Don't be so inflexible, my friend. From the moment you give me some idea as to where I might find Friday, there'll be no more need for this conversation. And if finding Friday means finding Raúl too, don't worry. You knew him from your student days. But I'm his cousin. And his sister-in-law, Alma, has already spoken to you. She thinks it's a good idea.'

'All I know is that Liberto had a friend over in Calle Bolivar. Behind Lezama park. Do you know where I mean?'

'A very close friend?'

'Very close.'

Carvalho simply shrugs and so, to get him off his back, the doctor consults a file and writes down an address and hands it to him.

'This conversation never happened.'

There are too many people around, so just in case, Carvalho tells the taxi-driver to pull over, and he walks the last few yards towards the crush of police cars, cops directing the traffic away and onlookers.

He joins the crowd, trying to push his way through to the front. When he succeeds, his gaze follows that of all the others: up at the windows of an apartment block where the police can be seen moving around inside as if deliberately putting on a show for the spectators. Pascuali is standing at one of the windows, listening to the forensic surgeon's explanations or looking over at the bed where the dead body of Friday, in his underpants, has still got the *atrezzo* of an overdose: rubber tubing round the arm, a syringe dangling from a vein. The surgeon removes it with gloved hands. To do so, he has had to step over another body on the floor: that of a youth who looks as if he is merely asleep, one forearm draped over his eyes.

'An overdose? The one on the floor as well?'

The forensic expert nods, and Pascuali punches the air with frustration.

'Take away everything you can, and then search the room thoroughly – under the paint on the walls if necessary.'

He goes back to the window, and the expression on his face changes abruptly. Among the crowd outside he can make out Carvalho, and he also sees another old acquaintance pushing his way through towards the detective – Raúl. Although he does not yet know it, Carvalho will soon meet Raúl again. Pascuali takes a walkie-talkie out of his pocket.

'Attention cars four and five. Take up position by the electrical goods shop on the corner. But don't let anyone see you. Our friend Carvalho and Raúl Tourón are standing close to the shop. Surround them without being seen. I repeat. Arrest them before I get there – I'm on my way now.'

He signs off and runs out of the room. Raúl meanwhile has moved alongside Carvalho, made himself known to him, and urged him to talk without looking at him, as if they were simply two more curious onlookers.

'I found the bodies before the police. I've been hidden here for several nights.'

'So what are you showing yourself in public for?'

'I didn't have time to get away. Anyway, I was curious. Friday said he had something to give me from Gálvez.'

But Carvalho has not taken his eyes off the parked patrol cars. He notices their doors opening, and a suspiciously large number of

*

policemen seem suddenly to want to take a stroll, a stroll in their direction.

'If you want to be arrested, and for Pascuali to keep his bargain and send you to Spain with me, stay where you are. Otherwise, make a run for it, because the cops are closing in.'

Raúl once again cowers like an animal at bay, then runs off as fast as fear can carry him. The police cannot understand why Carvalho just stands there passively while the other man is fleeing, and fan out too late to catch the fugitive. They reach Carvalho just as he is lighting a Rey del Mundo cigar in the open air, but with the relaxed gestures of an after-dinner smoker. They do not like this, and whip out their pistols with almost sexual excitement: 'Stop! Don't move!' one of them shouts hysterically, while a cautious circle gradually forms around this solitary smoker, who apparently has not realized the seriousness of what is going on. Pascuali comes panting up, and pushes his way through the circle. He stands in front of Carvalho, and then all at once reaches out, snatches the cigar from the detective's lips, throws it to the ground and tramples on it.

Hardened criminals look the same everywhere in the world, just like fools and madmen. Carvalho is with seven or eight of them, all much as might be expected, except for one tall half-blind man. He has realized Carvalho is not another old lag, and asks him for a light.

'The corrupt and corrupting state no longer distinguishes between virtue and vice, it simply puts a limit on them. My father once wrote: "There will never be a door. You are inside, and the fortress is as big as the universe."'

'Was your father a prison warder?'

The other man's patience must have been tried so often, and yet he is polite when he replies: 'My father was Jorge Luis Borges. The flesh and blood of literature.' He hands Carvalho a card, and presents himself. 'I am Jorge Luis Borges' natural son.'

He takes a notebook out of his jacket pocket and gives it to Carvalho.

'In Praise of Darkness, one of my father's best books. I copied it out by hand. I know it by heart. Do you love books?'

'So much so they burn in my hands.'

'What a fine image! It's true, books are like flames that sprout from our hands.'

'In my case, it's quite literally true. I burn them.'

But he has already spotted Pascuali on the other side of the bars. A jailer opens the cell door. Pascuali motions to Carvalho to come out, then sets off down the corridor. Carvalho follows him, but not before he waves farewell to Borges' son, who thanks him for it by starting to recite, in a strong, deep, serene voice:

> *And has neither obverse or reverse*
> *nor circling wall nor secret centre.*
> *Hope not that the straitness of your path*
> *that stubbornly branches off in two,*
> *and stubbornly branches off in two,*
> *will have an end. Your fate is ironbound.*

Pascuali has turned round and observes the scene. He comments drily: 'There are more lunatics outside the asylums than in them.'

'Have you arrested him for being mad?'

'For criminal impersonation.'

'But isn't he Borges' natural son?'

'Supernatural more like. And you can go.'

By now they're out in the doorway of the police station, and Carvalho has no reason to refuse the offer. But Pascuali holds him back a few seconds more.

'You broke our pact. You helped Raúl escape, after we had agreed I would help him leave the country without problems. You're crazy. Not even I can keep everything in the Raúl Tourón case under control, and you go and get mixed up in Robinson Gálvez's death too. And that's an even dirtier business. Did you know Robinson Gálvez was a shark who was blackmailing his former pals in the aquarium to get funds to take over the Malvinas? Do you know who his pals are? Even bigger sharks!'

And as if Carvalho were another shark, Pascuali heaves him out of the station with such force he almost falls down the front steps. Without turning round, Carvalho takes a deep breath and spits out the words, loud enough for the inspector to hear: 'You bastard!'

He desperately needs to get back to his apartment, to get in touch with Barcelona and Biscuter, to cook a meal perhaps – but if only he knew what or who for? He phones Alma from a public phone box, but she is evasive. When he reaches his apartment, he goes straight to the kitchen and considers the possibilities. He remembers a recipe he has seen in a magazine supplement, said to be from a Catalan woman in Sant Pol de Mar. *Pilota catalana*, on a bed of vegetables and squid slices. First mix minced pork with egg, breadcrumbs, garlic, parsley, sprinkle flour on it, and fry. Drain off the fat, and place the meatballs on a bed of spinach and slices of squid cut like thin pasta. A vinaigrette sauce with a touch of sherry vinegar and a little soy sauce.

'Is that you, Biscuter? I'm sorry, I haven't had a moment.'

Biscuter has a long list of complaints and needs, but yes, yes, the bank transfer has come through, and everything is in order for Carvalho's return.

'I'll prepare you a meal that'll have you licking your lips, boss. *Pilota catalana*, it's called, it's meatballs on a bed of vegetables with strips of squid. I got the recipe out of a magazine, it's by a woman from a place near here called Ruscalleda.'

The world's a small place.

'It couldn't be from anywhere else.'

'Are you surprised at the recipe?'

'Who wouldn't be?'

'My cooking is getting more sophisticated. When will you be back, boss? I've got news from Charo you might like to hear. I think she's coming back too.'

Carvalho need not reply, but Biscuter insists.

'What d'you make of that?'

'Good.'

'D'you know what she said when I called her? She said you were the love of her life.'

'Of all her life?'

'She didn't make that clear.'

Carvalho struggles to free himself more from Charo than from Biscuter, and returns to his cooking until he is interrupted by the door bell. He takes a revolver wrapped in a plastic sheet out of a jar of Italian pasta. He sticks it in his waistband under his apron. Then he goes to the door and peers through the spyhole. He opens the door to an Alma who is every bit as exhausted as he is.

'I want to eat something warm and comforting. I'm at such a low ebb, I don't think the tide is ever going to turn.'

Carvalho ushers her in, and describes the first course.

'But that's architecture, not cookery.'

'I have several other alternatives already prepared: onion tortilla with cod; sweet and sour lamb with herbes de Provence, and figs in syrup.

Alma cannot believe her ears. Carvalho is offended by her disbelief, and strides off to the kitchen to show her all the food is real.

'Incredible. And did you cook all that to eat on your own?'

'I was depressed, and anyway, I always keep the leftovers. In Spain I used to cook for a neighbour, Fuster, who's a friend. Here in Buenos Aires when I cook I fill the place with imaginary guests. Sometimes I have to throw whole casseroles of food that's taken me hours to prepare straight down the toilet.'

Now they have finished eating, and Alma allows herself to be drawn into Carvalho's silence; allows him to look longingly at her, to lightly caress her face and to play with the curls of her hair. She leans towards him, smiling and her body welcoming – but at that very moment the door bell rings, and Carvalho glances down at his watch and exclaims: 'What a stupid son of a bitch I am!'

Alma is taken aback.

'Don't worry. It's Don Vito. I'd forgotten I asked him to come.'

Alma pleads with her eyes for him not to go to the door.

'I'll get rid of him as quickly as I can. Stay out of sight.'

Don Vito slumps into the office armchair, exhausted by the tango that is his life.

'Your call made the love around me evaporate.'

'You should wear Fahrenheit by Yves Saint-Laurent. Nothing makes that evaporate. But now you're headed for the high spot of your career. You have to tail a cop, our friend Pascuali.'

'Are you crazy? So I get in a taxi and I tell the driver: follow that car, that police car over there?'

'Hire someone by the day – take on someone you trust, and pay them a fee.'

Don Vito's face lights up.

'Madame Lissieux! She was a women's rally driver champion in Europe!'

'So I'm giving you back the perfume of love. I need the complete list of all the people Pascuali visits in the next twenty-four hours. He's investigating men who are too powerful for him to summon to the station. I want to know who they are.'

Alma is waiting for him naked between the sheets, but she still has a few questions.

'The hunter hunted. But why Pascuali?'

'I've been hired by Robinson's son, a yuppie who takes a plane to go and have a cocktail in Mar del Plata and returns for a game of polo in Buenos Aires. Friday turned up, dead from an overdose. Raúl had been there. Sometimes he stayed in an apartment a young lover of Friday's had, behind Lezama park. He turned up one day and found two corpses. Overdoses.'

'The Captain.'

'I don't know. Robinson was busy blackmailing all his rich pals to get money to retake the Malvinas. I'm guessing Pascuali has a list of his victims, and will go and interview them in their homes. He won't bring them in to the station – class still counts. Vito will tail Pascuali, and within two days we'll have a list of all the offended oligarchs. I want to have a few tricks up my sleeve, because I reckon young Gálvez is playing a game of his own.'

'Robinson was a terrorist.'

'This Robinson, yes. The original Robinson Crusoe was the perfect example of bourgeois individualism and the providential philosophy of modern capitalism.'

Alma is so surprised at this comment that she sits up, and her as yet unaroused nipples pop out of the sheets.

'But that's what I say in my lectures!'

'Good for you. And after all these questions, are you still naked?'

'What do you think?'

As Carvalho embraces her bare body, he can feel it bristling all over with electricity; he buries his mouth into the fair curls of her pearly opening. He needed the taste of sex like an exile needs to kiss the ground of his home country on return. Alma does not say a word, does not groan, but her eyes go soft as he penetrates her, and her hands grip his back in recognition and acceptance at each thrust. Then the love-making – Carvalho is scared it is love – leaves them silent and inward-looking. Still half-naked, Alma seems sad as she sits in front of the logs of the fire and watches Carvalho tearing up a book and preparing to place the pages under a pyramid of wood for lighting.

'My God! Every time I see you, you're about to burn a book. Would you like the address of a psychiatrist?'

Ignoring her, Carvalho sets fire to the book.

'Which one was it today?'

'By Borges. *In Praise of Darkness*, one of his best books, according to his son. Borges' son, I mean.'

'Borges' son? Borges never had any children. They say he died a virgin.'

'He introduced himself as Jorge Luis Borges' natural son, and he looked a lot like him.'

'Where was this?'

'In Pascuali's cells. I forgot to tell you he kept me in there for a few hours. He was in two minds whether to crush a Cuban cigar of mine or to arrest me, so in the end he just trod on my cigar and threw me in the cells for a few hours. I was glancing at that book I'm burning now, and it says somewhere that we can never get out of the labyrinth. I already told you that ever since I was a child, I feel I'll never find my way home…'

'You're even sadder than I am, Pepe. Kiss me again, but not like before. Kiss me like an impotent lover.'

'Having to pretend twice so quickly at my age! First pretending to be potent, now impotent!'

But he does kiss her like an impotent lover, then moves away from her and busies himself with the fire.

In his best down-at-heel style, Don Vito is waiting in his car. He looks down at his watch too often. Then a taxi pulls up a few yards away. A strange being of indeterminate sex, body and face gets out. Pays off the taxi-driver through the window. Then turns towards him. It's Madame Lissieux, disguised as a women's rally driver champion of the 1940s, down to the goggles and gaiters. She waves effusively at Don Vito.

'Take a look at that! It's Fangio!'

But his expression changes when he gets out of the car and offers her the driving seat, after first kissing her hand in a gesture from a brilliantined gentleman to a somewhat ambiguous racing driver.

'You always rise to the occasion.'

'Who are we following? A dangerous criminal?'

'The most dangerous of all. The state.'

Despite the goggles, Madame Lissieux's professional concentration is obvious as she pulls out, ready to confront her fate.

'She drove as if life depended on it – my life more than hers; and overtook cars all the time so that Pascuali wouldn't get away from us. My only fear was Pascuali would notice and arrest us.'

Carvalho enjoys Buenos Aires cafés, where alongside the wooden panels and polished metal you can enjoy a space where time is on your side. Don Vito is playing the part of a man exhausted after an impossible day. He loosens his tie, and undoes the top button of his shirt.

'Have you any idea what it's like to follow a cop in a car driven by someone who is a cross between Juan Manuel Fangio and the Man in the Mask? And someone who, to top it all, is a woman: Madame Lissieux? Have you ever sat alongside a woman who crosses Libertador Avenue and Callao at a hundred and twenty kilometres an hour? Can you imagine what it was like when a cop came alongside at a traffic light to tell us we were speeding, and Madame Lissieux said: "Don't hold us up, my good man, we're following that police car"?'

'And he arrested you?'

'On the contrary. He cleared the traffic for us to get on with the chase.'

'Enough of words. Were you successful?'

With a theatrical gesture Don Vito throws a sheet of paper on to the table.

'It reads like the Argentine rich men's football team, without Maradona. These people have more money than Fort Knox.'

Carvalho puts the piece of paper in his pocket. Don Vito has recovered sufficient breath to start up a conversation with a young lady who is offering him the price for a night, without bed and board.

'That was not the reason for my approaching you. I simply wished to have the heady pleasure of sniffing your bosom and your armpits.'

'Dirty old man!'

Carvalho leaves Don Vito to his fate, and asks the taxi-driver to take him to the Polo Club.

'The one at Palermo, you mean?'

'It's called the Hurlingham Club.'

'Oh, right, the Hurlingham. That's where the seriously loaded people go.'

In the darkness under floodlights, their lordships are engaged in the inexplicable pursuit of a white ball. A sport of gentlemen, Carvalho reflects, watching as they finish their last chukkas. He picks out Gálvez Jr. from the other players when he dismounts and with a tired but reluctant gesture hands over the pony reins to a groom. He has spotted Carvalho at the rail, and waves in acknowledgement. As he comes over, he takes off his gloves.

'I'm going to have a shower. Have what you like to drink. Tell them you're with me – they don't like strangers.'

The barman stares icily at Carvalho – he has obviously decided he is not worthy to be in such an exclusive club. But before he can offend him with a far too educated sneer, Carvalho defends himself: 'Señor Gálvez asked me to wait for him here.'

Although Carvalho's attire does not permit him to judge just what level of intercourse he may have with the powerful Gálvez Jr., the barman decides it is sufficiently decent for him to be accepted into the sanctum.

'Would you care for something to drink, sir?'

'I'd like four fingers of your best whisky, with no ice.'

'Of the most expensive?'

'Of the best.'

'That's very subjective.'

'That's your problem.'

The barman bows and goes off. Carvalho feels a touch of Stockholm syndrome coming on as he examines with affection the stock types filling the room. Well-kept bodies in sporty clothes, but all of them slightly unreal, as if they were extras in a lifestyle shoot strangely out of date in the final years of the century. Then the head waiter comes over to his table with a bottle of whisky and a glass on a tray.

'The waiter told me your request, and I took it upon myself to interpret it. At this time of day, my choice would be a Glenmorangie, a single malt that is equally good before a meal or after. I've chosen this twenty-year-old malt, and allow me to remind you that if you add ice it will gain in bouquet but lose its smoothness on the throat. As you well know, whisky is not like wine, all of whose taste is on the palate and the tongue. Whisky is best judged in the throat.'

Carvalho accepts his choice. The head waiter pours five fingers of whisky, and the glass, bottle and tray are left at his disposition. He picks up the glass, sniffs at the contents the regulation three times, each time swirling the liquid around a little more in the glass, then takes a sip. His throat is well pleased. He nods at the head waiter.

'Excellent, Señor...'

'Loroño, at your service.'

'In my next reincarnation I'll employ you as my sommelier for whiskies.'

'Forgive my curiosity, but as what would you like to be reincarnated?'

'As a member of this club.'

The arrival of an impeccably dressed Gálvez Jr. cuts short the head waiter's reply.

'Would Señor Gálvez like his usual?'

Gálvez nods. Looks at his watch.

'Is your plane waiting?'

'No. I understand I must look like a stereotype. A plane of my own, and polo. Well, my father brought me up to have a plane and to play polo, to be the perfect English yuppie. In spite of everything, my father was an Anglophile, one of those who thought Argentina's problems began when we refused to become an English colony. I'm in charge of thirty businesses throughout the length and breadth of this country.'

'Real yuppies don't know that's what they are.'

'I've read a little, not much. Enough to know that it's not good to be a yuppie – to look like one, anyway.'

Carvalho gives him Don Vito's piece of paper.

'Whether he was senile or lucid, these are the people your father was blackmailing. He wanted money to retake the Malvinas peacefully and to fill the world with phalansteries.'

As he reads each name, Gálvez Jr. gives a low whistle. 'My God, my God, my God...' When he has finished, he looks up, perplexed: 'Had he gone completely mad? He wasn't even blackmailing any middle-of-the-road people. They're all the hardest cases you can find.'

'They must have been the ones he had the most damaging information on.'

'Well, the effect was devastating. Any one of them could have paid for his murder.'

'Does it happen often?'

'It happens. They're dangerous people. You can't take on the mafias – especially the public one. The public mafia – the people the subversives called the oligarchy – is by far the deadliest. Are there any copies of this list?'

'Pascuali has been to see them all.'

Carvalho can almost hear the yuppie's brain whirring as he thinks about this, and quickly comes to a conclusion.

'I'm going to have to do something similar. I'll go straight to the top. I'll call on Ostiz and Maetzu. I think they should know I'm aware of everything.'

The head waiter brings him his usual drink.

'Your mixed fruit juice, sir.'

Gálvez sees how Carvalho reacts to this, and laughs. 'A very Robinson drink. When I'm old, when I'm an adult, I want to be Robinson Crusoe.'

But business is business and, after a long, healthy and pleasurable drink, which Carvalho compensates with another unhealthy but no less pleasurable one, Gálvez tells rather than asks him: 'I want you to come with me to see Ostiz and Maetzu.'

A ray of sunlight picks out bronze glints in Alma's curls. Muriel stares intrigued at the gleams, as if tongues of the flame of knowledge were really sprouting from the teacher's head as she concludes her lecture.

'So Robinson is not an innocent myth, but rather an attempt to explain man's position in the world as that of an individual who can dominate it thanks to his experience, his intelligence and the support of Providence. Defoe sets out the philosophy of the ascendant, all-conquering bourgeoisie, and as such his proposal in Robinson is more realist than that of Rousseau's Emile. Rousseau's world contains the seeds of revolt and anarchist rebellion. Contemporary liberalism has reacted against the father of liberalism and denies the possibility of man as a noble savage influenced by his social environment. What's happened to didactic literature like this? What writer of today would dare propose a Robinson, an Emile, a Werther or an Ivan Karamazov to his readers? To offer role models like them, you need to have hope, even if it is an angst-ridden hope. Sometimes, hope may be a theological virtue. At others it can be just a historical one, or even a biological necessity. Or in the case of someone like Bloch, his non-religious hope is a bio-historical necessity, which conceives the future like a religion.'

She draws to an end, and the students start to leave. Alma picks up her things as well. She looks up, and sees Muriel standing by her desk.

'Excuse me.'

'Of course.'

'I read Robinson like you told us – or recommended us – to do, but my reading of it was different, an ecological one.'

'You could also read Robinson as an apology for your average Argentine, free to cook a barbecue in his weekend place. No, I'm only joking. But any great work of literature is open to many different interpretations. The reader is always freer than the author, and has centuries to impose his way of seeing it.'

Muriel whispers 'Thanks' and makes to leave. Alma watches her go. Her eyes show her professional enthusiasm, but there is something else in her voice when she calls out: 'Muriel.'

She is surprised her professor even remembers her name.

'I really like the way you participate in the class, and the work you do. You write very well, in the papers you hand in, at least.'

The young girl's voice fails her: she's so happy she feels like crying. Eventually she manages to stammer out: 'That's because I like your classes so much.'

'Where do you get your interest from? Does your family have anything to do with it?'

'No. Nothing. My father is a businessman, and my mother isn't interested in the least.'

'In the vacation I'd like to get together a literary workshop, nothing too serious, just for fun. Just a few of the students to write, discuss, look at texts. Would you like to join in?'

'Of course!' Muriel almost shouts.

Alma is pleased at this, and suggests they leave together. As they are going down the staircase, she has a sudden flashback and sees Robinson haranguing the students a few days earlier.

'D'you remember the prophet who was here the other day? Robinson?'

Muriel remembers the argument between her and the teacher, and says cautiously: 'Perhaps I didn't understand what he was saying.'

'That wasn't why I mentioned him. There's nothing left of any of them: Robinson is dead, Friday is dead, and I wonder...'

Muriel is astonished.

'Dead?'

'Yes, and I can't help wondering: what happened to the parrot? And the llama? What's become of the llama? Especially her, the poor thing.'

Don Vito has been telling Carvalho how his previous night's love-making went: 'She wasn't a whore, Carvalho. She was simply a merry widow.'

He senses that Carvalho is not in the mood, and has it proved when the Spaniard thrusts a *Clarín* newspaper in front of his face. The headline reads:

'Pacho Escámez murdered.
Police on the trail of the WHITE LADY.'

'Well, poor old Pacho. But he had a good life, there's no denying that. What have you or I got to do with his tragic end?'

'Try to put the widow's breasts out of your mind for a moment, and read the first few lines of the article at least. I've underlined them.'

'A blow to the back of the head has
ended the life of one of Argentine
television's best-known presenters. The
police are searching for this outstanding
professional's last regular companion,
known only by the initials M.F.M., said to
be a blonde woman with a marble-
white skin. The case has already been
given a name: The Producer and the
White Lady.'

'The no-good woman!'

'This edition of *Clarín* is five days old, which means either we
never read the papers, or we only read what we want to.'

'They're always full of corruption and sport. Look at this:
Maradona calls all Argentine politicians shits and says he only trusts
Fidel Castro.'

'I was sent the newspaper by an old client of ours: Don Leonardo.
He wants us to go and see him.'

The news has hit Don Leonardo hard. He's sporting several days'
worth of stubble, there's a glass in front of him that's obviously been
filled with *grappa* and emptied more than once, the ashtrays are
overflowing with cigarette butts. His luxurious apartment looks
uncared for. Don Vito and Carvalho wait for him to say something. He
goes over to the TV set, and turns towards them: 'Haven't you seen
the news bulletin?'

Carvalho and Don Vito shake their heads.

'I've recorded it on video.'

The screen fills with images of a swarm of journalists and
onlookers outside a courthouse. Pascuali is there with his men. A
blonde, white-skinned woman, wearing a headscarf and dark glasses,
is trying to force her way through the crowd. The TV presenter tries
to get a declaration, then gives up and gives his own report.

'There's a dramatic new twist in the case of the White Lady.
Marta Fanchelli Maluendas, the famous M.F.M., has come forward
of her own accord, and from her statement it is clear she was in no

way responsible for the death of the TV presenter Pacho Escámez.'

Then they see Marta speaking as close to the microphone as if she were kissing it.

'How could I kill anyone with a karate chop? I spend my whole life on a diet, I haven't got the strength to karate chop a fly.'

'But you know who did it.'

'Everything I know is in the hands of the magistrate and the police.'

She points to the policemen around her, and in particular to Pascuali.

'Inspector Pascuali here has been very polite and very intelligent.'

The presenter grabs back the microphone.

'That's very true, I'm sure. So now from the initials M.F.M. – or Marta Fanchelli Maluendas, we have gone to those of L.C.L., another palindrome, and the new target of the police investigation.'

Don Leonardo stops the video. Stands staring at the screen for a few seconds. Then turns back to them again.

'L.C.L. Leonardo Costa Livorno. Me.'

Don Vito is indignant.

'Who does that whore think she is?'

Carvalho tries to shut him up, but there is no stopping Don Vito.

'That no-good woman!'

Leonardo glares at him.

'Appearances can be deceptive. Marta. Marta is an extraordinary woman. I need to pour my heart out, Don Vito, Pepe – I can call you Pepe, can't I? Marta is an extraordinary woman. She gave all the love she had to my son; she tried to persuade him not to do the embezzling. She followed him to the Bahamas because she feared the worst, and she was proved right. He suffered a complete psychological collapse. She was – is – a woman full of love and life. She is in no way suicidal: it's my son who is the potential suicide, as she herself explained to me very clearly. Now I love her, and she loves me. That swine Escámez was blackmailing her. He told her that if she left him, he would come and tell me everything; and on top of it all, he was always trying to find her lovers who would help her with her career.'

'So you killed him?'

'Why not? I told her that's what I would tell the magistrate. It was me who killed him – in an outburst of rage at the ghastly proposals the old pimp was making to me.'

'Are you a karate expert then?'

'I know how to defend myself. I could have struck him with an iron fist.'

Don Vito shakes his head.

'That would be premeditation.'

Carvalho is also against the idea.

'Forget the iron fist.'

'Tomorrow morning I'm going to hand myself over to the police, and I want you two to tell them the truth – that is, how at first I hated her for what she had done to my son. I want the magistrate to know the whole story – how love was born of hate, not death out of revenge. I'll pay you whatever you ask.'

Carvalho and Don Vito exchange glances, and it is Altofini who gives their verdict:

'We don't charge for giving statements.'

The next day, Carvalho, Alma and Altofini switch their TV on to watch the news. The usual crowd of curious onlookers, journalists, Pascuali and two policemen who are leading Don Leonardo out in a pair of handcuffs. They pause while the presenter announces: 'Leonardo Costa Livorno, the self-confessed killer of Pacho Escámez, who this morning told the police the story of his love for the White Lady. Pacho Escámez tried to stand in their way, leading the woman in question into corruption and the white slave trade, as her lawyer put it.'

Then there is a clip of the lawyer: 'It was a passionate response to the evil procuring of a lascivious old man. An act of love. In the past, Don Leonardo had hated Marta Fanchelli for her relationship with his son, until the moment that is when he began to appreciate her great qualities.'

Carvalho switches off. Don Vito starts to mutter the words to the tango 'Cambalache':

Twentieth century, full of problems, loud and new
If you don't cry you don't get the milk

If you don't steal, then the fool is you.
Go on! Get on with it!
We all end up in the same stew.
Don't give it a second thought, fill your plate
No one gives a damn if you're honest or you're great
If you break your back day and night
If you murder, cure, or don't know wrong from right.

Alma sips her *mate* and comments:

'He'll be locked away for years.'

'They've already found lots of extenuating circumstances. He won't be inside for many years. It's only in tangos that crimes of passion lead to prison for life.'

Waiters in uniform and carrying silver platters. Carvalho watches them go by from a chair that seems to want to eat him. Gálvez Jr. is more used to such extravagant comfort, and has managed to drape his frame in such a way as to avoid the sucking mouth of the giant upholstered sea-slug. The two other men, Ostiz and Maetzu, are seated quite naturally and comfortably, and watch with amusement Carvalho's efforts to squirm and prod himself into a proper upright position. Ostiz, who is gaunt-faced and bald as a billiard-ball, has begun lecturing Gálvez.

'I'm sure you agree, Richard, that your father's body should not stand in the way of our relations, which should of necessity be excellent.'

Maetzu, a man with a sad drunk's eyes and half a kilo of platinum rings, underlines the message: 'Unfortunately, there's no way to bring him back to life, but anyway, by dint of hard work and intelligence, you managed to preserve the best part of your inheritance.'

Then Ostiz chimes in again, as if on cue: 'Richard, you must agree that your father – that poetic man, poetic and poignant – yes, that's the word, poignant – in his last incarnation as Robinson Crusoe, had something to teach us which we should not forget – the lesson of universal solidarity.'

Maetzu closes his sad, alcoholic eyes and adds: 'He was one of us, and we need to emphasize that we too think of others, that not everything comes down to creating wealth – which is also for others of course, but mainly for ourselves. We wealthy people of Argentina have got a bad reputation, and it's the fault of those Perónists. The days when Menem was first in power, and we demonstrated side-by-side with the trade unionists, are long gone. Why, even our wives were Perónist then.'

'Cartier's "Must", perfume and underarm sweat. I read about it in *Nuevo Porteño*.'

Carvalho's comment amuses Ostiz and annoys Maetzu. Gálvez nods for Carvalho to go in for the kill.

'My client and I would just like to add however that there remains the small matter of someone ordering the death of Señor Gálvez and his chauffeur.'

Ostiz and Maetzu look at each other and by mutual agreement call a waiter. One comes over, carrying a huge leather case, like those used for carrying architect's drawings. Inside there is a big sketch, and the two financiers have to get up and hold it open with all four hands, as if they were folding a sheet. It shows the river, between Buenos Aires and the sea.

It is Ostiz who explains the project.

'Our idea is to build an artificial island in honour of your father. It will be called the "Robinson Joaquín Gálvez" Island: we already have raised the initial capital, and it's quite possible we may be able to get Barbara Bush involved. We see this as almost entirely charitable enterprise, although we don't know if she agrees. You have a guaranteed fifteen per cent, Richard. Oh and by the way, Robinson Island, theme park, will give part of its profits to research into new diseases. We won't mention AIDS directly, so that nobody will associate that with your father.'

Once again, Carvalho supplies the voice like a ventriloquist on behalf of Gálvez.

'Why an artificial island? Aren't there any real ones left?'

'Yes, but they're so expensive! Anything in the Tigre is impossible nowadays; and besides, in Buenos Aires they're still fascinated with Le Corbusier's nonsense about constructing an artificial island.'

Gálvez Jr. nods, beginning to warm to the idea. Yes, of course a natural island would be impossible.

Maetzu starts to dream. 'I can just see it! In my mind's eye! The
"Joaquín Gálvez" Robinson Crusoe Island.'

Carvalho is still hoping that Richard wants to get back to the
question of his father's death, and makes a final attempt to try to raise
it.

'What if we returned from Never-Never Island? Do you have a
reply to the question...'

'Leave it for now, Carvalho,' Richard Gálvez orders him, as only
a captain of industry can give orders, and Carvalho reflects that
Robinson Gálvez was Richard's father, not his. So he sits back and
listens to the smooth flow of conversation between Gálvez Jr. and the
men who had ordered his father's death, how they agree with each
other, how they speak the same language, how they decide to drink
and eat together in the near future. Occasionally, Richard tries to
work out what Carvalho must be thinking, and to bring him into the
conversation.

'The real gourmet is Señor Carvalho here.'

'Is that true?'

'I hate gourmets, but I suppose to a certain extent, I am one, yes.'

'How interesting.'

Ostiz was the one expressing interest.

'I own vineyards and make a few wines. Some friends of mine and
I have set up a Gourmet Club. We dine privately at Chez Reyero, and
all we talk about is what we are eating, have eaten and are going to eat.
Would you be our guest, Señor Carvalho? And you too, of course,
Richard.'

'I can't tell a potato from an aubergine.'

'Would you allow us to invite you, Carvalho?'

'Would I allow myself to be invited by this bunch of bastards?'
Carvalho wonders. 'Say something,' he says to himself.

'Yes.'

The brilliantly bedecked yacht sails down the river. The mist is as
murky as the waters below, but the glow of the guests and the strings
of lights give their gentle progress its splendour. The boat is full of
the highest class of criminals – at least one archbishop, several
supposed politicians, the press, TV cameras. Gálvez provides the

offscreen commentary in Carvalho's ear on who all the most important guests are. Suddenly, Maetzu's voice rings out from the foredeck: 'Island in sight!'

The yacht drops anchor. A beaming Ostiz spreads his arms towards the waters of the river.

'There's the island!'

Carvalho cannot see it anywhere. But all the guests hang over the port side of the ship, and finally he spots a small concrete mixer on a barge. The load seems to be ready, and so Ostiz leans to ask the city mayor to finish the task, and the archbishop to give his blessing. The mayor helps the workmen tip the first load of concrete of what is to become the island into the river. The archbishop gives his blessing. Gálvez Jr. whispers admiringly into Carvalho's ear: 'They're putting twenty million dollars into it.'

He says no more, as it is time for the speeches and a soft but interminable national anthem. Gálvez takes Carvalho by the arm.

'Papa would be pleased; Robinson less so. Don't feel let down, Carvalho. The truth isn't always necessary. One has to wait for the right moment. Either it'll come, or I'll provoke it, but I swear to you his death won't go unpunished. How about having dinner with me? Let's go to Puerto Madero. They tell me the choice is better there than in La Recoleta. Now that Gato Dumas has gone, La Recoleta has become ordinary again. Wouldn't you like to? You don't seem very enthusiastic.'

'Drink to remember, eat to forget. How do you deal with those priorities?'

Gálvez thinks about this for a moment, then replies.

'Wasn't it the other way round? The important thing is to remember or to forget when we need to.'

Now they are installed at a table in an Italian restaurant that likes to consider itself the equal of the best Italian restaurants in the world – those in New York – and Carvalho is trying to follow the abundant, melancholy thoughts of Gálvez Jr. when a gloved hand comes to rest on his shoulder. Looking up, he sees it is Marta, the White Lady, with her pink smile and flowing golden hair.

'D'you remember me?'

'Whether you're Beatriz or Marta, you are unforgettable. But do you remember me? From Spain? The Frigola case? Do you remember Señor Frigola?'

But all she does is give a little laugh, as if he had paid her a compliment. Then she says, hurriedly:

'Leonardo is in jail. But not for long.'

'I know.'

At that point he notices that Marta is accompanied by an elegant-looking young man, who is waiting for her at a discreet distance.

'It's over between us – I mean, the relation there was between Leonardo and me. But we're still good friends. I go and visit him every week. Don't worry. I don't want any more suicides on my conscience.'

'You really are dangerous. Men just love to kill and commit suicide for you.'

Marta laughs crazily, and brushes Carvalho's lips with hers before slinking off to her table. Carvalho sits down again, and refuses to satisfy Gálvez's silent curiosity. Marta has eased herself into a chair opposite her companion, and takes advantage of the first glass of champagne to turn towards Carvalho and toast him in the distance. The detective returns her gesture. Gálvez finally admits his curiosity.

'Who is that? Might I be allowed to know?'

'She's a no-good woman, and no-good women can cost you your life or your fortune, or both. D'you like no-good women?'

'I know the man she's with. He's the son of Leonardo, who runs a lingerie business.'

'Didn't he join a sect?'

'I don't know the latest details. But to answer your question – yes, I like no-good women. They fascinate me.'

Carvalho spreads his hand, palm up, as if offering Gálvez the opportunity to take his chance with Marta.

'Go on then, but try not to kill anyone while you're at it.'

The no-good woman has been following their conversation, openly ignoring the stern words her companion seems to be addressing to her. She gives Gálvez Jr. a knowing look, which he returns, raising his glass too in a silent toast.

Chapter 4

Borges' Love Child

The oldest port area of Buenos Aires, far beyond the La Boca that tourists know. A man of around forty, badly dressed and unkempt, although something in his demeanour speaks of what used to be called 'good breeding' – but this might just be the cautious way he moves. He glances suspiciously up and down the street. Eventually decides to enter one of the abandoned shops. He seems to hesitate in his choice of a corner, but gradually relaxes and pulls out a syringe, then starts to prepare his heroin ritual. Shoots up. A broad smile spreads across his anxious features. A second man appears. A light behind him means the first one cannot see who it is. The addict's face shows only pleasure and trust. Then suddenly the newcomer's fist is raised, and starts to pound the other's face. He receives the blows without a murmur. His empty eyes watch as the fist smashes them shut in an explosion of star-filled darkness. He takes a dozen blows to the head, delivered by an ever more incensed attacker. Finally his body slumps to the floor, alongside the uninvolved, almost dainty shoes of his assailant.

A coffered ceiling, alabaster busts, marble, tear-drop chandeliers. A very theatrical setting for a press conference. Television cameras, journalists crowding round, radio reporters with phallic microphones stuck to their lips, the electric shock energy of important events.

Then comes the dramatic pause before a great announcement and a serious, deep voice declaims, as if from the heavens:

> *The span of heaven measures my glory.*
> *Libraries in the East vie for my works.*
> *Emirs seek me, to fill my mouth with gold.*
> *The angels know my latest lyrics by heart.*
> *The tools I work with are pain and humiliation.*
> *Would that I had been born dead.*

All the journalists – and not just the sports reporters sent to cover what they were told was a patriotic literary event – look startled, up at the ceiling to try to discover where the voice of this exotic god may be coming from. As the recital of the poem draws to a close, a strange figure steps out from behind the curtains: it looks as if it is Jorge Luis Borges himself.

'Borges!' everyone exclaims, even the sceptics and those who aren't even aware the poet is dead.

The imposing figure is in full control of the situation, and he takes advantage of the general amazement to stride to the centre of the platform, to stare gravely at the assembled journalists, and to declare in the most Borgesian of voices: 'Ladies and gentlemen, my name is Ariel Borges, and I am Jorge Luis Borges' love child.'

This announcement is greeted by murmurs, whispers, some whistled dissent, until the alleged son of Borges raises his arms to silence his audience.

'I am the biggest story of the century, and I'll even give you the headline for your pieces: The Best-Kept Secret in Universal Literature.'

Cameras flash, the TV lights snap on. The supposed Ariel Borges is besieged by the journalists' recorders, microphones, urgent questions:

'How did such a phenomenon occur?'

'My mother was the daughter of an eccentric English lord and a princess from Samarkand. She was a dancer, and she met my father during a tour of Argentina.'

'What kind of a dancer? A belly dancer?'

'My mother was an artiste, a contortionist. She could dance the dance of the cygnets like a spider – like Carlota von Ussler used to do, bent backward on all fours, spinning on her hands and feet.'

'How did your mother succeed in being fecundated by the undoubtedly eminent writer Jorge Luis Borges?'

'In order not to offend Aunty Nora or Aunty Victoria, my father – Borges, that is – never publicly acknowledged his paternity. My mother always explained this by saying that instead of semen, Jorge Luis had writing ink inside him, and to admit he could have had a child horrified him, because it was tantamount to saying all his inkwells had dried up.'

'How are you when it comes to inkwells?'

Borges Jr. does not even blink. Instead he bows, and from behind the curtains a scrawny rag of a woman steps out. Apart from a slight disdain, her face betrays no emotion. She looks like a tiny schoolteacher made up to look like an old woman refusing to admit her age. She is smoking a pipe, and pushing a supermarket trolley overflowing with books. As she hands them out to the journalists, she calls out their titles, like a soulless robot: *Secret Letter to My Father*, and *Universal History of Infamy*. As she does this, Borges Jr.'s voice booms out through the room:

'I am the son of a king and a princess, and through my veins flows the blood or ink that helped Wordsworth write his *Ode to Immortality*.'

Some hours later, he displays exactly the same attitude in front of the TV cameras in an air-conditioned studio, with a décor appropriate to the literary event of the century. In close-up, Ariel Borges repeats the phrase he pronounced for the assembled journalists: 'I always say I am the son of a king and a princess, and that through my veins flows the ink or blood that helped Wordsworth write his *Ode to Immortality*.'

The camera pulls back to reveal Borges Jr. next to a presenter who seems to have escaped from one of Jorge Luis Borges' literary fantasies. They are in bed. She is in her slip, while Borges is wearing a tweed jacket, his tie poking out from above the sheets, and his fingers interlaced around a cup of tea.

'So you are the happy fruit of a poetic encounter, an encounter between Borges and the descendant of a princess from Samarkand.'

'My granny.'

'That's right, your granny. There is something magical about that encounter. How did it happen?'

The son's eyes widen as he starts the story of how his life might have begun.

'My mother was performing in a small theatre in Palermo Chico that no longer exists, and my papa went to see her one night with all his usual group: Victoria Ocampo, Aunty Nora, Uncle Guillermo, who was Spanish, and Bioy. If only Bioy would say what he knew – but he doesn't want to share Borges with anyone. That night...'

His face fades from the screen, and a group of actors dramatize the flashback. The probable lack of truth of the scene is reinforced by the unreal way it is represented. The contortionist is still smoking her pipe as she wheels around flung backwards on hands and feet, to a simple piano accompaniment. Amidst the smoke and dim lights of the auditorium the figure of Borges can be seen, played by his alleged son. At a certain point in the dance, he stands up and begins to recite:

> Four-footed at dawn, in the daytime tall,
> and wandering three-legged down the hollow
> reaches of evening: thus did the sphinx,
> the eternal one, regard his restless fellow,
> mankind; and at evening came a man
> who, terror-struck, discovered as in a mirror
> his own decline set forth in the monstrous image,
> his destiny, and felt a chill of terror.
> We are Oedipus and everlastingly
> we are the long tripartite beast; we are
> all that we were and will be, nothing less.
> It would destroy us to look steadily
> at our full being. Mercifully, God grants us
> the ticking of the clock, forgetfulness.

The contortionist pauses in her dangerous dance. She has become a polyhedron of flesh, her legs crossed above her head as she peers out into the audience, as if trying to make out the poet. When

she does not succeed, still in her extraordinary position, she takes a
pair of glasses out of some unlikely fold in her ballerina's dress, puts
them on, and renews the puffing on her pipe. A few moments later,
she returns to her feet, and walks off down the theatre aisle, leading
Borges by the hand. He is big and shambling, as slow and clumsy as
if he were already blind. Both the aisle and the corridor they
disappear along look unreal; and at the same time the voice of Borges
Jr. can be heard commentating:

"And they transcended the corridors of memory itself until they
found themselves in the shared future of a bed of tears and lust."'

The corridor ends in a dressing-room; as the door opens, we see
it is entirely filled with a huge four-poster bed with baroque columns.
The contortionist drops Borges' hand and rushes to the bed, where
once again she twists herself in knots, but with her sex pointing out in
the right direction, ready to receive her lover, who leaps on her in a
sudden uncontrollable rush of desire and passion. Even though her
body is contorted on itself, she goes on calmly smoking her pipe.

Then we are back with the reality of the set, where the presenter
is poking fun at Borges Jr.

'Well! What you've told us is quite fantastic, in the Borgesian and
in the absolute sense of the term.'

'In the Borgesian and in the absolute sense, maybe. But not in the
relative sense of the word.'

'No of course, not in the relative sense. But tell me, what would
you like to be called? Borges? Borges Junior? Junior?'

'Anything but Junior.'

Carvalho is in his apartment, watching the interview with the alleged
son of Borges and the dramatization of his conception, beating a
bowlful of eggs as he does so. The presenter is asking: 'What would
you like to be called? Borges? Borges Junior? Junior?'

'Anything but Junior.'

Carvalho likes the answer. He goes on beating the eggs.

What is left of the world seen through a whisky glass? Shelves full of
all the bottles of drink available to the clients of Tango Amigo.
Carvalho has already found his answer, and can see that Alma is doing

the same, but without a filter. She is also puzzled at the vast array of bottles, but has no whisky glass. The club is filling up, as people sit at the tables with their marble lamps. Alma is softly drinking a soft drink, a milk shake made with a fruit she has not bothered to investigate. Carvalho's words reach her from afar.

'I swear the guy takes himself seriously. He was talking about his father as though he really believed it was Borges. But I know his face.'

'That's because he looks like Jorge Luis. If he didn't, there wouldn't be so much fuss.'

'But I've seen him somewhere before.'

'In an earlier incarnation, perhaps. Were you a contortionist in your previous incarnation?'

Carvalho gnaws at his memory, but just then the lights go down for the show to begin. Silence falls on the darkened room, like a veil as soft as the drink Alma is drinking, or the gauze covering her well-rounded breasts. Silverstein appears, dressed as an imagined English writer at the turn of the nineteenth and twentieth centuries, with more than a hint of Oscar Wilde, hair parted in the middle.

'Allow me to introduce myself. I'm the son of Oscar Wilde and the young Lord Douglas. My birth has been kept a secret because ever since I was a child I've shown disturbing tendencies, and my psychiatrist, an Argentine who's more of a Lacanian than a Freudian, suspects I might be Jack the Ripper. I went to a school for the natural sons and orphans of famous writers. That's where I got to know Arielito Borges, Macedonita Fernández, Osvaldita Soriano, Manolito Puig, and others whose paternity I could guess at, even though it was not officially recognized: ten little girls who were the spitting image of Jorge Asís, for example. In the school, they taught us everything except how to write, and when after a rigorous examination of our chromosomes it was found we had writers' genes, above and beyond those necessary to write for the magazine *Caras*, they were deleted. Our fathers couldn't bear the thought of competition. A lot has been written about the death of the father, but what about the death of the son? Don't fathers dream of the death of their sons as a way of warding off their own end? That's why I'm so surprised Arielito Borges writes.'

He puts on a child's voice. 'When he was little, Arielito was very stubborn. Just to annoy his father, he used to read the English writers in Portuguese. Which was all the more remarkable, as he could not read Portuguese. Arielito Borges, Borges Junior…but I think Adriana Varela is here, and wants to sing something for you about this genetic prodigy.'

The spotlight moves off him in search of the singer. Carvalho cannot tear his eyes from Alma's cleavage, until she covers his face with her hand.

'You won't get round me again.'

Applause as Adriana Varela appears. Silverstein goes to greet her. He kisses her hand, and welcomes her to centre stage.

'It's wonderful news, isn't it, Adriana? Whoever would have thought the old devil had something more than ink in his veins.'

'Veins have so much in them.'

'What's this tango called?'

'"Borges Junior."'

'By?'

'Borges Junior.'

The spotlights veer off into the audience. General amazement when they come to rest on the bulky outline of Borges Junior himself. Silence and applause – mostly silence. Silverstein has nothing more to say, and leaves the stage to Adriana. She sings:

> *Son!*
> *Borges Junior*
> *You are called*
> *By varicosed*
> *Whores*
> *By worm-ridden*
> *Professors*
> *So watch out*
> *Don't shout.*
>
> *Son!*
> *Borges Junior*
> *They cry*
> *Miracle-working*

Chromosomes
Would-be
Genomes
Don't let
Them get
You.
Son!
Make sure you make the most of it
And remember you did good
To turn me into a stud.

Don't leave me outside
Stark-naked in the rain
The fervour of Buenos Aires
Won't let me out again.

Take care with what you say,
Remember you are flesh of my flesh
Nostril of my nostrils
My lust of a single day.

Son!
Borges Junior
You are called
By varicosed
Whores
By worm-ridden
Professors
So watch out
Don't shout.

Son!
Borges Junior
They cry
Miracle-working
Chromosomes
Would-be

Genomes
Don't let
Them get
You.

Son!
Make sure you make the most of it
And remember you did good
To turn me into a stud.

Above the applause, Carvalho's voice. He has been staring the whole time at Borges' posthumous son, and now he roars into Alma's ear.

'I've got it! I saw that guy in Pascuali's cells!'

Two fists flashing in the middle of a ring. Skilful fists, driven on by the audience's enthusiasm. Peretti is fighting Negro Salta. Peretti is a middle-weight, about thirty years old, and looks as though he has never been caught square on the nose by any blow. He floats round the ring like a fencing champion, or a prince turned boxer. His opponent is a stolid punching bag from Salta province. He pits his strength and courage against the constant dancing of the prince of the ring.

'Go on, Negro! Smash his pretty boy's face in!' someone shouts from the crowd.

'There's no one good enough to even touch Peretti!' another voice replies.

'Boxing is for men!'

'Get up there and see if you're man enough to land one on his face!' shouts a blowsy blonde.

Her companion tries to calm her down. 'Don't go making a fool of yourself, because it's always me who gets into trouble.'

But the woman carries on shouting at the man who had criticized Peretti.

'You're all mouth and no balls!'

'Get into bed with me and I'll show you I've got more balls than that asshole who's with you!'

The blonde's companion sighs wearily. He takes off his elegant

overcoat and his white scarf, folds them carefully on his seat, turns to
the man insulting him, and without a word lands a powerful punch
on his chin. Soon all the public is joining in. The blonde woman is
trying to gouge out the eyes of the man who insulted her companion.
In the ring, Peretti's fists have done their work: one final blow spins
Negro Salta round and sends him crashing to the canvas. The crowd
roars. Peretti walks back ever so slowly to his corner, back to his
opponent. He leans on the ropes and gives a self-satisfied smile to the
audience, most of whom are still involved in a fight of their own.

The three Japanese businessmen seem to have agreed not to react to
Güelmes' explanations. All three are perched uncomfortably on the
edge of their seats, ready to get up and leave at any moment.
    'It's the letter of an unbalanced mind. A poor wretch who it's true
did collaborate at the start with research that fifteen years later – more
than fifteen years later – finally gave the results we wish to share with
you. Where was Raúl Tourón all that time? In Spain – and now he's
back looking for revenge. Trying to cause problems.'
    'We won't invest in projects with problems.'
    Another of the Japanese supports this.
    'It's you who have the problem, and it's for you to solve it.'
    The two who have spoken look across at the third, silent one. He
says something in his own language and immediately stands up. His
two companions follow suit, while a worried Güelmes half-raises
himself from his seat behind the desk. He does not really understand
what is going on, and it is no use him trying to gain a little time: 'Why
don't...'
    As they make their bows and leave, Güelmes does manage to
regain his composure and see them out like a minister should. Left on
his own, he mutters: 'What can that fool have said?'
    A half-open door in the office swings wide, and the Captain and
Font y Rius enter the room, followed by another Japanese man.
    'We know what he said: "These racists think all of us Japanese are
stupid."'
    Güelmes starts to pace up and down. The Captain sits calmly, and
Font y Rius follows his example, staring down at the tips of his shoes.
The Japanese interpreter waits politely for further instructions.

'We're the stupid ones. You two above all.'

The Captain points to Güelmes and Font y Rius.

'If you hadn't been so squeamish, Raúl Tourón wouldn't be a problem any more.'

Güelmes explodes.

'Who would have thought that bastard, that crazy son of a bitch would stick his nose into this of all things?'

Font y Rius protests weakly that after all, it was Raúl who made the discovery, but Güelmes bursts out again.

'He made the discovery, and that's all. Who developed it and turned it into a commercial prospect?'

'But we agreed we should respect Raúl's life.'

'Tell him to keep out of our business then!'

Deep inside, the Captain is pleased at the way Güelmes and Font y Rius are arguing.

'All that Raúl Tourón wants is to get in the way. That letter he wrote to our possible partners is a declaration of war.'

Font y Rius becomes sarcastic.

'A dirty war, Captain? The kind you like?'

'There are no clean wars.'

He gets up, goes over to the desk, picks up the letter and waves it as though it were incontrovertible proof: 'This is a declaration of war.'

He reads coolly, as though detailing the evidence:

'"...I should like to inform you that the offer that The New Argentina has made you through its associates Señores Güelmes and Font y Rius is based on usurpation. The writer of this letter is the biologist who fifteen years ago discovered a possible link between animal behaviour and the quality of animal feed. A sinister plot is now underway to rob me of the fruit of my labours. To demonstrate the validity of my claim, I would refer you to the information I sent to the Congress on Nutrition and Development held by ECLA in Ottawa in 1975, and to the article published in *Ciencia Latina* in January 1976, entitled *An animal is what it eats*."'

The room is silent. Güelmes has stopped his pacing, and is staring with contained fury at Font y Rius.

'I wonder how that jerk managed to get our Japanese friends' address. How he discovered they were in Buenos Aires. It seems to me he's not on his own – someone is helping him, and I don't mean that dumb Spaniard, or Alma, or Silverstein.'

'Less words, more deeds.'

The Captain seems to be speaking above all to Font y Rius, and he marches out of the room with a final sally, followed by the interpreter.

'I ask myself the same questions as the under-secretary – I'm sorry, as the minister. And I can only find one answer. A jerk holds our future in his hands. And don't imagine for a minute that I'm the only one threatened. All three of us are, and everything we've been trying to achieve.'

As soon as the Captain and the interpreter have left the room, Güelmes rounds on his companion.

'The Captain is furious – he knows how to conceal it, but underneath, he's furious.'

'So what? It's as if nothing had changed, as if we were still his prisoners. I don't want to be anybody's prisoner! What about you? What good is all the paraphernalia of power to you? You still think like a prisoner, like one of the Captain's prisoners.'

'And you? Aren't you a prisoner of your guilty conscience? The prisoner of a ghost, of an imaginary Raúl? The Raúl we all loved doesn't exist any more. Now there's only an animal in a corner that will die lashing out. We have to choose.'

'Choose to kill him, as your Captain wants?'

Güelmes dismisses the idea with a wave.

'This stress isn't good for me. Let's leave it for today.'

He takes an apparatus to measure blood pressure out of a desk drawer. He thrusts a finger in it, and checks the result. Wide-eyed, he stares at Font y Rius as if he is the one to blame.

'See that? My pressure's gone sky-high! Fourteen over eleven! Fourteen over eleven – d'you know what that means?'

He detains Font y Rius with a hand as he is about to stride out in disgust.

By now he is perfectly calm again.

'One of those two has to go. Either Raúl or the Captain.'

The buzz of young people chatting, consuming breakfasts, books, jokes reaches his ears like a distantly familiar sound landscape. Something he would rather not call his youth. Not because that would be nostalgia – good or bad – but because it seems to him inappropriate. It does not feel right. He wants to leave as quickly as possible. Font y Rius is unable to contain himself when Alma expresses her surprise at him agreeing to meet her in the university bar. He is too nervous to go along with her attempts to make their meeting more relaxed.

'I can't see any other solution. I can't hold them back much longer. If Raúl doesn't sort it out...they'll get him.'

'How did you manage to pass the message about the deal with the Japanese on to him?'

'Raúl came to see me. It was like an apparition, I can tell you. I was caught up in some boring administration, and to take my mind off it I looked out into the garden. The usual patients were there, with all their usual tics, and all the usual nurses and guards. But something told me there was a visual intrusion, and I soon saw what it was. Raúl. He was walking very calmly in among the lunatics, as if trying to work out where he was. A short while later, he was sitting opposite me. I tried to talk to him affectionately but responsibly. "Do you know what you want?" I asked him. "Everything. Or nothing," he replied. I tried to reason with him: "This is a bad moment for all or nothing. We have to make do with a little something. We can't win any wars, so we have to be satisfied with winning the odd battle. What is it you want?" "I want to be who I am." "Who you are, or who you were? It's impossible to be the person you were. Twenty years have gone by. For you, for me, for our memory." We can't even trust our memory. My career. My daughter. I think I know who has her." "Are you sure?" "No, I'm not sure. I was closer to her before they killed Robinson." Are you listening? "What Robinson are you talking about?" I lost my patience. "So you want to win back a daughter who doesn't know you, who wouldn't even recognize you? And who we don't know the whereabouts of? Wouldn't the cure be worse than the illness? Your career is easier to save." And it was then I made my mistake. Are you listening, Alma?'

'I'm listening.'

'I said to him: "Not all or nothing, but something, something you can hold on to, Raúl. Would you like to be a partner with us?" He replied: "A partner in exploiting a discovery I made and you stole from me?" I insisted: "It can't be all or nothing. The Captain is a bad enemy but a good partner." "You're all kidnapped people," he said. "You're living the Stockholm syndrome. You're partners with your own jailers." "Not all or nothing. Something, something, Raúl." D'you understand what I was trying to tell him, Alma? D'you understand my position?'

'I understand. You're the good cop, the Captain is the bad cop and Güelmes is the professional. When we were being interrogated we had time to learn all the roles.'

'You're so harsh with everyone else, but I think you're a little soft with yourself. It was me who gave Raúl the idea of getting mixed up in this, of interfering in our project. Once it was done, I thought I could suggest to them that they brought him in properly, and do a deal with him.'

'That's the Yankee method. Take things to the edge of the abyss, then do a deal. That's what we always denounced as the Kissinger school – his satanic way of calculating probabilities. So Vietnam was bombarded with napalm to ensure peace, and in Latin America the left was wiped out, so a deal could be done with the survivors.'

'But at least I have a position – you don't have one at all! You're all running away, like Raúl, but there's no way you can get back to the lost homeland of your memories!'

Alma stands up, angry with herself.

'Do a deal, do a deal!'

She turns her back on Font y Rius and leaves, but not before she hears him calling to her.

'Berta, Bertita.'

'Don't call me Berta, and especially not Bertita.'

'Alma, just remember, please. Either we did a deal, or we wouldn't get out of there alive. You did a deal too.'

The private club El Aleph, or the English Royal Academy of Borges Studies. A villa in a residential neighbourhood, wooden beams, and waiters who are wooden copies of English butlers but in flesh and blood, as if they were all called James. And James is what they are all called by the assembled guests, who are also dressed up, mimicking illustrations of Victorian life at the turn of the twentieth century. They are grouped in a circle around the man who is obviously their leader – a man who looks even more like an English aristocrat than the rest of them.

'This villainy has plumbed the depths: consider just how preposterously Borges' style has been satirized, when the master's work is the supreme example of how to avoid commonplaces. And what a commonplace! The grandson of a dancer from Samarkand and an English lord, and the son, no less, of Borges himself!'

One of the academics draws his own conclusion.

'Ostiz. The cur has no right to live!'

The chairman calls for silence and gestures for another academic to speak. This one is dressed up as a lord. Fair-haired and pale, he speaks slowly and carefully.

'In agreement with our chairman, Doctor Ostiz, this morning I disguised myself as Jude the Obscure from the novel by Thomas Hardy, and took up my position opposite this charlatan's house. I didn't leave a single window intact – I'm a good shot with a stone. Through the windows I could see the impostor's ashen face – even more disturbed, I imagine, now he is coming to realize the consequences of his actions.'

'James, bring me a scotch would you – an eighteen-year-old Langavulin in a brandy glass, with no ice or water,' the chairman orders, provoking an admiring reaction among the other club members.

'James, I'd like a sarsaparilla with water and a slice of lemon.'

Third academic to the same waiter.

'And I'd like a mulled wine with a little honey.'

But something is worrying the chairman. He is staring quizzically at the young lord's disguise, and asks him: 'Why are you dressed up as a nineteenth-century English peasant?'

'The master was a great admirer of English realist writers of the nineteenth century, especially Thomas Hardy. He told me one day,' he says, putting on Borges' most cavernous voice: "Martínez, nearly all realism is ghastly, and the worst of all is Spanish realism. In Latin America it is not so bad, because the realist writers from this side of the Atlantic wrote out of the fear they felt at having been abandoned over here. But English realism is something else, whether it is Hardy and his rearguard action, or Kipling – in it one can sense the energy of Empire. In every Empire there is a moon shining somewhere."'

This is followed by murmurs of approval, moist eyes. A few restrained gasps of 'wonderful, wonderful!' The chairman stifles a ripple of applause.

'Dirty wars have to be met with equally dirty measures. Our own history proves it, whatever the subversives or the riff-raff who protect them – all those people who call themselves defenders of human rights – might say. We have to give this impostor a fright. Yes, first we frighten him, and if he carries on...'

A lord draws his hand across his throat and gives a meaningful gurgle. Then he asks another waiter who has arrived to help the first James:

'A tea, James. Put the hot skimmed milk in first.'

Someone who to judge by his shyness must be a lesser lord comes up and whispers something into the chairman's ear. The chairman does not bother to excuse himself, but gets up and follows his informant out of the room. Waiting for them in a side-room that is as heavily wood-panelled as the rest of the house are Pascuali and Vladimiro.

'Inspector Pascuali has some information about the impostor.'

Pascuali is not just looking at his surroundings – he is positively smelling the carved wood, the polished metal, the rough gaucho beams and ceiling, as if they all gave off a very special perfume. He is holding a photograph of Borges Jr. reciting. The chairman clears his throat, and the inspector turns to show him the photograph.

'Is this the face of the intruder into the Borges universe?'

'Yes, the face of the faceless one.'

Vladimiro laughs at the inspector's wit, but none of the Borges archangels follows suit.

'I hope the police will take appropriate action.'

'I believe so. As long as he doesn't harm anyone, we will leave him alone.'

'But this man must have a criminal record.'

Pascuali points to a thick folder that looks out of place on a far too splendid desk.

'He has eighteen attempted frauds to his name. Some of which succeeded. It's like a game to him. He once pretended to be Lindbergh's son, the one who disappeared.'

'He's nowhere near old enough. So you aren't going to arrest him?'

'No. A short while ago I kept him in the cells because he was going around claiming to be Eva Perón's younger brother.'

'What are you going to do then?'

'Open file number nineteen.' All of a sudden, Pascuali loses his temper. 'What world do you live in? We have to make some distinction between real fraudsters and petty ones.'

Doctor Ostiz wrinkles his whisky connoisseur's nose. 'What you've just said smacks of demagoguery.'

The jersey is growing steadily as the old woman knits away, pipe clenched between her teeth. Borges Jr. sitting in the middle of bits of antique junk, holds up a piece of paper he has just taken out of an envelope. As he reads it, his hands start to tremble:

'"...cease your fraudulent activities forthwith, or the executors of the Borges universe will despatch you to the hell of infamy. The walls of your disgusting den will not protect you. Up to now we have smashed your windows. If you continue, we will smash your soul, if indeed you have a soul...you are no more than a thing, not even an animal."'

'Bad news?'

'An anonymous letter.'

'I must finish this jersey before they kill you.' The old woman pauses, thinks about what she has just said. 'Before they kill us.'

'How much have we got saved?'

'Enough for two funerals.'

The same sad expression with which he greets his mother's news accompanies him out of their house, along the streets, and up into Carvalho's office. He introduces himself to Don Vito, who is seated in Carvalho's chair, and explains why he has come.

'I know Carvalho, you see.'

'If you know him, you know me. As Confucius said: know your partner and you will know yourself.'

'Papa always thought Confucius was an invention. That every age put words in Confucius' mouth that he had never said, ideas he hadn't ever had.'

'The classics! Ah, the classics! That's what they are there for. Your father, Confucius, Gardel. My partner won't be long.'

Don Vito casts an impatient glance towards the door separating the office space from the rest of the apartment. Carvalho has just sat up in bed. He's slept in his clothes. He looks down at his body, feels it, grabs a fold or two of flesh.

'Too many *asados*, too much *chimichurri*.'

He gazes down and discovers an empty bottle of Knockando whisky on the floor by the bed, with a glass on its side next to it.

'Too much whisky.'

He has a foul taste in his mouth. He stands up, nearly falls over.

'Hangover, my old friend. At last we meet again.'

In the bathroom, the light from the bulb over the mirror shows Carvalho's surprise at seeing his own reflection: several days' growth of beard, dark circles round his eyes, toothbrush dangling from his mouth. He reaches out and touches the bulb. It burns his finger.

'Sun, suns inside. I wonder what the weather's like in Barcelona?'

He continues talking to the person reflected in the mirror.

'You'll never find your way home.'

He decides to rinse his mouth. Then he smears his cheeks with shaving cream out of a spray. He looks down at the container angrily, then up at the bathroom ceiling, as if trying to gaze at the distant southern heavens.

'I've just made another centimetre hole in the ozone layer.'

He surveys the ceiling as if he might find the ozone layer there. It's full of flaking plaster and patches of damp. He draws a furrow in his lathered cheek with a disposable razor. By the time he opens the door to the office, he feels somewhat restored, though a little weary. He studies the composition offered by Don Vito and Borges Jr.

'Señor Altofini, would you mind checking your paper to see what the weather is like in Spain?'

As if this were the most natural thing in the world to do at this time of day, Don Vito picks up a carefully folded newspaper from the desk, and stands up to let Carvalho sit down while he carries out his task. Carvalho sinks into the chair and listens as Borges Jr. launches straight into his story.

'I've come to ask your professional help on the strength of our long-lasting friendship. We met in one of those places where people really get to know each other: jails, police stations, lifeboats.'

'Now I remember. It was in a lifeboat.'

'It was in a police station. Do you remember Borges' son, who helped you through your moment of despair? A group of Borges fanatics who call themselves El Aleph are threatening me. They sent me this anonymous letter.'

Carvalho reads it. 'What does Aleph mean?'

'It's the letter alpha, the "a" of the Hebrew alphabet. But my father used it with lots of meanings, and no meaning at all.'

Don Vito has found what he was looking for.

'Here it is. There's an anticyclone over southwestern Europe. Do you want to know the high and low temperatures?'

'That's not the weather. What on earth has the weather got to do with temperatures?'

Carvalho nods thoughtfully. Waves the sheet of paper in the air.

'There are no fanatics worse than those addicted to a cultural myth. Especially nowadays, when nobody believes in anything. When they do find something to believe in, they can commit any crime in order to defend their belief. It will be an expensive investigation.'

'Very expensive,' Don Vito echoes him.

'Incredibly expensive,' Carvalho says, raising the adverbial stakes even higher.

'These fellows probably spend the whole day reciting quotations from your father's work.'

'Degrading them, you mean. Money is no object. My mother, and even I, have some savings put by after two long lives of forced labour. Mamma was the queen of contortionism at a time when her clients smothered her in mysteries and jewels. It's a shame she's so small, or there would have been more jewels.'

Don Vito thanks God that mysteries pass and jewels remain. Ariel Borges is suddenly carried away, and clasps one of Carvalho's hands between his two huge paws:

'I can prove I am my father's son!'

'You don't say.'

'When I was a little boy, my mother used to take me to see him in his apartment in Calle Maipú, though she always kept it from Aunty Nora and the Borges mafia. But papa did recognize me. He wrote as much in *The Self and the Other*, from 1964, when mamma went to see him to remind him of his paternity. It's a poem called "To The Son".'

> *It was not I who begot you. It was the dead –*
> *my father, and his father, and their forebears,*
> *all those who through a labyrinth of loves*
> *descend from Adam and the desert wastes*
> *of Cain and Abel, in a dawn so ancient*
> *it has become mythology by now,*
> *to arrive, blood and marrow, at this day*
> *in the future, in which I now beget you.*
> *I feel their multitudes. They are who we are,*
> *and you among us, you and the sons to come*
> *that you will beget. The latest in the line*
> *and in red Adam's line. I too am those others.*
> *Eternity is present in the things*
> *of time and its impatient happenings.*

Borges Jr. finishes his recital and looks expectantly towards Carvalho and Don Vito to see the effect. Altofini is truly amazed.

'You recite wonderfully.'

'Yes, wonderfully. It may be that my partner can take your case,' Carvalho adds. 'To investigate this club of fanatics who are threatening you. We're up to our eyes in work.'

'Up to our ears,' Don Vito insists.

'I am on the trail of an eternal fugitive, my cousin Raúl Tourón, who is no ordinary man. Perhaps you have run into him?'

'I don't leave home much.'

'Don't be surprised by my question. I ask everyone the same.'

'Questions like that may seem silly, but they can be effective, I know. My papa used to say...'

He is unable to finish, because an imposing figure suddenly looms in the office doorway. His gestures are offhand, but his eyes put a price on everything they encounter. When they have totalled up everything in the room, the newcomer's face assumes a sardonic grin. His disdain as he hands a business card to the attentive Don Vito is in direct proportion to the detective's unctuous charm.

'Getulio Merletti, Boom Boom Peretti's manager.'

Borges Jr. leaves the office, promising to stay in touch and to dedicate special editions to them. He bows his massive head to the newcomer, who does not even deign to notice him. Then he gropes his way down the unlit staircase, worried that his outsized body will betray his spindly legs. The violent sun outside brings him to a halt, but he is more concerned at the violent voice he hears.

'Are you blind like your father then?'

Borges recognizes Inspector Pascuali. Behind him he sees the two other policemen who always accompany him.

'You've got nothing on me.'

'So now you call yourself Ariel. That was your name ten years ago too, when you were Ariel Carriego.'

'There's no point you pursuing me. I've retired. I've recovered my true identity.'

'And how's your mother, the contortionist?'

'She's too old for contortions, poor thing.'

'It's in her blood. Do you remember when your mother Dora la Larga sold some poor fool a Philips shaver, telling him he could use it to contact UFOs?'

Pascuali motions towards the doorway Ariel has just come out of.

'Since when did a fraudster like you need a private detective?'

'He's an old friend. It was thanks to you I met him, in one of your cells.'

Too short to reach the shoulders of this Percheron man, Pascuali puts an arm round his waist and pushes him along the pavement. He falls in beside Ariel, who all at once looks sad and defeated.

'Borges – let's say your name is Borges, just for now. Today I want us to talk about Pepe Carvalho. But you're looking very pale. What's wrong?'

'I'm hungry. I always get hungry at this time of day. I'm a big man with a big appetite.'

Pascuali steers Ariel into the nearest bar. Half an hour later the policeman is staring fascinated at the remains of an ample *asado* for four, of which he has only had two sausages. He watches intrigued as Borges Jr. uses another huge hunk of bread to wipe up the remainder of the oil and meat juices.

'If I'd known, I'd have bought you a pair of shoes instead.'

'Don't be so sure. I eat a lot because there's a lot of me. I take size twelve in shoes.'

'But did you understand what I was saying? I'll forget your record. You can play at being a writer. I'll even protect you from those fanatics if you get close to Carvalho, Alma and Silverstein. You'll soon meet the others. They're looking for the same thing as me.'

'Raúl Tourón. It sounds like one of those nineteenth-century writers my father used to invent.'

'So your father made things up as well, did he?'

At this, Borges stares down at the remains of his food like a sad, forlorn puppy.

'Haven't you ever read anything papa wrote?'

'I'm one of the many Argentines who has never read Borges, and one of the few to admit it.'

In Carvalho's office, Altofini is giving a boxing exhibition while Carvalho looks on doubtfully.

'He leads with the left, but it's a feint. It's the right hook that explodes. Peretti's right and boom! There's no chin that can withstand it, believe me. He's an intelligent boxer – intelligent twice over, because there have been boxers who were only intelligent inside the ring. Outside, they were idiots. Peretti is…boxing's intellectual, like Menotti is football's intellectual.'

'Calm down, Don Vito, calm down before you have a heart attack!'

'I'm passionate about art. There are butchers who are artists – you can be an artist in any trade.'

'Yes, there have been some unique hangmen. And torturers who were perfectionists.'

'Don't try to twist what I'm saying. You and I for example are artists in our line of work.'

At that moment, Alma comes in.

'What about me?' she wants to know.

Altofini goes to greet her. He takes her hand, kisses it and proclaims: 'You're an artist and a muse!'

Alma strikes the pose of a flattered queen and asks somewhat haughtily: 'What are you playing at today?'

'Jorge Luis Borges' natural son and Boom Boom Peretti have

engaged our services,' Altofini tells her.

'It's strange, sometimes Borges looked like a blind boxer, and isn't Peretti the intellectual boxer?' she asks, looking towards Carvalho for an answer.

But Carvalho does not reply. Tongue-tied? Change in the moon? Lack of knowledge of the subject?

'It's not my day, week, month, or year,' he explains.

'How about the decade?'

'Shit.'

'My decade was the fifties to sixties: from fifty-five to sixty-five! That was Altofini on the crest of a wave, I had twenty fedoras, two top hats to go racing in, and half-a-dozen bowlers.'

Much to Altofini's horror, these remarks send Alma into a fit of uncontrollable laughter. Carvalho picks up on it, and is soon reduced to a similar state. Soon both of them are weeping with laughter.

'Can you imagine him in a bowler?' Alma says.

'And in two top hats, one on top of the other?'

Altofini is first perplexed, then full of hurt pride.

'A true gentleman should always wear a hat.'

Altofini is still annoyed with Carvalho as they get into the car that is to take them to their meeting with Boom Boom Peretti. He gives monosyllabic directions about how they should get out of Buenos Aires.

'South. Keep going south. Towards Mar del Plata. Boom Boom's country house is between Dolores and Maipú.'

Altofini has put his hat on, as if to defy his critics. Carvalho shoots him a glance as they speed along.

'You were quite right. With a hat on, you do look like a gentleman.'

'Aha…you have to know how to wear one, that's all. My family have always been great hat-wearers. My father, his father before him. And as for the women! My mother never ever went to any important occasion without her hat, and she had a hat for every occasion. Mamma!' Dreamily nostalgic, Altofini adjusts his hat in the mirror of the car flap. 'Don't get carried away. You have to turn left at the next side road. This car of yours is a disgrace. When Argentina was a rich and civilized country, we had the finest and best-kept cars in the world. D'you know when I first realized how bad things had become? When I saw that people didn't bother to fix the dents in their cars, or to whitewash their tyres.'

Their appointment takes them first of all to a private airfield. A light plane is circling to land. Eventually it does so, and once things have quietened down again, out steps Merletti. He's followed by several men with flattened noses and scarred eyebrows, and then by a spectacular blond youth who walks down the four steps from the Fokker carefully studying his fingernails. The last to appear is Peretti. He stands at the top of the steps, body taut and powerful, as if emphasizing the distance between himself and all those who have already left the plane. On the runway, he whispers something to Merletti, who comes over to Carvalho and Altofini in their car.

'The boss would rather talk to you at home. Follow our cars. If you lose us, remember it's the Estancia Angostura, twenty kilometres before Maipú.'

They do not get lost, and succeed in following the procession of cars up to a mansion that looks as if it has been transferred stone by stone from the English home counties. Merletti is waiting for them with his sour poker-face. He looks at Altofini's hat and cannot resist a sarcastic comment.

'You'd better jam it on tight: the pampas wind could blow it away at any moment.'

Don Vito decides to take his hat off and hold it in both hands. They go into the hall, where in spite of the almost luxurious décor, the number of misplaced or forgotten objects conveys a sense of insecurity, as if the mansion were not inhabited by its real owners.

'Boom Boom is expecting you. He couldn't come to Buenos Aires, because his next fight is a hard one. It's against Azpeitia, that brute of a Spaniard who only knows how to hold on and head-butt.'

'He's not a boxer, he's a goat,' Altofini confirms.

'Yes, but he splits everyone's eyebrows, and Peretti can't bear to get his face cut.'

'The face is the mirror of the soul, and therefore of boxing as one of the fine arts. The great master stylists have never had their faces cut. Look at Cassius Clay.'

'He was called Mohammed Ali,' Carvalho corrects him.

They cross the hall and go out into a central courtyard, almost a cloister, with a silent fountain in the middle. They skirt a myrtle hedge enclosing a majestic monkey-puzzle tree and head for a door leading to a gym. Peretti is already training with his sparring partners. His face is barely visible beneath his helmet, but there is a gleam of fierce determination in his eyes as he pummels his opponents. The young blond who was so worried about his nails is now risking damage to them as he pokes at a punchbag. His movements and blows are more a parody than an imitation of Peretti's inside the ring. Much more impressive than his weak punches is the enormous tattoo that almost covers his entire left arm. Merletti bangs a gong. Peretti's sparring partner drops his guard, but Peretti carries on punching furiously, and a right hook sends the other man sprawling. Peretti gradually realizes what he has done, and helps his partner to his feet. He apologizes. He takes his helmet off and once again becomes the 'intellectual' boxer the press is so proud of. He weighs up Carvalho and Altofini as Merletti brings them over. Merletti reluctantly makes the introductions.

'Carvalho and Altofini, private detectives.'

Peretti points first to Carvalho, then to Altofini.

'Carvalho? Altofini?'

'Yes, you got it right.'

'Those eagle eyes of yours,' Altofini agrees.

'It's easy. I was told one of them is a Spaniard, and you walk like a Spaniard.'

'How do Spaniards walk?'

'With no rhythm. To a Spaniard, walking is the shortest path between two points.'

'It's a theory.'

'A brilliant and true one,' Altofini agrees.

'Show them into the bar. I'll be with you right away,' Peretti orders Merletti.

He strides off, bouncing on the balls of his feet as if still in the ring. He is followed by the blond, tattooed youth, who has shown as little enthusiasm for the newcomers as he had for the punchbag. In the bar, Merletti serves them whisky from a smoked-crystal decanter.

'Are you sure you don't want ice and water?'

'I'd like to see how good it is first,' Carvalho replies.

They are interrupted by the voice and the presence of Peretti. The blond youth follows in his wake as ever.

'The Spaniard must be a whisky connoisseur then. Drink it without water or ice. It's a thirty-year-old Springbank. The people who gave it me said it was a decent one.'

'If it's a thirty-year-old Springbank, they weren't lying. It's excellent, and very expensive.'

'You mean you've tried it before?' Merletti asks sarcastically.

'In my clients' private planes they don't serve anything else.'

Altofini stares down at his glass full of water, ice and thirty-year-old Springbank.

'But a bit of water and ice helps you piss it out. It's the only way to get rid of whisky. You have to have kidneys like Boom Boom or the Spaniard here to drink it on its own.'

Peretti has installed himself in an armchair, and dominates the room. He tilts his head in the direction of his companion.

'Robert, my son.'

The blond youth nods briefly.

'What do you mean, your son?' Altofini wants to know. 'You don't look old enough! Did you adopt him?'

Carvalho tries to calm Don Vito's impetuous curiosity, and Peretti cuts short the discussion.

'He's my son, and that's that.'

Altofini is so eager to accept this that he is about to start speaking again, until Carvalho silences him with a stare.

'Now I'd like to talk alone with our visitors,' Peretti tells everyone.

Merletti and Robert leave. It takes some time for Peretti to feel comfortable with the new arrangement, but he gradually relaxes. He reaches into his sports jacket pocket and hands Carvalho a letter. The detective reads it without comment.

Dear Lorenzo. I've read about your success in the papers
and occasionally I've gone to Luna Park to try to see
you box, but the tickets are very expensive for someone
like me. How well I remember those months when I was
the young teacher and you the adolescent pupil, those
days when we were happy, the two of us together, men

twice over, as you used to say, and it makes me sad to see
myself as I am, a ruin and an addict for every drug but
nothing else, someone down on his luck in life and in his
career, someone who fears he is destroying himself. I need
your help. Not in the name of what we once were, but
appealing to your qualities as a human being, of which
I have so much evidence. Write to me at PO Box 3457.
I don't have a fixed address.

LOAIZA

Peretti waits for Carvalho to say something. He nods when the detective asks for permission to show the letter to Altofini. To gain time, Carvalho pretends to wait for his partner to read it. When he finishes, Don Vito is obviously trying so hard to seem unaffected that his face takes on a comic cardboard rigidity.

'Well?' Peretti insists.

'Did you reply to this letter?'

'Yes. I must confess, I replied out of a mixture of compassion and fear. Compassion because I once admired Bruno Loaiza a lot, and fear because a person who lives sordidly behaves sordidly.'

'Young teacher…adolescent pupil. What years are we talking about?'

'It was at the end of the seventies. I was an oddball who was part of the world of junior amateur boxing, but at the same time I had enrolled at university. A lot of lecturers were missing: some were political prisoners, others had been wiped out, or were on the run. Of the few that had stayed, Bruno was one of the most brilliant, like a link with the intellectual splendour of the days before the military coup. He was as brilliant as he was careless about his seductions. He liked to play moral and sexual Russian roulette. He didn't care who got the bullet. But I don't hate him for it, I feel curious, curious about myself perhaps, about the curious and uncontrollable youth I once was.'

'When did your relations end?'

'The most intimate part only lasted one academic year. We used to meet as friends, but as his drug addiction got worse we saw each other less and less.'

'Did you see him after you got the letter?'

'No. I sent him money. On several occasions. The letters he sent me became increasingly bitter and demanding. Threatening.'

Peretti is expecting Carvalho to continue with his questions, but the detective says nothing and Altofini does not dare intervene.

'Excuse me if I don't show you the other letters. They would only make this dirtier, more disgusting, as if he were trying to spoil something that was almost beautiful. It was a youthful mistake. At university I wanted to be a boxer and a wise scholar at one and the same time. I enrolled in several subjects. I met Loaiza in philosophy – I already told you he was a stand-in lecturer, a promising poet, who said he was fascinated because in me he could see a real, complete man. You haven't asked me, but I'm going to tell you so that it's out in the open once and for all, to lay my cards on the table. For several months, we had a homosexual relationship.'

'How many months exactly?' Altofini asks.

'Four months and seven and a half days, to be completely precise: not a second more, not a second less.'

'The Greeks, Plato, Turkish wrestlers. No reason to feel ashamed,' Altofini concedes.

'I don't feel ashamed or sorry for anything, but I can imagine exactly what might happen if the news gets out that I had homosexual relations when I was twenty. In this country you can throw your wife out of a window and they forgive you because you're a macho man, but homosexuality is only tolerated in a few comedians. I need to bring Bruno Loaiza under control. To find him. Confront him. To put a stop to his threats. I'm not worried about money. I'm worried about the absurd, crazy logic of a drug addict.'

By the time they leave Peretti's mansion, night has fallen. Carvalho drives in weary silence. Still wearing his hat, Altofini has also been silenced by all he has seen and heard. He turns it over in his mind, and after thirty kilometres or so leans over to Carvalho and makes an obscene gesture with two fingers of each hand.

'So they fucked each other up the arse?'

'Where else?'

'Of course, of course. And how well that queer talks! How right my master Victor Hugo was when he said: "what is well-thought is well said / in words straight from the head". Ah, the human condition!

The more a man develops his body, the more he admires the body of another man, as Plato said.'

'The Greek philosopher?'

'No, Plato Carrasco, an ex-brother-in-law of mine who ran a gym down by Chacarita cemetery. He was a loyal Perónist. He wanted to improve the Argentine race.'

A melancholy Carvalho is studying the market stalls, surprised at the names of the cuts of meat, at how few fish there are. Alma watches him staring thoughtfully at what's on offer: topside, sirloin, rumpsteak, offal. She goes up to him and accepts his silent contemplation until finally he speaks: 'One day you'll have to come to Barcelona, and I'll take you to the Boquería market. Spain is full of wonderful markets. In Galicia there are fish markets that look like underwater cathedrals.'

'You're obviously in full nostalgic denial mode. How do you fight against it? Do you always come to markets?'

'First of all, a crime. Then a market. That's where I come in.'

'What crime are you talking about?'

Carvalho invites her to look around.

'We're surrounded by dead bodies: cattle, lamb, fish, lettuces, turnips, celery. Someone ended their lives so we can eat them.'

'So butchers and stallholders are murderers?'

'Murderers or their accomplices. Nobody is innocent.'

Suddenly Alma sees the women selling their wares as accomplices to a crime. She stares at all the victims, especially the whole fish on slabs, imagines their quiet or thrashing deaths. Closes her eyes.

'How horrible! If you look at it like that, we're in a cemetery.'

'But these are the dead without burial. Their burial is here and here.'

He points to his head and stomach.

'I'll never eat animals again.'

'But is it any better to kill plants? Have you seen the face of a stick of celery when it's pulled from the ground? Some botanists say plants scream when they die.'

Alma stares at Carvalho as though he is the messenger of death.

'Did you come here to give yourself a fright?'

'I was already scared. Font y Rius has been playing games again, and he's brought Raúl back into the eye of the storm.'

They walk back to Carvalho's apartment, his bag full of death, his head full of plans for cooking.

'It's only by cooking that we can disguise tragedy and horror.'

Alma describes the talk she had with Font y Rius, but Carvalho seems uninterested in anything to do with Raúl. He is staring at the rain drizzling outside the windows. Alma is sitting opposite him with a *mate* gourd in her hands. Carvalho is cupping a glass of whisky on the rocks, amazed at the persistence of this Argentine monsoon.

'It's done nothing but rain for weeks. It reminds me of the rains in Ranchipur. I'm so old I can remember the version of *The Day the Rains Came* with Myrna Loy and Tyrone Power. Have you any idea who Myrna Loy was? I wonder what the weather's like in Barcelona?'

'The sooner you find Raúl, the sooner you'll be able to go home. You're like ET. Home! Home!'

'Font y Rius is off his head. He would be a psychiatrist, wouldn't he? But what about my cousin? Why is he playing Russian roulette like this? And who told you you would find me in the market?'

'Don Vito. He was very pleased that cretin asked you for help. That son of a bitch who passes himself off as Borges' son.'

'None of my clients are sons of bitches.'

'Well, he is. He's trying to destroy the old man's reputation, to tarnish his image.'

'Why are you so worried about the image of a reactionary like him? He made short shrift of you revolutionaries, and applauded the dirty war.'

'Who didn't applaud the dirty war? Even some of our own comrades did. We said: let them come and get us! That way they'll show the true nature of this fascist regime.'

'Arrogance in arms.'

'If we were arrogant, what was the system? Anyway, within fifty years Borges will be read just as a writer, not as an ideologue. Who nowadays is bothered by the fact that Virgil was Octavius Augustus' arselicker? Or that Defoe was a miserable police informer, or Verlaine a poor wretch?'

'I never got as far as Virgil. I've only read Jules Verne.'

'That's a lie. And just because you pretend you're not cultured, that's no reason to try to do down Borges. To do down his memory is to humiliate all of us who need it. We need at least to believe in the magic of our creators.'

Carvalho takes Alma by the arm, to try to calm her down.

'That's enough, I believe you. But my job is my job. D'you say all this kind of thing in your university classes?'

'I said exactly the same this morning to my students. I've only got a few truths and a few rights left, but one of them is to choose my own brand of cultural necrophagy.'

Carvalho reaches into one of his shopping bags and pulls out the lifeless corpse of a huge fish. When he sees the look of sheer disgust on Alma's face, he quickly drops it back inside.

'Don't I have the right to choose the bodies I eat?'

The Captain is wearing a Nike tracksuit as he performs sit-ups with weights on a mat in his office. A computer and files rather than books; a punchbag, a pulley, a rope hanging down from the ceiling like an upside-down snake. Muriel comes running in, arms full of books. She bends down to give him a kiss on the cheek in mid-sit-up.

'Are you running or flying?'

'I'll be late for university. I don't want to miss my class.'

By now the Captain has got up and is drying his sweaty face with a towel, but still flexing his legs.

'Which class is it?'

'Our lecturer Modotti promised she'd talk to us about Borges. She told us about the fake son who's appeared, and said she'd talk to us about the *Universal History of Infamy*. Did you see there's this asshole who's passing himself off as Borges' son?'

'Asshole? Is that the kind of language they teach you at university?'

'He's a joker. We have to keep our respect for true creators. It's the only magic we have left. The magic of poets.'

'But there are dangerous poets who infect the blood with the virus of destruction and self-destruction. Some of the subversives were poets. Urondo, Gelman. At least, they called themselves poets, but a poet has to be constructive.'

'I love Gelman! I haven't read any Urondo yet, but I really like Gelman!'

'You've read people like that?'

Muriel runs out of the room. As he watches her go, the tender smile on the Captain's face gradually freezes. He goes over to the punchbag and starts to hit it. His blows become harder and harder as he starts to shout: 'Magic, magic...magic!'

Muriel rushes to catch a bus, but her watch tells her she is still going to be late. She grows increasingly impatient as the bus nears the city centre and gets stuck behind a crowd of people in the street. When she looks out of the bus window, Muriel sees Borges Jr. on the pavement, enjoying a new-found importance that is confirmed by the passers-by who turn to stare at him as if they recognize him from the television. But the crowd is due to a van with a loudspeaker in the road that is crawling along beside Ariel. A threatening voice can be heard over the loudspeaker:

'That peacock strutting along the pavement claims he is the son of the greatest Argentine writer of all time. He is an impostor who can only exist in an Argentina full of impostors. In the name of our great Borges: spit in the face of the impostor!'

The bus sweeps Muriel's astonishment away with it, while Borges Jr. first of all hears the threat as if it had nothing to do with him, then belatedly starts to walk more quickly. An old woman stops and spits at him. Ariel speeds up, pursued by the stares of other passers-by and by the van, which is still calling on them to 'spit in the face of the impostor'. Eventually he breaks into a run, and scurries several blocks before coming to a panting halt at the doorway to Carvalho's apartment block. His bulk makes it hard for him to climb the stairs, and by the time he reaches Carvalho's front door, he is out of breath yet again. He tries to get his breath and his calm back, and finally pushes open the office door. Carvalho is at the far side behind his desk, and Borges Jr. has just enough breath left to walk over to the window beside him, and overcome his fatigue by staring down at the traffic and people in the street below.

'My father wrote in *El Aleph*: "This city is so horrible, that merely by existing and persisting through time, even though in the middle of a secret desert, it pollutes the past and the future and in some way compromises the stars. For as long as it persists, no one in the world can be valiant or happy..." Doesn't that sound like a premonition and at the same time a description of Buenos Aires today?'

'All cities pollute the past and the future. Cities and people.'

'I remembered what you told me the other day about your cousin. Papa was a deliberately hermetic writer, and in another fragment from *El Aleph* there might be a clue to your case. Your cousin is like Ulysses, who returns to Ithaca and finds nothing is like it was, isn't that right? Perhaps Penelope has simply undone all her weaving, and Telemachus is either dead or is still in hiding. Homer tells the protagonist of *El Aleph* that, like Ulysses, he lived for a century in the city of the immortals, that city which pollutes the past and the future.'

Carvalho reacts with surprise at this, and Borges Jr. falls silent.

'So?'

'So there will come a moment when your cousin makes the same discovery as Cartaphilus: "As the end draws near, no images of memory survive: all that's left are words."'

'There is something in that. Recently my cousin has been writing anonymous letters, but at least he is writing. His memories have run out. That's why he's become aggressive. He wants to stir things up, to cause trouble. No. He doesn't want to die. He wants to come back to life. He is attacking all those who betrayed him. He's even writing to some Japanese. He is entering the modern world. And there's no modernity without the Japanese.'

'My father wrote things about Arabs and the Chinese, but I can't recall anything about the Japanese.'

'Was your father ever interested in livestock feed?'

'Never!'

With his eyes and a wooden spoon, the chef is busy stirring the contents of various pans lined up on a xylophone of burners. In the staff changing-room next to the kitchen, four waiters are dressing as butlers with spare, practised gestures that give them the appearance of a group of Buster Keaton look-alikes. A bell rings. It is the service door, and as one of the waiters opens it wearily, he almost falls into Don Vito's embrace.

'Lorenzo? You are Lorenzo, aren't you?'

Don Vito will not take the man's silent no for an answer, and rapidly squeezes himself inside, asking again: 'Well, but Lorenzo is here, isn't he?'

The waiter is unimpressed.

'We're all called James here.'

He turns his head towards the others.

'Anyone here called Lorenzo?'

One of the other three waiters lifts his head without much enthusiasm.

'Yes, me. My name is Lorenzo.'

Don Vito pushes into the room, arms open to give another embrace to the real Lorenzo. When he sees the three men dressed exactly the same, he pauses, but keeps his arms out as he identifies the least bored-looking of the three.

'Lorenzo!'

'Vito?'

'The very same.'

Don Vito embraces him, and Lorenzo begins to remember who he is, while he is being dragged off to talk alone with him.

'Can't we go somewhere more private?'

'The problem is that this place is going to be in an uproar in a minute, and the club members may be off their heads, but they are very demanding.'

The other three men are already patrolling the kitchen in their butler uniforms, and in the changing-room Don Vito has to appeal to Lorenzo to keep quiet when he explodes at the detective's suggestion.

'But...d'you know what you're asking me to do? This is one of the most private of private clubs. How am I supposed to let you see the club files?'

Don Vito is a picture of nostalgia as he puts his arm round the other man's shoulder.

'D'you remember when you used to smuggle stuff and I watched your back? Altofini, your wife used to say, give Lorenzo a hand, he's always getting into trouble.'

'That's precisely why I don't want any now. The club members are dangerous people. True gentlemen, but very dangerous. They're either in power or friends of the powerful, one hundred per cent oligarchy, and I don't know what their real game is. To live out literature, they say. To play the fool, I say. But when they take their masks off, they're real bastards, cannibals. I'm called James, like the other three, and that's how I want it to stay.'

'Just a little glance at the files, Lorenzo. For old times' sake.'

Lorenzo weighs Don Vito up, from perhaps a very personal view of what he is worth.

'I pay my debts, but I'm repaying you not because you helped me stay out of trouble, but because you screwed my wife and gave me the chance to get rid of her, the old bat. I couldn't stand her any more, the Valkyrie.'

Touched by this confession, and anxious to cement the bond between them, Don Vito puts his hand on his friend's shoulder.

'To be frank with you, Lorenzo, I couldn't stand her either.'

'Now get out, and take this key with you. After midnight, this place is deserted.'

It is more like a quarter-past twelve when the door connecting the changing-room to the kitchen opens again. Don Vito tiptoes through the room. He emerges into a hall leading to the downstairs rooms of the El Aleph club, and guides himself thanks to the dim glow of emergency lights. He takes a piece of paper from his pocket and studies the plan drawn on it. He climbs the stairs to the first floor. Then he heads for the door he wants, checks on the paper it is the right one, and is just about to go in when he hears what sounds like a cough coming from an unknown source. He stiffens, waiting for a confirmation of the sound, but nothing happens, so he steps inside the room.

Once he is in the office, he can no longer hear how a second coughing sound from the room next door confirms the first one, nor see how a group of club members are clustered there expectantly. They are dressed like boxers from the early twentieth century: baggy pants, shirts with horizontal stripes, heavy leather gloves, hair parted in the middle and plastered down with brilliantine, moustaches in the style of the King of England or the Tsar of Russia. There is only one butler present: Lorenzo. He tells them triumphantly: 'The son of a bitch is in the office.'

The boxers are anxious to get on with it: they prance around on tiptoe, throw punches in the air. The chairman gives his verdict: 'It's time to give him his just desserts.'

The posse of boxers leaves the room. They look more military than sporting. As he watches them leave, Lorenzo's face takes on the imperturbable smile of James. But his teeth are bared, and he snarls as he says: 'Vito Altofini, now you'll have something to remember this cuckold by.'

Afterwards, Don Vito can scarcely recall that he had already opened the filing cabinet drawers, had taken out the files he was interested in, and had even put his glasses on to read them by the light of a little torch Madame Lissieux had given him.

That is because the door suddenly flies open and four boxers of the old school advance towards him, thumping their gloves and breathing heavily. Don Vito tries to regain control of the situation, but his words lack conviction: 'This is all a misunderstanding.'

By now the boxers are upon him. All he can do is lash out and try to kick them, as they circle round him and land knowingly aimed punches. There is a gulf between Don Vito flailing despairingly and the four men advancing and retreating as they hit him with deadly force and accuracy. So accurately that he eventually topples to the floor, his face a swollen mess. One of the boxers lifts his head by the bloody roots of his hair, and the others continue their beating. Don Vito, *ecce homo*, is already unconscious.

Vladimiro considers the information that a shamefaced Borges Jr. has just given him.

'So Raúl Tourón has come back from the dead and is breaking his old friends' balls.'

He starts to laugh. Borges stares at him with his sad hound's eyes.

'I've betrayed those people's trust.'

Pascuali's voice rings out from somewhere behind him.

'Don't start getting a conscience now. Didn't you betray the trust of all the people you and your mother have conned over the years?'

'There couldn't be conmen if there weren't people willing to be conned.'

'And I suppose there wouldn't be murderers without people willing to be murdered. Don't talk nonsense.'

'Those fanatics are still pursuing me. I'm frightened, I need you to protect me.'

Pascuali is even more scathing than usual.

'Sects. That's all I needed, literary sects.'

He waits for the duty policeman to finish the report, flicks his head at his men in a way that Borges does not understand, then heads off down the corridors that lead to the room used by the director-general whenever he comes to the police station. After a few words of muttered greeting, the inspector drops the file in front of his superior's short-sighted gaze.

'Can't you tell me what's in it? In a few words?'

'Sects. Literary sects.'

'Literary sects? What am I supposed to do with that?'

Pascuali still says nothing, so the director-general is forced to read the file. Afterwards, he peers at Pascuali over his glasses, as if trying to see him without any distortion. Then he stands up. He thrusts his fists on to the desk, and leans forward until his face is close to the inspector's. The director-general loves to thrust his face only centimetres from Pascuali's nostrils and shout at him.

'Sects? Have you any idea who the members of El Aleph club are? The crème de la crème of our business leaders. Their chairman is Ostiz. Does that mean anything to you? And there are top university people, as well as people who have a lot of money and a lot of power. What do you want? A search warrant? What else? Would you like me to question Güelmes, who's just been made a minister, about his business dealings with a Japanese group? What else? Would you like me to declare the constitution unconstitutional? To issue an arrest warrant for the president of the republic? Do you want me to be kicked out of my job? And all because of a two-bit swindler and a lunatic you're on the trail of? What does that son of a bitch want anyway? What does he want? To drive me mad? Like you do?'

Pascuali waits for the storm to subside without moving his face away or closing his eyes. Finally the director-general grows weary. He goes back to his desk. Takes an executive blood pressure gauge out of a drawer, and tests himself.

'Fourteen over eleven! Fourteen over eleven! It's never been that bad before!'

His words meet only the empty air: the door has already shut behind Pascuali's back. The director-general takes out his mobile phone and dials a number he has looked up in his personal organizer.

'Güelmes? Pascuali is pressing harder and harder. We have to do something. We must meet. Yes, fourteen over eleven – what about you?'

The doctor bursts rather than emerges through the door they are staring at so anxiously. Carvalho leaps up to intercept him, followed by Alma. The doctor whispers directions, which they follow until they reach the screen behind which lies a mummified Don Vito. He can hardly even move his swollen lips. Horrified by the brutality of the spectacle, Alma and Carvalho have come to a halt, but Don Vito beckons them forward. They cannot make out what he is trying to say, so Carvalho leans forward to pick up the murmured fragments. Then he nods and turns back towards Alma.

'He says we live in a world full of fanatics. He also says that in films the heroine always gives the injured hero a kiss when she visits him in hospital.'

Alma smiles at this, but when she leans over Don Vito she sees the only place she can kiss him is on the mouth.

'But I can only kiss him on the mouth.'

'I think that's what he wants.'

Don Vito manages to convey the inevitability of the situation. Alma kisses him fully on the mouth, doing far more than her mere duty. The first or last kiss of a true love story. Wet. Deep. Don Vito's eyes show he is in ecstasy, until they suddenly change to an expression of alarm as he jerks his head to try to tell them something. Carvalho and Alma stare at him, then at each other in surprise, and finally understand. They look round and there is Pascuali standing in the doorway. They follow him out into the corridor, and hear him muttering under his breath:

'I'm sick and tired of you two. Sick and tired. Wherever you stick your noses you stir up shit!'

They come to the end of the corridor, and in the main hall of the hospital Pascuali grabs Carvalho by the arm.

'I want to know.'

Carvalho sighs to show how patient he has to be with the inspector.

'What do you want to know? Vito Altofini has been savagely attacked by a group of fanatics, Borgesian fundamentalists.'

'Don't talk such crap! I want to know all the details of Raúl Tourón's blackmail, including what the Japanese have to do with it.'

'One of the people involved is the Captain.' He thrusts his face into Pascuali's and says again: 'The Captain. Is he too much of a Captain for you, inspector?'

Pascuali does not respond, even with a gesture. Carvalho and Alma try to take advantage of his disarray to leave the building, but he runs after them, and this time seizes Carvalho by the shoulder, forcing him to turn and face him.

'The Captain, you Spanish asshole, is a military man, a leftover from the military dictatorship. But sooner or later, we'll be finished with them – all our society needs are policemen, not military goons. We'll leave that to the Yankees.'

'It's a point of view.'

'It's the plain truth. I am the future, the only possibility of order we have.'

'There's the private police as well.'

'Such as you?'

'No. I'm the last of the Mohicans. I mean the private police who are and always will be on the side of order. I am on the side of disorder. I am disorder.'

Plates and cutlery polished until they shine, and laid out in an order the washer-up faithfully respects. Raúl squeezes out the last few drops of dirty water from the sponge. He surveys the kitchen. Everything is shiny clean. He smiles with satisfaction. Through the window he can see other neon signs advertising restaurants along the Costanera Norte. He slumps on to a stool. Rubs his face in his hands. The swing door opens and the kitchen supervisor comes in. He inspects the washing-up, and nods his approval.

'What an incredible day. We seem to have fed half Buenos Aires.'

'And the other half brought their dirty plates along too.'

Raúl takes the envelope his boss hands him, squeezes the edges to see how many notes are inside. He puts it away and mutters a thank you that the other man does not even hear, because he has already left the kitchen. Raúl stands up, takes off his apron, and sticks his head under the cold water tap. Then he picks up a clean kitchen cloth to dry off his hair and face. When he emerges red-cheeked from rubbing his face dry, he realizes he is not alone. He recognizes the intruder, and nods to him. Out in the street, the other man invites him to get into a huge stretch Lincoln with tinted windows. The person waiting for him inside the car smells of fresh perfume and has pink, child-like skin. The limousine sets off, and Raúl's host launches straight in: 'Let's get things straight from the start. I know who you are, and you should know who I am. I am Gálvez Jr., Richard Gálvez Aristarain. Do you remember? My father – Robinson, Man Friday. He was killed just a few weeks ago. My father promised to help you find your daughter. As I already told you, I found some references to the search among his papers. They're interesting. Nothing definite, but interesting. In his notes, my father referred to a conversation in which you talk about a recent painful and surprising revelation. Something that opened your eyes. Was that here in Buenos Aires?'

'No. In Spain.'

'Was it that discovery which made you decide to come back to Argentina?'

'Not exactly. I was already coming back when I found out.'

Gálvez Jr. is curious to hear more, but Raúl says nothing. He sighs.

'Well, anyway. Cards on the table. From the outset, I suspected my father's death was related to his attempts to blackmail a good number of my friends and colleagues in what you used to call the oligarchy. We don't know what to call ourselves. Any suggestions gratefully received. One of the most dangerous people he tried to blackmail was Ostiz. Does the name mean anything to you?'

'He was one of those who encouraged the military coup.'

'Almost all the serious money in Argentina encouraged the coup, but as well as that, Ostiz is a very dangerous customer. He likes delving into sewers and getting his hands dirty. I'm certain he killed my father, and then he helped pay for the first stone laid to create a Robinson–Gálvez theme park. No one can remember if there ever was a second.'

'What has Ostiz got to do with my disappeared daughter?'

'That I don't know, but in my father's notes I came across the following scribble: Raúl's daughter-Ostiz-Señora Pardieu.'

'Why are you willing to help me?'

'I am helping myself. I can't take on Ostiz directly, but I want to make him pay for my father's death. We knew who you were, and who Ostiz is, but we know nothing about Señora Pardieu. We've been looking into it, and she figures as a single mother who had a daughter in Buenos Aires in 1977. The name given to the daughter was Eugenia, but beyond that, we can't find any trace of either mother or daughter. It's a brick wall. With no chinks in it. So we have to go back to Ostiz. Why did my father make him part of the equation? Ostiz was one of the members of the oligarchy who arranged financial support for those who led the repression. That included the adoption of children of the disappeared, so it wouldn't be too far-fetched to suppose he helped with the single mother Pardieu's sinful labour. Who better than a single mother to disguise the presence of a military officer or policeman in the affair?'

'Is there any military officer with the surname Pardieu?'

'They wouldn't be so careless.'

Carvalho opens the filing-cabinet drawers. One after another. All empty. He spins round, afraid he has fallen into a trap. He goes to the door and opens it a few centimetres: no one to be seen from where he stands. He slides back into the room. Checks the desks. Nothing interesting in the drawers. He surveys the walls, the furniture, as if he is making a visual inventory. Then pulls a bulky object from beneath his raincoat. It's a petrol can. He sprinkles a trail across the room, like a signature that curls around the filing cabinets, over the desk and out with him to the staircase. He pours the rest of the can on the stairs. Stands back. Lights a lighter and uses it to set fire to a handful of rolled-up paper. Throws it at the trail of petrol. The fire catches, and snakes quickly up the stairs. Carvalho watches the flames take hold, then leaves the building with controlled haste. As he drives home he sees the flames in front of him, as if they were just beyond his windscreen. He imagines how different people will react. Pascuali. Pascuali's superiors. You are a pyromaniac, he tells himself. You already were.

The director-general shouts into his telephone. He hangs up and collapses into his chair, on the verge of tearful self-pity. He opens a desk drawer and pulls out his blood pressure apparatus. He is terrified at the figures it offers him. He looks up, and his terror becomes indignation when he sees Pascuali standing there patiently in front of him.

'Who burnt down the Aleph Club?'

'Perhaps the firemen could tell you.'

'The firemen? Balls to that! Here! Read this. Stop playing at being a policeman from some B-movie!'

He throws him a sheet of paper that floats in the air. Pascuali catches it. He reads it impassively, while the director-general says sarcastically: 'It's a list of the club members. Two ministers from this government, and God knows how many from every other government we've had! Right from the days of Sarmiento and Mitre! You want financiers? Take your pick. To start with, Ostiz himself, a boss of the bosses. He's the chairman of these lunatics.'

He stands up to impress Pascuali with his size and rank.

'I want that pyromaniac! I want order! I don't want to have to lose my temper because you are allowing all this disorder!'

This time it is the director-general who leaves Pascuali with words on the tip of his tongue. He strides down corridors, fending off people wanting to ask him questions, and takes an elevator to the bottom level of the car park. He signals curtly to the two policemen who try to accompany him, and they desist. He opens a heavy iron door. Beyond it lies an art deco-style meeting-room that has suffered from damp and age, and in the middle of it, a smiling Güelmes, who greets him with a warm hug.

'I wish I could be so cheerful. The Aleph Club has just gone up in flames, and the whole of Buenos Aires wants the head of whoever is responsible.'

'That's the Borges Jr. case. Unimportant stuff. You and I are going to continue a conversation from before, Morales, dear Morales. Let's sit down. We're going to sit down and relax a little.'

Morales is not sure that he can relax, but does so because a superior is telling him to.

'Morales: in both the Raúl Tourón case and that of Borges Jr., which is connected to it, as well as in a series of other illegal activities, we find the Captain involved. Do you know who he really is, by the way? Do you know where he lives?'

'That's a state secret I don't have access to.'

'I know the Captain personally. He has had many names: Lage, Bianchini, Gorostizaga. Now he calls himself Doreste. When I was in his clutches, it was Gorostizaga. I must admit I find it hard to say, especially when you have the tongue and your genitals swollen from the electric prod. Don't worry, I'm not going to talk about the past, it's the future that concerns me. We can't take on people like the Captain face-to-face, but they are getting in our way. They represent powers we no longer need, don't you agree? We can't stir up all the shit they are concealing, so we have to use the jujitsu technique. Do you know the rules of jujitsu?'

The director-general shakes his head.

'They consist in using your opponent's aggressive intentions to overcome him: his aggression becomes a trap. The Captain imagines he is all-powerful, but he has one weak spot – his relation to Raúl Tourón. It's not normal for him to be so obsessed with one person like that. There's something between them that we don't know about.'

'And so... ?'

'I propose setting up a task force to get hold of Raúl Tourón and find out what he knows. Nothing official. Not even Pascuali is to know about it. Once we've discovered what Tourón knows, if it is really important and can destroy the Captain, then we release him and let him use it – we'll stay alert, even help him like Captain Nemo did Ciro Smith in *Mystery Island*. If he doesn't know anything, we'll use the opportunity to hand him over to Pascuali.'

'What kind of task force?'

'You're the one who's director-general of national security. But don't worry. The Captain and others like him gave me a few lessons in how to organize that kind of group.'

Alma's arms are raised. She is gesticulating with her hands as if to underline the point she is making as she sits alone reading through a pile of written exam papers, as if she were talking and arguing with a student hidden somewhere among the sheets.

'How's it possible? "Metaphor" spelt with an "f"? And you don't even know the year *Martín Fierro* was published! What school did you go to? And you? How can you be so careless? How can you write Curcius and not Curtius? Curtius. It's Curtius!'

She throws her pen down on to the desk.

'I'm going to fail half of them. We can't go on giving degrees to generation after generation of ignoramuses.'

Her door bell rings. She looks up, glances at her watch, then gets up and goes cautiously over to the door. She is about to look through the spyhole when a voice from outside stops her in her tracks and makes her turn round, her face a picture of anguish. She tries to calm herself. Turns back to the door. Opens it. Sees a police badge in an enormous hand thrust in front of her face.

Carvalho is bending over to see how strong the flame is under a stew he is cooking. The door bell rings. He straightens up slowly. Goes over to the cutlery drawer and takes out a gun hidden at the back. He has this in one hand and is about to leave the kitchen, but pauses to taste the stew with a wooden spoon. His face shows a mixture of satisfaction and concern as he steps into the living-room. He crosses it and peers into the spyhole just as the bell rings again impatiently. Through the lens he can make out the distorted images of two policemen. He moves away from the door and gives a weary sigh.

'Coming.'

'It's the police.'

'At your service.'

Carvalho quickly hides the gun behind the books stacked on a shelf waiting to be burnt. Returns to the front door and opens it. Two policemen are standing there. One of them thrusts a badge in his face.

A patient on the point of death is having to put up with Don Vito recounting his exploits. Don Vito is still swathed in bandages, but by now he is sitting up in a wheelchair and is waving his arms about freely, and his half-uncovered face has got its lively expression back, despite the abundance of cuts and bruises.

'Forgive me if I insist, but my contribution was vital. The chief inspector – Mendoza – said to me: "Altofini, if it wasn't for you we'd already be surrounded: that is, done for." They were so desperate they had been on the point of asking the Rosario police to come to their aid.'

This is too much for the dying man. He sits up, and screams incredulously: 'Who on earth has ever heard of the Buenos Aires cops asking the Rosario force for help?'

'It's easy to tell you've only seen cops in the cinema. The Rosario police are very competent. They study things very closely. My mother was from Rosario, and she never missed a trick.'

The other patient lolls back, ready to die, and Don Vito is about to go on with his story when a police badge glints before his eyes. When he looks up, Pascuali is standing there. The two men's attention is momentarily distracted by the other's death rattle, especially his very last gasp, which is a gloriously indignant farewell to life.

'You see? I was the one keeping him going.'

Altofini repeats the story in great detail to Alma and Carvalho when he joins them in the police van. He weeps as he recalls the last words the other man ever heard.

'He was from Rosario, and I was trying to cheer him up by telling him how good their police force was. I've been arrested illegally. I'm sure there's a law against arresting convalescents.'

In the police station, Carvalho, Alma, Don Vito in his wheelchair, together with two or three of the usual suspects: a prostitute arrested for public disorder, a young couple sitting holding hands and hoping never to have to go home, a psychopath pacing up and down like a caged animal, police officers behaving like shepherds of psychopaths and a world full of suspects.

Students standing around in small groups. Muriel at the centre of the most agitated of them, as if an important decision is about to be taken. Finally one of the group, Alberto, is urged to get up on the platform from where Alma usually gives her classes. He calls for silence.

'Our lecturer Alma Modotti has been arrested on the ridiculous excuse that she took part in the burning of the Aleph Club. This unacceptable event is a warning there could be further human rights violations and means we must show our solidarity. We have to demand she be set free at once.'

'What about our exams?'

'This is no moment for jokes.'

'Or for scratching our balls either.'

Arguments for and against. The student on the platform and Muriel show their disappointment. Muriel moves her lips as though she is trying to say something, but either she cannot get the words out or they cannot be heard above the general uproar. Her face reflects her frustration through the journey home, and once she is in her room, she sits pressed up against the window waiting for her father to return. Eventually headlights sweep across the front of the house to announce his arrival. Muriel leaves her post at the window, goes out on to the first-floor landing, and bounds down the stairs two at a time to meet him. She hardly even notices her mother dozing in front of the television, a bottle of Grand Marnier next to a hand still clutching a glass. Muriel reaches the front door just as her father and the fat man are about to step in.

'Papa, I have to go out tonight. But before I do, I need to ask you a favour, something I want with all my heart.'

'What's that?'

'They've arrested one of our lecturers. You know who. Alma. Alma Modotti. They've invented a stupid charge against her: setting fire to a club. You know a lot of powerful people.'

'How do you know who I know?'

'Because I've got eyes in my head, and I'm not deaf. I know you're connected to military goons and to important cops.'

'That's all I need: to hear my daughter call me a military goon!'

'I'm sorry, that's what we call military people, even if they are our parents. But can you do something for Alma?'

Her mother is still dozing in front of the TV set, the fat man is hovering discreetly in the background and Muriel stands waiting for her father's verdict. The Captain has sat down carefully on the sofa, and is apparently quite calm, but his hands are tense, and so is the stare he directs towards his daughter.

'So the young lady would like me to use my influence among military goons, to use the prestige I gained fighting wars, fighting the Malvinas war, to go and see my superiors, however superior they might be, and to tell them: set Señora Alma free at once. Alma what? Ah, yes – Alma Modotti; because she is a literature professor and we all know literature has never done anyone any harm. And all professors are harmless teachers.'

'I don't know why you're being so sarcastic.'

'Excuse me, Captain, but perhaps it's time for the girl to know what kind of scum it is who manipulate things at the university.'

The Captain crucifies the fat man with a look.

'What is it she should know?'

'That not everything that glitters is gold.'

'Who told you to poke your nose in?'

By now Muriel is at the front door. She turns to give her father a last look.

'Are you going to do something or not?'

'Isn't this a country governed by the rule of law? Isn't it a democracy? Let justice take its course. I don't think it's ethical for me to use my influence.'

'So you trust the ethics of power? How often have I heard you say this democracy is a farce?'

'I say what I like, and I do what I think is right.'

Muriel opens the front door, and to the astonishment of the Captain and the fat man, leaves the house slamming it behind her. The noise rouses her mother from her befuddled slumber. She stares at the Captain and at the fat man with fear and hatred in her eyes.

'A shot. That was a shot. Who have you killed this time?'

Two policemen push the wheelchair where Don Vito is doing his best to appear even more prostrate than he really is. Alma follows them, watching to see if they know how to manoeuvre the chair properly. When Don Vito sees he has been left in one piece on the pavement, he salutes the two policemen, who return his salute. Alma takes over the chair handles and starts to struggle along the street, one eye open to the possibility of a taxi. Suddenly the look on her face changes from one of hopeful expectation to surprise and emotion. She has seen Muriel and two other students coming out of a side street. By the time they have drawn near, Alma's eyes are glistening. She caresses the boys' faces, and hugs Muriel, rejoicing in her warmth and tenderness. She gradually regains her composure, and adopts a certain ironic distance, although she has to wipe away the tears with the back of her hand as she comments: 'What kind of a country do you think this is? This is a democracy, you know.'

She points at the police station.

'Don't you remember what Alfonsín said? Some intellectuals need to be reminded that the difference between democracy and the lack of it is as great as the difference between life and death. What d'you think? I for one know I'm not moving from here until they let Pepe go.'

An assortment of beggars of a variety of sexes are waiting in line for their plate of food provided by a charitable institution. Loaiza is one of them. He still has the marks of a beating on his face. Raúl is in the same queue. He gets his food and looks around for a free seat at a table. He sits down opposite Loaiza, who is eating half-heartedly. Raúl wipes his mouth with a handkerchief before taking a drink from a tin cup. At this point, Loaiza notices him, and Raúl realizes he is being observed.

'Not hungry?' Raúl asks.

'I eat to live. There's not much of me, so I don't eat very much. Man is what he eats.'

'That's what many people have said. Aristotle. Feuerbach.'

Loaiza bursts out laughing.

'This country must either be in a very bad or a very good way. Look what the middle classes have come to! Someone who reads Feuerbach in a place like this! Are you an out-of-work philosopher?'

'I'm Batman, but in disguise.'

Loaiza offers him his hand across the table.

'And I'm Mirta Legrand, also in disguise.'

Raúl surveys the injuries to the other man's face, but does not say a word.

'Yes, a beating: you didn't ask, but I'm telling you. It had to be me, didn't it? Someone who suffers from a Dorian Gray syndrome and hates the idea of getting old. It was one of those beatings that really hurt and scare you. Coldly done. *Boom, boom, boom*, and they knew where they were hitting. A professional thug. That's the reward we get after all we've done for them.'

'If it's not indiscreet, what exactly have we done for them?'

'We have become marginalized. By making sure we're outcasts from society, we've enabled them to be part of it, to be the dominant sector. If there weren't any outcasts, how could there be any integrated people? It's the same question that used to be answered with the formula: for there to be rich people, there have to be poor people.'

'So you're a Marxist, are you?'

'No, just the opposite. I'm quite a Fascist. Of the masochist faction. A masochistic Fascist. I believe in the happy inequality of the human race. Don't laugh, I'm being serious. I believe in superior beings, in congenital inequality, in the power of the elite over the majority, in the fact that you can't compare the vote of any poor fool with that of a university professor or above all of someone like Bernardo Neustadt or Palito Ortega.'

Raúl is trying to work out if the other man is pulling his leg.

'You're a cynic.'

'In the ordinary sense of the word, yes. Not in the philosophical sense. As far as philosophy goes,' he stands up and shakes hands again with Raúl, who accepts the handshake automatically, 'I am Bruno Loaiza, a right-wing Nietzschean.'

'Are there any left-wing Nietzscheans?'

'What an extraordinary conversation for a place like this.'

He struggles to his feet again, and shouts out loud: 'Hcw many Nietzscheans are there in here?'

The only reply is the sound of forks scraping on tin plates.

Inspector Pascuali opens one of the files he has picked at random from the pile on his lap and begins to talk to Vladimiro, who is more concerned with looking in the rear mirror than listening to what his boss has to say.

'You know, it's surprising. All these people who are supposed to be looking for Raúl Tourón suddenly go crazy and start stirring up the whole of Buenos Aires. Then they go quiet again, and nothing happens in the case, as if they were all happy to see it drag on and on. The state couldn't care less. Our new director-general couldn't give a damn about any unsolved cases: he starts from the principle that there's no point trying too hard to solve anything that doesn't want to be solved.'

Vladimiro gives a grudging shrug of the shoulders.

'And you couldn't care less either. You've got the mind of a bureaucrat. But I get really annoyed that there's a madman loose in Buenos Aires, I get really annoyed that his cousin, that asshole of a Spaniard, thinks he can make fun of us all the time. I'm not going to let him get away with it. I'm going to make him pay.'

'Of course you are, boss, of course,' Vladimiro interrupts, trying to soothe him.

Pascuali punches the empty air, desperate to make some gesture.
'D'you know why I punch the air when I'm mad?'
Vladimiro shrugs a second time.
'Because if you punch your desk like they do in films, you smash your hand.'
Pascuali is delighted at his own joke.
'Here he comes, boss.'
Carvalho has come out of his apartment building and walks a block to his car. When he gets in and drives off, Pascuali and Vladimiro start to follow him. Carvalho stops in a nondescript street, as if he is looking for somewhere in the vast city. A beggar comes up and leans in his car window.
'How's it going?'
'Don Vito, you look like the chimney-sweep from *Mary Poppins*.'
Altofini gets in the car. He's pleased with his disguise and with himself. They roam Buenos Aires until Carvalho pulls up to let Altofini out again. He strides off purposefully into the recently fallen night, and Carvalho sets off again.
'Who should we follow?'
Pascuali moves in behind the wheel by the simple expedient of sliding along and pushing his assistant out of the door.
'You go after the beggar. I'll follow the Spaniard.'

Norman and six glasses of *grappa* lined up on the Tango Amigo bar. Norman is drinking so that Alma will scold him. But next to him, Alma is staring absent-mindedly at the inside of another glass full of whisky, while on stage Adriana Varela sings the last verses of her tango. Just as Norman is adding his applause to the public's, Carvalho arrives and installs himself alongside them.
'You're late,' Norman accuses him.
'Late for what?'
'For almost everything,' Alma warns him.
When Norman nods vigorously in agreement, Carvalho makes as though to stand up and leave.
'I can't bear people getting metaphysical on me at this time of night.'
'Have a drink and you'll soon see things the way we do,' Norman

says, grasping his arm.

Carvalho accepts, and nervously downs his first glass.

'On the prowl?' asks Alma.

'Widening my net.'

'I'll go and bring the funeral to a close,' Norman says lugubriously.

He goes over to the stage and ends the show, bidding the public farewell in a hoarse whisper. At the bar, Alma and Carvalho sit drinking side by side – she is a bit tipsy, he's catching her up fast.

'Will you come to Fiorentino's with me?'

'What's that?'

'One of the places Boom Boom Peretti frequents. His manager Merletti has asked me to go, but without Peretti. He's two hundred kilometres from Buenos Aires, training for his fight tomorrow. It seems there's a Basque who wants to smash his face in.'

'He'll never manage it.'

'We'll see. Are you coming?'

'I won't go without Norman. He's depressed. He wants to kill himself.'

'Give him a good fuck.'

Alma cuffs him good-humouredly.

'If I want to. But I don't. It's not my Mother Teresa night. It's my spiderwoman night, my murdering spider night.'

She draws her nails lightly across Carvalho's face.

'I'll ask Norman to go with us.'

Norman has left the stage and is taking his make-up off in his dressing-room. He mouths a goodbye to Adriana Varela when she appears in the doorway, and then stares at his face in the mirror with the make-up still half on. He puts two fingers up to his temple and pulls an imaginary trigger.

'Imprecise, imperfect, immature. Defined entirely by what I am not.'

He stands up as if he has suddenly had a brilliant idea. He goes over to the wardrobe, rummages among his costumes, and picks out a long maroon boa. He wraps it round his neck, and uses one end to fan himself with in front of the mirror. Then he puts more heavy liner on his eyebrows, and applies turquoise lipstick to his lips.

At the bar, Alma sees something that makes her blink and stiffen.

'Did you see what I see?'

Carvalho looks in the direction that has given Alma such a shock. Norman, dressed like a blonde from a 1940s Buick advert, is swaying towards them.

'Call me Nelly, please. Tonight I want to be Nelly.'

Carvalho puts his money on the bar and gets up to go.

'Count me out.'

'Is that how you reward Norman's efforts? Are you such a macho you can't play along?'

'Those Spaniards are more macho than my mother,' Norman says in a high effeminate voice.

Carvalho stops in his tracks. Comes back sighing. Offers his arm and his night to Norman.

'Miss Nelly, remember you owe me every dance tonight.'

'You will be mine, you Spanish bull, all mine.'

Hidden in the shadows, Pascuali witnesses the scene in amazement. He takes the cigarette dangling from his lips and crushes it on the floor. Then he follows the three of them out of the bar. He is still on their heels when they go into Fiorentino's, where a first glance reveals at least half a dozen people from the world of film and theatre seated under the protective gaze of icons from the past staring down from the walls. There's a quiet buzz of conversation, full of relaxed and mannered voices – a lot of the latest street talk, not quite so fresh jokes. Norman frees himself from Carvalho's grasp.

'My, the place is full of ostriches and peacocks! Who needs you? The night is mine. Tonight I'm anybody's. Let's see if I can pick up a starlet.'

'What about him and me?' Alma asks.

'Your boring old selves. This hasn't been your millennium, has it?'

Norman totters off, hips swaying. Carvalho spots Merletti over in a corner.

'I just have to speak to that bulldog over there in the corner. I'll be back.'

'So you're abandoning me as well? Why did I come with you two?'

'Pick someone up.'

Carvalho heads for the table where Merletti is looking bored in the company of Boom Boom's son and two young ladies. When he sees the detective coming over, he has a word with them, and by the time Carvalho has reached their table, he is on his own. Carvalho looks to see what has happened to his two companions. Norman-Nelly is trying to make it with a young – incredibly young – Argentine film actress who wants to look like la Benedetto. Alma is deep in conversation with an ageing actor who specializes in millionaire roles, or perhaps really is a millionaire.

'What about your friends?'

'And yours?'

'They're too young.'

'Mine are like something out of *Alice in Wonderland*.'

'How about a ten-year-old Talisker? They don't have Springbank here.'

Carvalho nods. While Merletti is ordering the whisky from a waiter, the detective watches Boom Boom's son kissing one of the girls. Merletti has seen it too, and his face hardens, his mouth hardens, and his voice hardens when he speaks again.

'Let's get straight to the point. I brought you here to talk behind Boom Boom's back, but to try to help him. He's an intelligent man, sometimes too intelligent for his own good, if you understand me. All this nonsense about letters, blackmail, and turning to you is rubbish. Peretti should never have got involved – his reputation's on the line. I'll kill the bastard!'

These last words come spilling out, as does Merletti's anger and the move to leap up and confront Robert, who has his tongue somewhere down one of the girls' throats, while the other laughs hysterically.

'Is kissing prohibited in here then?' Carvalho wants to know.

Merletti regains control. The whiskies have arrived, and he waits for Carvalho to take a sip.

'I'd like you to consider me a client, on the same basis as Peretti.'

Carvalho's face twists to show his surprise.

'I'll pay you to be the first to hear all you find out about Loaiza and his links with Peretti.'

'That wouldn't be ethical – either for me, or for you.'

'All I want to do is protect Boom Boom. If I didn't pay you, would that make it ethical?'

'No way. I'd be thrown out of the private detectives' union.'

'I don't think that's funny.'

'Don't worry; not many do.'

'I'll do anything to protect Boom Boom. As you can see, I even work as babysitter for his "son".'

'Isn't he his son then?'

'Adopted son, yes. Almost kosher. It took him nine months to get all the papers – a pregnancy, in fact.'

He laughs out loud, enjoying his own joke. Carvalho drinks thoughtfully. The ageing actor is nuzzling Alma. Norman starts to nuzzle the starlet. Carvalho makes up his mind.

'What do you know about Loaiza?'

'Enough for me not to burst into tears if he turns up in a rubbish dump one of these days with his balls shot away.'

Altofini has lit his lighter so that he can distinguish the bulky shapes lying around the embers of a bonfire in a warehouse yard in the Puerto Viejo. One of the forms gets to its feet. The gleaming teeth of a beggar are thrust under Altofini's nose, followed by a knife that gleams just as brightly. Altofini does not flinch, even when other beggars stand up, other knives and threatening objects are thrust towards him. He stands firm, clears his throat and says: 'Sorry to disturb you. Has any of you seen Mister Balloonman?'

The beggars are as taken aback as Vladimiro, who is hidden at a safe distance, or Loaiza, looking on from behind a barred window on the first floor of a warehouse. The newcomer has succeeded in getting everyone's attention. Loaiza is suspicious. Raúl's voice calls from beside him: 'Who's that?'

'He looks like a madman, but I don't trust him,' Loaiza replies.

Raúl looks down at the bonfire. Something in Altofini's movements seems familiar. Loaiza notices his hesitation.

'Do you know him?'

'I don't think so. Just for a moment, I thought I did. But I don't think so. For a moment I thought so, but no, it's nothing.'

'What did you think?'

'It was a false impression.'

'What did you think?'

'Don't get hysterical. I thought it was someone who is looking for me.'

'So they're looking for you too. And look – there's another voyeur over there.'

From Loaiza and Raúl's vantage point they can clearly see Vladimiro hiding behind some oil drums.

'It seems everyone's playing cat and mouse. Do you know him too?'

'I can't see him very well. But I think he's a cop. I think I saw him with Pascuali.'

'Pascuali! You do have good connections, don't you?'

Merletti cannot bear it any longer; he goes over to Peretti's son.

'The fun's over – we have to be getting back. Peretti told us to be back before daybreak, and it's two hundred kilometres. You know how he gets before a fight.'

'You go, uncle.'

The girls laugh. Merletti leans over Robert, takes him by the lapel of his jacket, and hauls him to his feet.

'I'll abandon you in Buenos Aires, nephew.'

'You wouldn't have the guts.'

Merletti drops him, turns round and heads for the bar. Carvalho is stuck halfway between Merletti and the youngsters. Robert calls to him.

'Why don't you have a drink with us, Mister Bloodhound?'

Carvalho sits with the group. One of the girls sidles up to him and starts stroking his arm. She looks like a fragile blonde with a wicked gleam in her eyes, but Carvalho instinctively draws his arm away. He surveys Robert, made up like an adolescent Helmut Berger.

'Don't you like my friends?'

'From the waist up, yes.'

Robert and the girls exchange hurt glances.

'Not from the waist down?' the blonde asks.

'No.'

'Why's that?' Robert asks.

'Because they've both got cocks strapped round their waists.'

'Cocks?' the blonde says incredulously.

'Cocks, pricks, whatever you call them. You're a pair of queers.'

'I'll scratch your eyes out!' the other blonde screams.

'Calm down. You're to blame for making it so obvious. Anyone can see your pricks from a mile off.'

'This asshole here was the only one to spot anything,' the first blonde says, pouting.

Carvalho leans forward smiling, almost friendly, towards Robert.

'Does your father know about the friends you keep?'

'I'll scratch his eyes out!' the blonde insists.

'My papa spends all day at his boom! boom! and at night all he does is sleep to get his strength back.'

All at once Carvalho lifts Robert's shirt sleeve, and part of the tattoo appears.

'From prison? Reform school?'

'I've got another one up my arse.'

'Do you want to see it?' the dark blonde suggests.

Carvalho gets up and walks over to the bar. Merletti is staring incredulously as he hears Norman's secrets.

'Have you been introduced?' asks Carvalho.

'This is some night! This girl here says she isn't in fact a girl, she's an actor who studied with a Russian.'

'Stanislavski,' Norman explains.

'If he says so,' Carvalho sighs. 'Tonight no one is who they appear to be.'

Alma comes up, blazing with anger.

'That guy was trying to touch me up!'

Merletti does not know what to make of her. Carvalho confuses him some more.

'Merletti, Boom Boom Peretti's manager. And this is Gustav Mahler, weightlifting champion. He hides it very well – he's a genius as a transvestite, but in fact he is a weightlifting champion.'

It is hard to tell who is more amazed at this, Merletti or Alma. Half-hidden at one of the few free tables in a corner of the night-club, Pascuali peers out from behind his glass, unsure whether to concentrate on the group at the bar or on Robert and the two blondes.

Altofini moistens his lips with his tongue to lubricate his words; the beggars sitting round him on the ground listen fascinated.

'In the fifties and sixties, between 1955 and 1965 to be more exact, there wasn't a decent swindle in Buenos Aires that Mister Balloonman and I weren't involved in. We sold a farmer in Mendoza a machine for finding truffles that we also said he could use to counterfeit money. I worked with my other half, with my *babbo*, with my *momma*. A family that worked like a well-oiled machine. My grandfather had fought with Garibaldi. All of us were anarchists of Italian origin who were carrying out to the letter the instructions Evita gave me when she made me a captain in her people's army.'

'Did you meet Evita?'

'Did I meet her? Do you know what you're saying? When I was seventeen, she got me out of reform school. Why are you here, kid? Not because you're an aristo, I'm sure. Aristo, me? I was so thin you could shine a light through me. No, Evita, I'm here because I stole. Don't you worry, she told me. Steal from a thief, a hundred years relief. Capitalism deserves to be ripped off.'

'That's what Evita told you?' another admiring beggar asks.

'That's what she told me. Evita, Argentina's Karl Marx!'

'Did you meet Karl Marx too?'

Altofini puts a finger to his lips.

'That's another story, far too long and complicated at a historic moment like this, after the fall of the Berlin Wall and so on...'

'When I was young I liked the Marx brothers' films,' the most talkative beggar comments.

'Karl was the eldest of the Marx brothers. He was the one who travelled and knew most. But Groucho was the funniest,' Altofini declares.

'Groucho was very funny,' the Marxian beggar agrees.

'So none of you have seen Mister Balloonman recently?'

'His health wasn't too good,' the beggars' spokesman replies.

'That's a shame, because I needed him to put me in touch with Loaiza the philosopher. Bruno Loaiza.'

'What's Mister Balloonman got to do with a philosopher?'

'That's just a nickname, because he was a teacher. I've heard he lives around here.'

'Ah!' exclaims the Marxian beggar. 'The professor. He's a

warehouse rat. He's probably inside over there. He's hooked on his habit. He's a loudmouth who thinks he's better than everyone else, but he's just the same as all of us. He's a homeless bum. And someone gave him a real beating just recently.'

'In there?' Altofini asks, looking towards the warehouse.

'If I were you, I wouldn't go in there at night,' the first beggar advises him. 'Even if you've only got one gold tooth, it's not worth the risk.'

'Everything on me is mine. Including the dirt.'

Reluctantly, Altofini sits down by the fire. Then he curls up like the others, studying their gaunt faces hypnotized by the flames. Absorbs destruction upon destruction. He swallows, and tries to go to sleep, but cannot avoid keeping one eye open. Inside the warehouse, Loaiza also has an eye open; he uses it to keep watch on Raúl, who finds it impossible to sleep.

'What or who are you hiding from? You're not an addict, you're not hooked on anything, you're an educated man. So what on earth are you doing here?'

'If I knew the answer to your questions, I'd have no problems. I'm hiding from reality. I don't want to accept reality.'

'An exile then?'

'Can you tell?'

'I can tell – I could before they went into exile, and I can now they've all come back. They never could accept reality.'

'And you can?'

'I know what it is, but it doesn't interest me. Seeing I can't destroy it, I destroy myself. But what you're running from finished a long time ago. What's still pursuing you? Ghosts?'

'Ghosts and real people too.'

'Pascuali?'

'He's not really after me. He's doing his job. The one who's really after me is a sinister figure linked to the secret services. Though I don't know why he's so obsessed with me either.'

'The secret services. Does your pursuer have a name?'

Raúl hesitates, but eventually sighs and carries on.

'A meaningless name, yes. The Captain. You have to have been in that dirty war to appreciate all that "The Captain" means. We never managed to find out what his real name was.'

Loaiza flops back on a pile of sacks and tarpaulins. He stares up at the distant roof.

'The Captain,' he says, thoughtfully.

Carvalho and Alma support Norman as they leave Fiorentino's. Merletti is the last person drinking at the bar. Pascuali goes over to the table where Robert and the two blondes are sitting.

'May I?'

'That depends,' Robert answers.

'Of course you can,' the light blonde says. 'I like a man with imagination.'

Pascuali sits next to the darker blonde. Robert and the other girl wink at each other and get up from the table.

'Film? Theatre? Television? What line are you in?' the blonde asks Pascuali.

'Sound and special effects.'

This takes the blonde aback, but not for long.

'Very special effects?'

'Extremely special.'

'Would you like to try one on me?'

'Here?'

'No, at my place.'

Pascuali lets himself be dragged off down a tunnel of night and silence. The ash blonde opens the door to her apartment. The inspector's silhouette appears in the door frame, then follows her as she switches on the lights in the different rooms.

'Sit down and pour yourself a drink. I'm going to slip into something more comfortable.'

Pascuali fills a glass with the only spirit that does not smell too sweet, and shouts questions at the woman in another room.

'You were saying that Spanish bloodhound Carvalho has business with Boom Boom Peretti.'

'That's what his son told me. Ready for the big surprise?'

Pascuali cannot take his eyes off the door where the blonde disappeared, and now reappears, turning down the lights as she comes in. She's wearing only a déshabillé. Smiles seductively, sure of her charms. Pascuali puts his glass down. She reaches the sofa, will not let him get up, but ruffles his hair. Then she lets the déshabillé fall to the floor. Pascuali stares at the naked body, but it takes him a long while to believe the evidence of his eyes: beneath the firm round breasts, the succulent navel, the tiny waist he could grasp in one hand, there hangs a short, thin, operated-on cock, pink as a lipstick. Finally he raises his gaze to the blonde's face.

'Don't you go for alternatives?'

'Alternatives? I can't see any.'

Pascuali stands up, confronting the darkly furious blonde. Pascuali smiles non-committally. He bends his head and kisses the girl's hand.

'Sweetheart. I've just realized it's very late and I have to go and breastfeed my babies.'

He tilts his head, turns for the door and leaves, leaving the false blonde with a scowl on her face and a parting shot on her lips:

'Who's going to pay for the time I wasted?'

Alma is beside herself with laughter, and Muriel joins in.

'No one was who they seemed to be, apart from the Spaniard with that dour poker face of his. Why does he always look so Spanish? So down-in-the-mouth?'

'Poor thing. From all you've said, he seems so, so…helpless.'

'Poor thing? Helpless? Carvalho? Help! And Norman was priceless, he looked just like one of those femmes fatales in 1940s Argentine films, one of those vamps who lead all men to their doom. But best of all were the two fake blondes with Boom Boom Peretti's son.'

'Did you see Peretti?'

'No, but I could. He's going to fight at the Argentine Boxing Federation. D'you want to come? D'you like boxing?'

'No, but I do like Peretti, he's so, so…'

'Helpless? Do you think all men are helpless?'

'No. Interesting, unusual.'

'And he'll seem even more interesting if I tell you something I shouldn't really tell you at all.'

Muriel looks at her expectantly. Alma leans over and whispers in her ear. Muriel's face registers her surprise.

'So when he was young, Peretti…'

'When he was very young. We have to find Loaiza. I'll see what the people who entered the university with him know. Even if in some cases I have to hold my nose, because they stink just the way he used to.'

'I'd love to get Boom Boom Peretti's autograph! I'll help you!'

'That'll make it much easier.'

'Are you laughing at me?'

'It's time for my class.'

'What's the class today?'

'About what Lionel Trilling has to say on Henry James.'

Muriel looks embarrassed, as if she does not dare tell Alma she is not going to the class.

'Aren't you coming?'

'I don't think so.'

'Got a date?'

'I want to get things straight once and for all with Alberto.'

'So Alberto's the one, is it? The smartest of the lot. The one who's going to have the most problems. Haven't you learnt a thing yet? What's your family going to say? It had to be Alberto, didn't it?'

Muriel cannot believe what she is hearing.

'You're talking to me like the mother in some old-fashioned film!'

The two of them burst out laughing again, holding each other tight.

'Some day you'll have to introduce me to your father, because you never talk about your mother.'

As ever when Alma mentions her family, Muriel cannot think of anything to say in reply. Alma gives a sigh and before getting up to go into the faculty, pushes three books under Muriel's arm.

'Here, take these. Read up on it at least.'

Alma is disappearing inside the building as Muriel shouts: 'If you see Peretti before I do, ask him for his autograph, please!'

Alma nods without turning round. Muriel reads the titles of the books: *The Liberal Imagination, The Opposing Self, Middle of the Journey*. Then Alberto bursts in, startling her.

'Caught you!'

'Idiot! You scared me. What did you catch me at anyway?'

Alberto seizes one of her books.

'The liberal imagination! That sounds like the Chicago School. Like neo-liberal crap. A Latin American or North American asshole.'

Muriel is not having a good day. She snatches back the book, shouts 'Cretin!' at him, and storms off. Alberto is baffled.

'It was a joke. An intellectual joke.'

Day is breaking when inside the port warehouse Loaiza starts to tremble, to drool – he shudders, shouts insults, curses, shivers uncontrollably.

'Do something! Do something!'

But Raúl does not know what to do. He goes over to the window with its broken panes and looks down into the yard. All the beggars have disappeared except for Altofini, who is still sleeping by the dead bonfire.

'For God's sake, do something!'

'What do you want me to do? Call the cops? An ambulance – that's it, I'll call an ambulance.'

Loaiza grabs hold of his arm.

'I don't want any ambulances or cops!'

Loaiza fumbles through his pockets and inside his clothing. He pulls a purse out of his filthy white T-shirt. His hands are shaking, but he manages to find a crumpled piece of paper. He hands it to Raúl.

'Ask this son of a bitch for money, tell him it's for me. Then score some dope for me. Go on, hurry, you asshole!'

He looks as though he is about to pass out, but in fact he is turning aside to avoid throwing up on the sacks. A stream of the foulest vomit Raúl has ever had to smell hits the floor just by him. Paralysed with disgust, he hesitates, still holding Loaiza's bit of paper in his hand. After a while, he goes over to the window. Altofini has got up. He's stiff: every bone aches. Raúl mouths some almost silent words. He is signalling as if to attract Altofini when he hears a noise beside him. He has no time to turn round. He does not see the strained, threatening face of the addict beaded with sweat, as he swings a heavy stick and clouts him on the head until he loses consciousness.

Altofini is still walking stiffly as he emerges from the dock. First he checks his pockets, then his appearance. Both of them leave a lot to be desired. He scans the horizon. A few cars pass by. An occasional taxi. He walks to the centre of the road.

'Who's going to stop for someone looking the way I do?'

When he sees Altofini leaving the warehouses, Loaiza slips out as well. He keeps close to the dock wall, fearful of being seen.

A car pulls up next to Altofini. Inside are Pascuali and Vladimiro. They look tired.

'On the early shift?' Pascuali asks him.

'Same as you, by the look of it.'

'Dressed for the carnival?'

'No, for transcendental meditation. Sometimes I like to dress like the dregs of humanity to remind myself of the human condition. *Polvus eris et polvus reveteris.*'

'You've chosen a poor place and a poor disguise to catch a taxi,' Pascuali says, commiserating.

'Yes, you two are heaven-sent. May I?'

He makes to get into the car, but Pascuali deliberately drives on a few metres. Altofini wearily accepts the challenge. He shuffles up to the car. Pascuali sticks his head out of the window.

'This isn't a taxi. What were you looking for round here?'

Altofini shrugs. He has nothing to say. Pascuali mimics his shrug and pulls off again.

'Police. You're all the same. Cops! The only good cop is a dead cop.'

He spots a phone box in the distance and starts toward it, but someone has beaten him to it. He turns back towards the port and stands staring at the empty warehouse.

The man on the telephone seems to have a lot to say. It's a desperate, shuddering Loaiza, who has the mouthpiece close to his lips and is speaking in wheezing gasps.

'No, I don't want to give my message to anyone. I want to speak directly to the Captain.'

Raúl is coming to. Blood drips down his forehead. He opens his eyes. The warehouse ceiling looms threateningly above his head. He is tied up. He struggles in vain with the ropes.

Altofini makes up his mind and walks towards the warehouse. He takes out a gun and a small torch from his inside pocket. He enters the building, walks along the different stacks. Climbs up rotten staircases. There are ashes from fires, excrement and tins everywhere. In one of the upstairs rooms, Raúl, tied up, calling for help.

'Is that someone there? Help me, please.'

Altofini has not heard him. He is still searching every corner, philosophizing on all the debris and destruction he comes across.

'We are nothing.'

He thinks he hears sounds. He cocks his revolver and edges towards where they are coming from. He hears them more clearly now. At last he stumbles on the storeroom where Raúl is lying tied up on the floor.

'I'm Raúl Tourón.'

'Oh, shit!' is Altofini's only comment as he bends to undo the knots. 'The world's a small place. What are you disguised as now, a bum? Who did this to you?'

Freed from his bonds, Raúl stands up and hands him the scrap of paper Loaiza gave him. Altofini reads it.

'Peretti? Boom Boom Peretti? What have you got to do with Peretti?'

'Nothing. But the man who hit me on the head and tied me up does.'

Altofini slaps his own forehead.

'Loaiza!'

'Do you know him?'

'I'd like to. So he was the one who tied you up? Has he gone far?'

'Why? He needed a fix. I wanted to help him. He gave me this address to ask for money. He was quite sure I'd get it, then all of a sudden he hit me.'

'What did you tell him? Did you say anything about your situation?'

'More or less.'

'Did you mention anyone? Pascuali? The Captain?'

Raúl nods.

'Shit! We have to get out of here as quickly as possible. I bet he's got the whole of Buenos Aires on their way here by now.'

*

Loaiza staggers up to the gate of a large mansion on the outskirts of Buenos Aires. He pushes it open. The effort is too much for him, and he collapses on to the gravel path. He scrambles to his feet, and manages to reach the front door of the house. He passes out again.

The needle of a full syringe hovers over Loaiza's dilated vein. The anxiety on his face gives way to a satisfied smile. He opens his eyes and blinks: all he can see at first is the fat man's blurred features and his huge bulk, which gives way to reveal the Captain, who stares down at the junkie contemptuously. Loaiza stammers: 'Captain. Thank you.'

'It's nothing. You got what you wanted. Now it's my turn. What is this valuable information you have?'

'Raúl. Raúl Tourón. I've got him.'

'Where?'

'How many doses?'

'A good question: how many doses. Give him a dose, will you?'

The fat man goes over to Loaiza and kicks him twice in the head.

'The soul of markets, Carvalho, is the ghost of murdered Nature.'

'That's exactly what I think. Did your father write that?'

'No, I did.'

Borges Jr. is accompanying Carvalho as he wanders through the Central Market surveying the displays of meat, fruit and vegetables.

'You've almost abandoned me, Carvalho. What's happening about my case?'

'We almost went to jail because of you. I think the Aleph business has stopped for now.'

'I read about the fire. Thank you. Fire does not purify, but it prevents.'

'Your father?'

'No, me again. I thought you must be looking for your cousin.'

'I've scarcely had time for that. I've been hired by Boom Boom Peretti.'

'Boxers are guided by their sense of touch.'

'Yours?'

'No, my father's.'

Borges stays a respectful metre away whenever Carvalho stops to talk to a stallholder. By now they are used to him, and do not dismiss him as a widower, old-age pensioner or queer.

'What are you going to cook tonight?' one of them asks.

'What d'you reckon for after a fight?'

'Chopped liver!'

'That's a good idea. *Fegatini con funghi trifolati!*'

'That's too many different things on the same plate,' the stallholder warns him.

'So tell me an Argentine dish I can make.'

'Have you tried our *carbonada?* Yes? What about *niños envueltos* then?'

'No way.'

'Well, take this down – it's good, and easy to make. Mix rice, minced beef and an onion sliced fine: add salt, pepper, the juice of a lemon and olive oil. Strip the leaves from a cabbage and cook them for two minutes in boiling water until they are soft. The rest is simple. You stuff each cabbage leaf with the mixture, roll them up and place them in a dish. Cover them with cold water, and cook them on a slow stove for three-quarters of an hour. They taste wonderful with any sauce.'

'It sounds like a Catalan dish to me. It sounds as if you cook them just like *farcellets de col*. Would you like the recipe?'

'Yes, please! The other day I made the one you gave me, and my old man was licking his fingers it was so good. Squid stuffed with mushrooms!'

Carvalho dictates the recipe for *farcellets de col* to a divided audience. Some of the women in the queue behind him write it down, while others protest loudly that this isn't the moment, that they are all in a hurry. Borges Jr. adds his contribution as the cookery class draws to its close and the pair of them set off again through the market.

'My father was in Catalonia shortly before he died, and they offered him bread brushed with tomato. Is that right? Bread and tomato! He would say, "what poverty!"'

He bows and makes his exit.

'I'll stop by one of these days to pay my bill.'

Carvalho continues with his search for the ingredients he needs to make the *fegatini*. Chicken livers, dried mushrooms, celery, onions, herbs. Carvalho's face reflects a calm anticipation of pleasure, tempered by the realization that the day is not yet over. Back in his apartment, he tries to keep the pleasure going by carefully preparing all the elements of his dish. He makes the pasta. He cleans and washes the livers and puts them on a plate. He puts the mushrooms to soak, and chops the onion and celery. He lifts a bottle of white wine to the light to see how much is left. The door bell rings and he goes automatically to open it. Then he pauses and decides he should take at least a minimum of precautions. He opens the door on the chain and is somewhat disappointed to see who is standing there.

'Altofini.'

But it is Raúl who enters first. He has forsaken his beggar's clothes and now looks like a sixties' lounge lizard, complete with hat. Carvalho checks no one has followed them, and shuts the door behind them. He goes over to the window and peers down into the street. Nothing unusual, it seems.

'The last time I saw you, you were doing your chimney-sweep number.'

'I went home to change. And look who I found in that rubbish dump. But I didn't find the person I was looking for: Loaiza.'

'I did,' Raúl says.

He thinks about it, and eventually explains what happened. Carvalho listens without saying a word. Raúl finishes, and waits for Carvalho to rebuke him.

'Did you see the Captain arrive?'

'Like I told you, I got Raúl out of the warehouse, and we hid in one of those old disused cranes that are almost falling apart. Then we saw the motorcyclists arrive as usual, followed by the car. The fat man and the Captain were inside. I can just imagine what happened in the warehouse. They must have been furious.'

'What about Loaiza?'

'I didn't see him. He must have been somewhere in the crowd, because it was like the Calle Florida on a Saturday. Everyone was there. Even Pascuali and his sidekick, the one with the name of a Bolshoi ballet dancer.'

'Let's be logical about this. Pascuali was following you to see if you would lead him to Raúl. There's no other explanation. We were

following Loaiza and ran into Raúl. The Captain was after Raúl –
Loaiza must have sold him the information. An open and shut case.
What about you? Are you still happy with your little soap opera?
D'you still want to be a fugitive?'
'I wish I were at least a fugitive.'
Carvalho loses his temper.
'What the fuck do you want?'
'I want people to stop shouting at me!'

'You mean you're going to see that joker?'
'He helps me relax.'
Merletti shrugs and nods to another man. Peretti's assistant
opens the door and in comes the flabby heavyweight bulk of Borges
Jr., who waddles over to the table where the boxer is resting, his hands
already in their gloves.
'Borges Jr. at the service of one of the world's great fencing
masters. Because you are not a boxer. You are a swordsman, and
beyond that, an angelic knife-fighter of the open pampas.'
'Did your father write about boxing?'
'No, he never got beyond knife-fighters.'
Borges takes one of Peretti's gloved hands and gives it a
ceremonious kiss. Then he withdraws without turning his back, half
Royal Hussar, half dashing croupier from a Mississippi steamboat.
The open door to the changing-room lets in a solid wall of noise from
the Argentine Boxing Federation, waiting expectantly for the main
bout of the evening.
The public are shouting as if trying to escape all their hundred
years of solitude and silence. The announcer jumps into the ring,
microphone in hand. In one corner stands a young Basque boxer with
his team. His long nose has been flattened so often it seems like a
second face jutting out like a wall. In the other corner, Peretti and his
seconds. In the front row of the public, Merletti, Robert and his two
girl friends. A little further back Carvalho, Alma and Muriel. The two
women are very excited.
'A world championship bout for the superwelterweight title!'
bawls the announcer. 'In the blue corner, the challenger, Aitor
Azpeitia!'

The public boos and jeers.

'Aren't you applauding your fellow countryman?'

'We're not from the same country. He's a Basque and I'm mixed race.'

'But you're both European.'

'I'm Afro-European,' Carvalho tells Alma.

The announcer raises his arm and the crowd falls silent.

'In the red corner, the current world champion, Boom Boom Peretti!'

Patriotic cheers and applause as ethnic ecstasy takes hold of the public in much the same way as the tongues of fire of the Holy Spirit took hold of the apostles. The boxers exchange pleasantries. Azpeitia is gruff and swaggering; Peretti elegant and disdainful. The bell rings. The referee gives his instructions. The two men touch gloves, and the Basque whispers in Peretti's ear as they part: 'I'm going to cut your face to pieces, pretty boy.'

Peretti smiles but says nothing. He goes back to his corner. The gong sounds. The two boxers circle the centre of the ring. They start jabbing at each other, taking the blows on the gloves. Then Azpeitia launches an attack, which Peretti dances away from. The Basque's punches are hard, but Boom Boom ducks them and suddenly unleashes a right hook that does not land full on his opponent's face, but hurts him nonetheless. Gasps from the public.

Muriel has shut her eyes. She does not want to see the fight, she simply wants to see Peretti win. Alma does watch, acknowledging the punches with a faint grimace, while Carvalho shows no emotion at all. Robert is shouting his father encouragement. Merletti does the same. The Basque butts Peretti in the face. Outraged, Boom Boom feels the effects with his glove. The referee cautions Azpeitia. Then more clinches. Peretti lands two more blows without much effect, and the bell rings.

Ten more gongs come and go, with the Basque soaking up punishment and trying all the while to use his strength to cut Peretti. The crowd jeers and insults him.

'Use your right, Boom Boom!' they shout. 'Smash him!'

Muriel is not enjoying it. She opens her eyes and looks round the hall. All of a sudden she starts in disbelief. Her father is there, and

next to him, the fat man. Muriel tries to hide behind Alma.
'What's the matter?'
'Nothing.'
But Carvalho has followed Muriel's gaze and has spotted the
Captain. Alma cannot understand what is going on, and
communicates this to Carvalho. He does not say a word, but from now
on, his attention is divided between the ring, the Captain and Muriel.
By round eleven, the Basque is tiring. He holds Peretti in a clinch
and deliberately head-butts him twice. The referee gives him another
caution. As they are stepping back, Peretti lands a fierce left to
Azpeitia's stomach, and when he tries to cover up, hits him with a
straight right to the face. Azpeitia stumbles and leaves his guard open.
Peretti steps in and lands a second right, followed by a stunning left.
The crowd drowns in ecstasy. Only the Captain and Carvalho appear
unmoved – staring at each other.
'Pepe! Where's the girl?' Alma says, suddenly realizing Muriel is
no longer with them.
'She doesn't like boxing,' Carvalho comments laconically.
But the roar of the crowd forces them to concentrate on what's
going on in the ring. The Basque challenger is down, and the referee
has begun his count. Peretti is the winner! The crowd goes wild.
Robert and Merletti hug each other. Alma looks desperately for
Muriel in the crowd. She has vanished. Peretti trots out to his
dressing-room and while his seconds are removing the tape from his
hands, Merletti gives an excited running commentary on the bout.
Peretti examines his face in the mirror, looking at the marks Azpeitia's
fists have made. He runs his fingers over his cheeks, and stops at the
huge bump on his forehead.
'Any longer and that son of a bitch would have messed up my
eyebrow!'
'Yes, he was a tough son of a bitch all right, but you flattened
him, Boom Boom. That punch to his liver left him chopped like pâté
de foie.'
Robert laughs hysterically.
An attendant comes in and says something to Peretti. The boxer
mulls it over, hesitating. Eventually, he nods. He dips his fingers into
a pot of cream Merletti holds out to him, and spreads it gently over

the bumps on his face. He turns round just as Alma and Carvalho enter the dressing-room.

'I've brought an assistant with me – Dr Alma.'

Peretti kisses her hand, much to her barely concealed delight. Carvalho takes the boxer to one side, despite Merletti and Robert's suspicious glances.

'Let's just say the plot is thickening,' Carvalho says. 'We've found Loaiza but can't actually get our hands on him. Your friend has strange relations – and I don't mean sexual ones. And also, it seems he was badly beaten up a few days ago.'

'I had nothing to do with that.'

'I believe you. But even more worrying than the beating he got is the fact he seems to have links to groups from the dirty war.'

This surprises Peretti. He exchanges a glance with Merletti that Carvalho catches.

'Bruno always liked playing with fire,' Peretti says, turning his attention back to the detective.

'Did he have those kinds of links when you knew him?' Carvalho asks.

Peretti thinks before replying.

'Bruno liked provoking people. There was a lot of repression in the university, and there was a strong official line, but Bruno liked doing down the lefties. He always said that potentially they were just as murderous as the military thugs in power.'

'Did you think that?'

'I didn't like terrorism, but I didn't support the dictatorship either. I've always stayed out of politics. They asked me to do like Palito Ortega or Neumann and put myself down as a candidate for Menem or for the "Radishes", the Radicals. Politics is an even more uncertain business than boxing. Between Perón and the military, I choose Jünger.'

'Is that a kind of tank?'

'No, a Prussian writer.'

'Politics only becomes a sure thing when it turns into boxing. I'm afraid Loaiza's dangerous liaisons will make their presence felt.'

'I'm a personal friend of the president.'

'I don't doubt it. All I ask is that you don't keep anything from

me. In the crowd tonight I saw a figure who represents a whole era –
the Captain, he's known as. He had power in the cellars of the
dictatorship, and still thinks he has now there's democracy.'

'You can trust me.'

Carvalho signals to Alma for them to leave, but she comes over to
Peretti and holds out a pen and piece of paper.

'Would you mind signing an autograph?'

Carvalho can't believe what he is seeing or hearing.

'Is it for you?' asks Peretti.

'No, it's for a student of mine: could you dedicate it to Muriel,
please. She was here, but she was too shy to come in.'

Peretti writes something and signs his name. He hands the
autograph to Alma, who looks at him gratefully. There is a worried
look on the boxer's face as he watches her leave with Carvalho, then
Robert rushes up to him.

'What did he say about me?'

'Why should he mention you?'

Merletti butts in.

'Go and have your medical check-up, then I'll explain.'

Carvalho and Alma leave the dressing-room and walk down the
centre aisle of the hall. Muriel is waiting for them at the exit.

'Where did you get to?' asks Alma.

'I don't know what came over me.'

'Here's the autograph for you.'

Muriel takes it and stuffs it into her bag. She does not know what
to say. Her eyes are red from crying.

'I'll tell you the truth. I saw my father in the audience.'

'So what?'

'You don't understand. He's very strange, very conservative. He's
always attacking university teachers. He says they corrupt innocent
youth. I gave him an excuse about coming home late, but I didn't tell
him I was coming to the fight with you.'

Alma puts an arm round her waist, and pushes her towards the exit.

'Parents. No one chooses their parents. You have to take them as
you find them.'

Carvalho's face is as sad as a funeral, the corner of his eyes mist
over. Half-hidden behind a column, the Captain watches them leave,

and then decides to head back to the dressing-room. He flattens himself against the wall just outside the door, from where he can make out what is going on inside, and hear the exchanges between Boom Boom and Merletti. The manager is trying to explain something to a furious Peretti.

'I had to do it, Boom Boom. You're an idealist. If it had been me, I wouldn't have brought in outsiders – I would have sorted it out amongst us: that's why I arranged to see the Spaniard in Fiorentino's, and that's where he met Robert and his "girl" friends. Robert's always playing at mixing the three or four sexes. That's why he was so worried about what the Spanish bloodhound might tell you, and dumped me in it.'

'What else are you hiding from me?'

'Nothing.'

'It was you who had Loaiza beaten up.'

'How could I, if I didn't even know where he was?'

'Don't lie to me again, it was you!'

'Yes, what the shit, it was me! What are you going to do when they find him? Set him up in a restaurant, or give him more money to buy drugs with? Shit only understands shit, I say.'

Peretti cannot stand any more, and punches Merletti half-seriously. Merletti slaps him in return, and in a few seconds they are really fighting, working off their anger but without seriously trying to hurt each other. Eventually Peretti collapses breathless on to the massage table, while Merletti turns his face to the wall as if trying to find somewhere to hide his body and his face. Robert, who has had nothing to do with the fight, walks out of the dressing-room without noticing the man listening outside, and carries on until he has left the Argentine Boxing Federation altogether. He shows little interest in the small crowd gathered round a big hefty man who is reciting poems to the jeers and laughter of people whose eyes and minds are still lit up by Peretti's flashing punches.

Robert climbs into a sports car driven by the ash-blonde from the other evening at Fiorentino's, who is now an effeminate male with dark fair hair. They kiss each other fleetingly, and pull off.

'There's always an incredible amount of tension on fight days. Everyone gets so aggressive.'

'Who won? "Daddy"?'

He bursts out laughing.

'Don't laugh at Boom Boom. He's a decent guy, very straight.'

'Very rich, you mean. Did they spoil his pretty face?'

He takes one hand off the steering-wheel and strokes Robert's face. 'Have they disfigured my little Robert's father's face?'

Robert slaps him. Hysterical, the blond boy loses control of the car momentarily, and brakes as he clutches the wheel with both hands.

'Are you crazy? You almost sent us off the road!'

'Show Boom Boom some respect! He's the one who feeds us, isn't he?'

By now the blond has recovered his composure. He looks down scornfully at the car.

'Well, he's not very generous with the cars he buys you. You deserve a Porsche, not this tin bucket. You're the Porsche generation.'

A car behind them is flashing its lights. The blond looks in the rear-view mirror. He does not like what he sees, and is even more upset when a siren starts to wail.

'The cops! We must have stepped in a dog's turd or something tonight.'

He brakes and pulls over to the pavement. The police car does the same. Glancing again in the mirror, he sees two plainclothes policemen coming towards them, one on either side of the car.

'Oh, no!'

'What's wrong? What's wrong?' Robert asks nervously.

But Pascuali has already stuck his head in the driver's side window.

'That's what I'd like to know: what's wrong? Drunken driving? Coke?'

'We're not drunk, and there's no coke,' Robert replies.

'You're driving in a zigzag though, is that the latest style? Anyway, it's a fortunate coincidence, because I wanted to talk to you.'

He points across at Robert. The ash-blond heaves a sigh of relief.

The human fauna in Fiorentino's is much the same as before. Still with traces of the bout on his face, Peretti is having a drink with his manager. Whenever someone comes over to congratulate him, he returns the compliment with a superwelterweight champion's smile.

'Trust me. You shouldn't have got anyone else involved in this.'

Merletti gets up and goes to the toilet. As he is washing his hands, he looks in the mirror and sees the Captain standing behind him.

'Did you speak to him?' asks the Captain.

'Bit by bit. Let me do it my way.'

'There's no reason I should.'

This leaves Merletti preoccupied. He dries his hands and leaves the toilet. By the time he arrives, Peretti is already at the night-club door, and they leave together. Merletti walks staring at the pavement, but lifts his head when he sees the Captain coming towards them. The Captain pays no heed to his warning look, and goes straight up to Peretti.

'Peretti...I'm a great fan.'

Peretti shakes his hand and tries to move on, but the Captain stops him.

'Not just a fan, but someone who can do you a big favour.'

Still smiling, Peretti tries to push past him. The Captain says only one word: 'Loaiza.'

Peretti is pulled up short. Merletti closes his eyes, knowing there is nothing to be done.

Carvalho jabs on the apartment light. Alma follows him wearily or reluctantly. Carvalho closes the front door, then steps ahead of her to open the communicating door between office and living quarters.

'You can come out.'

It is Raúl who appears from the bedroom. Alma whispers his name, as if talking to herself. Then she embraces him.

'What are you today? Cat? Mouse?'

'Mouse, as usual.'

Carvalho busies himself in the kitchen, while the other two sit in the office – chairs apart, hands joined.

'Aren't you tired of always having to escape?'

'It's almost become a bad habit. Sometimes I try to imagine myself in a normal life, living like a normal person, and it feels as though I am vicariously living someone else's existence. It's not me.'

'We're all tired of this. I can't get passionate about anything any more. Norman's the same. And the masked Spaniard here can't even stand himself. To top it all, I'm going to boxing matches.'

Raúl is about to say something, but thinks better of it. Carvalho balances the earpiece of the telephone between neck and shoulder while he tidies up the plates and cutlery on the kitchen table.

'Biscuter? Spain? Barcelona?'

He hangs up in disgust, then dials again, shouting hysterically.

'The day the Spanish telephone system bought the Argentine one, they should have declared the Third World War!'

His hysterical shouts bring Alma and Raúl running.

'Come on, tell me what's wrong,' Alma suggests.

Carvalho flings the phone at her.

'I can't get Spain. This phone is only connected to Patagonia.'

'Here, tell me the number.'

Carvalho tells her, but gets the code for Spain wrong.

'Overseas. Thirty-three for Spain. Three for Barcelona.'

'I think if you dial 33, you get France, not Spain.'

'So you're a telephone operator now, are you? How on earth do you know what the code for Spain is?'

Alma ignores him, and dials again, adding 34 for Spain. She waits.

'Biscuter? I'm calling from Buenos Aires. This is Señor José Carvalho Tourón's secretary. Don't hang up. While he comes to the receiver, I'll sing you a tango, like they do on all the best business lines.

> I was so good to you, but you treated me bad
> You bled me white, to the very last drop
> In six months you gobbled up all that I had
> My stall in the market, and everything in the shop.

Carvalho grabs the phone from her, and Alma spins away, dancing the tango all by herself. Raúl smiles bleakly.

'Biscuter? No, a madwoman. A madwoman who's going to have dinner with me. *Fegatini con funghi trifolati*, Carvalho says, while Alma mimics disgust. 'It's a dish I tried in a restaurant in Arezzo, the Bucco de San Francesco. First course, *risotto con carciofi*. I'm sick and tired of being here in this city full of Argentine men and women like the one you heard on the line. Have you found my uncle? No sign of him?

What's the weather like in Barcelona? It's snowing? They don't know what that means here. And Charo has called! It's snowing and Charo has called. Fine. OK. I'll call you.'

'If we're in the way…' Alma says.

'Of course you're in the way, but what can I do about it? And besides, I've made enough food for an army.'

'*Fegatini*! After the punch to the liver that Boom Boom gave the Basque,' Alma protests.

But she and Raúl wolf down the *fegatini*. It is Carvalho who hardly touches them.

'I thought liver disgusted you.'

'Cheer up, go and burn a book. I brought you one especially.'

She picks up her bag and takes out a copy of *Artificial Respiration* by Ricardo Piglia. Before passing it to Carvalho, she reads out: 'But it was not, he said, the laws of chance that I wanted to discuss with you here today. It fascinates all of us to think of the lives we might have lived, and all of us have our moments of Oedipal choice (in the Greek rather than the Viennese sense of the word), our crucial moments of decision. All of us are fascinated, he said, by thinking of this, and some people pay dearly for this fascination…'

With a resigned sigh, she hands the book to Carvalho. Carvalho performs his ritual, and when the flames have enveloped it completely, Alma switches off the light. The firelight flickers on the three of them, wrapped in their personal melancholies. Carvalho sits facing the fire, the other two have their backs to him. Alma comes over, and nestles her chin on his head, arms round his shoulders.

'So that Charo of yours called?'

'She hardly even asked after me.'

'She's a vixen, like all women. She can only think of you, and that's why she doesn't even mention you.'

She moves away from Carvalho. She looks at the forlorn Raúl, then back at Carvalho. Sighs a deep sigh.

'Children, children. Boys, boys! What can I do to help?'

Alma, Raúl and Carvalho are stretched out on the bed fully clothed. All three stare up at the ceiling. Carvalho is smoking a cigar, and Alma tries from time to time to waft away the smoke with her hand.

'It's dangerous for Raúl to stay here...' Carvalho says, breaking the silence.

'I couldn't care less any more.'

'Why don't you come back to Spain with me?'

But Raúl has already fallen asleep. Alma stares down at him anxiously.

'What's going to become of me without all this excitement? Are you sure you want to go back to Spain, Pepe?'

Carvalho avoids a direct reply.

'At this time of year there was still lots of daylight after school, and my mother let me play out in the street for a while. Only for a little while, because this was just after the civil war in Barcelona, and there were lots of rumours going around about vampires with tuberculosis who sucked children's blood. And one morning, my mother gave me a piece of freshly baked bread – or perhaps I'm just imagining it was freshly baked – and a handful of black olives, those really tasty wrinkled ones from Aragon. I can still taste them, still remember how happy I was to be free like that in the street. If only I could get back to that morning. That would be my real homecoming. My Rosebud. Do you remember *Citizen Kane*?'

'The land of our childhood.'

Alma gets up and goes over to the window. She is upset but calm as she looks down into the street. What she sees changes her anxiety to scorn. Two police cars have just pulled up stealthily in front of the building. Pascuali and as many as six others are getting out. They take up their positions on each corner and by the entrance. Pascuali motions to them to keep quiet, and opens the front door, followed by Vladimiro and two men in plain clothes. They climb quickly and silently to Carvalho's apartment.

He does not give them time to batter on the door, but opens it for them. He is in his pyjamas, and seems sleepy.

'What kind of time d'you call this... ?'

Pascuali pushes the door wide and enters the room.

'Search warrant,' Carvalho says, without much conviction.

'I've got it here,' Pascuali says, touching his trouser zip.

No need to be rude, Carvalho thinks to himself. By now, all the police are in the apartment. Carvalho follows them wearily. Alma is in bed, apparently naked, with the sheets drawn up to cover her breasts. The police search the room without paying her any attention. Pascuali watches them with a wry smile on his face. It's still there when in the kitchen he notes the three places set for dinner. One of the policemen thinks he has made an earth-shattering discovery when he kneels in the fireplace and shouts: 'They've burnt something here!'

Pascuali turns to Carvalho.

'Borges? Sábato? Asís? Soriano? Macedonio Fernández? Bioy Casares?'

Alma emerges from the bedroom draped in a sheet like a vestal virgin.

'Piglia, Ricardo. Born in Adrogué fifty something years ago.'

Vladimiro brushes past Carvalho, avoiding his gaze.

'So who was here? Raúl Tourón?' Pascuali weighs his next words to see the effect they have: 'Or Bruno Loaiza perhaps?'

'You and I have to talk in private,' Carvalho suggests.

'You don't know how delighted I am to hear that. I was just about to say the same thing.'

He does not even have time to cross Tres Sargentos, heading for San Martín. He is bundled rapidly into a van. They do not need to use violence, the pressure of round barrels on his back is enough for someone like him, well-schooled in threats. Inside the van, his brain starts to work almost normally again: neither the smell nor the way he is treated bear the hallmarks of the Captain or Pascuali. There is no point asking anything, so he keeps quiet. Even when the van turns off on to dirt tracks – to judge by the jolting suspension and the efforts of his four guards to cling to the van walls. The men have not even bothered to put on hoods. At first this relieves him, but on second thoughts it suggests they feel menacingly untouchable. He can smell water and rotting vegetation outside: the river or the Tigre delta must be close by. The van pulls up, and they are not worried either that he sees the face of the pilot of the launch or the route they take through the Tigre. The launch leaves the main waterways behind, while Raúl, in sympathy with the weeping willows, casts his eyes back at the elegant buildings disappearing in the distance: the Cannotieri, the Club de la Marina, the Tigre Club – uncertain images in his uncertain memory. There is nothing uncertain though about the giant trees rising pearled with damp from the labyrinth of rivers: gum trees, jacarandas, palms, monkey-puzzles, flamboyants, and huge clumps of bamboo and ferns, the sudden gift of hanging orchids, the smell of water spume and ancient, deep-down rottenness.

Nor do they prevent him seeing the abandoned garden or the house on stilts ringed with flood marks like different archaeological epochs. It is one of the hidden mansions of the Tigre, built from once noble woods, gloomy inside and with almost all its windows broken, and everywhere the penetrating smell of dampness rising from the floor to the peeling stucco of the ceiling. A table that looks too new for its surroundings stands in the centre of the main room, which has a fireplace with crumbling, over-ornate columns; behind the table sits a man with a smile on his face. He offers Raúl a chair.

'Are you all right? Did they treat you well? Given the situation, I mean. Let's not waste time, Señor Tourón. You may not know it, but the game is up: for the good of everyone, it has to stop. You're reaching the end of your journey, aren't you?'

'Who sent you? Gálvez?'

'There is more than one Gálvez.'

'You know who I mean. Richard Gálvez Aristarain.'

'Let's say it was.'

'There was no need to kidnap me.'

'Kidnap? Why use such an obsolete term? Let's live in the present. You are trying to find your identity and your daughter. You have been offered your identity back by your associates, but there's the problem of the Captain. Then there's your daughter. What about her?'

'Have you found out anything about the links between Ostiz and the mysterious Señora Pardieu?'

'We're looking into it.'

The interrogator signals to the four men to guard Raúl, and climbs a wooden staircase that creaks under his feet. In a much more rustic room than the ones on the ground floor, Güelmes and the director-general Morales are waiting for him.

'What next? Did you hear what he said?'

'You want to know what comes next? He's just given you the

whole script! He told us everything in two minutes. Richard Gálvez
is helping him find his daughter through Ostiz and someone called
Señora Pardieu. Morales, I want a report at once on all the people he
mentioned – Gálvez, Doctor Ostiz – that Borges fan you admire so
much, and the Pardieu woman. The one he called the 'mysterious'
Señora Pardieu. Go back and question him some more. Promise him
news, and get him to talk about why he came back. Let him talk – he
must feel like talking by now.'

He does feel like talking, especially because he thinks he can see
light at the end of the tunnel, without knowing exactly what that
might mean. Eva Maria. The vague outline of a baby who is now a
woman. He himself. What would he be like at the end of the tunnel?

'It all started in Spain. I had an argument with my father. He's a
strong character. I'm not. I told him I felt rootless. He couldn't
understand. But you have all the power my money and your scientific
knowledge can give you, he kept shouting. And in the heat of our
argument, he said something that horrified me. He said he had done
a deal with the Argentine military to win my freedom. He had given
them all my research and had promised they would hear nothing
more from me. As far as me and my group were concerned, that was
it. He gave up all idea of finding his granddaughter. He even gave up
all claim to having a granddaughter. I was his only son. He did not
even have a granddaughter.'

'Who did he do this deal with?'

'With Captain Gorostizaga. In those days, his name was
Gorostizaga.'

The Captain orders the fat man to leave, but the motorcyclists stay
lined up beside him. Merletti sits in a chair, crushed by his own
abjection and by Peretti's inquisitive stare.

'Is this another of your secret attempts at protection?'

'Don't jump to conclusions – let him speak.'

'That's right, don't jump to any conclusions,' the Captain agrees.
'I'll lay my cards on the table. I found out about Loaiza by chance. All
you asked us to do was to beat up an addict who was getting in the
way. I was looking for a mouse, and instead I found a cat. Loaiza and
I know each other of old. He was a collaborator in the days when we

THE BUENOS AIRES QUINTET

were cleaning the country of Bolsheviks masquerading as nationalists and Perónists. We were the only true nationalists. But Loaiza is not what he once was. He's a piece of human waste who is blackmailing you. No, don't deny it. I know everything. Everything. I'm not bothered about your relations, or even your tastes. I've known some very macho queers. You're a national symbol, and we don't want any more symbols destroyed like Monzón and Maradona were. Their problems should have been declared state secrets. Who else can the Argentines turn into myths? Come and see.' He takes Peretti over to a door, slides open the spyhole and steps to one side. 'Take a look.'

Peretti leans forward to peer through the spyhole. There is a bare room, and on the floor by the far wall Loaiza is in the throes of withdrawal, his mouth frothing as he writhes miserably in a pool of urine.

'I've been more effective than your friend Pepe Carvalho. Why did you bring that asshole Spaniard into this? We could have sorted it out as Argentines.'

'I told you so, Boom Boom,' Merletti agrees.

'Let him go,' orders Peretti.

'Who?' the Captain asks, startled at the order.

'Bruno. Loaiza.'

'I can't, I shouldn't. Was I wrong about you?'

'If you don't let him go, what are you going to do with him?'

'So I was wrong about you. My, my. I still respect you as a myth, but as an Argentine for me you're no more than a *pulastro*...a cheap whore.'

'I'm telling you to let Loaiza go,' Peretti repeats, grabbing the Captain by the arm.

The Captain tries to shake him off. Peretti punches him in the stomach so hard he clatters against the door of Loaiza's cell. The motorcyclists fling themselves on Peretti. They beat him with clubs, chains; they kick and punch him. Merletti tries to protect the boxer, but receives a beating too for his pains. By now the Captain has got his breath back, and is trying to pull the motorcyclists off their victim.

'Don't touch Peretti, you bunch of idiots!'

Too late. They have to drag both Peretti and Merletti to the car. The fat man is in the driving seat, as a distraught and hesitant

Captain watches them load the vehicle. To the fat man this is just another job, and he reflects on things divine and human to murmurs of approval from the motorcyclists with him, as the car searches for a particular spot on the dark highway. When he finds it, the fat man slows and brakes. A door is opened, and Merletti and Peretti are flung out into the roadside ditch. Merletti's face shows the punishment he has received, but Peretti's is one huge bloody mess. He sits covering it with his hands, as if still trying in vain to protect himself. Merletti does not yet understand what has happened, and stares blankly at the car in the distance. It has not gone far – it has pulled up slowly at a rubbish dump a few hundred metres further on. Two motorcyclists are lit by the headlights as they get out, open the car boot, and throw a body on to the waste tip. As the car speeds off again, Peretti runs to the dump, where the body is lying flat on its back, eyes open to the stars. It is Loaiza, Peretti confirms, staring after the disappearing car with impotent hatred.

'It's Bruno.'

It's Bruno, he says over and over again to himself hours later, as obsessively as he stares into a mirror at the bumps and cuts on his face that have needed a lot of stitches, at the bruises as big as tumours. In the solitude of the bathroom, Peretti cries for Bruno and for himself.

'The Dorian Gray syndrome. The face is the mirror of failure. Of our fundamental failure. That's what you used to say. Bruno. Poor Bruno. Poor Peretti. Poor Boom Boom Peretti.'

He comes out of the bathroom. Merletti is fast asleep on a sofa. Peretti goes over to a bedroom door and looks in on Robert's peaceful sleep. Then he goes out into the street.

The Captain returns home, and goes to his kitchen-office. He pours out a coffee and downs it in two gulps. The house is completely quiet. He climbs the stairs and looks in at his daughter's room. Muriel is sleeping, and the Captain goes over to the bed to stroke her face. She wakes up and smiles.

'I've got a secret.'

'Perhaps it's not a secret for me.'

'I was at the Peretti fight.'

The Captain says nothing, encouraging her to go on.

'I didn't like it…it was so brutal!' Before falling asleep again, she nods towards something on her night-table. 'Peretti gave me his autograph. Or rather, he gave it to someone else on my behalf. I didn't dare ask him for it.'

With this, she falls asleep again. The Captain picks up the piece of paper.

To a young lady I do not know, but who has chosen someone I think the world of to ask for my autograph.

BOOM BOOM PERETTI

Without a trace of emotion, the Captain puts the autograph back where he found it. He walks back down the stairs, pushes past the slumped body of his wife and collapses into an armchair in front of the television. Although he is nodding off to sleep himself, he switches it on to catch the early morning news bulletin. The images and words finally coalesce inside his brain: something has happened to Boom Boom Peretti. He forces himself awake, and manages to reconstruct what happened in the early hours of that morning.

Employees at Jorge Newbery airport rouse themselves and smile broadly at the man who has suddenly appeared. They shake hands with him, congratulate him.

'That's some beating you took, Boom Boom!'

'He sure caught you this time, didn't he?'

'On TV it didn't look so bad.'

The employee interviewed said they joked with Peretti as usual, but the boxer did not respond. He was concealing his eyes behind a pair of enormous sunglasses; his cheeks had strips of plaster on them, and he wore the collar of his leather jacket up. He went out to his plane and climbed into the pilot's seat. Signalled for the all-clear for take-off. Adjusted the controls. He had taken off his sunglasses and his jacket, and the destruction was plain for all to see.

'His face was smashed to a pulp.'

He took off, steering determinedly and without hesitation. He flew higher and higher. Then levelled out. All of a sudden, the plane went into a nosedive. Boom Boom's hands remained firmly on the controls, his face set in a grim mask. The plane crashed into a motorway with an enormous explosion.

'It was terrible because we not only saw it, but we heard it, if you know what I mean.'

The Captain finally realizes what has happened. Boom Boom has killed himself.

'Fairy asshole!' the Captain shouts, eyes like steel.

In Tango Amigo, Alma and Carvalho sit in silence, untouched drinks in front of them.

'What are you thinking?' Carvalho asks.

'And you?'

'Why must you always reply to a question with another question?'

'I can't get Peretti's accident – or his suicide – out of my mind. And I can't help thinking about Muriel. She's so sweet. Do you remember her at the fight last night? She wanted Peretti's autograph, but she couldn't stand the violence. That's why she got up and left.'

Carvalho has to look away.

'No? Wasn't that why she left?' Alma asks.

'Yes, what other reason could there be? But I don't know why you worry about her so much. She has her own family. She has her boyfriend. A commie, according to you.'

'I'm not so sure about the boyfriend. She can't make up her mind. She's worried about how her father might react. One of these days I'll have to have a word with him.'

Carvalho closes his eyes.

'Why don't we think a bit about Raúl? We ought to.'

'Raúl. That's true. He escaped by the skin of his teeth yet again, although I reckon Pascuali is about as keen to find him as...'

'As who?'

'Never mind. But it's true. We ought to be thinking about Raúl occasionally. He's the reason we are here, after all. Particularly in your case. Raúl is your only reason for being in Buenos Aires. What can have become of him?'

'He'll live to bury us all. Even if socially he does not exist. Hidden. Invisible. On the run. Wanted. All qualities I admire, and increasingly so.'

'But the show must go on.'

Norman has appeared on stage, dressed up as a woman like the other night at Fiorentino's. He addresses his audience: 'Forgive me for appearing like this, I'm no queen – a queer perhaps, but a queen, never! It's just that sometimes I get these metaphysical and even physical anxieties, and I start asking myself some fundamental questions. Is there really only one truth? Is there really only one market? Only one army? It's possible. The one real truth would be liberalism. The one true market is the one we can all see in front of us. The single and universal market, where you can buy everything you wish, but sell only what you're allowed to. The army. One. Only one. Who needs more? The US army. The US army and if need be the British army to take on ambiguous cases like Argentina. But there are other numbers that don't add up. Take the pyramids, for example. We all learnt in school that in Egypt there are three pyramids...but no, in fact there are lots more. And what about the sexes? There are two of them, aren't there? The female one with a hole all hidden and wrapped up in itself; and the male one with its prick that comes and goes; and my! how it goes! Tonight our tango is about sex. Honoured ladies and gentlemen, tonight it is my great honour to present the world premiere of the first tango in favour of fairies...'

Dressed as an effeminate woman more than as a man, Adriana has fake worry lines around her eyes, and aims her gaze at the trouser-fronts of all the men in the room:

With your suede shoes on
But your socks left off
A pair of silken trousers
And head in dainty hands
You were like sick jokes
Ghastly caricatures
Of waxwork women
And honey-scented men.

Queens or queers
Love daring only
To whisper its name

Faggots or fairies
Stinking like the cottagers
From public lavatories.

Caricature
Of effeminate women
Caricature
Of macho male
Caricature
Of a faceless person
Caricature
Of a young man in bloom.

Now you see them married
In every registry
Kissing in the streets
Openly in broad day
Now you've got the reins
Firmly in your hands
So why does no one sing
A tango in your name?

Queens or queers
Love daring only
To whisper its name
Faggots or fairies
Stinking like the cottagers
From public lavatories.

Caricature
Of effeminate women
Caricature
Of macho male
Caricature
Of a faceless lover
Caricature
Of a young boy in bloom.

So I offer you this tango
Without a moment's hesitation
Sex has always been
Something shared by three
There never were two sexes
Defined as separate and distinct
Whoever cannot think of four
Can never have two in mind.

With your suede shoes on
But your socks left off
A pair of silken trousers
Head in dainty hands
Stop being such poodles
Such caricatures
Of waxwork women
Or honey-scented men.

'Mamma, Boom Boom Peretti has killed himself. It's a real shame. He was such a gentleman.'

'Did you know him?'

'Since childhood.'

'You never told me.'

'You didn't like me mixing with kids who did boxing. The other day I went to say hello to him before his fight. He gave me a big hug, and he knew some of my poems off by heart. It makes me sad, Mamma.'

'Go out and get yourself an *empanada* to eat. But don't be long – we have to go and sell books in San Telmo.'

Borges Jr. goes for a walk in the park. He stumbles along, his bulky body a prey to its secret nostalgias and melancholy. He recites, as if praying: 'This city is so horrible that by its very existence and persistence over time, even though it is in the midst of a secret desert, pollutes the past and future and even somehow compromises the stars.' A few early-morning joggers pass by, but he is so short-sighted he does not realize that two of them running along in step with each other are the minister Güelmes and the director-general of security,

Zenón Morales. Borges waddles along as before, and the two runners carry on up the hill, slowing as they climb the gentle incline crowned with lawns and crisscrossing paths. Down below is a broad highway, and there is no one else to be seen.

'It's time, isn't it?'

The director-general looks at his watch and nods. The two of them have sat down, and are using their towels to wipe off the sweat, though their hands cannot compete with the flushed scarlet of their faces.

'There they are.'

A powerful car pulls up on one side of the highway at the foot of the park. One of its doors opens, and a man appears as if leaving jail, happy to see the ground stretching out above him to the brow of the hill. He touches his own body. Uses his hands to wipe off the grime that sleep has added to the already filthy state of his clothes. Feels all the bones of his body. Then realizes where he is, smells the damp grass, smiles with satisfaction. He starts to climb the hill, and when he reaches the top looks at the park and the grass around his feet. He notices a human presence on a bench surrounded by pigeons, and goes towards it, without catching sight of Güelmes and the director-general, who by now are standing watching him approach.

'There goes Raúl Tourón. I still don't understand what you're playing at, Güelmes.'

'Peter Pan.'

'Explain it to me so I can understand it for my own satisfaction. Peter Pan?'

'You scratch my back, I'll scratch yours. That man over there is Peter Pan. He never grew up. Nor have I completely. That's why I protect him. Because of what I owe him, and what you owe him as well, this is between the two of us. Let's allow Gálvez Jr. and Raúl to get on with it. Don't bring Pascuali into it. I've already organized my task force.'

'Pascuali least of all. He's nothing but a boy scout.'

'Raúl has almost tracked down the people who abducted his daughter. You should try to find this apparent single mother, the Señora Pardieu. It's my guess that by finding her, we'll get rid of quite a few people who are a nuisance that we've inherited from the days of the dictatorship. What were you doing during those years?'

'I was studying at MIT.'

'What did you think of the military?'

'I didn't like them, but I thought they were probably necessary.'

'What about now?'

'No, now they're no longer necessary.'

Güelmes takes the director-general by his arm, and gives it a conspiratorial squeeze.

Sitting on a bench, Borges Jr. digs into his pockets and pulls out handfuls of birdseed, as if he were a human silo. Out of the corner of an eye he notices another man has come to sit on the bench too. The newcomer stares fascinated at Ariel's attempts to feed as many pigeons as possible as they arrive from the four corners of the park. He is staring so hard that the poet's son feels it as an intrusion. He turns and sees the other man is in a similar condition to himself.

'Don't you like animals?'

'Yes, of course. I partly make – or made – my living thanks to them.'

'Did you breed dogs? Horses?'

'No, I just looked after them. I fed them.'

'Just like me. It's the life-cycle. Pigeons eat worms, we eat pigeons, worms eat us.'

'That's true enough.'

Borges is pleased with himself, or at least breathes heavily, giving that impression.

'Daybreak is like dusk. My father used to say: "the twilight of the dove, the Hebrews called the fall of evening".'

'Was your father a Jewish pigeon-fancier?'

'No, a writer. The greatest of all. Jorge Luis Borges.'

There is no trace of irony in the newcomer's voice when he comments: 'That sounds like an important name. Like an important man.'

Borges nods sadly. 'He was an important writer. I'm not so sure about him being an important man. He was on the run, like everyone else, like Ulysses. Do you know Homer?'

'I'm afraid not. Didn't he write tangos?'

'No, I mean the author of the *Odyssey*. About the myth of Ulysses. Just like me and everyone else, my father invented a return home for himself. But when he gets there, neither Penelope nor Telemachus exist, or are as he imagined them to be.'

'His mother? His little brother?'

'They're nothing more than myths. In the end, all that will remain are myths and the obelisk. Everyone will remember the myths, but who is going to remember the person the obelisk is dedicated to?'

All of a sudden, he holds his hand out in front of him. It is raining. He gets up, as if he were afraid of the raindrops.

'My name is Ariel Borges Samarcanda, and it's been a pleasure.'

'And I'm Raúl Tourón, and the pleasure was all mine.'

Borges shuts his eyes, and when he opens them again they are fixed on Raúl as if they wanted to absorb him.

'Raúl Tourón.'

'Does that mean something to you?'

'It sounds like a myth. It could be one of my father's inventions.'

'I am the name of one of my own father's inventions.'

'Is your father a writer then?'

'No, like me he's simply a survivor. It's taken me a while to realize it. As soon as we're born, we should be told: you are a survivor, the child of a survivor.'

Borges Jr. bids a ceremonious farewell to his bench companion, and moves away in a series of little shuffling hops, as if he does not know how to run. Raúl sits in the rain. He is enjoying getting wet, and his lips move as he recites to himself the poem that Borges Jr. had started:

> '*The twilight of the dove*'
> *the Hebrews called the fall of evening,*
> *when darkness does not yet hinder our steps*
> *and the oncoming night makes itself felt*
> *like an old, longed-for music,*
> *like a welcome downward path.*

Ariel skips along in the fine rain, leaves the park and charges down several streets like a prodded elephant until he catches up with his mother, who is struggling with a trolley piled high with books. The old woman scolds him for being so late, but then falls in behind him as he pushes the cart through San Telmo to the Plaza Dorrego. The square is already full of stalls and vendors, so the two of them have to make do with an adjacent street. Ariel tries to attract the attention of the passers-by, while his mother holds out books like a passive doll.

'The complete works of Jorge Luis Borges' natural son. *Letter to My Father! A Universal History of Commonplaces*!'

He repeats himself endlessly like a stuck record, although each time his voice sounds different. The old woman also continues obstinately with her half-hearted attempts at selling, the pipe dangling from her mouth as ever. Buyers are scarce, Borges goes on shouting, time goes by, the rain comes on harder than ever and the two of them shelter themselves and their books under a tarpaulin. Borges Jr. pushes the cart still piled high with his books. His mother helps as best she can, even though she seems to be leaning for support on the trolley rather than pushing it. The weight and the weather annoy Ariel, and his tango ruffian's grimace only eases when he abandons the cart in the entrance to his house and can finally return to his world of books and collected objects. He asks his mother for the money they have earned, straightens out the notes and carefully piles them on an old chest. While he is counting their savings, his mother knits and puffs on her pipe at the far end of the room.

'Barely four thousand pesos in two months. I'll have to eat the edition. It cost almost as much to have them printed.'

'Did you pay the printer?'

'Yes.'

'That was a mistake. You should have told him: if I don't sell them, I won't pay you.'

'But mamma, why should the printer suffer if the publisher and author can't sell the books?'

'He has to accept some risk.'

The old woman stops knitting and contemplates her son.

'Literature will be the death of you.'

'But I've always wanted to be a writer.'

'But the Borges idea is old hat. Finished. How about changing fathers?'

Taken aback, Ariel tries to find words that will chime in with his mother's ideas. 'You always told me I was Jorge Luis Borges' son.'

'The important thing to know is who gave you birth, not who helped with it. The writer they're all talking about now is Sábato. Why don't you write something like him and present yourself as Sábato's son?'

'But I don't look like Sábato. He's skinny, and tiny. He's a sad figure, in life and in literature.'

'Jorge Luis was no great tango dancer either. Let's see. Come here a minute.'

Borges Jr. trots resignedly over to his mother. She takes his hand, and looks him up and down.

'No two ways about it, you'll have to shave your head. Lose a lot of weight – it'll do you good. Grow a bit of a moustache. Make sure you look sad. Very sad, all the time. "The natural son of Ernesto Sábato": how does that sound?'

'I'd prefer Cortázar.'

'Cortázar! Cortázar!'

The old woman is upset. She picks up her knitting, and puffs again on her pipe.

'I don't know what people see in Cortázar. I couldn't get beyond page five of *Hopscotch*.'

Borges stares gloomily down at the street through the repaired windows.

'Today I met a man people are desperately searching for. Sitting on a bench in the rain. I know who he is. I could inform the people looking for him, but he doesn't want them to find him.'

The old woman has not heard him, and he does not insist. She goes on knitting and smoking her pipe, but throws her son a pitying glance and comments: 'Julio was very demanding. He liked to put his women into his books, and I was always ashamed to have so many people I didn't know reading about me.'

Chapter 5

Murder at the Gourmet Club

Carvalho's client is expensively dressed, although his sagging body, droopy cheeks and thick, ill-fitting glasses tend to undermine his rich man's image. He signs the cheque with a gold Cartier pen, and his other wrist reveals a Cartier watch and a gold identity chain of the same family. He looks up and hands Carvalho the cheque.

'I've never paid with so much pleasure.'

'Señor Gorospe, if it gives you that much pleasure, I'd be very happy for you to pay me the same amount again.'

Carvalho's satisfaction at the size of the cheque is obvious, and he makes no attempt to conceal the fact.

'Paying and eating are two things one has to do with pleasure and without fear.'

'Bravo! That's exactly how I feel! Do you like to eat well?'

'I like to know everything about what I am eating.'

'But our memory is selective: I can only remember the outstanding meals I have had. I can't even remember my wife. By revealing her adultery, you've saved me the maintenance I would have had to pay that cow. So you see, thanks to your investigations, I've saved a lot of money. Anyway, as I said, I always remember the outstanding meals, for example the ones I ate at Girardet's every time I was there. Have you ever been to Girardet's?'

Carvalho shakes his head.

'Well then, when you get back to Europe you must make a point of going. Although the great Girardet is talking of retiring, as Robuchon did. He'll also be retiring young. I can remember a *papillote* of scallops and crayfish I ate there that was truly remarkable, as was Troisgros' *Pantagruel potpourri* and the chicken in salt that Bocuse prepared. Something as simple as that! Chicken in salt! Girardet is the best all-rounder, but Troisgros has some wonderful recipes too. Did you know he invented something called *tango oranges?*'

'How do you make it? How do you eat it?'

'It's wonderfully simple, like everything Troisgros does. Oranges, grenadine, Grand Marnier, powdered sugar...but is it true you've never tried Troisgros' *Pantagruel potpourri?*'

Carvalho shakes his head a second time.

'Would you like to?'

'I wouldn't say no.'

'Fantastic! Tomorrow we're having one of our Gourmet Club dinners, and the pièce de résistance is Troisgros' *potpourri*. You must come! It's at Lucho Reyero's restaurant. He's a great professional and a gentleman. A black sheep from one of the oldest families of the oligarchy who's finally come to his senses and become a restaurant-owner.'

Delighted to have found a kindred spirit in the detective, Gorospe takes a card out of his pocket and hands it to Carvalho with the most Cartier of his collection of Cartier hands.

The curtains open on the small stage at Tango Amigo, and a shimmering, pearly Adriana Varela appears, only a few feet from her audience. The bandoneon imposes silence.

> They eat to forget
> They drink to remember
> A Croesus salad
> Rich as cheesecake,
> Woodcock in December.
>
> Stendhal aubergines!
> Tango oranges!

Slices of orange
A glass of Grand Marnier
Pomegranate juice
Sugar glacé.

Strips of orange peel
Pomegranate syrup
To create the perfume
Boil them up.

Stir the orange slices
In the Grand Marnier
A pink coulis on top
Decorate in your own way.

If anyone wants to know
What this has to do with tango
If you have to ask the question
You pay for the creation.

They eat to remember
What they've eaten in the past
They drink to forget
All they've lived and lost.

Lemon tangos
Vinegar tangos
Because nobody wants
Tangos sickly-sweet

Because the true gourmet
Eats to fill his fantasies
He doesn't count the cost
Of disguising the dead meat.

They eat to remember
What they've eaten in the past

They drink to forget
All they've lived and lost.

They drink to forget
They eat to remember.
Croesus salad
Rich as cheesecake,
Woodcock in December,
Stendhal aubergines.

Tango oranges!

Splendidly drunk, Alma is surveying Muriel's frustrated efforts to nibble at Alberto's ear. Carvalho and Norman have decided to pay no attention, and sit watching Adriana acknowledge the applause after her song. Alma's face reappears over the top of her glass, as she rediscovers her two companions:

'So she said to me: "Don't meddle in my life!" Fine, that's just fine. From then on, I dropped all the friendly stuff. I said: "I hope you hand in your comparative essay on Neruda's *Canto General* and Archibald MacLeish's *Conquistador* on time," then I turned my back on her and left.'

'Left who?' Carvalho replies, finally tearing his attention away from the night-club stage.

'So I talk and I talk, and it's like I'm speaking to a plank of wood. I was telling you about my fight with Muriel. She's become hysterical, unbearable. She's scared of standing up to her father, and scared of sorting out her relationship with Alberto. Just look at the pair of them. They're dying to go to bed together. And sooner or later they will. Why do I have to get involved in all this?'

'But are you talking about a student or a daughter?' Norman asks.

Carvalho does not much like this observation, and frowns at Silverstein.

'What do you mean by that?' Alma wants to know.

'That Muriel is only one of your students – intelligent, very nice, and so on, but only a student after all. It's not as if she's your daughter!'

'Norman,' Carvalho insists.

'You stay out of this, Pepe. I know that, Norman: I don't need you
to remind me. What are you doing talking to me like a stranger, anyway?
I'll give you a good kick in the balls.'

She thrusts her face challengingly at Norman.

'I don't want a fight, Almita,' Norman says, backing down.

'But I do.'

Norman leaves the bar laughing, and Alma lunges after him, but
Carvalho holds her back. She instantly collapses in his arms, looking for
comfort. Carvalho hugs her, and strokes her cheeks. He needs to feel
her skin, and when she speaks, her voice is thick with emotion too: 'I'm
more lonely than a lighthouse.'

'You've got us, your friends.'

But Alma bursts into tears. Carvalho does not know what to do with
her, so he hugs her more tightly.

'What's the matter now?'

'That bastard Norman! He said Muriel wasn't my daughter, that she
was only my student!'

'But that's true, isn't it?'

'What is it to him if I see her as a daughter, as the daughter I lost?'

Carvalho leans on the bar, lifting his hands to his head, then cradling
his head on his hands and elbows.

'What's wrong? Your head falling off?'

'I don't have the brain or the stomach for all these melodramas. And
I'm sorry, I don't feel like drinking to catch up with you. I'm going to
dinner at a gourmet club tomorrow night and I want to have the liver
of a choirboy.'

'There are choirboys with cirrhosis.'

Carvalho laughs despite himself, and Alma joins in. Norman comes
back over to them, relieved to see them both in good spirits. He puts
his arm round Alma's shoulders.

'So Almita, have you got over your little fit of bad temper?'

A centred, central, bull's eye of a knee homes in on Norman's groin.
He doubles up in agony, his groans made all the more theatrical by his
white face paint and the black eye make-up, make-up that darkly
condemns the continuing laughter from Alma and from Pepe, although
the latter is busily protecting his own crotch with both hands.

Norman is twisting and turning in his sleep, sweating and panting.

Suddenly he sits up and cannot believe what he thinks he sees: Carvalho standing at the foot of his bed. He looks round to make sure he really is in his bedroom. He is.

'What are you doing here?'

'I wanted to talk to you, but without Alma.'

'What's wrong? Has something happened to Almita?'

He leaps out of bed, and Carvalho stares at his erect penis. Norman realizes, and covers himself with his hands.

'Just look how it gets while I'm asleep, but then when I really need it, it all shrivels up.'

Carvalho does not seem particularly interested. Norman pulls on a pair of jeans that float around his skinny hips. He fills a cup with coffee that has obviously been in the pot for days. Coffee and coffee-pot are the usual brands. Norman has not bothered to wash. He rubs his eyes and yawns, waiting for Carvalho to explain.

'So, what's up?'

'Last night you had an argument with Alma over her relationship to Muriel.'

'She was hysterical, and so was I. I became hy-ster-ical.'

'It's true. Sometimes you seem like a pair of hysterical old women.'

'You can be quite hysterical yourself too.'

'OK, so I'm a hysterical old woman as well. But that's not the problem now. I have an idea who Muriel really is.'

'What do you mean?'

'Muriel is the Captain's daughter.'

Norman's jaw drops, leaving his mouth at the mercy of all the flies in Buenos Aires. He gradually recovers as Carvalho goes on: 'Muriel has never wanted to talk about her father or her family. Alma always thought it was because it was a difficult relationship: a father who was very authoritarian but who she loved, a mother who is sick or incapacitated in some way or other. When I went to the Boom Boom Peretti fight with Alma and Muriel, I could see that there was some link between the Captain and her. Afterwards Muriel herself admitted she had seen her father at the boxing club. She told us so.'

'This is like a Brazilian soap opera!'

'At first I was worried that Muriel was a spy planted by the Captain in our – well, let's call it our group. But if she had been a spy, she wouldn't have said her father was at the boxing match.'

'Have you said anything about this to Alma?'

'No.'

'Why not?'

'Because it's not quite so simple. Muriel appears to be the Captain's daughter – but is she really?'

Norman buries his face in his hands.

'That's enough, I think I know where you're heading.'

'Don't come the Method actor with me. It's not the moment. I went to see the grandmothers of the Plaza de Mayo. All I wanted to know was whether the Captain had been a normally registered father, with everything above board.'

'Well?'

'There are no records. It's impossible to tell even whether he is married or not, or when the marriage took place – it's as if a screen has been put up to protect the private life of a Captain who has too many names. His real one is Doñate, but Muriel is registered for Alma's classes as Muriel Ortínez. There is no trace of where he lives either, simply the mention: "classified information". Muriel is registered as the daughter of a single mother, and her surname is meant to be her mother's: Ortínez. But she is exactly the age that Alma and Raúl's daughter would be.'

'I don't want to hear it! I don't!'

'I haven't proved anything yet. How could I without blood tests? But at the very least, it's curious. I asked the woman who attended me if I could take away the Captain's dossier, but she would only let me look at it there. There was one scrap of paper that had fallen out of all the rest, where it talked of a meeting between Captain Gorostizaga – and that's one of the names our Captain uses – and all the members of the Tourón-Modotti family. There's nothing unusual in that, except that in this case there is a specific mention of a grandfather trying to establish what happened to his granddaughter. Can you guess the grandfather's name?'

Norman cannot and will not guess it. Carvalho shrugs and turns to leave the room.

'What are you going to do?'

'I'm going to have dinner at a Gourmet Club.'

'Don't make fun of me. Aren't you going to tell me the name of the grandfather who was in touch with the Captain?'

'Evaristo Tourón.'

He does not need to ask, but Norman nevertheless repeats the rhetorical question several times: 'Raúl's father?' Carvalho does not reply, and Norman does not really expect him to.

'What are you going to do?'

'I've called my uncle in Barcelona and left him several messages. He doesn't seem to be in his nieces' house. But I left the question for him: "why were you in touch with the Captain?"'

'You should ask Raúl that as well. Have you still heard nothing from him?'

'Not a thing. Vanished into thin air. And if he does reappear, I can't create false hopes. Just imagine if all this is mere coincidence and mistaken intuition on my part – and then it all explodes in the faces of Muriel, Raúl and Alma herself.'

Carvalho makes for the door.

'What, you're going just like that?'

'Just like what?'

'Aren't we going to have a bit of a cry together?' Norman asks to no avail, because Carvalho has gone, and Norman is left to shed his tears in utter solitude.

Doña Lina Sánchez de Pardieu purses her lips primly as she asks: 'How old do you think I am?'

Carvalho knows she is eighty-two, but also knows he cannot tell her that.

'That's hard to say. Somewhere between seventy and seventy-two?'

'Eighty-two!'

It sounds almost like a shout of triumph at her capacity to defeat the ravages of time.

'And that's despite not being able to look after myself, like a lot of others do. My husband was a military man, on horseback, the cavalry, though it became a tank regiment. I know every barracks in Argentina where there are tanks and armour. My five children were born in them – and the youngest is María Asunción. I named her after an aunt of mine who was from Santander in Spain – do you know it? I loved her a lot, the way children always love spinster aunts. It's true, isn't it? The

way they love grandparents too. Just like I loved my grandparents, and
my children love me, except the ones María Asunción has had. It's as
though I don't exist for her. I haven't seen her in twenty years. She
writes to me, calls me on the phone. Though less and less. I don't even
know where she lives, but I know she must be very unhappy, because
her letters are increasingly sad and odd. Would you like to read the
latest?'

Freedom of movement in the Leopoldo Lugones geriatric facility
depends entirely on the old people's ability to get about, and when
Doña Lina stands up she reaches for a stick hanging from the arm of
her chair and accepts Carvalho's assistance. As they shuffle along the
corridor to her room, she recalls her absent daughter.

'My other children come to see me sometimes, although it's not very
often. They never write or ring me. María Asunción never visits me,
but she writes all the time.'

The room is for two people, and in the other bed lies the statue of an
old woman who does not move, but stares endlessly up at the ceiling
tiles.

'She's a vegetable. She doesn't feel anything, or remember anything.
She doesn't even cry.'

She reaches for María Asunción's letter in a sandalwood box which
starts to play the 'Barcarolle' when she lifts the lid. She hands it to
Carvalho, and while he reads it, her lips repeat the words she seems to
have learnt by heart:

> *Dear Mother,*
> *I know you are well, and I'm taking advantage of*
> *feeling a little better in my own mind to write to you and tell*
> *you I'm fine too and that I love you, although I can't come*
> *and see you for the usual reasons of not being able to get there.*
> *Ernesto's job takes up a lot of his time, and I'm part of that.*
> *You are a military widow, so you know we do not have the*
> *same freedom of movement as civilians do, and on top of that,*
> *Ernesto has always had very special tasks assigned to him.*
> *Next time I'll send you a photo of me. One day when*
> *I'm feeling pretty – do you remember how you used to say I*
> *was the prettiest girl in Rosario when we were in the*

barracks there, and the prettiest in San Miguel when we
were stationed in Tucumán?
  A million kisses,
  Your daughter

MARIA ASUNCION

'Her handwriting isn't as nice as it used to be. You can see her hand
shakes. I reckon my poor María Asunción is ill, and she doesn't want
me to worry. She was such a lovely girl. Her father used to say it was all
planned: I started with her feet and kept on right up to her head.'
  'Do you know her husband?'
  'No.'
She is not trying to hide anything. She really never has met her son-
in-law.
  'Do you know his name?'
  'Doñate, I think he's called Doñate.'
  'Don't they have any children?'
  'I don't know. María Asunción never told me so.'
  'Where does your daughter live?'
  'All I know is, it's somewhere in Buenos Aires. She must live in a part
where there are lots of trees and birds, because she often mentions
them in her letters.'
  She insists on seeing him to the door. How did you find me? Mutual
friends. He does not want to tell her that in the document where María
Asunción is listed as a single mother, she is said to be the daughter of
Antonio Pardieu Bolos and Adelina Sánchez Fierro. Before Carvalho
leaves the old people's home in Mar del Plata, he telephones Don Vito
and arranges to meet him as soon as he gets back to Buenos Aires.
  'I haven't got long. I don't want to miss my dinner tonight at the
Gourmet Club.'
In the Patio Bulrich, Altofini recalls the days when he was a
conspicuous consumer, even before buying was known as consuming,
and being rich was not yet called having great purchasing power. He
looks himself up and down in the shopfront mirrors, after examining
button by button and stitch by stitch almost all the goods in the tailors,
the imported shirt shops, the delicatessens and champagne stores

which evoke for him nights of splendour and tango.

'It was a good idea of yours to meet here, Pepe. The Patio Bulrich is the symbol of the new consumer Buenos Aires; but I still don't understand why we couldn't meet where we always do, in our office.'

'I didn't want anyone bursting in on us, or people overhearing what I have to say. We're at a very delicate moment, Don Vito.'

'We are personally, or the world is?'

'The world doesn't exist, but we do. I'm talking about the real reason for me being here in Buenos Aires. My cousin. I've come to the conclusion I've been looking in completely the wrong direction. I think I didn't want to know the truth because deep down I didn't want to go back to Spain. I know who kept Raúl's baby when she was abducted, and I have to find his lair before Raúl does. But I have to do all this without Alma knowing, because either I do find the people responsible and things come to a head, or I've got it all wrong, and I'll have created false expectations in her.'

'What can I do to help?'

'We have to follow the girl so she can lead us to her home.'

'Have you identified her?'

'I think so. She's one of Alma's students.'

'Good God!'

Don Vito's face takes on an expression of theatrical amazement, which it keeps through all their journey and through the thousand times he expresses his astonishment before they pull up at the faculty exit where they expect to see Muriel. Carvalho leaves it to his partner to philosophize on the paradoxes of Buenos Aires: 'Twelve million inhabitants, and we all know each other!'

'The girl now goes by the name of Muriel Ortínez Ortínez. But on her birth register she is Pardieu Pardieu, and there is no record of a home address. That is confidential information, which gives some idea of what kind of VIP her father or parents must be.'

He parks his car close to the faculty. In the fifteen minutes before the end of the lecture, he goes over Muriel's personal details with Don Vito. As he does so, he realizes he is emotionally affected, as if he were describing a very special member of his own family, someone who needed protection.

'She shouldn't know you're following her. I don't want to scare her.

Don't get her worried. Don't arouse her suspicions.'

'Why are you talking to me as if I was an idiot?'

'I can't do it, she knows me.'

Muriel comes out in a group of students, though it is Alberto she is closest to. He has tied his long blond hair in a ponytail with a black band, and is explaining something with a show of great affection.

'She does have a family likeness,' Don Vito concedes.

In the soothing kitchen of Chez Reyero, a meeting of cooks and kitchen assistants is taking place. In amidst the shouting and gesticulating, one man is noticeable for his passivity. His large starched hat and his haughty expression mark him out as a French chef, not merely because he is sneering so openly at his companions, but because his mouth is shaped that way because of the millions of times it has had to pronounce the diphthong 'eu'. His scorn is more than matched in return by that of his workmates, and in particular by the union representative Magín, who is the one addressing the meeting.

'Brothers.'

'What about us women?' shouts one of the female kitchen workers.

'Brothers and sisters. I understand your position, but as I see it, the only mistake is that the management did not inform you that on your day off there would be this special dinner.'

'They're taking away our only day off for a miserable extra payment!' one of the chefs protests.

'Why don't the gourmets' wives do the cooking?' the first woman adds.

'You're perfectly right, but the owner committed himself to the dinner, and he can't pull out now, just a few hours before it's due to take place.'

'How about a compromise solution: those who want to stay can stay, and those who want to leave can go,' another chef suggests. 'What's the *grand chef* going to do?'

'He's a frog-eating French scab of a strikebreaker,' a strident second female voice declares.

The *grand chef* replies disdainfully:

'*Moi, je suis un artiste. Ce soir je deviendrai heureux de pouvoir faire la cuisine pour les plus importants gourmets de Buenos Aires. Je ne comprends pas des actitudes gremialistes, corporativistes par rapport à l'art magique de la cuisine.'*

'Oh, shut up!' everyone else shouts in unison.

'Hands up all those willing to stay,' Magín says, leading by example. Three others follow suit – two assistant chefs and a woman.

'Brothers, it's a promise we should keep. In times like these, when workers are more or less defenceless, we shouldn't give our boss the excuse he needs to throw us all out on the street. If tonight's a success, he won't be able to get rid of us. I don't know whether we'll be able to cope if I'm on my own as the *maître* and in the kitchen there are only the *grand chef* and three assistants.'

'Tell the Great Exploiter that he can count on the *grand chef*, the *grand maître* and three great potlicking, arselicking sons of bitches.'

The words are from the same irascible woman assistant, and they cause uproar. Several of those who are planning to stay try to get at her, but Magín soon leaves them all to it, and sets off through the restaurant in search of Don Lucho, the proprietor. He is an elegant man in his forties, dressed somewhere between Milan and London, standing in his office which is carpeted in green and has a practice golf hole in it. When he hears tapping on the door, Lucho Reyero reluctantly lowers his putter. Magín pokes his head in.

'Excuse me.'

'Well? What has the Supreme Soviet ordained?'

'I'll be in charge of waiting on table, the *grand chef* is keeping his word, and so are three assistants. That's all you can count on.'

'The others aren't going to last long here. I want you to make their lives hell so they leave as soon as possible.'

'I'll do what I've said I will, but I'm no bounty-hunter. It was their day off, and they're entitled to decide what they do with it.'

'OK, Lenin. Just make sure everything goes perfectly, otherwise the day after tomorrow I personally will organize a lock-out, and they can all go and run hotdog stands.'

Reyero waves the other man out. Left on his own, he goes over to a bar, takes out a cut-glass decanter and serves himself a large tumbler of whisky, which he downs like water. Then he stares out of his office window down into the restaurant, pleased at the impression of harmonious luxury created by the wooden panelling inlaid with white and purple, the heavy curtains and the rest of the décor.

'Ladies and gentlemen, the show is about to start.'

Magín has made his way back to the kitchen and casts an eye over the different courses. First course, seafood *papillote* with scallops and crayfish with coriander (scallops, crayfish, onion, spring onions, butter, white wine, tomato sauce, chopped coriander, pepper; salt and pepper to taste). Main course: *Pantagruel potpourri* (knuckle of beef, ox and lamb, with shoulder of salt lamb, chicken legs, oxtails, carrots, turnips, leeks, sticks of celery, French beans, red beans, rice, vinegar, peanut and walnut oil, butter, shallots, cloves of garlic, parsley, chervil, thyme, bay leaves, cloves, sea salt, pink pepper, sugar, bouquet of herbs, mustard, gherkins). Desserts: *tango oranges* (oranges, grenadine, Grand Marnier, powdered sugar), *kiwi sorbet* (kiwis, freshly-squeezed orange and lemon juice, in a chilled glass), *Mont Blanc aux marrons glacés* (*marrons glacés*, Chantilly cream, Chartreuse) and *soufflé aux fleurs d'acacia 'Liliana Mazure'* (bunches of acacia flowers, Armagnac, eggs, butter, confectioner's custard, caster and icing sugar, salt). Magín likes to see work well done, even though this spirit of perfection is not shared by his trade union colleagues – but Magín himself does not identify with what he sees as the *grand chef*'s abject submission.

At that very moment, chef Drumond is inspecting the different preparations with the satisfied look of an emperor's quartermaster general. He claps his hands in childish delight, and dances a waltz with a whisk for partner. He waltzes over to the giant freezer, and opens the door. Great hunks of meat hang down – sides of beef, whole lambs, pigs' carcasses, and on the marble slabs a whole array of produce from the galactic supermarket. Then, despite the freezing temperature, chef Drumond's face turns bright scarlet.

Güelmes accepts the Havana cigar Ostiz proffers him half-heartedly, as if he might change his mind at the last moment. They are in the most private room of the newly rebuilt El Aleph Club. On one wall an inscription in gold script by Borges reads: 'In republics founded by nomads, the contribution of outsiders is indispensable for all building tasks.'

'I can't spare you much time. I have a pressing engagement this evening.'

'Dinner at the Gourmet Club.'

Ostiz is forced to accept that the Development Minister is aware of one of his weaknesses. He waits for the minister or Morales to make the first move. It is not going to be the director-general of security who does so; he is taking his orders from Güelmes, and the minister takes orders from no one. He has got everything calculated in his mind, in his eyes, and in the measured way he goes on.

'One of the guests at that dinner is Captain Doñate. I believe that is his real name. He only uses it on occasions like this: but I've no need to tell you anything about Captain Doñate, have I? Captain Doñate is your own personal household cavalry, and you are his bedside financier.'

'Captain Doñate is a hero of the Malvinas war.'

'And of the dirty war.'

'I still prefer to call it our war against subversion.'

'A foreign writer who came to the first book fair under democratic rule in 1984 told me it felt as if Argentina hadn't changed at all. Of course President Alfonsín, a democratically elected leader, made the speech, but alongside him were the same president of the writers' union who had been there through all the years of the dictatorship, the same cardinal, and in the second row, the same virtual head of the employers' association, namely yourself.'

'Videla and the other military men have already paid the price for their dictatorship.'

'But not their civilian backers.'

'What do you want to do? Put eighty per cent of the population in jail?'

'Don't exaggerate. By the end it was only a few of you.'

'Right at the end. But I don't think you came here to discuss the ins and outs of the military government with me.'

Güelmes stays silent, knowing his silence and sense of security will unnerve Ostiz, however much he is used to playing Russian roulette.

'A weak link has appeared in the chain you and your friends formed during that military government. Captain Doñate kept the daughter of a "disappeared" couple, and it was you who organized the operation to conceal the fact. It was you who financed Doñate and his group, you who organized the splendid isolation which he abandons now and then to commit acts of kidnapping, torture, murder, all with complete impunity…'

'Prove it.'

'For now we can prove the relationship between María Asunción Pardieu, Ostiz and Captain Doñate in the case of Eva María Tourón, daughter of Raúl Tourón and Berta Modotti. Eva María Tourón was registered as the daughter of a single mother, María Asunción Pardieu, and given the name Muriel Pardieu Pardieu. In fact, María Asunción Pardieu was married to Captain Doñate. And now she no longer calls herself Pardieu, but Ortínez, and Muriel believes her own real name is Muriel Ortínez Ortínez. And even the false birth certificate has disappeared. Are you beginning to remember now?'

Ostiz avoids Güelmes and appeals directly to the director-general.

'Is there any proof of all this?'

'It's been collected by someone who doesn't much like you, Ostiz. And with good reason.'

Ostiz closes his eyes, then stares indignantly down at his cigar. It has gone out. He takes three deep breaths, then relights it. He puffs on it a few times to make sure it is properly lit, then addresses the two men.

'Before I accept any of what you are saying, I'd like to know what I stand to gain from this.'

'It's more what you don't lose.'

'You aren't after me?'

'No.'

'Only Captain Doñate?'

'That's right.'

'Can you get to him and keep my possible involvement a secret?'

'We want nothing better.'

'So what use am I to you?'

'We want concrete proof of the Eva María Tourón case so we can start legal proceedings against Captain Doñate. In exchange, your name will not appear anywhere. No one will find out that you created the infrastructure for the Captain to continue to operate under civilian rule – the New Argentina Foundation, the house you bought him registered in the name of one of your front men, the security system that has made him invulnerable. No one will find out you had a few awkward disappeared people killed, and most recently – only yesterday it seems

– you arranged for the death of Gálvez, also known as Robinson Crusoe.'

'That idiot started to spoil everything. It was his son who told you all this, wasn't it?'

Güelmes says nothing.

'But Richard Gálvez won't be satisfied with just getting rid of the Captain. He's going to want my head as well.'

Güelmes beams at him.

'Try not to offer it to him. We won't.'

'So what do we do now?'

'Wait for Tom Thumb to find the clues we've left him that lead to the Giant's lair.'

Magín has left the restaurant to get some fresh La Recoleta air. Night is falling. He is nervous, and lights a cigarette. He looks up at the restaurant sign and the front of the building, the upstairs light in Don Lucho's office, and Don Lucho's shadow standing there, golf club in hand. Don Lucho puts the club back in the golf bag. He pours himself another large whisky, and drinks it as though he were still thirsty. He goes over to the street window and peers through the blinds. He spots Magín out on the pavement staring up at his window, lets the blind drop and goes back to his desk. All of a sudden he pulls open a drawer. In it is a black pistol, a shiny Luger that smells as though it has recently been greased. He picks the gun up, caresses it, aims it at targets only he can see. He lowers his arm, puts the Luger back inside the drawer. He thinks desperately, then opens the drawer again, picks up the gun and wipes his fingerprints off with a cloth. He puts it back again when he thinks he hears voices in the street outside the restaurant.

The most expensive Jaguar of all the Jaguars in Buenos Aires has pulled to a halt. A uniformed chauffeur opens the door and Gorospe gets out. He gives instructions, and heads for the restaurant. Magín is waiting at the door for him.

'Don Leandro, welcome.'

'What's wrong, Magín? Why no doorman?'

'Today is a rest day for the restaurant staff. Those of us working are volunteers,' Magín replies. When Gorospe twists his mouth in distaste, he hastens to add: 'Don't worry, sir. Everything is under control.'

In the kitchen, the French chef is finishing off one dish and supervising another with irritating precision. There are only three people – a woman and two men – to help chef Drumond, who suddenly recovers his Spanish when he tastes a stock that does not meet his approval.

'Lighten that stock for me! How long was it in the *frigidaire*?'

'Since Alfonsín's time,' the woman sniggers.

Much to Drumond's annoyance, this sets the other two off laughing as well, so hard that one of them loses his glasses in the stew. He looks to right and left to see if anyone has noticed, then snatches his spectacles out of the boiling pot as quickly as he can. He wipes them and puts them on again. Taking advantage of his companion's momentary blindness, the other assistant gives the woman's breasts a quick fondle, although she warns him off, gesturing that it is too dangerous.

A couple in their forties enter the restaurant, keeping a respectful ten yards behind Gorospe. The man's skin shines from a recent massage by an Austrian masseuse weighing ninety kilos and with a blonde ponytail; she glows as if she has just emerged from thalassotherapy in the Mongo Aurelio Club, with Roman baths thrown in.   She looks like a good-looking recent divorcee who has just remarried a perfectly matched divorced husband. Magín bows, and Gorospe comes to greet them.

'Dora, Sinaí, how splendidly happy you look!'

'Leandro – the first to arrive, as ever.'

'So that I can give you the first kiss.'

They exchange the ritual *mwaa! mwaa!* but Gorospe clings on to the woman, and his hands stray down her back to grope her behind. She smiles icily and pushes him away, while her husband interjects: 'Watch those hands, Gorospe, watch those hands of yours. Where is your wife, by the way?'

'I didn't bring her, so you couldn't get your hands on her.' He laughs out loud at his own joke, and then goes on, suddenly serious: 'No, that's not true. I divorced her.'

'When? You kept that quiet, didn't you?' Dora exclaims.

'It was on Thursday. It was raining, and I had nothing to do. You know how sad it can be in Buenos Aires when it rains. I always get divorced when I have nothing to do.'

Dora laughs. Magín thrusts a tray of *kir* aperitifs at them.

'May I offer you an aperitif the chef has invented: Roederer Premier champagne with a few drops of Napoleon mandarin liqueur.'

'I love drinking kir without the blackcurrant!' Dora gurgles. 'I can't bear blackcurrant. What a good idea of the chef's!'

'Have you been at the Golf Club?' Gorospe asks.

Sinaí shakes his head, unable to speak because he is busy trying the aperitif he has been offered.

'Who goes to the club these days?' he says eventually. 'It's full of this regime's nouveaux riches. Mmm, delicious! This kir is delicious!'

'De-li-sh-ous,' Dora echoes him, breathing out the 'sh' endlessly until the final hissed 's' entirely robs her of all her remaining breath.

'Forgive me, but this cocktail is for pansies, Magín: what we need is a good Sauternes or a dry sherry, or my own favourite, a chilled tawny port with a slice of lemon.'

Magín cuts him short by handing him a glass he has prepared especially. The connoisseur's eyes light up.

'A cold tawny port with a drop of lemon!'

Gorospe kisses Magín, who does not know where to put himself.

'You're the finest Perónist *maître* I've ever met.'

'You're too kind.'

Carvalho arrives on foot. He looks at his watch and at the restaurant front. He starts to read the illuminated menu next to the door, when a stern voice rings out: 'We're closed to the public tonight.'

'I'm not the public. I was invited by Señor Gorospe.'

Magín looks him up and down. He does not look like one of Gorospe's usual guests. He lets Carvalho into the restaurant, where Gorospe, Dora, Sinaí and Dolly and Hermann – whose bulk and appearance betray German origins – are still on their aperitifs.

'One has to eat to live,' Hermann is saying, 'but just occasionally one has to live to eat.'

'Especially if everyday life is one long diet, boring but healthy,' says Dolly. 'Have you tried the Atkins diet?'

'I don't believe in any theological approach to eating. I believe in the pleasure of food,' Gorospe replies.

The group turns towards the door when they hear Carvalho and

Magín come in. Magín's embarrassment and Carvalho's hesitancy arouse their curiosity. He is obviously not one of them.

'This gentleman says he is...'

'This gentleman is my guest,' Gorospe cuts him short.

He takes Carvalho by the arm and leads him over to the others.

'Allow me to introduce you to a great Spanish gourmet, Señor Carvalho. This evening he represents the historical memory of Spanish cooking, which forms such an important part of our Argentine taste – well, for those of us of Spanish origin, at least. But beware Carvalho, this place will soon be full of yids, macaronis and krauts.'

Everyone laughs at Gorospe's little joke. As he is presented to the group, Dora in particular catches Carvalho's eye, but when she opens her mouth to speak, out comes a catalogue of ethnic stereotypes.

'So you're Spanish? How wonderful. Well, I guess you already know that we pure-blooded Argentines – that is, those of us who have been here for more than three generations – have a low opinion of all foreigners: we see Italians as odd-job men, Spaniards as slow on the uptake, and Jews as restless, unstable, potentially subversive.'

Gorospe leaves Dora to philosophize into thin air as he whisks Carvalho away to show him the restaurant. His presentation is interrupted by the entrance of twin brothers.

'The Ferlinghettis!' Gorospe cries like a circus ringmaster. 'Two peas in a pod stuffed with money and whisky!'

Magín serves all the newcomers an aperitif. He tries to make amends with Carvalho.

'My family's from Spain too. From Santander.'

Carvalho refuses the proffered kir and points to what Gorospe is drinking.

'I knew our Spaniard was a true gourmet,' Gorospe chortles.

The group is almost complete – the only ones missing are the Fieldmanns, Cari, Sara, Ostiz and Doñate.

'Is Doñate coming?' Sinaí asks, intrigued.

'The mysterious Doñate?' Dora insists.

'Yes, he's coming,' Gorospe says curtly.

'As ever, he'll arrive at the very last moment,' Ferlinghetti number one adds, 'just as somebody is saying: "Doñate is going to be late."'

'So say it, then he'll appear,' Dora suggests helpfully.

With all the bubbles and alcohol the guests have livened up considerably, and Gorospe has to shout to draw their attention to the latest arrival.

'Audrey Hepburn!'

A thin, waif-like woman has made her entrance. Everyone's rush to give her a kiss takes Carvalho aback. It is as though they are worried they will not get there in time.

'How beautiful you look, and how thin! And yet you eat all the time, it's not fair!' Dora says.

'I burn off the calories,' Cari replies. 'And I only very rarely allow myself excesses like tonight.'

One of the Ferlinghetti brothers is the last to kiss her. He makes such a meal of it that his brother stares daggers at him. At that precise moment, the Fieldmanns come in. Isaac and Raquel, their skins tanned by many hours on the golf course, the oldest of the guests. The greetings ritual all over again. Don Lucho descends from his office eyrie, humming a popular song:

> Have this one on me
> I've no one to rely on
> So lonely, far from home
> I need a shoulder to cry on.

'Everything going to plan, Lucho. The only guests missing are Sara, Ostiz and, of course, Doñate,' Gorospe informs him.

'You invited Sara?' Don Lucho asks.

'She is a member of the Club.'

Lucho tries to hide his annoyance, but is put out still further when he spots Carvalho.

'He's a great Spanish gourmet,' Gorospe tells him soothingly.

'We know that,' Dora reproaches him, 'but you haven't told us what else this mysterious fellow does.'

'I'm a private detective,' Carvalho explains.

Gorospe is not at all pleased that Carvalho is so open about his profession, but nothing will make his broad smile slip.

'How private?' Dora wants to know.

'As private as they come these days,' Carvalho tells her. 'In the future all our police forces will be privatized, and so will our prisons.'

'Well, let's hope no one gives you any business tonight,' Don Lucho says. 'No one is to kill anyone, understood?'

Some of the guests show they are curious about Carvalho, but most of them cannot get over the fact that there is a stranger in their midst. The tension is relieved when a dynamic, angular woman appears in a wheelchair, propelling herself along as if she was competing in the paraOlympics. 'That's Sara,' Gorospe whispers in Carvalho's ear. Everyone expresses their delight at seeing her, except Don Lucho, who glares blackly at her. The guests try to make room for Sara in the centre of their group, but she refuses forcefully. There is little time for them to adjust their attitude from one of compassion to the normal enjoyment of someone's company, because the financier Ostiz commands everyone's attention by the simple expedient of coming in and throwing his arms wide. His eyes flicker across Carvalho's face when they are introduced and the detective says: 'I think we've met before somewhere.'

Ostiz makes no reply beyond a knowing smile.

'Dinner is served!' Gorospe shouts. 'You know Doñate will only appear when we've all sat down. It's magic.'

Everyone takes their seat, the couples sitting as far away from each other as possible. Lucho grasps Sara's wheelchair and pushes her towards the table, leaning over to whisper in her ear as he does so: 'You bitch!'

Sara pretends she has not heard. Still smiling and cheerful, she hisses back at him: 'Cuckold, cuckold!'

Lucho leaves her at the table and withdraws upstairs to his office.

'Magín, start serving the entrées,' Gorospe orders. 'Doñate is late.'

No sooner has he pronounced the words than Doñate appears in the restaurant doorway. Carvalho tries to conceal his sense of shock. Doñate. The Captain.

Magín goes into the kitchen. The plates for the first course are ready.

'To whet their appetite,' chef Drumond says, his French accent returning as he surveys the hors d'oeuvre: '*Sashimi de thon frais mariné au soja, artichaut déguisé et la marinade de légumes nouveaux aux agrumes, carpaccio de morue... Merde!* they are supposed to be served one after the other, but...'

'They'll eat them anyway,' Magín says.

All at once there is a loud clatter of pots and pans. The cook with the boiled glasses has thrown a pan at the other, younger man. The woman shrieks and stands in front of her lover to protect him.

'Whore!' the myopic cook shouts. 'D'you think I didn't see you? You've been fondling each other all evening!'

He snatches up a big kitchen knife and lunges after them, but Magín and the other man manage to stop him.

'Calm down, all of you,' Magín shouts. 'You,' he tells the woman, 'put your apron on and come and help me serve.'

Magín and the kitchen maid make their way into the restaurant. Their faces and the dishes they are carrying announce the start of the meal. The Captain is being presented to everyone, Carvalho included. They look each other up and down.

'José Carvalho Tourón, private detective.'

They manage not to shake hands, merely nodding their head.

'We share a first name then. José Doñate, retired army officer.'

'No one here believes you're retired,' Sinaí reproaches him.

To judge by the suppressed laughter that escapes them despite the respect the Captain inspires, the others obviously all agree with him. Ostiz takes him aside to say something, but apparently Doñate is only half-listening and half-looking at him, because he is busy ogling Dora and trying to warn Carvalho off at the same time. With Dora he is all charm.

'Dora, if the other ladies present weren't just as beautiful, I'd say you are truly beautiful tonight,' he says.

'You poet!' Dora replies simperingly.

But his charm does not extend beyond Dora. Carvalho has heard his growled comment to Ostiz: 'Go fuck yourself.' Ostiz tries to make him see reason, but to no avail. Sinaí gets up self-importantly and directs their attention to the wines displayed on a nearby buffet.

'I would have preferred French wines, perhaps a bottle or two from South Africa, but Gorospe insisted I choose *from my own vineyards!*'

Everyone applauds.

'I'll only say a few words about them because I know you are all experts. I've chosen a Côtes de Arezzo as the sparkling wine – the champagne let's call it, because our Argentine sparkling wines are every bit as good as champagne. Then an '89 Riesling Sinaí which is a good honest drink, and also, in honour of my wife here' – more applause – 'a young Château Dora which can be drunk with another more full-bodied wine, the Château Margaux Francesca, named after my mother, which despite its name is not an imitation of a Château Margaux but a fine Merlot wine in the best traditions of Mendoza.'

'Very good!' Gorospe bellows. 'As you all know, when it comes to wines I'm a nationalist, whenever I can't have a good French wine instead, that is.' The others boo and hiss. 'That reminds me of a story I once heard about that great poet of negritude, Senghor – who was Senegalese – who, when he was asked "Do you know a lot about Senegalese cooking?" replied: "Enough to prefer French cooking."'

Loud whoops of approval, but mostly the gourmet guests are already busily sniffing the hors d'oeuvre, tasting a little with the tips of their forks, and generally swooning with pleasure.

'Mmm, how delicious!' some say.

'What subtle flavours! What texture!' say the others.

'What do you make of this, Carvalho?' Gorospe wants to know. 'Try this tuna *sashimi*. It smells of the sea, has the consistency of air and glides across the tongue.'

'It glides,' Cari enthuses.

'Smooth is the word,' Ferlinghetti opines.

'Smooth and gentle, like a French kiss,' Sara suggests.

'What are you thinking about, Sara?' the Captain wonders. 'Isn't Lucho eating with us?'

'We begged him to, but he refused,' Gorospe replies, pointing up towards the office.

Don Lucho is surveying the dinner guests from his hiding place. He points the Luger at Sara in her wheelchair and mouths silently: *bang! bang!* Meanwhile in the kitchen, the female assistant in her waitress's apron is beside herself with rage.

'This is a trap! I'm off!'

She undoes her apron and flings it on to the kitchen table. Unfortunately it lands straight in the pot full of squid stuffed with mushrooms. Drumond and her husband try to stop her leaving.

'Lupe, I'm sorry. You're right, I'm a hopeless cuckold.'

'Of course you are, at last you've got it. You're a miserable cuckold, nothing more!' she shouts at him.

'There's no need to insult me, Lupe!'

'You were the one who said it.'

The cook grabs the kitchen knife again and flings himself on his wife. The younger man steps in between them, and whacks Lupe's husband on the head with a heavy copper pan. A dull thud. He falls to the ground, and the other three stare down at him in panic. There is a different kind of panic in Magín's face: he has served some of the *papillotes* but is looking for the waitress to bring in the rest. Eventually she appears through the swing doors, still unsteady on her feet, but carrying the two required plates. She places them in front of the Captain and Carvalho, nervously staring down at a bright red stain on her blouse front.

'Tomato sauce?' the Captain asks.

'No, it's coulis. Tomato coulis,' the waitress mumbles.

'I'm sorry, this is a very difficult day, not everything can be perfect,' Magín apologizes.

'But this *papillote* is perfect. It's *merveilleuse* – tell the chef so from me,' Dolly says, trying to smoothe things over.

'Chef will come and explain the intimate details of the menu to you,' Magín informs them.

'But not just at this moment,' the waitress adds hastily.

'Whenever he gets the opportunity,' Magín insists.

Magín follows the waitress out to the kitchen.

'Did you hear that?' Ferlinghetti number two says. The "intimate details" of the menu. He talks a good meal.'

'Cooking made mankind what it is. There is a materialist theory about the origins of language which says it was born around the fire when primitive man was grilling some bison ribs or cooking the first *pot-au-feu*,' Carvalho tells his companions.

'Would that be a dialectical materialist theory?' the Captain wants to know.

'Of course,' Carvalho replies. 'The man who launched the theory is a dialectical materialist. He is called Faustino Cordón.'

'A Marxist? Do Marxists eat?' Dora asks incredulously.

'I've met Marxist gourmets,' says the Captain.

'Dead or alive?' Ferlinghetti number one quips, pleased at his own joke.

His brother's laughter is cut short by an icy glare from the Captain.

'Pleasure admits neither ideology nor violence,' Gorospe purrs. 'A good dinner table calms spirits and brings people together.'

'Does pleasure admit patriotism?' Dora wants to know. 'Who is willing to leap to the defence of Argentine cooking, for example?'

Her suggestion meets only dismissive snorts, which Gorospe puts into words.

'The problem is, there is no such thing. There is excellent food in Argentina – *asado* or *empanadas* for example. But there isn't really anything that could be called Argentine cooking. There's a big difference between food and cooking.'

'Do you think the same way?' Dora says, staring at the Captain. 'I've heard you're a true patriot.'

The Captain meets her gaze and gives her a long, careful reply: 'Well, patriotism is one thing, food is another. The flavours we cherish most are those in our memory. They're bound up with how our taste has developed – that's why we like *asado* or whatever our mothers or grandmothers cooked for us. But it's true that Argentine cooking cannot compete with that of many other nations. For example – our most sophisticated dish is *matambre*, rolled meat loaf. And our most patriotic contribution is *carbonada*, our meat stew! As Borges might have said: what paucity!'

The others applaud.

Magín has followed the waitress into the kitchen. He looks around, bewildered that no one is to be seen. Then the cold-storage door opens and Drumond and the younger cook appear, hurriedly shutting the door behind them.

'Where's Santos?' Magín asks.

'My husband's left,' the waitress explains. 'He changed his mind and walked out.'

'Son of a... !' Magín screams. 'Now what are we going to do?'

'We'll manage,' the waitress says.

'Drumond, I'd like you to explain the details of the menu to the club members,' Magín says.

Drumond is drinking deeply from a huge glass full of gin with a splash of tonic and lemon juice.

'Do you think it's the moment to be drinking?' Magín asks.

'*Bien sûr.*'

He boards the train in Retiro station, with its distant echoes of Victorian splendour, its historic iron rails that have fascinated him since childhood, as if the iron had become a malleable part of his own existence. He gets off where the old English-built railway ends and boards a modern tourist train, resisting the temptation to get off again at each of the suburban stations that have been turned into shopping centres. Gradually the built-up city gives way to houses with gardens, and then finally the trees of northern Buenos Aires announce that they are nearing the Tigre delta. He does not recognize anything in the terminal, which has also been turned into an American-style shopping mall, so Raúl hastens to get out to the Tigre canals, his sense of hope a mixture of expectation and fear, the same kind of tremulous hope he felt as a child when faced with this maze of dark waters, and imagined that paradise could exist. He is to meet his contact on the boat going to Puerto Escobar, and as soon as he sits by the port bow he is joined by one of the people who took him on his first trip here. They were not supposed to speak to each other, and they remain silent as the boat makes its way to one of the river stopping points, next to a dilapidated row of diesel pumps. The two of them get off, then board a waiting launch. Raúl recognizes the route from the previous occasion, and then there is the same house almost swallowed up by vegetation, rotten from damp and a lack of care, but still beautiful to live in – it even crosses Raúl's mind to ask how much it would cost to buy it.

He is met by the same man as before, who motions him to sit down, and gets straight to the point.

'I am in a position to give you excellent news. The investigations we have made can help you in your search. Your daughter is alive. She is being brought up by Captain Doreste, whom you know as Gorostizaga, or the "Ranger", as his military nickname had it.'

Raúl is on the verge of tears, and his voice is strangled when he asks: 'Where is she? How can I get her back? What proof do I need to show?'

He can feel the other man's eyes on him, and realizes there must be a second part to his proposal.

'The proof depends on an agreement.'

'An agreement between whom?'

The sphinx in front of him takes his time, not to think what to say but to see if Raúl's vehement emotions will push him further.

'I'm willing to make any agreement that returns my daughter to me.'

Satisfied, the sphinx now speaks.

'That's a good start. You have been in contact with Richard Gálvez Aristarain, who told you about some things his father, the famous Robinson, had found out. And what Gálvez discovered coincides with our own investigations.'

'But who are you?'

'We are who we are. Don't look a gift horse in the mouth, Señor Tourón. Gálvez Junior got involved in this to get revenge on Ostiz, whom he blamed for being behind his father's murder. And Ostiz does lead to the Captain and your daughter, but he is not to appear in any of this. You are to present a lawsuit against the Captain and his wife, whose maiden name is Pardieu, and who was part of the farce of the adoption of Eva María Tourón as the daughter of a single mother. The girl is now called Muriel Ortínez Ortínez and is almost twenty.'

Muriel's name sounds familiar to Raúl, as if he had heard it somewhere recently.

'Gálvez won't agree to leaving Ostiz out of this.'

'We'll take care of Richard Gálvez.'

'Why are you helping me? Who are you?'

'You go and find your daughter and sort out the Captain. We'll look after everything else. In this dossier you'll find where the Captain's family lives, how you should proceed so they don't take flight, and the name of a firm of lawyers who are willing to help you. Don't get the grandmothers of the Plaza de Mayo mixed up in this, or we won't supply you with all the proof you need. For the next few hours, the Captain and his troupe of motorcyclists won't be at his home, and we've taken care of the two guards there. So the way is open for you to reach María Asunción Pardieu – she's the Captain's wife, who lives under an assumed name because Pardieu is the maiden name they used to register her as Eva María's mother. You are to enter the house, go up to the woman you find there and say: "I am Raúl Tourón and I am Muriel's father."'

Up in his office, Lucho Reyero takes a woman's photo from the desk top. He stares at it, tears in his eyes. Then he starts to speak:

'Of course I always knew there was a risk you'd leave me, but why with that dyke, that ghastly lesbian? What's she got that I can't give you? And to think she had the nerve to come here!'

He stands up and goes over to the interior window. He stares down at Sara and insults her. 'Filth! Dyke! Disgusting lesbian!'

There is a knock at the door.

'Who's there?'

Magín's voice reaches him from the far side of the door.

'Don Lucho, there's hardly anyone left in the kitchen. Something strange is going on.'

'Get lost, Magín.'

With that, Don Lucho returns to his voyeuristic contemplation of the restaurant, where the guests are deep in conversation.

'I'd like,' Gorospe says, 'those who have not had much to say so far – our young actress friend Cari, Carvalho and Doñate – to give their opinion of this Sinaí Riesling.'

'It's pure fruit,' Cari exclaims.

Sinaí pulls a face, but keeps on smiling.

'I'd say it isn't exactly a Riesling, but is closer to a hock, which is similar to a white Burgundy but with more of a spring-like bouquet, as our young friend here has correctly observed,' Carvalho says, pointing to Cari.

'I agree with the attribution and am a great fan of hock, which I tried in Germany when I was military attaché there. The Germans call the bottle *Bocksbeutel*, because they say it is shaped like…'

'Shaped like what?' Carvalho asks slyly.

'Yes, yes, like what exactly?' Dora eggs him on.

'Gorospe will tell you, he's more forthright than I am,' the Captain says evasively.

'Like bulls' balls,' Gorospe says.

Everyone laughs. Ferlinghetti number two wants to lead the conversation back to the wine.

'In fact, hocks are nothing like Riesling – Rieslings are drier, more perfumed, more subtle – and they have a bouquet which is a *mélange* of lime, acacia and orange blossom, with very occasionally a hint of cinnamon.'

'What a poet!' gushes Cari.

'No, it's just that he's read the *Larousse des Vins*,' Ferlinghetti number one corrects her.

At this point, a red-faced Drumond sweeps in, closely followed by Magín. His entrance is greeted with a round of silent applause. Drumond drops his chin like an actor, and launches into his speech, gathering confidence as the words flow in a fluent Spanish with a French lilt.

'Tonight I am offering several *hommages* to French nouvelle cuisine. The first course I learnt from my master Gérard and his *minceur exquise*, or cooking to lose weight.'

Señora Fieldmann gives her husband a sharp jab in the ribs. Until now, both of them have devoted themselves to eating rather than talking.

'Gérard, in Sainte-Eugénie! Do you remember we went there, to eat and lose weight?'

'Eating to lose weight?' Gorospe says suspiciously. 'Back to the theology of food, the theology of guilt! But go on, Monsieur Drumond, go on.'

'The scallops were a tribute to that great Swiss master of subtlety, the magician Girardet.'

'A round of applause for Girardet!' proposes Ferlinghetti number one.

A short but enthusiastic clapping of hands.

'And the *Pantagruel potpourri* by Troisgros is a playfully symbolic dish in honour of the Argentines' love of meat, because it has beef, veal, pig, lamb, chicken and oxtail in it, all of them cooked differently. It's baroque but light, aimed at bringing out the flavour and the texture of each of them, cooked in walnut or peanut oil to give it that final touch!' Drumond says triumphantly.

'*Chapeau!*' exclaims Dora.

'And for dessert I have allowed myself to go from the exquisitely obvious choice of Troisgros' *tango oranges*, a tribute to Argentina's worldwide fame, to Bocuse's *Mont Blanc aux marrons glacés*, with in between Gérard's *kiwi sorbet* – which you can use as a sort of *trou normand* before you start on the meat *potpourri*, and a crazy fantasy invented by Troisgros: an acacia blossom *soufflé "Liliana Mazure"*!' Drumond declares, at the height of his oratorical powers.

'Wonderful!' all the guests exclaim.

'Just one question,' Carvalho says, interrupting them. 'Why is the acacia blossom *soufflé* called *"Liliana Mazure"*?'

Drumond smiles coyly.

'What would cookery be without mystery? I don't mean to be rude, *mon ami*, but permit me to take that little secret with me to my grave.'

This speech is received with delirious enthusiasm by the gourmets, especially the women among them. Dora even climbs on to a chair to clap her hands above all the rest, and to take photos of the chef. Drumond leaves the restaurant beaming, with an exit he has studied for weeks.

'What would cooking and life be without mystery?' Sara says.

'You yourself are a mystery,' Ferlinghetti number one says.

'My only mystery is that I'm a cripple and different.'

Ferlinghetti number two puts his lips close to Cari's ear, nibbles it, and whispers: 'Are you different like Sara? Different? Really different?'

Cari laughs a little inanely.

'Food awakens the memory of food,' Gorospe declares. 'Dora and Sinaí, do you remember that unforgettable lunch we had at *Le Carré de Feuillant*? It might not get the most Michelin stars, but it is always excellent, and that was where we ate that wonderful civet of game. In the autumn of 1990...'

'Two,' Sinaí finishes the sentence. 'It was 1992. It's true, that was a wonderful meal. The only thing that spoiled it for me was that on their wine list they had Catalan and Spanish wines, but none from Argentina.'

'A Dutch colleague of mine gave me an extraordinary South African wine to try in Holland. A Jacobsdal Pinotage. It was so good I sent to Cape Town for more,' Fieldmann says, still eating and casting his eyes greedily at what the others have left on their plates.

'All he ever remembers are good wines and our arguments,' his wife reproaches him. 'I think he must write them both down in his diary.'

In the kitchen, Lupe is still slumped in a state of shock on her chair. Slowly what has happened appears to sink in. The young cook is keeping a watchful eye on her as he gets on with his tasks. Drumond only has eyes for the dinner. The cook goes hesitantly over to Lupe.

'There was nothing else we could do!'

Lupe finally succeeds in emerging from her stupor, and stares at her lover with increasing fury.

'Murderer! He was the father of my children!'

Drumond waves at them to stop arguing. Lupe struggles to her feet. Her eyes roll wildly as she searches for something on the kitchen table. She sees the knife her husband had wielded and before Drumond can intervene, plunges it into her lover's stomach. He reacts as disbelievingly as a cook can after being stabbed and before falling stone dead to the floor. At this moment, Magín comes in from the restaurant. He stares at Drumond. Lupe sees nothing. Magín holds his head in his hands.

'What about the dinner? What are we going to do about the dinner?' he asks eventually.

Drumond stubbornly refuses to speak. From the restaurant can be heard the twitter of female voices, the deeper boom of the men fighting to impose their point of view.

'It's a cliché to say you can't eat well in Germany,' Hermann is pontificating. 'You only eat badly in today's Germany because it has lost its traditions due to a poorly assimilated development and because it has been invaded by all kinds of barbarians.'

'Do you mean the Yankees?' Sinaí asks.

'The Yankees, the Turks, the Poles and the *ossies*,' Hermann specifies. 'The people from the east don't know how to eat, and they don't have anything decent to eat anyway because of the state those communist hordes left them in. But I can remember my grandmother's cooking...it was wholesome, full of taste, the food of peasants and farmers.'

'Hell is other people,' Dora muses. 'I believe that. Nothing could be more true.'

'Did you think that up?' Ferlinghetti number one wants to know.

'No, Sartre did.'

Magín reappears from the kitchen. He is carrying as many plates as he can in his hands, or balanced on his arms.

'Good God, Magín,' Dora says. 'Why don't we help you?'

At this, most of the women guests stand up and head for the kitchen. Magín is balancing far too many plates to be able to stop them, but he shouts: 'No!' so imperiously that they all halt in their tracks. Magín places the plates in front of each guest with all his remaining aplomb and dexterity, and then excuses himself.

'Do forgive me for shouting, but a kitchen without mystery is not a kitchen. The food would not have the same flavour if you all knew the secrets of chef Drumond's inner sanctum.'

'That's true. This postmodern idea that customers in a restaurant should be free to wander round the kitchens is like putting a condom on your palate,' Gorospe says.

Cari laughs out loud.

'Palate condoms? Leandro! What are we to think of you?' Sara cries.

'Think what you like. The truth is the truth.'

By now, all the sorbets have been served. Dora closes her eyes and talks with them tight shut.

'It's true. They open a pinprick in the soul for all the other delights to come rushing in.'

'Food for pansies,' Gorospe grumbles. 'Sorbets are nothing but food for pansies.'

'What have you got against homosexuals, Leandro?' Cari asks him.

Gorospe gets to his feet, waddles round the table, and kisses Cari on the hand.

'Nothing. *Bebamus atque amemus...mea Lesbia...*'

Some of the guests smile at this, although Carvalho is amazed how famous Don Vito's Latin sayings have become. Nobody dares say what he or she is thinking. Magín waits for them all to finish their sorbets. He is a bundle of nerves as he pours out the wine, not always in the right spot. When he disappears again into the kitchen, Señora Fieldmann bursts out:

'What's wrong with that fellow?'

'We are not concerned with what's wrong with him,' the Captain declares. 'Tonight is an exceptional night, and our only duty is to eat.'

'To savour,' Gorospe corrects him.

'I can hardly wait for the *Pantagruel potpourri*,' Sinaí says. 'Whatever else we may say, meat is what Argentina is all about. I once saw the great Jorge Luis Borges put away a gigantic steak, even though I remember the poem he wrote in *Fervor de Buenos Aires* where he talks about his horror of butcher's shops.'

'Recite it for us, Sinaí!' Gorospe roars.

'It's not the moment,' Sinaí excuses himself.

But Dora and the others insist. Gorospe addresses Carvalho: 'Not only does Sinaí recite like an actor, but he writes poems as well, doesn't he, Cari? When we get to the Château Margaux, he'll perform for us.'

Eventually Sinaí yields to the outcry, and starts to recite:

> *Viler than any brothel*
> *The butcher's shop seals the street like an insult.*
> *Above the doorway*
> *A blind cow's head*
> *Presides over the uproar*
> *Of cheap meat and marble slabs*
> *With an idol's distant majesty.*

'Bravo!' the other guests shout, applauding wildly. 'Wonderful! Marvellous!'

Hermann engages Carvalho in conversation. 'I admire people who are skilled at expressing themselves. I'm hopeless at it, despite being German, from the homeland of the best poetry in the world – Hölderlin, Heine, Benn, Hofmannsthal.'

'And Brecht,' Carvalho adds.

'Brecht? Possibly. I don't like him much. He wants to be subversive, and uses poetry or the theatre as a pretext. Isn't that so, Cari?'

'What's that?' the actress says absently.

'As an actress, what do you think of Brecht?'

'Brecht?' Cari stammers, anxiously flicking through her mental archive of playwrights.

'You don't think much of him, do you?'

'Aha!' Cari says forcefully.

'You see? What does a subversive message have to offer today's generation?'

His question is for anyone to answer.

'Oh please,' Señora Fieldmann says, still chewing, 'the *toilette* is for talking politics.'

'Why in the *toilette*, Rebecca?' asks the Captain. 'Everywhere is a valid place to talk politics, and I'll pick up Hermann's gauntlet. And I'll tell you, my friend, that even though today's generation is not affected by any subversive message, subversion is not born or destroyed, it simply changes form. Nowadays the subversives are hiding in all the non-governmental organizations. Why do you look so surprised? Or are some of your children in NGOs too? If they are, keep a close watch on them. Evil exists in life and in history – if it didn't, how could we tell what good was?'

'That's very true,' Ferlinghetti number one agrees.

'In life as well?' Cari wants to know.

'Yes, in life too,' the Captain says.

'Are you always able to distinguish between good and evil?' Sara asks.

'Always,' he replies.

'Congratulations.'

'Thank you.'

'But what room is there in your morality for mistakes?' Carvalho asks.

'If you catch them at the start, they can be corrected; otherwise, they have to be rooted out. Co-existence is so difficult, we have to guard against destroying ourselves due to a mistake.'

'But just imagine that someone you know, someone you love, makes that mistake,' Carvalho insists.

'Are you talking about anyone in particular?' the Captain enquires.

'I don't have the pleasure of knowing your world.'

'I've created a world for myself. I don't allow others to decide for me. I decide for myself.'

'The stainless-steel man!' Sara exclaims. 'What about feelings?'

'My feelings are a personal matter, and don't change. As soon as you start changing them, they become obscene.'

The Captain raises his wine glass in a toast to Sara, then to Carvalho, and especially to Ostiz, who does not return the compliment. Then the military man drinks with everyone else except Carvalho, who is staring at him defiantly. At this point Magín comes in to remove all their plates, and when the guests find the space in front of them free, they start to fill it with noisy conversation on all sides. Magín serves more wine, then finally starts to bring in the *Pantagruel potpourri*. The extravagance of the dish is reflected in the gourmets' faces, which shine as though they were about to take first communion. Gorospe stands up and taps his spoon on a wine glass to silence the hubbub.

'Ladies and gentlemen. Once every two months we meet in this Gourmet Club to eat.'

Laughter from the others.

'To talk of "eating" as directly as that might seem brutal, but in itself, the act is not an aesthetic one: it is very primitive. We kill to eat, and we eat to survive. Every animal does this – but it is only man who has converted this primitive act into culture, who has elevated it beyond animal instinct into a cultural act. I don't want to spoil your pleasure, girls and boys, *companions of a lifetime's adventures...*' Gorospe pauses until the laughter at his tango reference dies down: 'but I would like to draw your attention to what we are about to eat. *Pantagruel potpourri!*

On the one hand, a vulgar anthology of all the meats we Argentines are so fond of; on the other, the glory of the first modern literary work devoted to the joys of pleasure and of culture: Rabelais' *Gargantua and Pantagruel*. Just look at it!' and when several of them do not follow his command, he repeats: 'Look at it! What do you see?'

'A butcher's shop,' Sara says wickedly.

The dining table explodes with laughter. Even Gorospe has to chuckle.

'OK. But thanks to culture, the brutality of so much dead meat has been transformed into a poem, into a marvellous synthesis of flavours and fragrances. So before you sink your knives and your teeth into this feast, I'd like to propose a toast to culture: to culture, which saves us from being mere cannibals and murderers!'

Everyone gets to their feet.

'To culture!' they cry, raising their glasses.

Then everyone attacks the *potpourri* as if they really were cannibals. Meanwhile, up in his office, Lucho Reyero takes off his jacket, his waistcoat, his trousers, his suspenders, his socks, shoes and shirt. He seems completely stunned as he twists trousers and shirt to make a rope. He stares up at the ceiling, until his eyes fix on the light fitting in the centre of the room.

Tango Amigo before the public arrives. The barman is wondering about the meaning of life, Adriana is practising the opening of 'Tango Oranges' with the orchestra, Silverstein is muttering his monologue to himself, but gesticulating as though the audience were already in their seats. His arm stays in mid-air, because he sees Raúl come into the club, pausing at the lit-up doorway to try and make out where everyone is in the darkness. Silverstein's two hands are scarcely enough for all the gestures the fugitive's sudden appearance evoke in him. He comes over, and Silverstein stiffens at the words Raúl whispers in his ear, then follows him out without a word of explanation to the others, as if something far more important than anything Tango Amigo can offer him is guiding his steps. In the taxi, the two men respect each other's silence until Silverstein realizes they have reached Villa Freud.

'Font y Rius?'

'I wasn't going to ask Güelmes along, was I? These days he represents power.'

Norman's eyes signal his agreement, and he trots along behind Raúl when he gets out of the taxi at the clinic and strides across the gravel path up to the side door where Font y Rius' office is situated. He is waiting for them beyond the glass panels, and does not ask a thing when he opens the door for them, takes off his white coat, feels in his jacket pockets, smoothes down the bare sides of his head rather than any actual hair and sighs resignedly. His first reaction comes when they are all back at the taxi.

'I'll get rid of him. We can go in my car.'

Font y Rius pays off the driver, and once he is installed behind the wheel of his own car, he turns to Raúl.

'Are you sure about all you told me?'

'Absolutely.'

'And who are these people who first of all abduct you, then lead you to the solution of your problems?'

'Why does that matter?'

'Why does anything matter at this stage?'

This leads Font y Rius into a lengthy monologue that lasts from the car leaving the centre of Buenos Aires, travelling through the suburb of San Isidro, and down towards the bridges over the river at the Tigre delta, with its promise of the open pampas beyond the last lines of houses where the city has already lost its name.

'When they killed my poor Alma and I was held by the military goons in the Navy School of Engineering, I thought my life was over. I was sure all of you were dead. Berta, Norman, Pignatari, Güelmes, you Raúl, and all the others, the ones who really had been killed, whose names only a few of us remember and will continue to remember: even if they were only their assumed names, they were every bit as real as the ones their parents had given them. No one can deny we acted out of altruism, a suicidal altruism maybe, but altruism should be enshrined as one of the great traditional virtues. And then mysteriously, I didn't die. Something happened and we all survived. I thought to myself: someone has performed this miracle, God bless them. After that, I didn't believe in altruism. I was only concerned about myself. I even began to hate the two sisters, Berta and Alma, because I could see it was their influence that made me a militant. They did the same to you, Raúl. Not you, Norman, you never knew why you were doing it. No, don't thank me. But it's very hard to grasp the dialectic between altruism and survival. When we became partners with the Captain, we were playing a dirty trick on ourselves, even though Güelmes tried to argue that it was simply another dialectic, like the master and slave when their relation reaches the point where the slave is as powerful as the master, and ends up destroying him. That's the trap a whole generation of Argentines has fallen into. Look at Alfonsín, look at Menem. The result is obvious. You don't change the culture of power, it's the culture of power that changes you. Do you follow me? And where exactly am I headed? The only way we can win is by destroying the Captain and all those like him, so what we are doing now is winning our war. Do you agree or don't you?'

He grips the steering-wheel even more firmly, and does not seem to realize that his companions remain silent, and will never give him the answer he is looking for.

In the kitchen, Magín, Drumond and the waitress are still at their posts.

'We can't count on her any more,' Magín moans, 'look at her, she's completely out of it.'

'I'm going to serve the desserts, if it's the last thing I do. *Mon dieu! Qu'est-ce que j'ai fait pour mériter ça?*

The kitchen maid comes round, and stares at them wildly.

'Out of respect for the dinner I haven't called the police,' Magín tells her, 'and I haven't said a word to the boss – he's locked himself up in his office anyway. It's too late to do anything more.'

'When they have all drunk their last glass of Armagnac, when they've exhaled the last breath of smoke and finally gone home, call the police and if need be, here are my hands for the cuffs. *Je suis disposé pour le sacrifice! Moi, le plus important élève de Robuchon!*'

'What are you two talking about?' Lupe asks, finally fully aware of where she is. 'Why did you kill my husband? Murderers! And where's my Santos?'

'She's going to scream!' Magín shouts in panic.

Lupe screams at the top of her voice.

'Murderers!'

The guests in the restaurant turn towards the noise, as Drumond and Magín try to grab the waitress.

'Did you hear someone shouting?' Señora Fieldmann asks the others.

'They're killing a pig in case we ask for more,' says Ferlinghetti number one, cackling at his own wit.

With that, most of the guests turn their attention back to their plates, although Señora Fieldmann is still half-listening to what is going on in the kitchen, where the *grand chef* and Magín are busy gagging Lupe and using a Souvenir of Mar del Plata apron as an improvised straitjacket to tie her up. They have no idea what to do with her, until Drumond points to the cold-storage room.

'In there!'

Drumond opens the door, and Magín pushes Lupe inside. As he does so, he thinks he sees something very odd and tries to get a better look, but Drumond quickly shuts the door and stands guard in front of it.

'Let's leave her in.'

'But I thought I saw…'

'Nothing. You saw nothing. As my great maestro, Michel Gérard –

or was it Robuchon? – told me one day when I was very nervous because things weren't coming out right: *Drumond, cessons de jeter de l'huile sur le feu, voulez-vous, et d'alimenter une polémique stérile...* Either you cook, or you argue.'

'I must admit you're a professional to your fingertips, Monsieur Drumond.'

'My dear Magín, ideologies and fashions may come and go, but professionalism, *elle reste!*'

In his office, Lucho is still staring up at the improvised rope dangling from the centre light like an invitation to suicide or an escape from Alcatraz. He picks up a portrait of his wife, and rubs his genitals with it.

'Sow,' Lucho says, poking his tongue out. 'Now you'll see what it takes to be a man!'

He flings the framed photo against the wall, where it shatters in pieces. He strides determinedly towards the rope. He barely even notices the din from the restaurant below.

'This dish reminds me of all those ideas about a well-done piece of work being the only true ethical value. Otherwise ethics is so relative!' Sinaí observes. 'But a well-done piece of work is exactly that. That's why I appreciate Borges, even though he's not exactly from my world, of my ideological persuasion.'

'Borges was a right-wing anarchist,' Carvalho suggests.

'That's too much of a simplification!' Gorospe protests.

'I don't know if he was on the right or on the left, but he was an anarchist. Like me. Like most extraordinary people. Like all of you. But he wrote well, and I know a lot of his work by heart,' Sinaí concludes.

As he says this, he is staring hard at Carvalho. The detective cannot imagine why, and glances furtively to the left, the right and behind, in case something is going on that he is not aware of. Eventually Sinaí makes his mind up, and launches into: '"A couple of years ago, although I have lost the letter, Gannon wrote to me from Gualeguaychú, telling me he had sent me a version – possibly the first to be published in Spanish – of the poem *The Past* by Ralph Waldo Emerson, and adding in a postscript that Don Pedro Damián, whom I surely recalled, had died some nights earlier of a pulmonary congestion..."'

THE BUENOS AIRES QUINTET

A round of applause obliges him to stop there.

'Can you guess where that fragment comes from?'

'The opening paragraph of the epilogue from *El Aleph*,' Ostiz says, proud of himself.

'Borges! Borges! Borges is like a pig or the Virgin Mary, every bit of him is useful, and he is useful for everybody,' Sara complains. 'Personally, I prefer Sábato. He's not so chewn over.'

'But I can't bear Ernestito ever since he turned into a mendicant friar searching for those disappeared *lumpen*, I can't bear him or what he writes.' Sinaí scolds the speaker. 'And anyway, to compare Borges to Sábato is like comparing the Holy Trinity to the Pope, to any Pope.'

'Well said, Sinaí, well said!'

In a few more minutes, bottles of wine have almost completely filled the table. Magín comes in to clear away the plates. There is a lot of food left over, but the wine is slipping down their throats like water, is being drunk as if they were parched in a desert. Despite her composed exterior, Señora Fieldmann is completely drunk. She keeps trying to grab her husband's genitals, which he protects desperately between mouthfuls.

'Is this your first trip to Argentina?' Sinaí asks Carvalho.

'Yes.'

'And what do you think of the Argentines?'

'Why don't you come straight out and ask him what he thinks of Argentine women?' Gorospe cuts in. 'Come on, Sinaí, you can recite whatever you like, but don't ask him such awkward questions.'

Sinaí stands up, enraged.

'I ask whatever questions I like…and who are you to criticize me anyway? You're just a pen-pusher – a rich one, but nothing but a pen-pusher nonetheless!'

'For heaven's sake, Sinaí,' Dora protests.

'Me, a pen-pusher? I'm the foremost publicist in the Southern Cone!'

'I sell my wine by the bottle, but you line your pockets because you're thick as thieves with Menem and his cronies, all those building labourers in silk shirts!' Sinaí yells.

'If it wasn't for official orders, your wine wouldn't even be good enough for vinegar!'

'Gentlemen!' Hermann intercedes.

'Let them be. You know they always get over it,' Dolly calms him.

Gorospe and Sinaí lean towards each other over the table until their faces are almost touching. After a few moments, they draw back.

'What a horrible sight you are close-up,' Sinaí comments.

'And you look like death in a Bergman film,' Gorospe responds.

Sinaí sits down again and returns to Carvalho.

'OK, so don't tell me your impression of Argentines, men or women. The women are all bitches anyway! They're all food for psychoanalysts, and sooner or later they end up taking us to see them as well, the same psychoanalysts who are busy screwing them. But tell me what you think of Argentina! What do you make of this Argentina of ours?'

Carvalho thinks what he will say. First he drains his glass of wine. The Captain is quick to fill it again, and maliciously encourages him to respond.

'We're waiting for your answer. A foreigner's judgement can be very interesting. What do you think of this Argentina of ours?'

Carvalho looks as foreign as can be.

One last time, Lucho Reyero surveys the dinner guests below him, all waiting in silence for Carvalho to give his answer. Lucho has made a decision. He moves the chair underneath the improvised rope hanging from the light fitting. He climbs on to the chair. Ties the trouser leg round his neck. Pulls on it to make sure it is securely fastened to the chandelier. He closes his eyes and kicks the chair away.

Carvalho looks round the table at all of them. Finally he decides to speak: 'I don't think it exists.'

'Argentina doesn't exist?' Sinaí asks, taken aback.

'What's this man saying?' Ferlinghetti number one wants to know.

'Where are we then? In Paraguay?' Cari smirks.

'Let him have his say,' Sara objects.

'This gentleman, from Spain no less, is only repeating what Borges once said: Buenos Aires is terribly ugly; to which Pepe María Peña found the brilliant reply: the problem is, Borges is blind.'

Sinaí laughs again at his own wit.

'What did you mean when you said Argentina doesn't exist?' Sara insists.

'Well, I'd say that Spain doesn't exist either, or Europe, though San Marino probably does. Complex realities don't allow for metaphysical abstractions.'

'Ah, I'm beginning to understand,' Gorospe says with relief. 'Let him go on, vintner.'

Sinaí accepts, and leans back in his chair to listen to Carvalho's explanation.

'There are a lot of possible as well as real Spains,' Carvalho goes on, 'just as there are a lot of possible and real Argentinas. Who can describe such complex phenomena?'

'But you can choose a characteristic. Something that has struck you more than anything else,' the Captain urges him.

Carvalho thinks about this. In the end, he gives a deep sigh and looks first at the Captain, then at Sinaí.

'The gaps.'

'The what?' Sinaí asks.

'The gaps left by thirty thousand human beings, the gaps left by the so-called "disappeared".'

The silence that follows is as thick as a béchamel sauce tinted with squid's ink. With sarcastic curiosity, Sara surveys all their faces. Even the Fieldmann couple have stopped eating, though their mouths are still full.

'Let's leave it there,' Gorospe begs. 'But thank you for the simplifying sincerity of a foreigner.'

'Simplifying?' Sara queries.

'The same old clichés! Tango, Maradona, the disappeared!' Ferlinghetti number two roars.

In the ensuing weary silence, Ostiz' voice rings out with particular clarity. 'Thirty thousand disappeared, you say, and you say you notice their absence, the gaps they leave. But I say too few people disappeared, I think there are still too many of that riff-raff that need exterminating.'

By now he appears to be speaking directly to the Captain, and his final words are for his ears only. 'All those who didn't disappear for ever come back to life, Doreste. They haven't really disappeared. The next time we'll have to learn the lesson from the unburied dead.'

'The radicals, those damned *Radishes* are the ones to blame, with their need for catharsis. The Radicals are shit.' Sinaí is on his high horse again: 'Of course, the Perónists are worse still. But the disappeared were AIDS. They were like our moral AIDS problem. You, Señor Carvalho, are unaware of what it was like here when Perón died and the subversives felt they could do exactly as they pleased. Not even the Perónist mafia could control them, as we saw when the General Labour Confederation withdrew its support from that excuse for a president Isabelita Perón, and the acting head of state Italo Luder declared a state of emergency and authorized the Armed Forces to wipe out the armed left-wing subversives. It was us the subversives were coming after. It was a life for a life. Here in Argentina, just like in Chile, in Uruguay and over there in Berlin, we won the battle against communism for the West. What are thirty thousand disappeared? How many of us would they have killed if they had won? The Process of National Reorganization, the military Process, was not only inevitable, it was a godsend. The military leaders themselves were another matter. Videla was the only one big enough for the job that needed to be done.'

'With enough balls,' Dolly thunders.

'But we should at least thank Señor Carvalho for being so sincere with us,' Sara timidly suggests.

'Of course, clichés can offend, but...' Dora starts to say, but is cut short by Sinaí.

'Don't get me wrong. I don't want to kill or mistreat anyone at all. I've never so much as killed a fly.'

'Others did it for you,' Sara accuses him with her most charming smile.

'And not for you?'

'For me too.'

'But I have the right of self-defence!' shouts Sinaí. 'We were their targets! They were coming to strip us of our land, our industries, our religion, our values, our sacred order. Isn't it true, Captain?'

He realizes his mistake as soon as he has said this, and bites his lip. The Captain gives him a thunderous look. Sinaí addresses Carvalho.

'As for you, Señor Carvalho, I should like to be friends with you, and tomorrow at your residence you will find a selection of my best wines. It will be an honour to me for you to taste them.'

Sara's voice imposes itself on the conciliatory hush.

'Congratulations, Señor Carvalho, for having escaped alive. But another time, don't mention the rope in the hanged man's house.'

This provokes fresh scandal. The Captain and Carvalho glare at each other.

'Didn't you hear a heavy blow?' Señora Fieldmann is still alert to other developments.

Lucho is flat out on the floor of the office. His nose is bleeding. The failed hangman's rope swings above his head. He is whimpering into the dripping blood. All of a sudden he realizes how ridiculous he must look, and sits up on the parquet floor in his underpants. He feels his nose, and then looks down and sees his body spattered with blood.

'Blood!' he exclaims, looking all around him uncomprehendingly.

Magín and Drumond are still shoulder to shoulder fighting their Great War.

'What about the desserts?'

'Ah yes, the desserts,' Drumond muses. 'Shall I help you serve them?'

'It's unheard of for a *grand chef* to serve at table,' Magín reproaches him.

'You're right,' Drumond says emphatically.

So Drumond helps Magín load himself up with plates of *tango oranges*. Magín looks like a pastrycook scarecrow: he is balancing the dishes on hands, arms and shoulders. He staggers to the door of the restaurant, where all the proprieties are beginning to go by the board.

'If you accept my proposal, I'll take you by plane to my *estancia*,' Ferlinghetti number two is telling Cari.

'What about my film shoot? It took me ages to learn my lines,' the actress complains.

'Who's your producer?'

'Ponti Asiaín,' Cari says.

'We're great friends. He moors his yacht next to mine in San Isidro,' Ferlinghetti replies, his voice deep and encouraging, his eyes like a snake.

Dora gets up and demands that Gorospe let her sit next to Carvalho.

They change places, and she drapes herself affectionately over his arm.

'I've come to convince you that Argentina isn't as bloodthirsty as you might think.'

'There's no real need for you to convince me of something I already believe, but it's a great pleasure anyway to have you sit next to me.'

'Did you hear that?' Dora asks the others. 'He's a gentleman! A Spanish gentleman!'

The physical contact between them is real. Carvalho's knee presses against Dora's thigh. Seen this close to, she is a truly beautiful woman, and her low neckline reveals an enticing skin. Dora cannot help notice Carvalho's interest in her cleavage, and whispers to him: 'He may be a gentleman, but he stares in quite a different fashion.'

'That's because I like what I see. And the closer, the better.'

'Is that a proposition?'

'I'd really, really like to talk wines with you.'

'Me too,' Dora says, drawing closer to Carvalho's ear. 'Don't pay any attention to these people, they're all reactionary bastards. They were all in the Triple A murder squads. López Rega had them all organized even before Perón died.'

Carvalho looks at her in surprise. She has drawn back her head a little, and smiles at him like someone who has been very daring.

'Is Sara like that too?'

She smiles absently at him again, but then leans forward once more to whisper in his ear. 'Sara is a lesbian bitch who stole the restaurant owner's wife from him. You may be interested in her, but she isn't interested in you.'

Drawing back again, her face is a picture of sweet innocence.

'Are you a subversive then?'

'Before I became a woman-object I wanted to be a social scientist. Science is neutral. It doesn't belong to the Triple A.'

'Science belongs to whoever controls it.'

'Do you think that of women too?'

Gorospe's voice breaks in on their private conversation.

'Sinaí, your wife is making indecent proposals to my Spanish friend here.'

Sinaí looks over at his wife with drunken but tender eyes, and recites another poem:

Flee, galactic hind, if you think you flee
because your flight leads back
to find me at the limits of your madness
your one and only possible stallion.

'What did I tell you, Carvalho? Our vintner is a poet. I bet he wrote that himself.'

'Yes, you can tell,' Sara says sarcastically.

'It's among the most beautiful of all the poems he's dedicated to me,' Dora purrs, taking his hand across the table and staring into his eyes besottedly.

The telephone has burst in on them once, twice, and finally becomes unavoidable. As there are no waiters, it is Dolly who answers, and then shouts above the din at the table: 'Pepe Carvalho! A call for Señor Pepe Carvalho!'

The detective goes over to the phone, observed closely all the way by the Captain. At the far end of the line, Don Vito's voice gives him instructions.

'Don't say who you are talking to. Just say yes or no.'

'Agreed.'

'I have to inform you that in following the girl I arrived outside what appears to be the Captain's real home, and not observing any security guards was about to effect an entry when I saw three other people approaching. Can you guess who one of them is?'

'No.'

'Your cousin Raúl. And with him there's a very odd guy, white-haired, thin as a rake, who skips around like a ballet dancer.'

'Yes, I know who he is.'

'The other looks a lot less happy to be there. He's tall and has thinning hair.'

'I know who he is too. So it's a musketeers' reunion. And there aren't three or four of them: there are five. With two others, they make up a quintet.'

'Am I to let them go in first? Or do I get in ahead of them?'

'Do you remember the maiden name of the lady of the house?'

'I've got it written down. Pardieu. María Asunción Pardieu.'

'Ring the bell or knock on the front door, ask for her by name, and explain to her everything we know and what we want.'

'Don't you prefer me to wait for you?'

'We haven't had the desserts here, and I don't want to miss them. I'll explain later.'

The kitchen door swings open. The sight of the head waiter literally covered in desserts leaves all the guests dumbfounded. As if it were the most natural thing in the world, the *maître* wobbles over to the table and like a circus performer slides each plate into perfect position in front of each astounded diner. He bows, and goes off to fetch all the remaining dishes. The guests stare at each other in amazement, then turn as one to survey the door to the kitchen. A few seconds later, the *maître* reappears, and performs the whole operation a second time with unerring accuracy.

'To start with, *tango oranges*,' Magín explains. 'The *marrons* and the *soufflé d'acacia* are still cooking. These things must be done just right.'

He bows again and backs out of the restaurant.

'Well... did you all see what I saw?' Gorospe asks, unaware that he is stating the obvious.

In his office, Lucho Reyero picks up the clothing scattered all over the floor, and puts it on. He even dons his jacket and tie. When he is fully dressed in his crumpled clothes he looks like an aristocratic tramp. He studies himself in the mirror. He fixes his tiepin, and carefully places a white handkerchief in his top pocket. He is pleased with the effect. He goes over to his desk and takes out the pistol. He snaps it open. It is fully loaded.

Magín enters the kitchen. Drumond is examining the individual soufflés in the oven, which have all risen magnificently.

'You won't be able to serve these on your own. *Pas possible!* They'll all collapse as you come back for more. *Tragique!*'

'I'll go and see if Lupe has calmed down.'

Drumond tries to stop him, but in vain. Magín opens the cold-storage door and halts in amazement. The two dead kitchen assistants are hanging from meat hooks. Lupe is lying on the floor, frozen solid. Magín feels for a pulse.

'She's dead!' he exclaims in horror, unable to grasp all that's been going on. He turns round. Drumond is a couple of feet away, waving a huge cleaver to stop him coming out of the storage room.

'Don't say anything. Don't do anything.'

'Let me out of here.'

'Dinner isn't over. I don't want you to spoil it for me.'

Magín cannot think of a suitable reply to this, and cannot react quickly enough to prevent Drumond locking him in the room.

'I'm really sorry, you were a true professional,' the *grand chef* shouts from the far side of the door.

'And the soufflés? Who is going to serve them?'

'It's a disgrace for a *grand chef,* but I'll have to do it.'

'They'll collapse! By the time they reach the table, they'll look like *quiches lorraine!* It'll be a disaster!' Magín shouts at him with increasing desperation.

Drumond thinks this over.

'That's true.'

'What do you imagine?' Magín scolds him. 'That you're the only professional in this city, this country, this world? Do you mean to insult the Argentines by saying I'm not as professional as you? What am I trained to do? Count dead bodies or serve soufflés?'

'Serve soufflés, of course,' Drumond replies.

'And that's what I intend to do,' Magín's voice comes back, encouraged at this glimmer of hope. 'Everyone gets what they deserve, including all those in here.'

Drumond appears to agree wholeheartedly. He throws away the cleaver, opens the cold-storage door and lets Magín out. He points him towards the restaurant. As soon as he enters the room, Magín is the complete *maître* once more, and he starts to withdraw the empty plates. He gestures to attract the guests' attention.

'I propose a forty-year-old port, a Noval grand reserve. The *sommelier* chose it before he went home. But if you prefer, there are chilled liqueurs or Armagnac and cognac.'

'Excellent! But Magín, what on earth is going on in the kitchen? You're the only person serving. Whatever happened to the waitress?'

'She had a sudden indisposition.'

'I must say, the kitchen is a disaster tonight,' Dolly complains with a bewildered shrug.

'If only it were just this kitchen,' Señora Fieldmann chimes in. 'Can you find staff in Buenos Aires? They say there's a crisis in Argentina, but you can't even find girls from Paraguay. My sister, who lives in Paris, says it's easy as pie there – her servants are a Polish couple who play the cello. They are extraordinary!'

'Although it is slightly unorthodox, as a token of the satisfaction it has given him to have such connoisseurs as his guests this evening, the chef and myself will be serving the *soufflés aux fleurs d'acacia "Liliana Mazure"* ourselves.'

Magín considers he has said all he needs to say, and disappears back into the kitchen.

'The *potpourri* was delicious, but this is undoubtedly the other star dish of the evening. A soufflé with acacia flowers!' Gorospe enthuses.

'How wonderful!' Cari trills.

'Tango oranges are a dish for pansies that anyone can make, but this is a real invention. It was Troisgros who first thought of it, and I've taken the liberty of bringing his recipe along with me.'

Gorospe takes a piece of paper from his pocket and hands it to Sinaí. 'Read this.'

'Why me? Cari should read it, she's the actress.'

'You read it, you're the poet.'

Sinaí stands up and starts to read.

'"Preparation time: thirty minutes. Cooking time: eighteen minutes."'

'So little!' Dolly exclaims.

Sinaí gives her a thunderous look and goes on:

'"A hundred grammes of bunches of acacia flowers, two centilitres of cognac, two egg yolks, five egg whites, a teaspoon of butter, an eighth of a litre of *crème pâtissière*... "' he pauses. 'This isn't enough even to get started.'

'It's a recipe for four people. Go on.'

'... "powdered and icing sugar, salt...Preparation – first, take two whole bunches of flowers and put them to one side. Then pluck the rest flower by flower..."'

As Sinaí goes on reading with his practised, professional delivery, Lucho is at the door of his office ready to come down. He is standing to attention, and slips the pistol into his jacket pocket as if about to depart on an epic mission. He turns back to the mirror and confirms how dishevelled he looks. He is past caring. He turns back again and sets off for the door. He opens it, and stares down at the distant guests for a second or two before he begins to walk slowly and stiffly down the staircase. At that precise instant, Drumond and Magín appear from the kitchen loaded with trays of soufflés. The guests receive them with applause. The soufflés are placed majestically in front of each of them.

'When I think how I love acacia trees, and here I am about to eat the flowers,' Cari says sadly.

'When I was a girl I loved little rabbits, but now my favourite meal is rabbit stew,' Señora Fieldmann adds dreamily.

'And what about little birds?' Gorospe asks. 'Song thrushes have to be drowned in wine for them to have any taste.'

'And in Brillat-Savarin's time, they ate a certain little bird raw because it had such flavour,' Ferlinghetti number two says.

This is a bit more information than Cari needs to know. She starts to retch, and though at first it seems funny, soon the retching is ghastly, uncontrollable, her body arching brutally – until all of a sudden she vomits massively all over Señor Fieldmann's trousers.

'Why don't you do something?' Señora Fieldmann complains to her husband.

'What's that girl up to?' Dolly asks disgustedly.

Not only are Señor Fieldmann's trousers soaked in vomit, it has also splashed on to his wife's Versace dress. Drumond tries to rescue the situation.

'Please, don't look! There's nothing wrong with the dessert!' He picks up a spoon and tries a mouthful from Sinaí's plate, despite the latter's indignation. 'Don't look, just eat!'

Everyone screws up their faces in disgust. Drumond and Gorospe go and try to help the increasing numbers of casualties. Magín collapses into a chair and pretends he is not there. Also divorcing themselves from the general panic, Carvalho, the Captain, Sinaí and Sara taste their soufflés, then nod to each other enthusiastically. Gorospe interrupts his humanitarian efforts and takes a mouthful from his own plate.

'Exquisite!'

Then he rushes off again.

Ostiz and the Captain take advantage of the confusion to talk to each other. The financier does not look directly at the Captain, but he has harsh words for him. Carvalho picks up scraps of their conversation.

'You went too far.'

To which the Captain replies: 'So you're feeding me to the lions?'

Lucho has reached the bottom three steps. He cannot make up his mind whether to complete the descent. He stares at the tragi-comic scene in front of him. Eventually he takes the gun out of his pocket, descends the final three stairs and heads towards what is left of the banqueting table.

'Lucho! Luchito!' shouts Dora, the first to have spotted his presence. 'So you finally decided to join us?'

In a fraction of a second, all the other guests suddenly see the gun and the wild-eyed man wielding it.

'What's got into you, Lucho?' Gorospe asks nervously.

Lucho raises the pistol. He stares at Sara and points it at her. The two of them glare at each other. He takes aim, Sara propels her wheelchair violently backwards, and Drumond is left in the line of fire. A shot rings out, and the chef crumples to the floor. Any of the guests who were not already hysterical take the opportunity to join in now. Sinaí pulls a gun from his shoulder holster and aims at Lucho. The Captain knocks the gun down, and the bullet zings away harmlessly.

'We shouldn't be killing each other,' says the Captain, staring pointedly at Ostiz.

Lucho stares down numbly at the gun in his hand. The Captain strides up to him.

'Give me that.'

Lucho hands it over. The Captain turns round, gun at the ready. All the guests are sprawled over or under the table. Only Carvalho appears unaffected. He has one hand hidden inside his jacket, and meets the Captain's gaze defiantly.

Raúl takes charge, even though he is surprised at how easily they enter through the iron gate into the garden and that they are all alone on the avenue of trees leading up to the house, and can see that the quickest way to the secret heart of the beast is by marching straight up to the front door. The three men look anxiously in all directions to try to spot any danger – they even glance up into the sky, in case they should be spotted from there, or suddenly hear the forbidding voice of some god or other; but no, the house grows steadily larger and closer, and all at once they have to do something because they find themselves at the bottom of the steps leading to the main door. Again it is Raúl who takes the lead, and without waiting to see how his companions are faring, presses the bell once and once more: then the three of them wait, trying to sense what is going on inside, until they hear footsteps and a distorted shape behind the bevelled glass. The door opens – and it is Don Vito who welcomes them with a sad, knowing smile.

'Vito Altofini, Carvalho's partner. I was expecting you – come on in.'

None of them can think of anything to reply to their surprise host, so he leads them through the wide hall with its flight of stairs to the upper floors, and into a living-room filled with heavy cane furniture upholstered in bright clashing colours, the opposite of the pale, former blonde, former beautiful woman sitting there rubbing her hands on her skirt as if trying to get rid of invisible stains.

'Doña María Asunción, these gentlemen are here for the same reason as me; and I'd particularly like you to meet Don Raúl Tourón, who is Muriel's real father.'

At this, the woman stares up at the ceiling, and Don Vito helps her by explaining to the new arrivals: 'The girl is upstairs. We agreed to talk about what had happened without disturbing her. She's in her bedroom. But now that you're here, Don Raúl, you're the one who has to decide.'

'Let things stay as they are.'

Don Vito asks the woman to go on with her story. Before she speaks, she has a drink of some dark liquid from a glass on the round lace-covered table beside her.

'I'm discovering it's as hard for me to talk as it was to stay silent.'

She has to take another drink.

'At first I didn't know what on earth I was doing. He would tell me – do this, do that, and I did it. I was brought up in a military background, where I was educated to be a soldier's wife, to go from garrison to garrison, first following my father, and then my husband. With my father everything was black or white, but in broad daylight, but living with my husband meant being submerged in darkness. We were not supposed to know or to speak: we couldn't even say who we were, or where we lived. I've been another of the disappeared ever since he became an expert in the dirty war, and though at first he taught me how to behave, soon he did not even bother with that. He took it for granted that I should accept everything, that I was merely there to watch and applaud whatever he did. The truth is I didn't start to revolt until it was pointless to do so, and so of course I did not bother. I don't even raise my head when I see them come and go. They come in, go out: they don't even look at me; they don't even see me.'

'The girl, Doña María Asunción. The girl. She was what we were asking you about.'

'Of course, of course. And that's what I'm talking about. We used to live in anonymous military installations that could not be identified from outside. One morning he brought the baby. She's ours, he said. Just like that. She's ours. I didn't ask him about her parents. I never asked him about anything that I sensed was happening in the Navy Engineering School and all those other places. He told me that within twenty-four hours we had to move to an address that we could not give out even to our closest family. Not even to your mother, he said. You'll be able to go and visit her. And whatever you do, don't say anything about the baby. He gave some sort of confused explanation that she was only mine in legal terms, and that since my real names appeared on the birth register, I would not be able to appear in public with him, and would have to change my name. We could not have friends. Leaving the house became a difficult, nocturnal business. Whenever we went out together it was more or less in disguise, so bit by bit we stopped going out together. I stopped going out altogether. I've hardly been out in the past fifteen years – whenever I do, those horrible flies, those motorcyclists follow me everywhere. They're there to protect me, the fat man says. He's almost the only person who talks to me.'

'And what's your relation with the girl?'

'I barely have one. I used to, but not any more. When she arrived, it was the end of my life. I'm dozing when she goes out, asleep when she gets back. Occasionally I ask her: is everything all right, Muriel? And she's learnt from childhood to reply: yes, Mamma, everything's fine. She's very affectionate, poor thing, she forgives me everything. I hear her arguing with him, standing up for me. She is the only one on my side. When she was tiny, I tried to be a mother to her, but he wouldn't let me: he was both father and mother, always. He organized his time and his postings so that he could be with Muriel as much as possible, and when he wasn't around, the fat man took over. They didn't trust me.'

'Why was that?'

'Perhaps because they realized that deep down I didn't love the girl.'

'You didn't love her?'

'Are you her father?'

'Yes.'

'I'm really sorry. But no, I didn't really love her. I felt sorry for her, and I think I always treated her well, but I didn't love her. She was your daughter. I'm sorry. I know it was wrong, but try to understand – my husband organized everything, he was the one responsible.'

'She didn't love her. She didn't love her.'

Silverstein mutters this to himself, trying to understand, and is inwardly surprised at Raúl's strength as he continues with his interrogation to the bitter end.

'The bitter end. The bitter end.'

Silverstein keeps up his running commentary on what's going on. And all at once Raúl raises what must be the bitter end of the affair.

'Would you be willing to testify all you have said to a judge?'

Without a moment's hesitation, she replies: 'Yes.'

Raúl looks up at the living-room ceiling. Muriel is up there. All it would take would be to climb a few steps, and he would have his daughter back. But Silverstein puts a restraining hand on his arm, and Font y Rius decrees: 'Not just yet, Raulito.'

Raúl Tourón nods his agreement, and Don Vito adds his weight to the decision – not that Raúl or anyone else has asked him to. Tourón turns to the woman, who is sadly surveying her past in the bottom of her empty glass.

'It's best if you come with us before they get back. We need to lay charges and have you confirm them as soon as possible.'

The woman breathes out a sighing 'yes' through weary lips, then accepts Don Vito's arm as she struggles up out of her chair and staggers to the door on legs almost as unsteady as Altofini's.

In the midst of a gaggle of police cars and ambulances, Pascuali looks up at the sky over Buenos Aires in search of a star that might shed some light on this dark and confused night, but his search is interrupted by the dinner guests starting to leave the restaurant. He and the Captain exchange curt salutes. The inspector's jaw drops when behind the Captain it is Carvalho who appears.

'So you're here too? You're ubiquitous!'

'No, just a man of many talents: among them, a gourmet.'

Vladimiro comes running up.

'Boss, there are three bodies in the cold-storage room!'

Pascuali rushes into the restaurant. The Captain and Carvalho do not appear surprised at the news.

'Who knows what happens behind the scenes at even the best restaurants!' the Captain comments drily.

'If we did, we'd never go to another one,' Carvalho replies.

A distraught Gorospe is trying to recover his prestige with words of consolation to each departing guest. Before stepping into her limousine, Dolly stares hard at Carvalho. The Captain notices the exchange of glances.

'It could be a mistake. Sinaí is a very jealous man.'

'My whole life is a series of bigger and better mistakes.'

'Well, that's the end of the gourmet truce.'

The two men are about to go their separate ways when the detective remembers a forgotten incident and catches the Captain's attention by mentioning it.

'I saw you the other night at the boxing match.'

'Boxing?'

'Boom Boom Peretti.'

A flicker of alarm appears in the Captain's eyes.

'Your daughter was with us, with Alma and me.'

'I don't know what daughter you're talking about. I'm not even married.'

'I could have sworn you realized Muriel was there.'

The Captain growls a warning.

'Don't go too far. If you do, I'll be waiting. And the abyss.'

'Well, each to his own, and I'm going home to bed. As you say, the truce has ended, but it seems to me a lot more things have ended for you, Captain. Among them your friendship with Ostiz, for example.'

Doreste does not flinch at this, or even at Carvalho's parting shot.

'Say hello from me to your wife, maiden name Pardieu.'

The Captain strides off. His face is drawn into such a tight ball it seems what little flesh is left on it must explode. As he charges along the pavement, he almost collides with Ostiz and his personal bodyguards. They do not speak, and Ostiz's face is a picture of scorn. Then the fat man comes puffing up, and the orders the Captain barks so alarm him that he looks around at all points of the compass as if to spy out an imminent invasion. Although the Captain walks with dignity to his car, the fat man rushes ahead as if scared that he too might suddenly disappear.

Carvalho watches as the ambulancemen take out Drumond on a stretcher, and policemen lead out Lucho in handcuffs. Carvalho goes over to the stretcher. He leans over and asks Drumond something, much to Pascuali's annoyance.

'Why do you call the soufflé "Liliana Mazure"? What makes it different?'

'I add some drops of champagne, in honour of a woman friend who really likes champagne,' Drumond whispers to him.

He is carried off to the ambulance. Pascuali is bemused, and even more so when Carvalho exclaims: 'How odd!'

'What's so odd?'

'I wonder how and when he adds the champagne? Normally you can't mix champagne and *crème pâtissière*.'

Pascuali cannot and never could understand why Carvalho is so preoccupied with this.

'Why was it so important to know?'

Carvalho looks at the inspector as if he is a complete idiot. But his superior air does not last long. His eyes are telling him he will have to get used to a new and disturbing fact: among the crowd of onlookers outside Chez Reyero is his uncle. The one and only Evaristo Tourón. His American uncle. His European uncle. And he also has to take in the fact that as the Captain beats his retreat led by the fat man and the motorcyclists, he comes up against Don Evaristo, and cannot look him in the face.

The European Uncle

There's a nobody who is everybody's victim
He's the anonymous king of disasters
The excuse you're forced to invent
For so many unsolved crimes.

MARIA ELENA WALSH
Magoya

Pascuali is thinking that if the Polack Goyeneche were not dead, then this must be him. A singer of the age and rough-hewn appearance of the Polack is walking along the pavement, ignoring the traffic and the passers-by, and singing out loud: *Corrientes 348, second floor, with a lift, there are no porters or neighbours...*He is still singing when he reaches Corrientes 348, and is forced by the police guard to go round the area cordoned off for Pascuali and the forensic expert. Pascuali is obsessed with the singer. If Goyeneche had not died, he could swear it was him, down to the yellow shoes. The old guy goes up to the entrance to Corrientes 348 and reads the plaque where it says that on this spot the tango was invented, an apartment block which has ended its days as a parking lot. He nods wistfully, and only then appears to notice all the hubbub around the cordoned-off area, in the middle of which is a parked car. Inside the car an even older man is sprawled dead at the wheel, his eyes wide open and something very odd dangling from his mouth. Vladimiro reacts more quickly than his boss, who still seems fascinated by the singer, and tugs until he finally manages to remove the object from the dead man's lips. He waves it in the air, and as it opens out, sees it is a pair of women's knickers. Wet ones. The examining magistrate draws Pascuali and the rest of the assembled police's attention to them by shouting out: 'A pair of panties. A soaking pair of panties.'

But Pascuali is still staring absent-mindedly after the old singer who now has wandered off, unconcerned about what is going on around the car.

'Are you listening, Pascuali? A pair of wet panties, Pascuali. Hello?'

'Sorry, I thought I was seeing a reincarnation. Goyeneche the Polack died, didn't he?'

'The tango singer? Yes, of course.'

'Well, I thought I just saw him. At any rate, I know that old singer guy who just went by. I know him from somewhere. What were you saying?'

'I was saying that what was stuffed in the stiff's mouth was a pair of wet panties.'

'Wet from saliva, I guess.'

From saliva, Inspector Pascuali repeats to himself, sitting in front of his computer back at the police station. The details he called up appear on the screen. Abraham Gratowsky, born Warsaw in 1913. Immigrated to Argentina in 1943. Concert violin player. Artists' agent. Boyfriend and manager of Gilda Laplace from 1949 to 1963. Current address: The Pauline Sisters Old-Age Pensioners' Home. Criminal record: none. After he has read the notes, someone presses the right buttons and the dead man's life is delivered neatly printed into Pascuali's hands. He takes the pages back to his desk, and sits forward in his chair to read them through again. His lips move as he makes mental notes. Then he leans back in his chair and mutters to himself: 'Gilda Laplace.'

He remembers how his mother used to be fascinated by the actress, and his eyes moisten with the damp fog of time.

Adriana Varela, her eye make-up blotched and all her paper handkerchiefs thrown into the waste-paper basket. Norman is a hapless witness to her grief, and shrugs apologetically as Carvalho and Alma enter the dressing-room.

'What's the matter with her?'

'Someone killed the Great Gratowsky.'

In his ignorance, Carvalho asks: 'Was he a magician?'

Norman is indignant that this foreigner does not know someone so famous in Argentina.

'In the fifties and sixties, he was one of our best-known agents. He was still highly thought of. By those who still have a memory, that is.'

Adriana's memory summons up the image of herself as a youngster. She starts to sing a classic tango:

> *When fortune, that sad bitch*
> *Lying and betraying*
> *Leaves you out in the cold*

In the stalls sit the pretend judges of a pretend talent contest. One of them is an already ancient Gratowsky. He likes what he hears. He leans over to the man who makes all the decisions and whispers in his ear: 'I can't bear women who sing tangos, especially the old ones that Gardel or Rivero made famous, but this girl is different.'

'Are you listening to me, Norman? The Great Gratowsky gave me his seal of approval. When I'd finished, I saw the judge turn and say something to him. He smiled, then stood up and clambered on to the stage. He came towards me, hands outstretched. I took them in mine – they were lined and old, but still oh so elegant. He seemed even more abashed than me. He said: "You're too young to know who I am. I'm called the Great Gratowsky. I can spot a star among a million constellations. And you're going to be a big star." After that, he was always like a godfather to me. He wasn't in the business any more, but the talent spotters listened to him. I went to see him several times in that horrible old people's home.'

'Don't cry, sweetheart, please don't cry! You're just like a tango. Don't become a walking tango, please! The old man lives, he lives in your memory. What more do you want? How many people have gone for good? How many of them don't even live on in someone's memory?'

Carvalho cannot contain himself any longer: 'Tango!'

The dressing-room mirror reflects Adriana's features: she has recovered completely by now, and is busy putting the final touches to her lips. She stares into the glass at the image of Carvalho behind her, and behind him Alma and Norman's vaguely encouraging presence.

'Pepe, I have a job for you. I want you to get on to it straight away. I want you to find out who killed the Great Gratowsky.'

'I don't know if I can take the case. I might be going back to Spain.

The circle is complete. All that's left to decide is not down to me.'

He is staring at Alma, who reacts uncomfortably, as if she does not like what she is hearing.

'There are some loose ends. Too many of them.'

'All that's left is what to do with the Captain and what my uncle sees fit to tell us.'

The police consult the label hanging from the handle: 'Murder at Corrientes 348'. He pulls open the drawer of the mortuary store and shows the body to a couple of around fifty. The woman's hormones suggest a great struggle between male and female. Alongside this hard-edged woman, the man is a let-down. The surgeon unzips the plastic body bag and the dead man's face appears. The woman stares coldly at the old man's features, closes her eyes and nods: 'It's Papa.'

The man agrees: 'Papa.'

'Señora...'

'Gratowsky. I didn't want to lose my maiden name.'

The man agrees again: 'No. She never wanted to lose her maiden name.'

'Do you have to repeat everything I say even in circumstances like this?'

'Repeat everything you say? Do I do that?'

He is trying to bring a touch of humour where none applies. The woman's expression is harsh rather than grieving. The forensic expert tries to build a bridge of sympathy between the two of them.

'In successful marriages, couples end up not only looking like each other but thinking and talking like each other.'

The woman casts a scornful glance at her husband.

'You mean I'm this jerk?'

The police expert looks from one to the other in search of similarities, then looks down at the dead body.

'No, it's strange. In fact, your husband looks more like your father. I've never seen a son-in-law so similar to his father-in-law.'

The woman goes on repeating insults against the smartass forensic expert all the way home on the bus, all through a brief, uncomfortable supper, and into their gloomy bedroom. Everything looks grubby and old, as if waiting for an unlikely face-lift. The woman sits on the bed, and removes her stockings, sloughing them off like cast-off skins. She stares down at her swollen feet, massages the varicose veins on her calves. A grimace of disgust appears on her harsh face, directed either at herself or at the world in general. Her husband comes into the room. He looks simple and contented. He is carrying a framed photograph, which he hands with a flourish to his wife.

'Ruth, your father.'

She gives him a dirty look, and her expression stays the same as she stares down at the photograph. It is from forty years earlier. It shows a middle-aged man, still young and forceful-looking, with a younger woman who is posing like a film star. In the background is someone who is her twin sister, a paler version of her. Ruth throws the photo on the bed.

'The dummy and his whore. Couldn't you find a photograph of him with my mother?'

She defies her husband, eyes blazing. He is crushed, and she goes in for the kill.

'You men are all the same.'

Don Vito is in full flow. Carvalho waits patiently for him to finish, swivelling round in his desk chair.

'It might be too much to say that the Great Gratowsky and I were like brothers, but first cousins, definitely. He used my services several times – he was a real skirt-chaser, and skirts always mean problems. Men always feel they have to find themselves by looking up as many skirts as possible.'

'Even if they are Scottish kilts?'

'That depends on the Scots person underneath. But the love of the Great Gratowsky's life was Gilda Laplace.'

Gilda Laplace was part of Argentine folklore when he was a child: Perón, Evita, Hugo del Carril, Gilda Laplace.

'She still works as a TV presenter. I saw some of her films in Spain when I was a teenager; she always seemed really beautiful to me.'

'She had a twin sister, who was just as pretty. They worked together for ten years: "The Laplace Sisters". They sang, danced, made films, worked in the theatre and in radio dramas. Then Lidia Laplace vanished from the limelight. She went back to her private life.

In fact, everyone knew it was Gilda who had the real talent.'

'Was she called Gilda in honour of Rita Hayworth?'

'No, poor thing. What else could she do? Her real name was Hermenegilda.'

'You start with the artistic lot: theatre, television, film people. I'll look into the family and the Laplace sisters. For as long as I'm still in Buenos Aires – I could be leaving tomorrow, next week or never at this rate.'

Don Vito has his hand on his heart, and breathes out the words with a sigh: 'You will never leave Buenos Aires, even if you do go away from it. Oh, and by the way, after all we've achieved together, after risking our necks so many times, do you mind if I keep the office? I'll even keep your name on the door. Your presence is guaranteed in my life and in the memory of private detection in Buenos Aires!'

'Don't make me cry, Don Vito. I'm going to see Gratowsky's daughter. Talk to my uncle about the office. He owns the apartment.'

He is already on the stairs when he hears his partner's shouted last words: 'It's so central, you see.'

Isaac and Ruth Gratowsky, a neighbour informs Carvalho. Her name has swallowed his up, and even though she is not at home and Isaac is, her presence fills the apartment. The living-room gives off an air of increasingly hard times that Carvalho immediately recognizes: the end of something, the end of everything. Isaac recalls his father-in-law dreamily:

'An insurance policy? I knew that deep down he loved her. Sometimes – but promise you'll never breathe a word to Ruth – sometimes I used to go and visit him. On my own. She would never have agreed to it. But he was always pleased to see me. We old folk appreciate visits.'

'But your wife hates them.'

'My wife is a very special person. She doesn't trust anyone, and I can understand that: life made her that way. She never forgave her father for abandoning her and her mother and going off with Gilda Laplace – and all the others, because he was a real ladies' man. When he saw what he wanted, he was quick on the draw.'

'Still nowadays?'

'You bet!'

He lowers his voice, as if the skinny presence of Ruth was fluttering somewhere around them.

'Sometimes we used to go out to a brothel together. But don't tell Ruth. She's very tough. Very complicated. She works as a masseuse, and she is allergic to the creams she has to use. Poor thing. She's scared she'll have to quit.'

Ruth Gratowsky in a white overcoat, hands smeared with cream, is bending professionally over a female body and pummelling its back. Her face betrays no emotions, but the hands work knowingly up and down the back, buttocks, thighs and shoulders of the anonymous but shapely body. A bit overweight perhaps. Ruth Gratowsky's voice is as strong as her hands:

'If I'm doing it too hard, tell me.'

'No, that's the way I like it. Keep going.'

The massage comes to an end. After a brief flash of nudity, the woman puts on her bathrobe. Ruth wipes her hands clean, and a frightened look appears in her eyes when she sees that red blotches have reappeared on her skin. Her customer leaves the room, but not before she has stuffed some notes into Ruth's overcoat.

'Thanks a lot, Señora Fersanti. You're always so kind.'

Left alone, Ruth peers desperately at her hands. She looks up to the skies as if searching for someone to blame, and from the skies comes a voice: 'Ruth Gratowsky, you are wanted in reception.'

Carvalho is glancing in through a half-open door. One woman is applying make-up to another, in a way that reminds him of a dentist's, because the person receiving the treatment is lying almost flat in a chair like those in a dental surgery. The make-up girl is rhythmically patting the other woman's double chins. Carvalho watches fascinated, but his curiosity is cut short when an unknown hand slams the door shut. The hand belongs to Ruth Gratowsky, who frowns at him.

'You wanted to see me?'

'Ruth Gratowsky?'

'Who else would it be? It was Ruth Gratowsky you asked for, wasn't it?'

Carvalho nods and offers her a chair.

'Why don't you sit down, make yourself at home.'

Carvalho himself sits down, and after a moment's reflection, Ruth does the same.

'First of all, let me express my deepest sympathy.'

'D'you mind telling me what your sympathy is for?'

'So you're from the Bette Davis school. At least you talk like Bette Davis. I was offering sympathy for a daughter who has just lost her father.'

'I lost my father forty years ago. He abandoned my mother and me in this city while he went off to play at being the Great Gratowsky.'

'So can I feel sympathy with you for that?'

'Why? Do you know how it feels to have a father abandon you forty years ago? Not in Buenos Aires of course, from your accent you're a Spaniard.'

'My father had a proper sense of the ridiculous, and never abandoned anyone in his life. Not even a mangy old cat we had at home called Negrín.'

'Was it a black cat then?'

'No. His name was in honour of a Spanish Republican leader, Juan Negrín. But you wouldn't have heard of him.'

'I can't even remember the names of our own politicians. What's our president called?'

'Menem, I think. Is that right?'

Ruth gives a sigh and says defiantly to Carvalho: 'Detective? Insurance inspector?'

Carvalho puts on his broadest, most disarming smile.

'Private detective.'

Ruth gets up at once. For her, the conversation is over, and she is about to stride off when Carvalho's voice pulls her up short.

'A private detective who could cause you problems cashing in the insurance policy your father left you.'

The phantom of a vanishing dream flickers in Ruth's eyes, and all of a sudden Carvalho feels sad and truly sympathetic. He mutters an apology and leaves.

One by one, Don Evaristo surveys all the components of Carvalho's living-room-cum-office, as if drawing up a mental inventory of all the changes his nephew has made. He also has one ear pricked for the lengthy phone call Carvalho is making to Barcelona, as if calculating how much it is going to cost, and whether the detective is likely to return to Spain without paying it. From the conversation, it seems as though someone has come back.

'So Charo is going to stay? She's going to start a business? I don't know, Biscuter. I don't know. There are lots of loose ends to tie up.'

The conversation goes on and on to no purpose, in Don Evaristo's view. People have lost all respect for the telephone, he thinks, and talk and talk without realizing that beyond the person they are talking to, in the basements of the telephone companies there are Lilliputian accountants rubbing their hands with glee at the profits they are making thanks to all these blabbermouths. He had never exactly thought of his nephew as a blabbermouth, but now there he is, his lips stuck to the mouthpiece and one arm folded over his head like a chimpanzee, as if he were trying to build a protective wall round himself.

'No, Biscuter, there's no way I can tell you.'

So if he can't tell him, what more is there to say? Don Evaristo pretends to drift off to sleep, to avoid having to listen to his nephew and to the endless chatter from Don Vito, but in reality he is keeping a weather eye open on the people coming and going in the office, until finally he sees Raúl outside the door and then coming towards him slowly, unkempt and cold – cold with him, his own father – even though he does bend and aim a kiss in the general direction of his cheek. Even Carvalho has put the phone down to see how their re-encounter goes, and Alma appears from the room next door, where she has been closeted with Font y Rius and Silverstein. Alma has shed floods of tears from eyes that look drowned in too many conflicting emotions, and is waiting for the old man to say something. No one looks at him, but they are all waiting for him to say something.

'The Day of Judgement,' is what he eventually does say, knowing they all wanted to hear more. 'So our Berta didn't die after all.'

Then he adds, sarcastically: 'Of course, how could your great leader die?'

By now he cannot interrupt the outpouring of his anguished feelings.

'At my age I don't have to apologize for anything. I didn't ask you to take on the Argentine army, the whole of Argentine society or the CIA, which was determined not to lose the Cold War anywhere in the world, and especially not here in America. I didn't ask you to play the fool. I had to deal with the consequences of something I had nothing to do with. Is that clear? That's why I am not going to apologize to anyone. I did things as I saw fit, just as you had done. I was able to do something to save your lives, but I had to pay the price.'

'Eva María?'

Don Evaristo has stood up, and now raises himself to his full height to confront his son face to face.

'She was a means to an end – to saving her and saving the rest of you. When I met Captain Gorostizaga…'

'Doreste.'

'Dorwhatever! What does it matter what his real name is? I used my influence – it will make you laugh, but it worked better than all your intellectuals, priests or human rights people put together – and I managed to reach the Captain.'

'What influence did you have?'

'Milk.'

By now he is sitting down again, and his tired eyes strain to see the effect his words are having on Raúl.

'Can you remember what my main business was in those days?'

'You ran a wholesale milk delivery business.'

'That's right. I had a contract to supply a lot of the army barracks, and that contract meant some juicy kickbacks for the top military men. It was Don Evaristo here, Don Evaristo there, what can we do for you, Don Evaristo? My son's been taken in, just some silly young people's nonsense. We'll see what we can do, Don Evaristo. What does he think is so funny?'

Silverstein has doubled up laughing.

'What I'm telling you is true, every word. I had very good connections in this country, the bribes I paid stood me in good stead with the commanders, and so I got to talk to the Captain's superiors. You had lost everything, and Eva María was in an orphanage, without any legal identity. You Raúl were alive, so I did a deal to hand over all your research and to keep quiet about what had happened. Berta was dead, or so I believed at the time, and anyway, it wasn't only you I got out, but all those who had been picked up with you, in your apartment.

That meant the fellow who's so amused over there, Alma, and Pignatari – where is Pignatari, by the way?'

'He's dead!'

Silverstein says between guffaws: 'So this guy saved our lives because he sold the army milk!'

'At least I had something to sell: you lot had nothing, either then or now; and either that bonehead stops laughing, or I'm not saying another word. What is there to laugh about anyway? Isn't the Captain still around? Do you think you're more powerful than I am? What are you going to do when the Captain comes to get you again?'

This time it is Raúl who speaks, without looking his father in the face.

'No one is judging you. We knew something must have happened for us all to be saved so miraculously. We didn't want to know the details, until I came back because I wanted to feel I belonged somewhere. Anyway, the Captain is no threat any more. At this very moment there's a warrant out for his arrest.'

'Idiots! People like him never get arrested!'

'Tell Adriana I'm off the case. I'm leaving. Going back to Spain with my uncle. I'm handing the Great Gratowsky case over to Don Vito. I don't have the heart to tell her myself.'

Alma refuses to believe what she is hearing.

'You're telling me you're going back to Spain? That you're never going to visit Tango Amigo ever again?'

'No, this is my last tango show. And with a quintet, no less. The Quinteto Real. Or the New Buenos Aires Quintet, as the posters say. After that, it's goodbye.'

There's a bottle of Bourgueil wine on the table, compliments of the house, and on the platform five old tango masters are tuning up with a skill born of a lifetime's practice. They are in the wine club in the Calle Contreras, the kind of place that advertises alternative theatre venues and plays born of the alienating madness of a city steeped in identity. Luis Cardei and Antonio Pisano on the bandoneon, Nestor Marconi and Antonio Agri on the violin, Salgán on the piano, De Lio on the guitar. Carvalho cannot take his eyes off the casual virtuosity of Agri, who used to play the violin for Astor Piazzola. He is an elegant old man with worried eyes that are full of the music he lives and breathes. The instruments start up their dialogue, with the bandoneon taking the lead and making room for itself. To Carvalho the bandoneon seems like the objective correlative, while the piano, guitar and violin fill in behind. The bandoneon is a stabbing spotlight, weary of illuminating only battlefields of defeat. Raúl, Norman, Font y Rius and Alma are excited. They are paying attention to the music, but are also busy discussing their meeting with Muriel this evening – we can't let this evening go by without talking to her.

'Shall we call her Eva María?'

'I prefer Muriel.'

'Let her choose.'

Carvalho is a stranger outside the group, which is caught up in an adventure that is exclusively their own concern. It has nothing to do with him, or Raúl's father, or Güelmes.

They leave the wine club and set off for their meeting with Muriel.

'Callao on the corner with Corrientes.'

Font y Rius says goodbye.

'Aren't you coming?'

'I'll pick up the pieces afterwards. Remember, you can always get a discount at my clinic.'

Carvalho's car is commandeered, and he finds himself hired as driver, although no one asks him if he agrees. There is a lot of traffic, and lots of police on duty for what looks like a large demonstration.

'Is it the mothers of the Plaza de Mayo?'

'No.'

'The old-age pensioners?'

'No. It's for the "night of the pencils".'

The night of the pencils. While in the back of the car Raúl and Alma continue to go over the details of what to say to Muriel, in the front seat Norman explains what to Carvalho what that means.

'At the start of the dictatorship, the military arrested some secondary school students, just children. They accused them of putting out a "subversive publication", and killed them all. Well, one survived. We call it the "night of the pencils" because they were young schoolkids.'

Norman turns round and looks at Raúl and Alma, who are

oblivious to anything that might happen in the car or in the wide world outside. He comments: 'I was reading an article in *Nuevo Porteño* about Paco Urondo's kids. The elder one is a boy, who grew up with his father. And there's a girl, who was kidnapped by the military and was one of the disappeared. They have met again after all these years. The boy is a living book of memory, because he had the time to realize what it meant to be Urondo's son. But the girl needs everything explaining to her, everything, including the fact that her father was a great poet. None of these kids can ever be normal. Muriel will never be normal.'

When they get to the corner of Corrientes and Callao, Alma dives into a shop selling Argentine books and records. The three men stand watching the demonstration go by: thousands of young people, veterans already of years of marching, of so many defeats, with the image of Che Guevara waving over their heads, and above that too the shout of 'Venceremos!' It's like an optical illusion that the seventies are still with us, Silverstein says to himself over and over again, the years when it seemed we were on the verge of winning, until the sons of bitches came and wiped us out, wiped us out once and for all, in Argentina, in the United States, in Italy, in Germany. To Carvalho it seems as though the loudspeaker vans are groaning under the weight of all the drums and triumphant anthems. Alma reappears from the shop and hands him a bag.

'Here. Records and books to teach you something about us. The records are for you to listen to. The books are for you to burn.'

Alma's beautiful eyes are telling him: farewell, farewell, my masked Spaniard, I'm saying goodbye first, before you say goodbye to me. But perhaps Carvalho does not want to say goodbye. Perhaps Alma wants Carvalho to say: 'No, I don't want to say goodbye.'

Carvalho's lips move as if he does want to say something. It's not very clear what that might be: perhaps he wants to ask Alma – do you want me to stay? After you've got Eva María back will you devote a part of your lovely green eyes to me? Will I be an indispensable part of the everyday life of your green eyes? But Raúl is shouting that there she is, there's Muriel. She is marching with Alberto in the first row of a group of students. Alma runs to join her, followed by Raúl, then Silverstein, who apologizes to Carvalho but rushes off for his appointment with history, only to return a few moments later after kissing Muriel on both cheeks to tell him breathlessly that he is leaving because he has to go to Tango Amigo to present Adriana. Carvalho and Silverstein join the march alongside others who are relieved to find that for a few hours at least they can dispel the demon of forgetting. Then they push past the security guards and reach the pavement, where crowds of curious onlookers judge this attempt to go back down the time tunnel respectfully but without great enthusiasm.

Muriel seemed very serious when she saw them coming. Alberto had his arm round her shoulders. She looked Raúl up and down with great curiosity. She said: I know everything already. That was all. They all march on and on.

Carvalho has changed his mind. He does go to Tango Amigo one last time, but keeps his promise of not saying goodbye to Adriana. He has to watch her lunar expressiveness one last time, to seek out the thrill of her neckline for the origin of her voice in the spot where women bury all sense of time and place to reproduce the species, where the division of work is made between victims and executioners, tortured and torturers. Silverstein has promised him that tonight he will hear the first tango of the future, a tango beyond Piazzola, through the looking-glass of tango.

'I wrote the words, and they're dedicated to you.'

Güelmes is in the club. Drinking and observing. First he waves to Carvalho from the far side of the room, then decides to come over.

'Great atmosphere, isn't it?'

'I didn't realize you came here.'

'I come quite often, but I don't like to bother Silverstein. We lead parallel lives. In fact, it was Alma I was hoping to see. And you. Are you satisfied?'

'Why?'

'Because it's all over. The Captain's little group has been split up. We're free at last!'

'What about the others?'

'What others? The Captain was a useless leftover. He had to be dealt with for us to get back to democratic normality.'

'What does that mean?'

'It means that corruption and state violence are in the hands of civilians, not the military.'

'And what about the Captain's civilian friends?'

'When can you remember any civilians paying for their sins? The only civilian linked to the barbarity of this century who paid at all was Alfried Krupp. Let the Captain's civilian friends be. Their servants can pay in their place. The military and the police.'

'What about Richard Gálvez? He was chasing those civilians to avenge his father's death.'

'Richard Gálvez? Do you really think someone like Richard Gálvez could give the state sleepless nights? Sometimes the state needs to remember it has a monopoly on violence.'

Silverstein appears in the spotlight, his hands full of coloured pencils.

'It is especially gratifying to see the presence of power amongst us tonight. The minister Güelmes is doing us the honour of taking a moment to cover the shortest distance between poetry and life, that is, the tango. Just so long as it is clear this is not setting a precedent, let's have a round of applause for the minister.'

He waits for the applause to finish, without joining in, and then shows the audience what he is holding.

'These pencils have travelled through time to write history with the uncertain hand of schoolchildren, full of spelling mistakes. The future may be imperfect, but less so than the past. I could shed floods of tears tonight to the sound of the drums of our most glorious defeats. I could allow other people to learn by their mistakes and to have the right to a different kind of anger. Do you think I'm talking about politics? You couldn't be more mistaken. I'm talking about the splendour in the grass we witnessed in Buenos Aires tonight, that confirmation of what Wordsworth wrote in his *Ode to Immortality*:

> *Whither is fled the visionary gleam?*
> *Where is it now, the glory and the dream?*

'Which means, translated into Argentine – grab the dough and clear off! Adriana Varela is about to sing the saddest verses – for example: "you should not, know not, you cannot, you will not return". What she sings is not a tango, but within it there are the shards of all the shattered tangos, all that is somewhere above and beyond Piazzola. Through the looking-glass of tango.'

Adriana strides onstage and starts to sing or recite, recite or sing a poem with only perfectly placed, occasional bursts of disharmony from the violin, bass, piano and bandoneon:

> *Recall that nothingness and its world*
> *The four corners of your protection:*
> *You should not, know not, cannot, and will not return;*
> *Four ancient pasts of pewter and amethysts,*
> *Four wars, four corners, four doors,*
> *Four hells.*
>
> *When the angel comes to paint your memory*
> *In innocent and pretty water-colours*
> *Trading in death, trading in desires*
> *In the freest levels of your self-obsessed body,*
> *Even if they cast you from the pre-ordained paradise*
> *In memories you will always find fulfilment:*
> *Earth, water, air, fire, and time.*
> *Useless for memory to invent journeys*
> *Beyond those four protecting horizons,*
> *Well-known faces only lead*
> *To the snares of underwater voices*
> *On a badly-recorded tape that's close*
> *To the expressive wholeness of silence.*
>
> *Like an hourglass built from shifting sands*
> *You'll sink into the dark corners of desire*
> *Foreigner in the city of a thousand exiles*
> *Your absence will mark the start of a union of dreams*
> *A deception that does not even exist*
> *Wandering through this city of useless certainties*
> *That lead neither to origins or to extremes.*
>
> *They'll give you a name like they call wolf*
> *The fear sheep have, like they call fear*

The ill-repute the shipwrecked sailor earns by drowning.

Twelve wars, twelve corners, twelve doors,
Twelve hells.

But if you float down through this surrendered city
To where the shades of all that lives reside
Worlds toppled into dark and filthy waters
Trees like rubber, endless streets,
With no birds or stars to forget your presence
No sounds, no waltzes.

No sun or moon, only the emptiness of a thousand absences
Only the echo of a last and final word;
Float down to that city to try to bury time
Under cyclopean weights of saturated rocks.

If you float down

If you float down you will not recognize a single shadow
Or yourself be recognized by any shade
And this will not be your home even if your home
Was a makeshift model of this ruin,
The desecrated tomb of your forgetting.

Recall that nothingness and its world,
The four horizons of your protection:
You should not, know not, cannot, and will not return.

By the end, everyone is out of breath: Adriana, Carvalho, the audience. Güelmes is the first to recover. He whispers in the detective's ear: 'Was that tango? Tango as chamber music, perhaps.'

The helicopter circles over the forest, looking for the clearing and the flags put out to mark the landing spot. It lands, and the door is opened for Captain Doreste, who leaps out as the rotor blades come whirring to a halt, ignoring the difficulty the fat man is having in following him into a void that seems impossibly daunting. Doreste glares at the man who is there to receive them, straw hat twirling in his hands.

'Why did we have to land here? Why couldn't we fly straight to Paraguay?'

'The helicopter wasn't authorized any further. You'll be taken to the Puente de la Amistad, and you can cross into Paraguay through Ciudad del Este.'

'And run the risk they recognize me at border control?'

'Here nobody recognizes or controls anyone. Your Paraguayan contacts are waiting for you in Ciudad del Este.'

A jeep is ready for them in the trees, its wheels deep in the muddy red earth typical of this land close to the mighty Parana river, a few miles downstream from Iguazú falls. The Captain is fed up of hearing the fat man panting along behind him, and does not want to hear how they turn to groans when the other man's body gives out as he tries to clamber into the jeep.

'I don't feel well, boss. My chest hurts.'

'You need legs to get into the jeep, not your chest.'

Sweating from the tropical heat and his own anxiety, the fat man finally succeeds in scrambling up alongside the Captain, who is sitting there ice-cool, muttering to himself: 'Our four eyes are not enough. We're in other people's hands.'

'But you can trust these people, boss. You scratch my back, I'll scratch yours, that's their motto.'

'You could trust them in the days when there was order around here.'

The bridge is submerged under an endless caravan of tourists, all flocking to Ciudad del Este so that they can pay Paraguayan prices for anything and everything that this universal Ali Baba's cave can offer them.

'It could take us an hour to get across in the jeep.'

The driver turns to face him. He is dark-skinned, and his breath smells of spicy food.

'Why don't you go on foot? They'll be waiting for you on the far side of the bridge. It would be quicker.'

'Who is on the other side?'

'The general.'

'Elpidio?'

'That's right.'

The Captain smiles, and the fat man gives him a wink.

'So everything is in order, boss. If Elpidio is there, everything is just fine.'

The Captain strides across the steel walkway of the bridge, pushing his way past the obsessive buyers drawn to the travelling bazaar that is Ciudad del Este, with its fake labels from Paris or from the vast consumers' city that is the world, all stuffed into huge warehouses as if an army was in massive retreat, spilling on to muddy streets where water from broken drains mingles with puddles from the most recent rains. The fat man struggles to keep up, from time to time begging the Captain to have pity on him and take a moment's breather, because his chest is hurting as if he had a huge boulder pressing on his breastbone.

'One day we'll be back. They're not going to get away with taking my child from me so easily. One day we'll return, and I'll explain how it was me who saved her from what her parents were. I brought her up like a princess, like my princess. One day we'll be back, I swear.'

'Can't we have a rest, Captain?'

The fat man is beginning to realize he is never going to make it across the Puente de la Amistad. He can barely walk. There's a shooting pain in his left arm, and his chest feels like stone, a stone that hurts. He cannot breathe. He spreads his arms to get air into his lungs and to cry out, to ask the Captain for help. But Doreste strides on and does not even look round. He has spotted Elpidio at the boundary marking the start of Paraguayan territory, and although he hears the fat man collapse to the ground, slowing still further the trickle of cars able to cross the bridge, all he does is turn his head once and shout:

'This way you'll be buried in Argentina. You're lucky!'

When he reaches the other side, General Elpidio points back to the group of people gathered round the prostrate body of the fat man sprawled between two cars. Doreste shrugs. Elpidio is a man of few words.

'You're safe here. But times have changed.'

'But not your people.'

'No one believes in ideals any more. Communism has been defeated. We have to adapt. It's the drug traffickers who control and guarantee everything now.'

'What about arms trafficking?'

This sets Elpidio laughing out loud, revealing a set of teeth carefully repaired in Chicago. 'A million dollars this cost me,' he says, tapping the gleaming capped teeth. 'Arms? You're already thinking of buying arms? Look. Here in Ciudad del Este, on the main streets the tourists go to buy their Cacharel shirts, their sable furs and their Japanese word processors: they're all fake or smuggled in. But on all the others, where the tourists never go, they sell arms and drugs. But are you really thinking of buying arms this early in the morning?'

The Captain looks back one last time at the fat man saying his last goodbye to this world. Belatedly, an ambulance siren sounds, and the vehicle starts to thread its way slowly through the two opposing queues of cars.

By the time it reaches the body, the Captain has been introduced to Elpidio's friends, has been given a gun which he sticks in his waistband, and handed a new passport. He stares at his image in the photograph, and starts to memorize his name.

'Juan Carlos Orellana. I like it. I always liked being called Juan Carlos.'

There is nothing sordid about the old people's home, but there is nothing pleasing about it either. There's a garden with old folk shuffling around on their own, as if they had already accepted their ultimate solitude. A few old women are knitting or embroidering, others are singing. One of them is reciting a poem, although no one is paying her any attention:

> *Do you remember you wanted to be Marguerite*
> *Gautier? In my mind I see your face so sweet*
> *When we dined together that first time*
> *On a wonderful night that never will return.*

> *Your scarlet lips with their accursed flame*
> *Sipped from a crystal cup the finest champagne*
> *While your fingers plucked at the whitest flower*
> *He loves me...he loves me not...and I was in your power!*

A group of men has found sufficient fellow-feeling to organize a game of bowls, while a few nuns stroll about keeping the peace in this nondescript garden. But the old man Don Vito and Madame Lissieux have come to see is having nothing of it.

'Old farts. That's what they are. Nothing more, nothing less.'

'Don't say that, Don Aníbal. Old age is a treasure-house of experience.'

'Treasure-house of shit, you mean.'

Madame Lissieux embraces him with a tender look and then with tender words: 'How can anyone who looks as splendid as you think that? Every age has its regrets and its desires. A man is a man until the day he dies. The Great Gratowsky, for example.'

Don Vito strikes while the iron is hot.

'A skirt-chaser, wasn't he? Fancy dying with a pair of knickers in your mouth. That's really dying with your pants on, isn't it?'

Aníbal laughs wickedly and shows his own toothless mouth.

'But he didn't have a tooth in his head, like me.'

'He had all he needed, apparently.'

Don Vito takes advantage of the fact that Madame Lissieux appears to be looking elsewhere to make a vague gesture towards his crotch.

'Oh, that? I don't know how he was getting on, but I can't even use mine to piss properly – those butchers have operated on my prostate four times already, and yet it's still the same. Take a look.'

He starts to unbutton his trousers and pull them down, but Don Vito stops him by nodding towards Madame Lissieux.

'I'll take your word for it.'

'I'll just show you the tube and the bag for my urine.'

'There's no need,' Don Vito winks at him. 'I've been there myself.'

'You too?'

'I had a prostate as big as a hernia. Take it from a fellow-sufferer. But Gratowsky still did what he could in that department. I bet he had fun with some of this lot.'

'With these relics? Not likely! Sometimes we would sit here and think to ourselves: who could ever have slept with any of these old cows?'

At this point Madame Lissieux returns, light-hearted and content.

'What lovely old ladies they are!'

The old man shrugs his shoulders in disgust and sets off along the path. He walks with feigned cheerfulness until he reaches one of the rooms and opens the door. The dark rectangle lights up when the old man feels inside, finds a switch, and all of a sudden bulbs blaze out around a frame containing a huge photograph of Gilda Laplace taken in the 1950s.

'The Great Gratowsky's shrine!'

The twice-life-size portrait of Gilda Laplace is not the only nostalgic cult object in the room. There are a whole series of the stars of stage and screen from the same era, which have Don Vito and Madame Lissieux struggling to see if they can remember them all. There are photographs of Gratowsky in his prime; on nights of celebration with his artists; at social events; the photo of a woman typically 1940s or 1950s, with a young girl who already has a sour expression on her face – Ruth Gratowsky and daughter; the Great Gratowsky as a young concert violinist; another of a group of young people who have just arrived in Argentina, all of them looking pleased to have left the European tragedy behind – one of them is Gratowsky. Aníbal goes along confirming their guesses as to who is who, but stops when he comes to this last photograph.

'Who are these?'

'He never said much about this group. All he said was that they were European Jews, people who had escaped with him, but nothing else. He was very, very Jewish.'

'He was tight-fisted?'

'No, he wasn't tight-fisted at all. But he felt very Jewish, about Israel and everything, you know what I mean. He was organized – he went to Jewish meetings.'

Madame Lissieux drives them to the Once neighbourhood. Aníbal has told them about a Jewish cultural centre between Uriburu and Pasteur that the Great Gratowsky used to frequent.

'It's an organization that supports the Jewish communities here.'

The reception is full of posters of Israel, Zionist propaganda and offers of trips to the Promised Land, courses in Yiddish and Hebrew. The man in charge is a master of silence who does not want to become the slave of his words.

'All I can tell you is that Abraham Gratowsky was a good Jew.'

'I don't doubt it. He followed the Scriptures.'

'Being a good Jew doesn't just mean following the Scriptures. You have to be an active Zionist too.'

'Of course, international Zionism.'

The receptionist does not like this particular form of words.

'Words can have more than one meaning, depending on who uses them. "International Zionism" was invented by people who wanted to wipe out the Jews.'

Don Vito calls on Madame Lissieux to testify to his innocence.

'No, no, don't get me wrong! Lots of my best friends are Jews, I admire their genius, like Einstein. Isn't that so? Kirk Douglas. No, sir. I'm no enemy of the Jews, and I'm delighted to hear that Abraham was a Zionist, a militant Zionist. Did he contribute money to the cause?'

'As long as he could, yes. Lately it was all he could do to keep up with his insurance policy and the old people's home. But he was always active, and was well aware of the dangers facing the Jews in Argentina.'

'Are you in danger then?'

'Have you forgotten about the bomb attack on the Israeli embassy? What's happened to the perpetrators? How many Nazis from before and from now are hiding in this country?'

'Could you give me any details of how Gratowsky was active?'

A voice that sounds familiar to Don Vito cuts short his questions.

'No, he can't.'

He turns round and there is Pascuali, a fact that Don Vito immediately communicates to Madame Lissieux.

'Madame, allow me to introduce the best policeman in Buenos Aires – Inspector Pascuali. He is going to be our ally in many future adventures.'

'What adventures are you talking about?'

'My associate, Señor Pepe Carvalho, is on his way back to Spain this evening, and I have assumed full control of Altofini & Carvalho, Partners in Crime, with the invaluable assistance of Madame Lissieux here.'

Pascuali is heard to mutter: 'Stupidity is never born and never dies. It simply changes form.'

On the way to Ezeiza airport, Pascuali alternates the hard cop warning them not to go on investigating the Gratowsky case...'It's got nothing to do with skirt-chasing. It's related to the blowing-up of the Israeli embassy'…with the soft cop paying particular attention to Madame Lissieux, as demonstrated by his taking them to Ezeiza in a squad car with siren blaring.

'What case were you involved in? I read about a woman in some of my reports, but then there was nothing more. Was it Borges' son?'

As soon as he says the words, a lightbulb flashes in Pascuali's mind. He shuts his eyes to visualize the scene more clearly. That old tango singer outside Corrientes 348. The man who looked like the Polack Goyeneche.

'That fake Goyeneche! So now he's the spitting image of Goyeneche, as if he had come back to life!'

Neither Madame Lissieux nor Don Vito have the faintest idea what he means, until Pascuali uses the car phone to speak to headquarters.

'Put out a search call for a fake Polack masquerading as Goyeneche. I have an idea it could be Arielito Borges Samarcanda. And keep an eye open, he must be up to something.'

'Arielito as a tango singer?'

They reach Ezeiza, where Carvalho was expecting only Don Vito to come and see him off. He kisses Madame Lissieux on the hand, and greets Pascuali with a coldness he does not feel. The policeman tells him: 'I came to make sure you really were leaving.'

'I on the other hand knew you would be left here at the Captain's mercy.'

'The Captain's vanished.'

'They've dropped him for now. But he'll be back. Either they kill him, or he'll be back.'

'I don't ask questions. He's gone, and that's enough for me.'

Don Vito quickly sums up the Gratowsky case, exaggerating what he knows about its connections with Zionism and anti-Zionism. Gilda Laplace? No, she's got nothing to do with it. But Pascuali lets slip: 'We've traced her to a plastic surgery clinic. She's having her tenth face-lift.'

Carvalho does not want to know about any more loose ends – he has enough of those waiting for him in Spain. There will be time enough for him to feel a new nostalgia, a nostalgia for Buenos Aires and perhaps for Alma. Don Vito hugs him so hard he almost crushes him, Madame Lissieux gives him the farewell kiss that Alma refuses, Pascuali tips two fingers to an imaginary hat brim and turns on his heel. All these gestures stay with Carvalho until their first stopover in Rio de Janeiro. His uncle has already dozed off by the time Carvalho settles in the seat next to him and tries the Argentine wine offered by the crew. He even starts to flick through the pages of the *Clarín* newspaper, but does not get beyond the front page headline: 'Richard Gálvez killed in air crash'. He died with his lawyers in attendance, and from some remaining stock of incredulity inside Carvalho there rises a nagging doubt that forces its way out in an expression of dismay. So Richard Gálvez is dead. No wonder it had suddenly become so easy to track down Muriel, no wonder the Captain had been dealt with. If he had been able to, he would have turned the plane back to Buenos Aires, but there is nothing to be done, it is already fast disappearing down the plughole of the future. When they reach Rio, he wakes his uncle and makes sure he totters into the right airport lounge, but still at the back of his mind is Gálvez's death. Power. So real power had taken a hand to make sure things came out as required. He remembers what Güelmes once said: 'The importance of me being in power is that I'll be able to look after Alma.'

Carvalho feels on edge. All he wants to do is carry on drinking so that he can doze through the wait, especially when his uncle finally wakes up properly and insists on striking up a conversation. The illuminated panels on the walls offer all kinds of escape, and if he could, he would have loved to head off to some city in Australia, given that he did not really believe Australia existed anyway. A couple sitting next to him are talking in Catalan. They are discussing their trip in voices strained by the discomfort of being between two seasons and two continents. 'But the traveller who is fleeing sooner or later has to end his flight,' Carvalho sings to himself, whistling the tune. The young Catalan woman stares up at him, her head on her companion's shoulder: 'Have you come from Buenos Aires?'

'Yes. And you two?'

'We spent a week there. What about you?'

'Several months.'

'You must know a lot about the place.'

'Tango, the disappeared, Maradona.'

The girl looks perplexed, and her boyfriend turns to Carvalho with an ironic smile.

'I've heard of Maradona, of course. But he's ancient history. Ronaldo, Ronaldinho is the new king of football. Tango – do they still sing tangos in Buenos Aires? And what disappeared are you talking about? Are they something to do with the *X Files*?'

This plants a seed of doubt in Carvalho's mind, which is still there when the postmodern glass palace of Barcelona airport comes into view. Has he really been in Buenos Aires? He never even got to see Cecilia Rosetto. It is then he remembers Alma gave him a present to prove he had been in her city. So he did have proof of his stay there, in addition to her green eyes, an image already being swallowed up by the quicksands of his memory. He opens the package he had stuffed into his shoulder bag, and several CDs fall out, plus a whole pile of books. Edmundo Rivero singing Discépolo. And the fattest book, *Adán Buenosayres*, by Leopoldo Marechal, also starts with a song:

> *The little white handkerchief*
> *I gave to you*
> *Embroidered with my hair...*

And it goes on:

> *Gentle and smiling (as so often in autumn in that most graceful of cities, Buenos Aires) shone the morning that twenty-eighth of April; the clocks had just struck ten and at that time, wide-awake and demonstrative in the early sunlight, the great capital of the south was a dense corn-cob of men and women shouting and arguing for their right to possess the morning and the earth.*